Abby,

To the sand scoop! :)

Trouble on TREASURE ISLAND

A *Beach House Mystery*

wolfprintMedia, LLC
Hernando Beach, FL 34607

Copyright ©2023 by Seth Sjostrom

For information, contact wolfprintMedia, LLC.

Trade Paperback
ISBN-13: 978-1-7375300-6-0

1. Kate Harper (Fictitious character)-Fiction. 2. Nick Mason (Fictitious character)-Fiction. 3. Mystery-Thriller- Fiction. 3. Beach House Mysteries Series-Fiction 4. Trouble on Treasure Island-Title.

First wolfprintMedia edition 2023.

wolfprintMedia is a trademark of wolfprint, LLC.

For information regarding bulk purchases, please contact wolfprintMedia, LLC at wolfprint@hotmail.com.

United States of America

Trouble on TREASURE ISLAND

Kathi, for your inspiration.

Special thanks to Jen, Teri and Jenn.

Trouble on TREASURE ISLAND

for Kathi

Trouble on TREASURE ISLAND

One

Kate Harper turned her car into the drive. Her luxury SUV's tires crunched over sand and shells as she pulled to a stop. While her company preferred traditional cement surfaces, she found it rather satisfying. If the driveway screamed beach, she couldn't wait to see what the rest of the waterfront house had to offer.

The rustic driveway belied a stunning residence perched right on Sunset Beach at the southern tip of St. Petersburg's Treasure Island. The house had a modern feel to it. Framed perfectly between two palms, the home could be a postcard for the property management company that Kate represented.

Opening her phone, she eyed the numbers in the email and matched her fingers on the keypad. A slight whir and satisfying click welcomed her to her temporary coastal home. Swinging the door open, the hallway made a straight line through the center of the house to a massive set of French doors. The sparkling, light blue waters of the Gulf of Mexico beckoned through the enormous expanse of glass.

Ignoring the rest of the house, Kate marched directly to the wall of doors and promptly flung them open. The light onshore breeze and the almost imperceptible yet memory-tingling scent of saltwater air teased her senses. A broad grin swept across her face as she placed her hands on the deck rails and took in the unimpeded ocean view.

With a nod of approval that her company had once again struck gold with the magnificent property, she turned back to assess the rest of the house and catalog her work over the next few weeks. A series of surfers eyed a set of incoming waves, each striking off in robust paddles to get in front of the swell as the Gulf waters propelled them along. One by one, they dropped off their boards and splashed into the water as the power of the wave ran out, calling an end to their rides.

Kate thought of adding pairs of surfboards and paddle boards for renters to try their own hand at tackling the waves. She smiled. It was a pleasant touch that would sign in the rental listing.

Heading back into the house, she paused as her foot sank slightly on a board. Looking down at the deck, Kate pressed with her toe as the board underneath felt mushy and gave an inch or two of travel as her weight settled on it.

"Might as well start my list now," she said.

Pulling out her phone, she busily scribbled a note. Starting with the view before her, Kate made observations regarding the magnificent view, the private beach access and the multi-level decking that maximized the grand Gulf vistas. Turning toward the house, she took a step, her foot plunging through the rotted board. Grimacing, she gently tugged, only to find her foot decidedly stuck.

A boisterous voice called out, a little too cheery for her current disposition, "Need a hand up there? 'Cause it looks like you need a hand."

"Uhm, yeah, I suppose I do. But I have to ask, why are you on my deck?" Kate seethed through a grimace.

"Fair question. How about we discuss that once you're free," the voice suggested.

Kate paused to consider the proposition, "Fair enough. You can come up. The front door is unlocked. I warn you; I carry pepper spray."

"Warning received. I'll see you in a minute," the voice said as it trailed alongside the house.

Kate fumed as she waited. Irritated with herself for carelessly landing in the awkward predicament. Annoyed that the trespasser slash rescuer was traipsing through her company's new property.

The surfer appeared in the opening of the French doors. A wide grin splashed across his face. Unfortunately, Kate's own demeanor was not nearly so jovial. With a friendly nod, the surfer collapsed to one knee to pry the boards apart in order to extricate Kate's foot.

Kate's head swiveled around, curious about what the stranger was doing and at the same time averting her eyes from her own spectacle. As the man pulled back on the adjacent board, Kate gained enough relief to pull her foot through the jagged wooden trap.

Rising from his kneeling position, the surfer offered a warm smile, "There you go. I apologize for the intrusion; the former owners didn't mind. It's kind of a popular access point to some of the best waves around."

Kate's face morphed from unmoved to decidedly sour, "Well, the house is under new ownership now. I'm sorry, but we mind."

The surfer studied Kate for a moment before nodding with his ever-present smile. "Being neighborly kind of worked out this time, huh?"

Kate flushed, "I mean, I'm grateful. You being there and all. Kind of saved the day."

Cocking his head, the surfer frowned.

"It's a company property. We have rules…for our guests," Kate shrugged.

"I see," the surfer nodded with dejection in his tone. "You know, I can help you fix the place up. Even put in a boardwalk along the alley so surfers wanting over the dunes stay off your property."

Kate scowled, eyeing the surfer. Flecks of grey telling his age versus the chiseled body and telltale surfer's disheveled appearance. Sand and salt caked against the stranger's skin.

"I do handyman work from time to time. I'm even licensed and bonded," the surfer assured her.

Kate looked at the hole where her foot was. "It does appear as though the house could use a...handyman."

The man smiled.

Kate snapped, "Bring your credentials in the morning. I'll pay you to do a walk-through and we can discuss bringing you in to do a few projects."

"Yes, ma'am. The surf report comes out early," the man said.

"What does *that* matter?" Kate frowned.

"It's the difference between eight and ten," the man grinned.

"Oh, it's eight," Kate said. "And bring coffee."

Appreciating the woman's swagger, the surfer picked up his board, "Eight o'clock. I'm Nick, by the way. Nick Mason."

"Kate. Kate Harper. Here's my card. Call me if you have any problems or unexpected surf-related delays."

Nick studied the card, "Property managers, huh? Nice place for a rental."

"I'll see you tomorrow, Nick," Kate held the French door open for the surfer/handyman to step through.

$\mathcal{T}wo$

Kate had run through the house making a list of things she needed to do or order for the home. Unfortunately, she found a few more items appropriate for Nick, the handyman-surfer, if his credentials checked out.

Taking advantage of the house's fantastic sunset view, she settled into a chair on the upper deck. Kate gingerly tested each board carefully as she went. Pouring a glass of wine, she opened her store-bought salad and enjoyed watching the waves roll in. Facing due west, she could watch the sun make its stunning splash into the Gulf and beyond.

The beach had emptied save a stray couple or late evening jogger enjoying the cooler evening air and onshore breezes.

Finished with her meal, Kate opened up her laptop and worked as the sun faded and the moon made its presence known, providing a splash of light dancing on the waters of the Gulf.

Engrossed in her work, she ignored the first sounds that struggled to filter through her ears. The sounds repeated, signaling her brain that something was amiss. Tilting the screen of her laptop, she peered over its edge out toward the beach.

A pair of shadows streaked by. The lead shadow let out a terrified shriek. Kate set her laptop aside, placed her hands on the rail, and stared out at the moonlit scene. One shadow appeared to chase another. The shriek belonged to a female voice. The trailing shadow looked male to Kate from her vantage point.

Grabbing her phone, she raced toward the house. Pausing abruptly as in the excitement, she nearly forgot about the weak floorboard. Stepping over the hole, she danced into the house and through the living room, down the stairs and circled back to the lower back deck that led to the beach.

Flinging the door open, Kate ran along the home's boardwalk and out to where she saw the darkness-shrouded subjects run. Scanning the length of the beach, she jogged in the direction of the chase, but even with the moonlight aiding her, she couldn't find them. Standing still, she listened hard over the melodic crashing waves, trying to hear additional screams or signs of distress.

Hearing nothing, she relented to return to the rental home. As she retraced her steps, she used the light from her cell phone to aid the soft glow of the moon. A series of fresh footsteps in distinct sizes were clearly visible in the sand. About to head back up her boardwalk, a flash in the corner of her eye gave her pause. Shining her phone light down, she bent and retrieved the glistening item from the sand.

Holding it up to the light, she found herself in possession of a ring. Inspecting it, she found it rather grand as it dazzled in the beam from her phone. A large princess-cut diamond gleamed practically illuminating the night.

Instinctively, Kate turned and cast her gaze in the direction the shadowy chase had vanished in. Flipping the ring thoughtfully between her thumb and finger, she decided there was little doubt it was time to call the authorities.

Carefully slipping the ring into her pocket, she dialed 911 as she marched up the boardwalk that stretched over the dunes separating her from her beach house. Her eyes were as much focused down the beach as where she was walking as the dispatcher answered her call.

Kate hardly knew where to begin. Stammering, she struggled to voice her concern over the events of the evening. "I...I uh, need to report an incident. There was a chase on the beach," Kate said into the phone.

"A chase...on the beach, ma'am? Are you sure it wasn't just kids playing? That is a common occurrence on the beach, even at night," the dispatcher questioned.

"No, I mean, yes, I understand that. This was different. There was a female who let out a scream and another person seemed to be chasing her," Kate said. "And I found a ring. It looks like a diamond ring. It was right in the path of their tracks."

The operator sighed, "Ma'am, I will send an officer out to check the beach. Just bring the ring to the nearest precinct in the morning. I'm sure everything is just fine. The shriek you heard might well have been the young lady realizing her ring was off her finger. You probably did the owner a tremendous favor by finding it. Good night."

The phone went dead. Kate studied the blank screen and retrieved the ring from her pocket, holding it up to her porch lights. Shaking her head, something felt off to her. If the shriek she heard was of someone realizing the diamond ring was missing, why wouldn't they have stopped to scour the beach?

With a final glance back at the sand, she retreated into the beach house. Kate instinctively spun the deadbolt as she pressed her back into the door. Still twirling the ring in her fingers, she headed upstairs to her bedroom. Sliding out a bureau drawer, she placed the ring gently amongst her garments.

Three

Kate was awakened by sirens screaming past the beach house, only to stop a short distance away. Her chest tightened and her heart skipped several beats as her fears had come true. She witnessed an atrocious crime taking place. A crime that she had failed to help prevent.

Bolting out of bed, she quickly tossed on clothes as she slid her feet into sandals. Slamming to a halt in front of the dresser, she pulled the ring out and stuffed it in her pocket. Racing down the stairs, she burst out of the house and hustled down the street to where a great commotion was beginning to take shape.

Kate didn't need to go far. A few blocks away at the public beach access, a dozen police and emergency vehicles had arrived. Their blue and red lights emanated an eerie strobing glow over the area. A crowd of onlookers and excited reporters assembled behind a hastily erected police barricade.

Slithering her way to the front of the throng of spectators, Kate found herself only to be held back by an open palm thrust forward by a young officer.

"Sorry, ma'am, this is an active crime scene," the officer spat.

"I'm the one that called it in, well, the initial call, anyway," Kate pleaded.

The young officer frowned, "I'll take your information and pass it along to the detectives. They can follow up with you should they see fit."

Kate danced in her spot, not ready to be turned away so quickly. Her eyes widened as her hand dove into her pocket and produced the ring she had found in the sand, "I have evidence!"

Holding the ring proudly in the air, she beamed at the perplexed officer. His face twisted in confusion as he eyed the jewelry. As the officer reached out for it, Kate yanked her hand away, "I'll give it directly to the detective, thank you."

Scowling, the officer slumped his shoulders. In a huff, he turned away. As Kate waited, she realized that she had drawn the interest of the crowd and the reporters covering the scene. Several flashes from photographers' cameras forced her to blink her eyes.

It wasn't long before a man in street clothes, with a gleaming badge hanging from a chain around his neck tailed the now irate junior officer.

"Officer Handley says you may have some information on this case and apparently have evidence that…," the man laughed, a wide grin spreading across his grizzled face. "You wouldn't relinquish to anyone other than the detective directly. I am Detective Connolly."

Handing Kate his card, he glanced around at the encroaching crowd. With a nod of his head, he beckoned her back behind the police line, "Come with me."

Officer Handley looked shocked at the development as he watched Kate whisked along by the detective. With a shrug, the young officer returned to manning his post.

The detective leaned over his shoulder toward Kate, "So, let's start with this evidence of yours…."

Kate fished in her pocket and held her tightly clenched fingers over the detective's outstretched hand. Opening her fingers, the ring fell into the detective's palm. Holding the piece of jewelry in the shine of the strobing police lights, the detective studied the ring. "How is this evidence?"

Taking a breath, Kate shared her encounter from the deck that evening and how she ventured out onto the beach in search of the potential assailant and victim, only to find the ring at her feet.

"Quite a bit of luck to find this out on the beach at night like that," the detective mused. "How are you so sure this has anything to do with what is going on out here?"

Kate frowned, "I guess I don't know. What *did* happen out here?"

The detective looked grim, "I'm afraid a body was found."

Kate's gut tightened as she gasped, "A woman? Was she murdered?"

"We have a lot of investigation to do here," the detective said, tight-lipped.

Placing a hand over her mouth, Kate choked, "She was. Right after I saw her...."

"Why don't you take me again through what you saw, step by step and then tell me how you came upon this ring?" Detective Connolly said.

Swallowing hard, Kate recounted in precise detail the shadowy chase that she witnessed, rushing out onto the beach and turning to head back to her beach house, finding the ring.

"The ring was just right there at your feet?"

"Well, yeah. I was using the flashlight tool on my phone, and it picked up the shine from the diamond," Kate said.

"And why do you think it is linked to what happened here?" Connolly restated.

"There were two pairs of fresh footprints in the sand right about the line where I saw the shadows running along the beach. The ring was right between them," Kate informed the detective.

Connolly looked thoughtful for a moment, "And you don't know the two people who raced by your beach house?"

Kate shook her head, "No. I couldn't even make them out clearly. I wasn't even sure the 911 dispatcher would take me seriously."

"Serious enough that an officer was sent out. It was just dumb luck that he used the alleyway to the beach as part of his route," Detective Connolly shared. "Otherwise, it would have been a rather unforgettable, and unfortunate trip to the beach for some tourists in the morning."

The detective waved a forensics team member over to collect the ring and place it in a baggy. Turning back to Kate, he said, "Let me have an officer collect your information. You have your I.D. on you?"

Kate patted her pockets and shook her head, "No, I ran out when I heard the sirens. I didn't think..."

"You're a potential material witness to a crime," Detective Connolly said. As the officer walked up, he directed, "Take Ms....."

"Kate. Kate Harper."

The detective nodded, "Escort Ms. Harper home. Capture her information and get a copy of her driver's license."

The officer nodded and held his hand out for Kate to walk toward the police line where a half dozen officers made space for them to exit through the crowd. Several reporters were snapping photos as they made their way away from the scene.

When the officer left, Kate closed the door tight and ensured the deadbolt was solidly locked in place. The flashing lights from the response vehicles down the street filtered softly through her windows, a strobing beacon that the horrific events of the evening had in fact taken place.

Both exhausted and jacked up on adrenaline, Kate tried to understand what she was supposed to do at the moment. Returning to bed made sense, but she couldn't imagine sleeping.

Making chamomile tea, she leaned against the kitchen island as she waited for the water to boil. Sitting still in the center of the quiet house helped to settle her nerves and allow the fatigue to seep back into her system.

The water ready, she tore at the tea bag, only then realizing how much her hands had been shaking. Concentrating on freeing the bag from its thin paper sleeve, Kate finally succeeded, dropping the tea into her cup and splashing the hot water until it neared the rim. Even the aroma as it wafted through the air gave comfort. Like an enormous sigh, it filled her with a sense of calm.

Cupping the mug in her hands, she walked through the house, turning lights on and off with her elbow as she passed. Uncharacteristically, she lit up every crevice on her way to the upstairs bedroom. Closing the door behind her, she was unsure whether she was more comforted in the confines of the closed bedroom or if she preferred to hear any noises that might emanate from the rest of the house.

Crawling to the middle of the bed, she crossed her legs holding the tea close to her. Deciding the quiet of the house was too much, she flipped on the television, finding a lighthearted romance that she had seen half a dozen times. The familiarity brought her comfort.

As the mug of tea emptied, Kate's eyes grew heavy. With a yawn, she reached the cup to the nightstand and allowed her body to sink slowly into the bed. As her heavy eyes closed, she kept the movie playing in the background like a friend with a hand on her back as she slept.

Four

Kate woke with a start. She was momentarily unsure of where she was, as exhaustion had overwhelmed her, if for a few precious hours. In a near trance-like state, Kate marched through the house, completely drained after the chaotic evening she had endured.

Shaking her head, Kate tried to fend off the haze of sleep as her mind fought to reconcile the input mercilessly bombarding her senses. The sun shot daggers through the wide berth of French doors as she shuffled down the steps onto the main floor of the beach house.

Instinctively, she veered toward the kitchen and the coffee pot she so desperately needed consolation from. The knock at the door made her jump as a chill shot through her spine. Spinning, she faced the front door which loomed menacingly after the horrors of the evening.

Kate stared down the hall as a fist pounded distinctively louder against the heavy wood front door. With a wary eye, she shuffled toward the door. Smashing her face against the frosted glace, all she could see was the mass of a man standing on her doorstep. Kate's heart accelerating its pace, she placed a hand on the handle as she flipped the deadbolt. Flinging the door open, she stared menacingly as she squinted against the easterly rising sun at the hulking silhouette on her doorstep.

"Business casual, I like it," a cheery voice called out as Kate's vision tried to compensate for its weariness against the morning light.

As her focus improved, she saw Nick, the surfer-handyman, smiling back at her.

Kate was taken aback by the realization that her appearance was being absorbed by the man's smug expression.

"It's eight o'clock!" Nick sang cheerily.

Kate glanced at her phone which she had clung to since her visit to the crime scene, "It's seven-fifty."

"If you're not early, you're late. I was here at seven forty-five."

"Of all the vagabond surfers, I have to get the one with a sense of promptness," Kate said. She glanced at the coffees and nodded, "One of those for me?"

Nick nodded and fished one out of the cup holder and handed it to her.

"Thanks, I need that," she admitted.

"Rough night?" Nick surmised.

"I think…I think I may have witnessed a murder…or at least the murderer and the victim," Kate said, her voice soft and shaky.

Nick reeled back, "Gosh, I'm sorry. Are *you* okay?"

Kate offered a nod that exuded little confidence, "I'm fine. A little tough to wrap my head around."

"Do you know…the people involved?" Nick asked, following Kate into the house.

"No," Kate said, sipping the coffee like it was a magical serum. "I was working on the back patio last night. I heard…I don't know what I heard, a shriek of some sort. It caught my attention. I saw someone being chased. It was dark. I really couldn't tell."

"Well, that's unsettling," Nick said.

"I went out on the beach to see if I could figure out what was happening…"

"You went out on the beach?" Nick asked, his eyes wide in shock.

"Well, yeah. I couldn't be sure and if someone needed help. I couldn't just ignore them," Kate said, her face screwed in a perplexed expression. "I didn't find anyone, but I did find tracks in the sand and what I think was a ring that I'm not even sure is connected. Anyway, a few hours later, I heard the sirens. I went to the scene and spent much of the night with the police explaining what I saw and found. Sorry I'm late and for my rather haggard appearance."

"For what it's worth, for rolling out of bed in a panic, I'd say you look pretty good," Nick said. His face fell as his words resonated, "No...I mean...just..."

Kate laughed and waved him off, "It's fine. I think I understand what you meant. Why don't I clean up and put on some proper clothes? Can you get started on the deck? I'll be right down."

Nick nodded, placing his notepad and tools on the counter.

"And thanks again for the coffee," Kate said, her head craning around the corner of the stairwell before she ran up to change.

"You bet," Nick looked up from the arsenal of tools he had laid out and watched Kate disappear. Chuckling to himself, he grabbed his prybar and headed for the back deck. Looking out onto the beach, he tried to picture what the woman must have gone through the evening prior.

Unlatching the door, he swung it open and kneeled down to begin prying up the damaged boards. Pulling up the suspect board that captured Kate's foot the day before, the door opened.

Looking up, he saw Kate in the immaculate persona he had met the day prior. He flashed a brief smile as he noticed how refreshed she looked. Even her sleep-deprived eyes couldn't hide her radiance.

Holding the plank up for her view, he said, "Here is your captor. I'll check the other boards for rot. Most likely they suffer from over-pour as the gutters struggle to contain Florida's famous rain bursts."

Kate nodded, "The thunderstorms come in quick and powerful here, don't they?"

Nick laughed, "They do. I'd like to think things cool off after they blast through, but sometimes all they do is raise the humidity even higher."

"It's not so bad right here along the beach. The coastal breeze is just enough to make it rather pleasant. Besides, that view...," Kate said, looking longingly at the Gulf waters lapping at the shore.

"It's a nice spot, that's for sure," Nick said. "This is your life, visiting beachfront properties?"

Kate let out a grin, "It's a pretty good gig."

"A little tough to put down roots, isn't it?" Nick asked, locating another board that warranted replacing.

Kate looked surprised, "A surfer concerned about putting down roots?"

"We can have families too," Nick defended. "Besides, that's how we find our favorite surf spots."

"Like spots behind private homes that you trespass through to get to?" Kate scoffed.

"Sure, like those," Nick grinned.

"I should let you do your work. Besides it looks like you are going to be yanking up where I'm standing," Kate said, backing into the house.

Closing the door behind her, she felt unusually comforted by the handyman's presence that morning. Known for her steel core, she admitted to herself that the night's events had shaken her.

By midday, Nick and Kate had come to the decision to replace the whole deck, ensuring a uniform look that wouldn't take away from the grand view and would be free of maintenance for years to come for the management company.

Kate watched the surfer-handyman toil in the hot Florida sun and rising humidity for hours as she peered over her laptop on the kitchen island. Watching Nick wipe the sweat off his brow for the hundredth time, she decided it was time he took a break.

She carefully opened the door so she didn't startle him, as he was perched precariously on the support beams. Tossing the last of the old boards to the ground below, he squinted through the midday sun at the woman in the doorway.

Kate observed the bare deck structure and laughed, "If you can somehow find your way back to safety, how about you cool off for a bit? I'll order us some lunch."

"I could eat…and get out of this sun for a little while," Nick admitted.

Letting his prybar drop in the sand next to the pile of loosened boards, he carefully tightrope walked his way to the open French door. With his last step, he lost his balance, wobbling side to side before Kate's hands reached out, grabbing him by the shirt and yanking him inside the house. The force sent her toppling backward with Nick landing arms outstretched on top of her.

For an awkward moment, they froze in that position, his face hovering directly over hers. Twisting into a wry grin, Nick breathed, "Thank you."

"That was a close one," Kate admitted as Nick rolled to the side and away from her.

"You'd think a surfer would have better balance," Nick grumbled as he held out his hand to help Kate up from the floor.

"Maybe one without sunstroke," Kate scoffed, accepting his hand. Kate noticed Nick's hand was strong, yet gentle, raising her to her feet with ease. Once more, they found themselves nose to nose. Pulling away, Kate flushed, "I should, uh…I'll order us some lunch."

"Yeah," Nick nodded, instinctively taking an additional step away.

While they waited for lunch to arrive, Nick hastily assembled the first section of new boards. Hauling the small outdoor table and chairs, he placed them on the freshly laid deck. Finishing just in time as the doorbell announced the delivery of their food.

Searching for Nick, Kate wandered the house with her arms laden with their lunch order. Seeing his smiling face peering through the French doors, Kate frowned. Stepping through the door Nick opened for her, she admired his handiwork.

"Wow, you work quick," Kate said.

"I figured I could get enough done that you could enjoy lunch beachfront on your own patio," Nick said, clearly proud of his accomplishment. Eyeing the extensive section on the south side of the deck, he warned, "Just don't step over t. Those aren't screwed down just yet."

"So noted. This looks great. I don't think I realized how weathered the decking was. Now that I see these new boards, it really makes a difference," Kate said, placing their food on the table.

Pulling the chair with the most direct view of the beach out for her, Nick held his hand out, offering the seat. With a slightly bashful look, Kate accepted.

Sorting out the food, she laid Nick's lunch in front of him as he pulled out a chair adjacent to hers. "I got you rock lobster street tacos. Sounded like something a surfer might eat," Kate said, as she opened the lid on her salad.

"Surfers have their own diet? Kind of feel like you may have watched an inaccurate wildlife show on the habitat and rituals of surfers," Nick laughed. "But, yes, this looks great. Thank you."

"I just mean, when in Rome…eat as the Romans do. I try to eat, drink, visit the places the locals do whenever I am working on a new property. It helps me get a sense of the place," Kate defended.

"If that's the case, maybe I can show you…er…share some of the hotspots around Treasure Island and St. Petersburg," Nick offered.

Kate smiled, "That would be great. Nothing better than an insider's view from a local."

Nick leaned back after taking a bite of his sandwich and gazed at the ocean, "This is an amazing view."

"It's gorgeous," Kate agreed. "This place will be easy to fill, creating wonderful vacation memories for families and couples."

Cocking his head at the edge of the large deck, he mused, "What do you think about a tiki bar right there? It would add some outdoor entertaining space with a commanding view of the beach and provide a bit more privacy against the neighbors."

"And against the proposed surfer trespass zone," Kate said, warily holding a forkful of salad.

"I prefer friendly neighbor boardwalk," Nick corrected.

Kate laughed, "I'll think about it. It would be added expense and time to the project."

"I'll do it, gratis," Nick shrugged. "There is a small easement between the two properties. While not an official public beach access, the locals have used it used for years. That won't stop. Might as well make it official with proper controls for privacy and security."

Kate looked thoughtful, "You are unusually diplomatic for a surfer-handyman."

"I wasn't always a surfer-handyman," Nick admitted. As Kate's eyes widened for more explanation, Nick smiled and shook his head, "Story for another day. Now, it's time for me to get back to work. We have a schedule to keep."

Kate watched Nick gather his empty lunch items and rise from the table. She admired his tenacity, surprised by his remarkably adept powers of persuasion. Not completely deterred, she leaned against the rail and studied the proposed boardwalk location between the adjacent properties.

Diving back into his work, Nick completed another plank. Looking up, he eyed Kate visualizing his proposal.

"I still can't believe you ran out there in the middle of the night," Nick called out, using his pencil to space the next board in line. "Especially after hearing what sounded like a scream."

Peering at her phone's screen, Kate took a few shots of the proposed tiki bar site. Turning to Nick, she shrugged, with a wry smile pursing her lips, "I'm not sure I can really explain, either. I just got a sense that something was wrong and wanted to see if I could help. I couldn't just stand by and do nothing." Kate eyed the beach and sighed, "I clearly didn't do enough."

Nick set his tools down to face Kate directly, "It wasn't your fault. You noticed. You investigated and called the police. You did what you could. Putting yourself in danger wouldn't have helped."

"No, I suppose not," Kate said, her voice lacking confidence in the response.

Admiring her tenacity, Nick offered a sympathetic nod and grabbed another board.

The late afternoon sun hung over the Gulf, the coastal breeze fighting to offer relief from the oppressive swirl of heat and humidity. Kate opened the door revealing a completely refreshed deck.

"Wow, this looks great!" Kate said, setting down a lemonade pitcher and pair of glasses on the table they shared lunch at.

Nick swung from the rail he was adjusting, "Yeah. It had good bones. It just needed a little sprucing here and there."

"No more devious foot snares?" Kate asked, prodding the boards with her toes.

"Not for another decade or so. No," Nick said. Eyeing the lemonade, he used the back of his wrist to swipe salty sweat from migrating and stinging his eyes. "That for me?"

"Looked like you could use a reprieve," Kate said, pouring a glass full for him.

Nick eagerly accepted the beverage as condensation instantly beaded on the surface of the cup, "Thank you." Taking a moment to fully appreciate the cool liquid sliding down his throat that at least for a moment cooled his core.

Pulling out his to-do list, he said, "With the deck done, I can start going to work on fixing that leaky fixture on the outdoor shower tomorrow."

"The weather report looks good for swells in the morning. Why not start around ten tomorrow?" Kate suggested, hiding her smile behind her glass of lemonade.

Nick's head snapped up, and he raised an eyebrow at her, "You've been doing your homework."

Kate dipped her shoulder in a slight shrug.

Eyes wide, Nick suggested, "Why don't you join me? Have you ever been?"

"Me?" Kate gasped. "No."

"Then come on. It will be fun. I can teach you everything you need to know," Nick urged.

After the slightest moment of hesitation, Kate shook her head, "Maybe some other time. I have a lot to get done around here and meet with realtors tomorrow."

"All right," Nick conceded. "Raincheck then. I will see you at ten tomorrow. Just do me a favor… Don't go chasing after shadows on the beach that might be murderers."

"That's funny. That is just what the detective said," Kate frowned.

Nick set his lemonade glass down and began collecting his tools, "Smart guy."

Watching him methodically place his tools into their cases, Kate chuckled, "See you tomorrow, Nick."

With a nod, Nick walked down the steps to the lower deck and around the house to his truck.

Kate sipped her lemonade, watching the surfer-handyman and, reflecting on the surprising depth of the man who initially trespassed onto her company's property. Leaning against the rail as he disappeared around the corner, she admitted to herself that having him there all day was comforting.

She was grateful for the presence of someone else at the house after the events of the previous evening. Hearing the activity on the back porch helped her mind from straying with continuous flashbacks and urges to recheck the locks on the doors.

The house, once again quiet, sent a shiver down her spine. Turning her attention to the beachgoers, she watched as couples and families enjoyed the sand and waves. For the time being, they would be her source of comfort and companionship. At least until the sun went down.

Five

Nibbling lightly at the back of her pen, Kate sat with her feet propped up on the deck railing, scribbling notes for her to-do list. The beach had all but emptied as the brilliant sky filtered through an artist's palette of ever-darkening blues mixed with crimson, orange and pink until just the tip of the sun peaked over the edge of the horizon.

Kate's eyes became more vigilant, peering over the pages of notes at every movement her peripheral vision picked up on. The entire process was exhausting. Her efforts were daunted by distraction and worry.

Having had enough, she cradled her laptop and notepad, retreating into the house. Her hand on the door handle, she froze in place as a shrill scream emanated from the beach. Spinning, gripped in fear, she scanned the beach. Her thumping heart pounded as her instincts screamed for her to go inside.

Her eyes caught the mild calamity as a mother scooped up her child, intent on chasing after her beach ball that bounced along the sand driven by the evening breeze. The distraught child was calmed as a beachcomber headed off the ball's escape and returned it to a grateful child and equally pleased mother.

Glad the scene was nothing more than a child fearful of losing their prized toy, Kate was fuming with herself for allowing her nerves to get rattled. Without Nick there working on the deck, she had found herself jumping at every shadow of a palm frond dancing in the breeze and the clatter of the air conditioner spooling to life.

Pushing into her house, she set her things down and returned to the French doors and their breathtaking view. Despite her own reconciliation and effort to calm herself as she took in the view, itself offering respite, she quickly flipped the deadbolt on the doors.

With a sigh, she receded to the confines of the beach house for the night. Perched on a tall kitchen chair, she admired the beach view from the safety of the windows while she worked. Lost in her reports, she nearly jumped when a loud knock at the front door was followed by an insistent urging from the doorbell.

Spinning in her seat, she stared down the hall toward the foyer. Instinctively, her eyes darted around for something that would make a useful weapon. Shaking off the idea as silly, Kate proceeded down the hall and down the steps to the front door.

Peering through the frosted glass windows that stood on either side of the doorway, she could see an impatient shadow leaning into the doorbell once more. Smashing her eye to the peephole, Kate saw a young man in a ball cap shifting back and forth on the front step. The logo on the hat caused Kate to slump her shoulders, feeling rather silly.

Flinging the door open, Kate was flustered, "I'm sorry to make you wait. I was on the opposite side of the house."

"Your order, ma'am," the young man stated flatly, thrusting a bag out in front of him.

Kate patted her pockets, realizing her purse was upstairs. "I nearly forgot I had placed the order. Let me run and get you a tip."

"There's already a tip on the bill. Have a goodnight, ma'am," the boy said, launching himself away from the house the moment Kate had a grip on the bag.

Kate watched the young delivery driver jump into his car and quickly pull away. With a sigh, Kate shut the door, setting the bag down to ensure the house was once again locked tight. Snatching the bag from the entry floor, she marched upstairs.

Spreading the bag's contents onto the counter, she opened the tubs of soup and salad, casting them a half-hearted glance. She was growing more and more annoyed with her newfound jumpiness. In a huff, she snatched her food and settled on the living room sofa.

Not one to watch the news on television, she was compelled. Flipping on the remote, the murder on Treasure Island dominated the broadcast. The newscaster was emphatic that tourists had nothing to fear at Sunset Beach, assuring the tragic incident was a unique and singular event.

A reporter on the scene summarized the events, reviewing the horrific scene as his cameraman did his best to capture video of the scene where the body was found and the investigation continued. While the report was descriptive, it offered no new information that Kate had not already known about the incident.

Taking a bite of soup, she nearly spit it out as her own image was splashed on the screen from footage taken early that morning. The words "Key Witness" scrolled under the video that showed her speaking to the detective and handing over what the reporter described as crucial evidence.

Shifting back to the studio, the newscaster concluded there were more questions than answers to the tragedy that occurred on Treasure Island.

Flipping off the television, Kate, decidedly losing what little appetite she had, placed the lids back on her dinner and shoved them into the refrigerator. Pulling a glass out of the cupboard, she poured a rather healthy glass of red wine and headed up to the third floor where she was sleeping.

Stepping out onto the third-story veranda only accessible through the master bedroom. The space made her feel safe, even as she tentatively looked out at the moon-swept beach.

Enjoying the cooler evening breeze and the palms' rustle, she felt at peace for the first time in nearly twenty-four hours.

Kate's mind drifted sublimely, romanced by the power of the Gulf's surf crashing against the shore. The ocean's powerful yet delicate dance was always soothing and invigorating for Kate. Taking a sip of wine, she relished the moment.

Even the stray nighttime beachgoer failed to give her pause and lure her attention. From the safety of the balcony, she was free to enjoy the stunning sight. The nerve-settling wine didn't hurt either, she conceded to herself.

Couples slowly sauntering, arms wrapped around each other's waists made Kate smile. Strollers enjoying an after-dinner march along the beach, their pants rolled up, shoes in hand as they walked just within reach of the lapping waves.

"This place is going to be perfect," Kate whispered to herself.

In the midst of the occasional couples, one late-night beach walker caught her eye. Focusing her attention, her brain fought to decipher why this one individual stood out. Instead of enjoying the ocean view or even looking ahead on his path, the lone figure was studying the houses that lined the beach. One by one, the shadowy image seemed not only to be looking at the houses, but seemed to stop and peer into the windows, especially those illuminated by interior lighting.

As the figure reached her balcony, Kate drew back from the railing. Lining her body up with a shadow cast from the roofline, she stood stone still, observing the observer. She hoped she had shrunk back into the shadows before she was detected. The faint dot of a cigarette illustrated the shadow lingering longer than Kate would have liked.

Ultimately, the shadow relented and moved on. Kate continued to spy on the figure's journey, moving to another dark space she hoped would provide concealment. Watching the shadow repeat the exercise at the next house, the glowing dot of the cigarette almost appearing to dance through the night, Kate got a chill that ran the length of her spine.

Deciding her night of beach gazing was over, she shrank back into the house. Closing the doors behind her, she forewent her norm of leaving the night open to the bedroom so the lullaby of the waves could serenade her asleep. Despite having no access other than the bedroom itself, leaving the doors open wasn't an option in Kate's mind.

Resisting the urge to dive into the center of the bed and pull the covers up to her chin, she was compelled to walk the entire house, checking and double-checking each door, lock and window. Only when she was convinced the house was as secure as she could make it, Kate retreated to the bedroom, leaping into the bed and melting under the pillowy covers.

Poking her head out, just so her ears crested the bedding to take in any deviation from the silence that prevailed. Her eyes wanted to close, but, instead they remained fixed on the rotating ceiling fan, watching it make its infinite journey around the center of the room. Ultimately, the hypnotic spin took hold, sending her into an exhausted slumber.

Six

Kate sprang from her bed. Embracing the invigorating refresh of a new day, she awoke with a fiery spirit, not allowing the haunting details of the murder investigation to rule her nerves.

Slinging open the French doors of the master bedroom, Kate felt the blast of the early morning coastal breeze. Taking a few steps out on the veranda, she paused to admire the aquamarine waters Treasure Island was famous for.

With a grin, she reasoned, how could anyone stay down and gloomy with a view like that? A glance toward the spot the man with the cigarette stood threatened to send her a shiver, instead, she shook the thoughts away and focused on the waves.

Spying specks of surfers enjoying the smooth swells, Kate wondered if one of them was handyman Nick. One looked up as he waited for a set to roll in and offered a friendly wave to the spectator on the balcony, answering Kate's question.

Peeling back from the rail, Kate retreated into the house, determined to get a pot of coffee brewing before she got wrapped up in the details of the day. The amazing piece of property she was enjoying was going to delight families, but first, she had to get the house ready.

Just pouring her second cup of coffee, Kate was surprised to hear the doorbell ring. Glancing at the clock, she reasoned the handyman-surfer was ready to start the day early. Setting her cup down, she headed for the door.

Flinging the door open in dramatic fashion, she blurted, "Well, you're early."

Kate nearly jumped back as she realized a stranger was standing on the doorstep and not Nick.

Offering a toothy smile, the man announced, "I'm sorry for the intrusion, ma'am. I'm with the neighborhood safety association. I am making the rounds to ensure everything is ok and make a catalog for the police with any residents who may have seen anything or who have security cameras which may have captured...unusual or suspicious behavior over the past couple of evenings."

Kate frowned, wanting to close the door on the man. Every instinct told her the man standing on her front porch was a fraud. She had worked with enough neighborhood associations to know the man's inquiry was false, especially in light of an active police investigation.

"I'm sorry, I go to bed pretty early. I haven't seen anything of particular interest. We are in the process of updating our home electronics. In fact, a security system is being installed today," Kate decided a fib was the best defense against another fib. In her head, she was thinking her lie wasn't such a bad idea.

"Of course, of course," the man waved his hands in front of him. "This is a safe neighborhood, and we just want our neighbors to know we are doing everything we can to keep it that way."

"I appreciate your efforts," Kate forced a smile, her hand on the door swaying it slightly toward closing.

"Say," the man craned his neck to peer into the home's living space, "quite a view out that back deck, I bet."

Kate was taken aback by the man's assertion. Her mind seized on the reality that he might have well been the man staring up at her balcony the previous evening. Feigning calm, she replied, "Yesterday was my first full day here. I honestly haven't had time to enjoy everything this house has to offer."

"I see," the man offered a sinister smile, his neck still craning to get a better view of inside the house. "Well, I won't keep you. If you see or hear anything, please give me a call."

Handing Kate a card, the man finally took a small step back. Kate studied the card, it was generic aside from a name, Tom Smith, and a phone number printed on a template background of a Florida backdrop.

Lingering awkwardly, the man seemed to study Kate for her reaction or contemplating his next step. The moment gave Kate a chill as she shuffled back further into the house.

To Kate's relief, Nick appeared at the foot of the stairs, his surfboard in hand. Nick's presence was enough to make up the man's mind as he dipped his head in adieu and scuffled quickly down the steps, squeezing by Nick and out to the road.

"Everything all right?" Nick asked, shooting Kate a concerned look.

"Yeah," Kate nodded. "I think so." She watched the man hurriedly turn the corner of the driveway and disappear down the street.

"What was that about?" Nick pressed, walking up the steps, pausing in front of Kate.

Kate's eyes moved from down the drive to the man on her doorstep. It wasn't the first time that she was relieved to see the surfer-handyman. "I don't honestly know. A veiled attempt to surveil the house and see what I knew about the incident the other night," Kate said.

"What do you mean, a veiled attempt? Who was that?" Nick frowned.

"Come on inside. I'll pour you a cup of coffee," Kate suggested.

Nick leaned his surfboard against the house and followed Kate inside. "Do you mind if I rinse off first? I don't want to track sand through the house. I can use the outside spigot."

"The guest bathroom has towels. Help yourself," Kate nodded, heading toward the kitchen.

Reaching into the cabinet, Kate pulled down a cup for Nick.

Kate's mind reeled as she struggled to reconcile the events of the past forty-eight hours. She was uncharacteristically unnerved. The uncomfortable feeling propelled her. She wanted to understand what had happened. She wondered if she could have somehow prevented it. She wondered if the information she provided the police was helpful at all. Now she had to ponder, who was that man that showed up on her front door and what was his connection to the murder of the poor girl who ran past on the beach?

Kate jumped as Nick appeared in her kitchen, his surf shorts and tank top replaced with work clothes. His wet items were cradled in his arms.

Reeling, Kate turned away and took a breath. Slapping an open palm to her chest, she cursed, "You have to get a grip on yourself!"

Collected, Kate reached under the sink, pulled out a grocery bag and handed it to Nick to stow his clothes.

"Thanks," Nick accepted the bag and stuffed his shorts and top in it. "I saw you on the news. You're brave. I might question how smart you are, but brave for sure."

"Thanks…I think," Kate frowned, sliding a cup of coffee across the island to Nick.

"I just mean you seem to march headlong into a scene. Well intended but a bit dangerous," Nick said.

Kate shrugged, "The police were there. I certainly didn't mean to become a spectacle."

"Lead witness, they called you," Nick reported.

"I witnessed little," Kate admitted.

"Maybe enough to gain some unwanted attention," Nick said, taking a sip of his coffee. "This is great, by the way. Thank you."

"Fresh from Kona. I did a project there and became friends with one of the coffee farmers. Great people, great coffee," Kate said.

"Kona, huh? You'll have to let me know the next time you have a job there and you need...a handyman," Nick quipped.

Kate switched into shrewd work mode. She eyed the surfer warily, "We'll see how you do on this job."

Nick sensed the doubt in his temporary boss' eyes.

"I'm not just a surf bum, you know," Nick defended.

Kate added a raised brow to match her "we'll see" comment.

"Tell me about this visitor of yours. What was that all about?" Nick asked.

Settling into the tall pub-style chairs pulled up next to the kitchen island, Kate cradled her coffee close, "He claimed to be part of a neighborhood safety committee collecting information on behalf of the police. He gave me his card."

Kate slid the card across the island to Nick.

Picking the card up, Nick studied it and scoffed, "Nothing screams illegitimate about this."

"Yeah," Kate nodded. "I've worked with hundreds of neighborhood associations. Even the busybody ones don't interfere with police work."

"You should call it in. He could be connected to the crime...or worse, the murderer," Nick suggested.

"I thought about that. He was definitely screening to see if I was a witness. I am wondering if he caught me spying on him spying on the house last night," Kate said.

Nick sat upright in his chair, concern creasing his brow, "What?"

Kate shared the incident with the cigarette-smoking man from the beach the previous evening. Nick's face grew more concerned the more Kate shared. "I'm sure it's nothing," Kate shrugged, her ragged nerves belying concern.

"So, you saw what might have been this guy on the beach last...," Nick prodded.

"I saw *someone* on the beach last night. Lingering, looking at each house on the beach. Most people look at the ocean or the beach ahead of them. This person was looking at the houses, studying them. It made me a bit ...uncomfortable," Kate admitted.

"Kate, I am really worried about you," Nick admitted.

"It *is* unsettling," Kate agreed. "This has certainly been one of the more unusual starts to a project."

Nick looked thoughtful as he sipped his cup of coffee, "You sure you're all right?"

"I'll be fine," Kate nodded, her voice lacking its usual confidence.

Studying Kate for a moment, Nick finished his coffee. Pushing away from the table, he announced, "Well, I should get to work. If you need anything..."

"I'll follow the sound of hammering or whatever it is you'll be doing," Kate assured.

Reluctantly, Nick grabbed his grocery sack of clothes and headed to his truck to swap it for his tool bag.

Kate watched him leave as she gathered the coffee items and put them in the sink. With a slight hum, she conceded to herself that she was indeed comforted by the fact that she would not be in the house alone.

Absorbed in the details of what she needed to put the property manager's spin on the interior of the house, she nearly jumped when Nick poked his head through the French doors that led to the deck.

"I've seriously got to get a grip," Kate chided herself.

"What?" Nick asked.

Kate shook her head sheepishly, "Nothing. What's up?"

"I'm sorry if I startled you," Nick said as he stepped into the room.

"Nonsense, I was just immersed in my work, that's all," Kate said, straightening in her seat.

"Hmm," Nick grunted. "You know, no one would blame you for being a little jumpy. Not with everything that has gone on."

Kate shot Nick a stern glare, "I'm fine."

"All right, all right," Nick acquiesced. "So, not to add to your worries, but I found some cigarette butts by the fan palm on the edge of the property."

Nick held the butts out in his gloved hand for Kate.

"Along the path you and your surfer buddies take?" Kate asked, pulling out a sheet of paper towel for Nick to lay the butts down.

"No," Nick said. "On the other side of the property. They weren't there the other day when I did my inspection."

Kate wrinkled her nose, "Why would anyone stop there to smoke?"

As the words tumbled out of her mouth, a chill ran down her spine. She looked away, seeking the calming presence of the ocean to quell her nerves. Her mind was not so easily deterred as it immediately went to the cigarette-smoking man on the beach.

"Kate?" Nick called softly, bringing her back into the moment.

Kate observed the handyman-surfer who cast her the most genuine, sensitive look she had ever received.

"Are you going to be okay here? Maybe you should get a hotel or something," Nick suggested.

"No. I'll be fine. No one is after me and with the increased police presence, Treasure Island has probably never been so safe," Kate said, almost as much to console herself.

"Maybe we should at least prioritize a security system, just to be safe," Nick pressed.

Kate nodded, "I won't argue with that. We have been converting all of our properties to infuse more tech, anyway. I'd be lying to say it wouldn't make me feel a bit better."

"I'll start designing a system right away," Nick offered.

Kate cleaned up, but instead of tossing butts in the trash, she slid them into a Ziploc baggie and sealed the top.

Nick noticed Kate's handling of the discarded cigarettes. His mouth opened to say something, but with a shake of his head held his tongue. He elected to let the woman manage the situation her way. A slight grin of appreciation at how Kate's mind worked creased his lips. Instead, he pulled out his pad and began drafting the plans for a tight security system.

Seven

Kate ran back and forth from meeting various realtors and rental posting sites to the house to keep whittling down her readiness list. Leaving Nick full reign of the house was not typical for Kate. She usually lorded over contractors as they worked on the properties.

Returning from late afternoon iced tea with a dolphin cruise company that gave discounts for rentals in return for advertising their service, Kate sat her satchel on the kitchen table. With a keen eye, she studied Nick working on installing a new range hood.

Using his shoulder, he pinned the unit to the overhead cabinet while he strained to align the mounting hardware. With a giggle, Kate marched over and questioned, "Is that usually how you do that?"

"Yes. Is there another way?" Nick grunted.

"Let me hold it in place so you can actually see what you're doing," Kate volunteered. "Unless that goes against some code, like men stopping to ask for directions or something."

Relenting, Nick backed out of his awkward position wedged between the stovetop and range hood, "No code. Just a modest pride hit."

"No shame in getting a little help now and then," Kate said. "What do I need to do?"

"Just hold this here and I can align the venting and attach the screws," Nick said.

Kate eyed the appliance and snaked under Nick's arm, her back scraping across his chest as she took over.

"Perfect," Nick whispered, his breath softly tickling Kate's ear.

With his own hands free, he made quick work of the installation. Kate remained dutifully in place, her arms outstretched, her body frozen in place as Nick worked around her.

With enough screws in place, Nick tapped her shoulder lightly, "That's good. Thank you."

Kate let her arms fall and spun, finding herself face-to-face with Nick. The moment seemed to shock them both as they stared into each other's eyes until Kate ducked and with a pirouette danced free from their close-quarters exercise.

"I suppose I should knock a little off my bill. That saved me twenty minutes of struggling and a crick in my neck," Nick said, putting the remaining screws and bolts into place.

Having moved a respectable distance away, Kate shrugged, "You can help me with some advice. The local charters, restaurants and services like us to put their information in our renter portfolios. I never list anyone that I haven't tried. Have you ever gone on Captain Jack's Dolphin Cruise?"

Nick looked over his shoulders, squinting his eyes thoughtfully, "I've heard of it. Seen the boats pull out of the harbor, but never been on a tour."

"Well, he gave me a pair of tickets for tonight's sunset cruise. You can come...that is...if you don't already have plans. I mean, to check it out," Kate's words stumbled the more she spoke.

Nick cocked his head, studying her for a moment. He almost seemed to enjoy the escalating discomfort in Kate's invitation. With a smile, he nodded, "I can go."

"Great. We can have the tourist and local perspective," Kate blurted.

"Right," Nick said as he began stowing the packing materials for the range hood back into their box.

"It's in a few hours if you wanted to get cleaned up and meet at the marina," Kate suggested.

Nick slanted his head and shot a curious eye towards Kate, "I need to get cleaned up…for a dolphin cruise?"

Kate twisted as she shuffled her feet on the kitchen floor, "Well, you've been working hard. Might be tight quarters, just thought you might want to freshen a bit. Maybe knock some of the sawdust off."

"I'll finish up and take off," Nick agreed. "Oh, I got the security system ordered. It should arrive in a couple of days. I just had it shipped to my address. I hope that's all right."

"I should have paid you in advance for that!" Kate exclaimed, moving toward the kitchen table she had turned into her de facto office to grab her checkbook.

"It's okay. You can settle with me when everything is done," Nick waved her off.

Kate looked concerned, "Are you sure?"

"Because I'm a surfer and I am unlikely to have a balance in my bank account?" Nick laughed.

"No, I…" Kate's face flushed.

"I'll see you at the dock," Nick smiled, gathering up the box the range hood came in.

Kate watched him leave, her mind grappling with the way the afternoon conversation unfolded.

Eschewing her professional clothes for a light, flowy sundress, Kate made her way to the boat docks lining Boca Ciega Bay just off of St. Pete Beach. Eyeing the placards above each slip, she found the one with her outfit's name on it.

Scanning the docks, she searched for Nick. Voices behind her from the boat caught her attention. Spinning, she found Nick leaning against the railing, a beer in hand, laughing with the boat captain.

"You found us!" Nick gleamed, raising his can in the air.

Kate walked up to the small gangplank that connected the boat to the dock, "Permission to come aboard."

"Permission granted," Captain Jack walked over to assist Kate across the threshold and get her feet planted on the deck of the boat. "Your friend Nick, here, was just telling me about a time when he saved a sea turtle."

"Oh, not just a rescuer of damsels with their feet stuck on old decking, but of sea creatures as well," Kate said.

Nick grinned, "A little Loggerhead. I was surfing near Sebastian Inlet. Saw the little guy with some old fishing line wrapped around his front flipper. It was binding, so he wasn't able to swim the currents very effectively. I rode the next wave in, grabbed some tools from the truck and swam back out to find him. Performed the surgery right on the deck of my board."

"Wow!" Kate exclaimed, genuinely impressed with the story.

"He almost seemed to hang out with me as a show of gratitude while I surfed that evening. Truth is, I think he was just trying to get the kinks out of his flipper before he swam back to where he was supposed to be for the night," Nick said, clearly proud of his exploit.

"We take conservation of Florida's wildlife seriously aboard the *Captain Jack*," the tour operator proclaimed. "Well, it's about time to shove off. Can I get you something to drink? We have canned wine, spritzers...."

Kate eyed the beer in Nick's hand, "A beer would be fine. Thank you."

The captain nodded and dove into the cooler, producing an icy beverage for his passenger.

"Where are the rest of the passengers?" Kate frowned, staring at the dock.

"Special trip just for you. Tonight was a glitch in the scheduling software. You two get the boat to yourselves," Captain Jack grinned as he pulled in the gangway and started the engines. Calling to Nick, he asked, "You want to get the lines and cast us off?"

"You bet!" Nick exclaimed, launching himself across the boat to slip the knots and free the boat from its tether.

Kate leaned back in her seat. She slipped her sunglasses over her eyes and enjoyed the golden sun sparkling off the water as the boat made its way out of the marina and into the bay.

"Boca Ciega Bay's shores are shared by Gulfport, St. Petersburg and St. Pete Beach. The bay is home to dolphins, manatees, brown pelicans and tons of other wildlife that enjoy the protected preserve," Captain Jack announced.

"It's beautiful!" Kate said, taking in the magnificent view of the crystal waters.

It didn't take them long to see their first pod of dolphins. Kate rose from her seat as Nick crowded next to her to watch the playful swimmers race alongside the boat, riding its bow wave.

"Bottlenose dolphins, like these, live right here in Boca Ciega and similar bays along the Florida coast," Captain Jack explained.

"There are eight! I found eight of them!" Kate squealed excitedly.

"Inshore dolphins live in tight family groups of right around ten or so. Offshore pods can range to over a hundred," the captain said, finding a line that allowed the boat to avoid other traffic but retain the attraction of the fun-loving dolphins.

"They're wonderful," Kate said, enjoying every moment of watching the dolphins. Her attention was drawn to a smaller dolphin swimming close beside a larger one. "It's a baby!" she hissed.

Nick laughed, "You like critters."

"I do," Kate nodded.

"Me too. One of the many reasons I love living here. I can swim, surf and kayak right alongside them," Nick acknowledged.

"I'll be sure to put that in the rental brochure," Kate said.

"You must travel to a lot of great beach areas like this," Nick suggested.

Kate stared through her amber-tinted glasses at the dolphins, "I do. Each one has its own special character."

"That's why you're hired to do what you do. Share your appreciation for each property," Nick acknowledged.

Offering a smile, Kate refused to shift her focus back to the dolphins gliding in and out of the boat's wake.

Captain Jack swung the boat knifing between Isla del Sol and Pass a Grille and out past Cabbage Key toward the open waters of the Gulf. The towering Don Cesar hotel gleamed in its pink hue against the evening sun, a recognizable beacon of the historic site.

Heading north, Captain Jack paralleled the coast.

"Recognize that building?" Nick asked, pointing toward the shore.

"That's the beach house!" Kate exclaimed.

Captain Jack let off the throttle, the resistance of the water naturally applying the brakes. Whipping out her phone, Kate snapped a flurry of pictures and did her best to stabilize the view for a short video.

"It's such a great location!" Kate acknowledged, as the boat rocked softly in the light swells.

A pair of paddle boards slowly drifted by, occasionally dipping their paddles in the water to maintain their momentum.

Kate took in a deep breath, admiring the area. Her gaze stopped abruptly as she spied a man strolling slowly along the beach, his attention on each house as he passed. What struck Kate the most was how the man was dressed in jeans, not exactly beach attire.

Flipping her camera's video recorder on, she zoomed in on the man as she passed by. As he disappeared down the beach, Kate put her phone away. Tugging at Nick's arm, she asked, "Did you see that?"

"See what?" Nick frowned.

"That man. On the beach," Kate said.

Nick looked confused, "There are lots of men on the beach."

"Dressed in jeans?" Kate asked.

"I suppose not," Nick replied. "Why?"

"Possibly nothing. Possibly something. It's difficult to tell anymore," Kate admitted.

Captain Jack nudged the throttle and brought the boat around in a smooth arch, "The sun sets fast on the Gulf. We should start heading back."

Kate's gaze remained fast on the beach. Her eyes scanned for the man or any other anomaly that dared to stand out. She never did see the man again, even as they passed the beach house and several hundred yards after it.

The dolphin family picking up their trail as they entered Boca Ciega Bay recaptured Kate's attention, allowing her mind to focus on more pleasant things than suspicious men. Kate and Nick leaned back in their respective seats as Captain Jack spun the boat and let it drift just in time to see the sun set.

Nick raised his nearly empty beer can in the air. Kate leaned over and clinked hers with his. "This was nice," Nick said.

"It was," Kate admitted.

With just enough light left, Captain Jack restarted the boat and began the low wake push into the marina. Expertly sliding the boat into its berth, the tour operator killed the engines. Grabbing the front line, he launched himself onto the dock and made quick work of securing them to the cleats.

The boat steadied, he held his arm out for Kate as she climbed out of the boat with Nick hopping onto the dock beside her. With a cautious smile, Captain Jack beckoned, "Well-"

"Captain Jack, you provide a wonderful tour. Your dolphin friends are clearly fans and that makes me a fan. I'll be happy to place you in our rental guide," Kate proclaimed.

"That's wonderful," the captain said. With a wink, he added, "It's John, by the way."

Instinctively, Kate's eyes glanced up at the placard hung over the boat slip.

"Captain Jack has a better ring to it than Captain John," the tour owner shrugged.

Kate laughed, "Either way, it was a lovely trip. Thank you...John."

Nick thanked the captain and waited for Kate to make her way from the dock and back on land.

"Do you have time for dinner? My treat," Nick suggested.

Kate hesitated for a moment. She had to admit, her stomach was beginning to growl, "Sure. I could eat. What do you have in mind?"

"I know a place," Nick grinned.

Kate followed Nick's truck to a restaurant nestled directly on the water. Situated just across Blind Pass Inlet that separated St. Pete Beach from Sunset Beach where Kate's beach house sat, the local restaurant was brimming with activity. Locals and tourists merged into an enjoyable medley of beach lovers.

The bar was lively as pirate and tiki-themed drinks were poured. A hostess instantly greeted them, offering Nick an especially warm smile that he shrugged off.

Stopping in front of a table that seemed mere feet from the water, the hostess sat menus down for them, "Good to see you again, Nick."

"Thanks for saving us a spot," Nick said, pulling out Kate's chair for her.

"Don't tell Frank. You know he doesn't like it when we do that," the hostess warned.

"Ahh, I'm one of his best customers," Nick grinned.

"He only likes you because you shared your favorite surf spots with him," the hostess teased.

"He likes me because I faithfully pay the rather lofty tab I ring up here," Nick laughed.

"That does help," the hostess nodded as she scurried away.

Kate sat across the table silently observing the exchange, "You're a regular."

"Regular enough," Nick admitted, straightening in his seat. "I like the atmosphere."

"The water view is amazing," Kate admitted, watching a boat maneuver through the inlet, its lights shining a path on the water.

Pulling at the menu, Kate scanned the options, "What's good?"

"If it was brunch, I'd say a Mimosa and the Godiva white chocolate French toast," Nick replied without hesitation. "For dinner, I'm a fan of the grouper and coconut rice. Caught straight out of the Gulf."

Kate found his selection on the menu and read the description. Satisfied, she laid the menu down on the table.

"Wine?" Nick suggested.

"Maybe a glass. I've got to navigate unfamiliar roads, so I need to keep my full wits about me," Kate said. "What few aren't frayed from witnessing a murder? Or at least the events that led up to one."

Nick nodded. A waitress came over and took their orders. "If it's any consolation, I think you're holding up well. If anything, you're a little too bold," Nick offered.

"I have to keep moving. Besides, I'm never one to allow bullies to win," Kate snapped, resounding defiance in her voice.

"I can see that," Nick laughed.

"Today was nice. Getting out on the water, seeing the dolphins. It was very…relaxing," Kate said.

"Relaxing? You relax?" Nick teased.

Kate cast a playful scowl, "I do make my living staying at beach houses. Eventually, the setting takes hold. I think that's the beauty of the properties we rent. Busy people, couples, families…get an opportunity to escape their busy home lives. The water draws all of that frantic energy away and just replaces it with peacefulness."

"That's how I came to surfing. Being on the water, feeling its power. Mighty and untamable, yet it can be gentle and giving," Nick said.

"A poetic surfer," Kate smiled.

"Just the ocean speaking through me," Nick said, his voice trailing off thoughtfully as he watched the lights of the opposing shore dance off the water.

As the waitress arrived to place two glasses of wine at the table, Kate lifted her glass, "To the call of the ocean."

"May she always land us gently back on the sand," Nick held his glass to hers.

Before long, the waitress returned with two plates. Kate observed as Nick bent his head for a moment before lifting his fork. She didn't comment, but appreciated the sentiment.

Digging into her own plate, a figure at the bar struck her eye. A man sat at an awkward angle in his seat. As she looked up, the man averted his eyes, turning his focus to his drink as if concentrating intensely on its contents.

Kate dipped her head toward her plate, her eyes pinned to the bar. The man returned his gaze only to realize he had been caught staring back. Pivoting his head away, he fixed his posture so that his body was properly aimed at the bar instead of its awkward twist toward Kate's table.

Nick paused, his fork hovering in midair above his plate. His eyes studied Kate before following her gaze toward the bar. The man abruptly pulled several bills out of his pocket and slapped them on the bar. Pushing his chair out, he purposely avoided eye contact with Kate and Nick, before slipping outside.

Kate pivoted in her seat, watching the man. Thinking himself free of scrutiny, the man casually strolled towards his waiting vehicle, lighting a cigarette on his way.

"You know that guy?" Nick asked.

"He was watching me," Kate said.

"Are you sure? I mean, the water is this way. People tend to look out at it," Nick suggested.

"He wasn't looking at the water. He was focused on me. When I looked up, he turned away like he had been caught. *And*, he lit a cigarette in the parking lot," Kate said, convinced the man was of suspicion.

"Lots of people smoke, Kate," Nick said.

Kate eyed the handyman-surfer, "You believe in so many coincidences?"

"I believe there are some strange things happening around you, around your beach house," Nick admitted.

"It was the news broadcast," Kate announced. "Ever since it aired."

Nick looked thoughtfully at Kate. His eyes joined her search for answers but since he had none, he held his words in reserve.

Despite Kate's arguing, Nick insisted on following Kate back to the beach house. As her car pulled into the crushed-shell drive and his truck eased to the curb, a car parked directly across the street pulled abruptly away.

Nick hopped out of his truck watching the taillights speed away. He eyed the spot the car had been parked. Splitting the bookend palm trees that framed the house, the car was positioned to be in immediate view of Kate's front door.

In a jog, he met Kate as she climbed out of her car. He tried to hide his concern, but Kate was astute, cocking her head, "What?"

"Nothing," Nick's voice was thin and unconvincing.

"You know, you didn't need to follow me home," Kate said. Her eyes danced over Nick's as if to interpret his intentions.

"I'm all for keeping you safe, even if it means giving into a shared paranoia," Nick scoffed.

"Oh, it's paranoia, is it?" Kate reeled playfully.

Nick shrugged, "Laced with a certain amount of truth."

Following Kate to her front door, he waited for her to unlock it. He stopped at the bottom step so that he didn't impose any supposition in his insistent presence.

Spinning from her open door, Kate smiled, "Thank you for seeing me safely home…and for joining me on my private dolphin excursion."

"Thank you for having dinner with me, so a salty old surfer didn't need to eat alone," Nick returned the affection.

Suddenly, they both froze. A murmur of voices from the side of the house caught their attention. The hair on the back of Kate's neck rose as a frigid chill knifed through her. Both of their heads snapped toward the voices.

With Nick in the lead, Kate bound down the steps as the two careened into the side yard. The lights from their phones illuminated a pair of startled trespassers.

Planting their feet, Nick and Kate stared down at the intruders. A giggly couple, their arms wrapped around each other, shoes dangling from their hands, sauntered toward the beach.

"Is this not the beach access?" a girl asked, her mildly dazed eyes sparkling in the phone light.

"Not the public one. It's a few blocks down," Kate informed her. "Go on ahead. Just be careful out there."

The girl's eyes widened, "I know. I saw the news. Creepy, huh? Good thing I've got my strapping beau with me."

The young man whose chest she slapped grinned, "I'm sorry to intrude. We'll find the proper public access on the way out."

Nick stood tall, his arms crossed in front of him, "Be sure you do."

The boy nodded, leading his girlfriend down the rough path toward the beach.

As Nick and Kate watched them disappear over the dunes, Kate laughed to Nick, "So, *now* you're concerned with trespassing."

Nick wasn't amused, "Well, things have become a bit less relaxed around here."

"I suppose we did just barrel around the house, in the dark, ready for a showdown," Kate admitted.

Nick winced, "Probably not the smartest thing to do."

"Well, I had my big strapping…handyman-surfer to protect me," Kate laughed to Nick's rolled eyes.

Nick followed Kate once more to her doorstep. Like before, he paused at the bottom step, watching her open the door and slip inside.

"Goodnight, Nick," Kate called.

"Goodnight, Kate," Nick replied, watching her close the door. Only when he heard the telltale click of the deadbolt did he retreat to his truck. Scanning the road and the sidewalks, satisfied no one was staking the house out, he started the truck. Hesitating for a moment, he put the truck in gear and drove away.

Eight

Kate double-checked that the door was locked behind her. The house was never completely dark as the massive view-enhancing windows let every speck of spectral light in. The interior was cast in a soft blue, growing brighter the closer you got to the beach side of the house.

Embracing the tranquility also meant accepting the loneliness, a thought that encouraged her to flip on the series of hallway lights despite the twilight glow.

Tossing her keys on the kitchen counter, Kate glanced at the clock. It had been a long day. Part of her preferred to stay up and work, but another part begged her to call it a night and get some much-needed rest.

Gliding her fingers across the top of her closed laptop, she spun defiantly. She would resist diving back into work and head upstairs to the master bedroom. The house was solidly built, shielding it from exterior noises which was both pleasant and a bit unnerving at the same time.

Walking up the steps, Kate's senses told her she was alone. The dark recesses of her mind caused her to jog up the stairs, casting a brief backward glance, nonetheless.

Flipping on the bedroom light, she gathered her garments and headed to the shower. Turning on the water, Kate quickly undressed and slipped in. She breathed deeply, letting the water flow soak her head, allowing the water to snake its way down her body. The heavy water felt wonderful against her tense muscles.

Letting the shower do its work, Kate actually began to relax. The sensation of the water made her lose track of time as the troubles of the world salted away. As she closed her eyes, letting the water cascade over her face, the perilous thought of her senses completely inhibited and vulnerable in the confines of the shower got the best of her imagination.

The thought of someone sneaking through the house and weaving their way to stand in waiting, right outside the hazy glass of the shower, was too much to bear. A shiver streaked down her spine and all at once, the healing magic of the shower was washed away. The tensing of her muscles, overworked nerves and wandering mind had all returned to plague her.

Shutting off the water, Kate pushed the shower door open, letting the steam billow out into the room. To her relief, there was no one lurking outside her bathroom. Her ears fought through the final water drops eking out of the shower head. Each splash to the floor below echoed throughout the tiled chamber. Straining, she found the house peacefully quiet.

Shaking off the irrational thoughts, she toweled off and slipped into her nightgown for bed. Turning off the lights, she hopped into her bed. The open French doors beckoned in the cool night breeze and the waves sang a melodic lullaby, but despite the inability of any outside presence to gain entry on the high balcony, she begrudgingly rolled out of bed. Closing the doors and spinning the deadbolt, Kate once more dove into bed, sliding her feet under the covers.

House secure and flights of fantasy finally put to rest, she tried to follow suit herself. Squeezing her eyes shut, she had hoped for the second evening to succumb to exhaustion. For a moment, it seemed like her hopes would be realized.

Suddenly, her eyes flashed open and she shot up. Listening intently, she swore she heard the creak of the steps leading up to the main floor patio, a section on Nick's to-do list that hadn't yet been addressed.

Slipping out of bed, her eyes darted around for an improvised weapon. Snatching the television remote, realizing how useless that would be, she cast it aside. Grabbing her robe from the closet, she spied a pair of her high heels. Lofting one in her hands, she held it spike out, a lightweight tool capable of delivering an alarmingly painful blow, she reckoned.

Ignoring her mind screaming about false confidence in her makeshift weapon, Kate snuck out of the bedroom and down the steps. Leaning forward so that her eyes would crest the obstruction of the stairwell as soon as possible, she peered out through the main floor French doors.

Kate's heart pounded as her ears picked up the sound of footfalls on the new decking. Corroborating the detection of noises, her eyes saw a shadow splash across the deck, creeping toward the patio doors.

Knifing through the house's own dark shadows, she streaked to the bank of switches and with a flat palm blasted them all on, bathing the house in light. The sudden burst caused whoever was lurking outside to panic. The heavy footfalls scampered across the wooden deck and down the steps toward the beach access.

Darting to the far wall, she flipped on the outside lights, illuminating the exterior of the house. Makeshift weapon in hand, she flung the door open. Leaning her head out, Kate's senses were on high alert.

She could hear the crunchy, pounding of sand as the intruder ran out onto the beach and out of sight. Kate ran to the edge of the patio, leaning out as far as she could. She tried to catch a glimpse of whoever was sneaking around her house.

Straining her eyes into the night, she merely caught a figure disappearing into the shadows of nearby houses in a clean escape.

Quickly retreating back into her house, Kate slammed the doors shut and spun the deadbolt. Leaving the outside lights on, she shut off all but the under-cabinet lights of the kitchen. This afforded her a view out while most of the interior would be consumed in glare from parties outside the house trying to catch a glimpse inside.

Kate's heart continued to pump vigorously. She was less scared at the moment than confused about what to do next. She contemplated the severity of the incident. Not one to rely on others to resolve her problems, she felt this one was too big to manage on her own. The coincidences following the attack on the beach were just too great for this to be a random prowler.

Digging in her purse, she extracted a card. Reading it, she punched the numbers into her phone.

The robust knock on the door made Kate jump despite her resolve to take control of her nerves. Wiping at the bit of tea that leaped from her mug at her reaction, she strode down the hall, determined to greet her visitor with poise.

Flinging the door open just as a second series of raps rang through the beach house, Kate was met with an unshaven face that looked conflicted to be there.

"Ms. Harper," the man at the door said.

"Come in," Kate said, holding the door wider. "Thank you for coming."

Shutting the door behind her guest and flipping the locks in place, Kate followed the man through the house as his eyes bounced around the impressive coastal home.

Reaching the kitchen, Detective Connolly squinted through seemingly tired eyes, "Why don't you tell me exactly what is going on and why I was awakened from an admittedly much-needed night of sleep."

Kate filled the detective in on the events of the previous evenings leading up to the most recent intruder.

Detective Connolly leaned against the kitchen counter as he took in the tales of beachfront snoopers, rogue cigarette butts and uninvited late-night visitors. The detective pursed his lips and tapped his fingertips together in a bit of a thought-inducing pyramid.

The room fell into a heavy, awkward silence before he finally spoke, "So, since the night of the attack on the beach and your discovery of what might be evidence tied to the case, you have had figures on the beach staring up at your house, apparently creeping around your bushes smoking…what…several cigarettes, surveilling your house from cars parked across the street and now coming onto your back patio in the middle of the night."

Kate twisted, her face trying to display indignance, "That's right."

The detective brought his hands up to his lips before speaking, "And you are only now telling me when all this happened mere yards and days away following the tragic event."

Kate shrugged, "I didn't want to bug you if it turned out to be nothing. It's just, I don't believe so many interlaced events to be a coincidence."

Detective Connolly's stance softened, "You know what? Neither do I. From what you have described, someone, likely related to the events of the other night in some way, has been casing the beach, trying to determine who might have witnessed the murder or anything leading up to the murder."

Kate was shocked at the detective's stance, fearing he was going to belittle her insights and observations, "Thank you. I wasn't sure how you would react."

"I'm not a fan of you running out into the night…to collect murder investigation evidence or to chase after possible intruders," Detective Connolly admitted. "But, I think your sense of circumstances is pretty astute."

"Am I in danger?" Kate asked.

Detective Connolly looked serious, "I don't know. If it is someone interested in the case, like a reporter…no. If it is the murderer himself looking for people who may have witnessed the chase or the murder, you might be."

"What do I do?" Kate sighed, relieved to have the police officer take her concerns seriously.

"I'll have an officer out front on a short leash to your house and the others between here and the crime scene," Detective Connolly announced. He looked compassionately at Kate, who was clearly frazzled, "I can stay…"

"No!" Kate gushed. "I'll be fine. Thank you."

The detective studied the woman for a moment before resolving to leave her in peace, "Well, I am a phone call away. If it is this time of night, I may be a bit disheveled, but I'll be here."

Kate nodded in appreciation at the assurance.

"I mean it," Connolly pressed. "Don't hesitate to call."

"I won't," Kate said, walking the detective to the door.

Detective Connolly swung the door open and spun, "Sincerely, your instincts are sharp. Trust them."

Kate's lips forced a smile at the compliment that she was not sure she earned, "Thank you."

With a nod, the detective walked down the steps, glancing over his shoulder as Kate closed and locked the door.

Turning away to once more retreat upstairs, she mulled over the fact that the detective didn't discount her experiences. She shuddered to interpret that her concerns were real. She was somewhat comforted in the fact that the detective would send an officer her way to keep an eye on the house. Kate was also more than a little concerned that the detective felt there was a valid need to have her house under watch.

Trudging up the steps, she cast her robe aside. As she did, she realized why Detective Connolly kept eyeing the counter with an awkwardly raised brow. Her sole high heel shoe lay without its mate next to the stove. Shaking her head at herself, she reeled, plopping backward onto her bed. Enjoying the fan circling overhead, she locked her eyes on its centrifugal motion, allowing its rotation to lull her into sleep.

Tossing and turning, waking in a palpitating start each time the air conditioning kicked on, she burrowed deep into her pillows, desperately stealing as much sleep as she could. Launching herself up, she wandered to the street front bedroom. Sliding her fingers through the blinds, she created a hole for her to see through. A police cruiser, its running lights casting a slight amber glow on the street in front of her house, gave her some comfort.

Striding with a bit more confidence, Kate flung the doors of the master bedroom open to once more allow the call of the waves to sing her to a more fitful sleep.

Nine

Kate felt like she had barely drifted to sleep when her alarm chimed. With a groan, she rolled over, a flailing arm slapping haphazardly for the snooze button. The moment she had successfully reached the button to provide her another fifteen minutes of much-needed sleep, a loud, insistent knock at her front door breached her attempt at continued slumber.

With a heavy breath, she scrambled out of bed. Grabbing for her robe where she usually kept it, she glanced down, finding it on the floor after casting it unceremoniously aside when she desperately lunged into bed after she visited with Detective Connolly.

Bounding down the steps, her robe barely clung to her shoulders, she skidded to a stop in front of the door. Only then, realizing what a mess she was likely to be, she scowled, tussling her hair. "Who is it?" she called, hoping it was merely an early delivery for her house.

"It's Nick!" a voice called from the other side of the wood slab.

Kate's head fell dejected, eyeing her disheveled appearance. Trying her best to straighten as much of herself up as possible, she reluctantly opened the door. With a forced vibrant smile, she cooed, "Good morning, Nick!"

The surfer-handyman stood on the doorstep, shuffling a bit awkwardly as he glanced back at the patrol car, "Everything okay?"

Kate sighed as her eyes gave a slight roll, "Yeah, I guess the excitement continues."

Nick looked concerned, his voice reticent, "What happened?"

As Nick walked into the beach house and Kate slung the door closed behind him, she winced, "I had another late-night visitor."

Nick's eyes went wide, "What?"

Kate described what she heard and saw, admitting that she called the police detective. Hearing the last part, the surfer-handyman was clearly relieved.

"Well, I'm glad they are taking it seriously. I hope you are too," Nick said.

Nodding slowly, Kate admitted, "I am."

Nick sighed, eyeing the distraught property stager, "Are you all right?"

Kate looked up, her face showing she didn't know how to answer the question.

"I tell you what," Nick offered. "How about I go get us some coffees, and maybe one for the officer out there? You get ready for the day and we'll tackle how to make you feel safer in your own home...or whoever stays here."

Kate looked into Nick's eyes as she pulled her robe tight and nodded, "I'd like that."

Nick spun on his heels, "Lock up. I'll be back in a bit."

Kate followed him to the door. As he cast his eyes over his shoulder, Kate called, her voice dripping with grateful sincerity, "Thank you, Nick."

"No problem," Nick assured and walked briskly to his truck.

Kate watched him climb into the cab. She offered a slight wave with her fingers over crossed arms to the officer maintaining vigil over her house and her neighbors.

When the next knock at the door arrived, Kate was put together and ready for the day. She swung the door open with a great deal more exuberance than earlier that morning.

Nick paused with a pair of coffees in a tray. His eyes swept over the woman that had somehow morphed from sleepy and frazzled to elegant businesswoman in the time it took for him to consult with a barista.

"What?" Kate snapped, her eyes sinking to a scowl.

Nick shook his head, "Nothing. You just...you look good. Ready to start the day, I mean."

Kate studied Nick for a moment before snatching a coffee, "Thank goodness these things come in extra-large and you had the where-with-all to get one."

Nick laughed, "You kinda screamed extra-large coffee when you opened the door."

"Thanks, I think," Kate scoffed.

"The officer was alarmed by someone tapping on the door. By the time he had gotten out the sentence he wasn't supposed to accept anything from civilians, he had the cup in what appeared to be very grateful hands," Nick said.

"I'm the grateful one. I don't think I would have slept without him out there last night...and Detective Connolly stopping by," Kate admitted.

"Detective Connolly himself, huh?" Nick scoffed.

Kate cast Nick a slight look. The moment her lips hit the edge of the coffee cup, her senses were overwhelmed with the comforting sensation of the first sip of the hot beverage.

Her shoulders softened and her visage was sublime, "Thank you."

"No problem," Nick said. His own look was serious, "How about we prioritize that alarm system today? I'll place a call right away to see where the shipment is."

Pulling away, Nick dialed his phone and delivered a very adamant, stern discussion with the clerk on the other side and then the clerk's boss.

Kate was both taken aback and intrigued by the new side of Nick that she witnessed as he navigated a confirmation that the system would be delivered that day. Spinning, a triumphant look splashed across his face, "Your security system will arrive by noon. I'll start installing it myself right away. By evening, this beach house will be more secure than the local bank."

Kate looked relieved, "I am lucky to have had you trespass on my company's property, aren't I?"

Nick cocked his head, "Luck…fate…I like to think of it as the community taking care of the community. You see us surfers as trespassers. I see us as fellow lovers of this coastline and we'll do what we can to protect it from anyone who would serve it harm."

Kate reeled at the implication of his words, "I'm sorry, I didn't mean…"

"It's okay," Nick waved her off. "I get property belonging to people, but the ocean… the Gulf…rivers…they belong to nature and all who revere her. The funny thing about 'us surfers', we'd do anything to preserve the sanctity of these spaces and all the people who are welcome to enjoy it, respectfully."

Kate studied Nick for a moment and then smiled, "I like that. I have been giving thought to the beach access. I think it will serve the owners, the renters and the community alike. In fact, after last night's disruption, I think separating the easement with the property makes strategic sense as well."

Nick looked pleased, "I think you're right. It will add to the privacy and security of the beach house."

"Don't look so smug. I am only looking at the best interest of the property management company. The fact that it helps you and your fellow surfers is only coincidental," Kate snapped.

"I'll take it any way you wish to give it," Nick smiled.

The inference made Kate sour as she turned her head away in protest. Reluctantly, she returned her gaze to the kitchen island and Nick, only to retrieve her coffee.

"You know," Nick scowled. "Maybe you should think about staying at a hotel. At least until all this blows over."

Kate clearly did not relish the idea, "No. I'll be fine. If I can't feel safe here, how can the families that we rent to feel safe?"

"Treasure Island is a very safe place, in general," Nick assured.

"This is a magnificent house in a fantastic location. I'm not going anywhere. No one is going to scare me away!"

Nick smiled at Kate's perseverance. "That's one of the many things I like about you, Ms. Harper. You are a strong and mostly reasonable woman."

"Mostly?" Kate snapped.

Nick merely offered a smile in return, "I should get to work."

Awaiting the arrival of the security equipment, Nick set to work on the remainder of his to-do list. Tackling the squeaky boards on the exterior stairs and beginning the process of cleaving out the community access easement separating the property Kate's company-owned and the neighboring house.

As he carried his tools from the house to the side yard, something caught his eye passing through the ground side entry to the house. The enclosed concrete pad provided access to storage for kayaks, paddleboards and surfboards as well as connected the under-the-house parking to a stairwell that led to the kitchen.

Deep scores in the paint and wood frame of the door made him freeze in his tracks. Dropping his tools, he ran his fingers along the depressions, rubbing the flaked paint and wood splinters between his fingers. His stomach tightened as he realized why the imperfections existed and why he hadn't noticed them before.

With considerable hesitation, he ran up the steps to the kitchen entry and pushed his way through.

Kate, working at the kitchen island, lifted her head up, "Hi, what's up, Nick? Need something?"

Swallowing hard, Nick choked, "I need to show you something…downstairs."

"All right," Kate shrugged, setting her work down on the counter and rising from her seat to follow Nick. She cocked her head in curiosity as she walked.

Leading Kate to the side door on the ground floor, Nick paused, turning to Kate. Running his fingers along the doorjamb, he revealed several markings. Paint chipped to bare wood and deep gouges between the door and the frame were unsettling finds.

Kate looked up at Nick, her voice hesitating before she choked, "Does this mean…?"

"Someone tried to gain access to the beach house…yes," Nick nodded, his tone grim.

Taking a step back, Kate's eyes remained fixed on the discovery. Her lungs swelled as she inhaled a decidedly deep breath. To Nick's surprise, Kate's inhale wasn't one of fearful contemplation, but one of determination. Her eyebrows furrowed into something just short of a scowl. Looking up at the surfer-handyman, Kate proclaimed, "I've about had enough of all this!"

Nick was taken aback by the petite woman's steadfastness. A slight smile creased his own lips in appreciation for the strength that Kate demonstrated. "What are you going to do?"

"I'm going to find out who is stalking the house and the other houses along the beach. If it is related to the murder, then others might be in danger. I'd just as soon take danger head-on than allow it to sneak up on me and take me by surprise," Kate spouted.

"A reasonable tactic, provided you keep yourself safe," Nick said.

"Safer looking for trouble that is trying to find me, than pretend it isn't there while curled up in my bed," Kate fumed.

Studying the woman, Nick had to admit to himself that she was more attractive than ever with her solid stance. "What's the plan?"

"First thing first, the best offense is a good defense. Making myself feel safe in the beach house is the first step," Kate said.

Nick nodded, "The security system will be up and running by sundown."

"I am going to find out what the police know. Are there people I should be on the lookout for? Is there a reason someone is poking around the houses along this beach? Is there someone specifically targeting me?" Kate shared her newly formed to-do list out loud.

Nick looked impressed, "How are you going to get the police to share all of that with you?"

"I'm their star witness, remember?" Kate smiled, pulling out her phone.

Nick laughed as Kate paced along the walkway alongside the house, dialing the Treasure Island Police Department.

Detective Sam Connolly pulled into the drive, the crushed shells and slight rumble of his unmarked police car announcing his arrival.

Nick had already gone to work installing metal plates at each of the house's primary entry points. Leaving the lower side entrance for last so that the detective could inspect it, despite the cavalcade of photos Kate had snapped of it as evidence.

Kate left Nick to his work to go greet the detective. She found the detective in front of his car, inspecting the façade of the house.

"Detective Connolly, thank you for coming," Kate called, instantly redirecting the detective's attention.

Detective Connolly smiled and, with a heavier southern drawl than usual, replied, "I said I would, Ms. Harper."

"Yes, you did, Detective," Kate admitted.

"So, why don't you show me what you found," Connolly said, his arms pushing out in front of him to illustrate he'd follow her lead.

"It's right back here," Kate said, heading towards the side of the house.

"Easy enough access," Connolly noted. He paused momentarily as he turned the corner and found Nick with his tools in front of the suspect door.

The detective eyed the tool bag on the ground and then the handyman.

"Nick is the one who found it," Kate announced, halting in front of the door.

"I came out to work on the rear steps and found the chipped paint. Under closer inspection, it was pretty easy to see someone had pried at the door with a tool leaving some deep gouges," Nick said.

The detective scarcely looked at Nick when he spoke but instead studied the door frame. As Nick did earlier, Detective Connolly ran his fingers along the wood, feeling the depressions with his fingertips, "And there is no chance this was here before?"

Nick shook his head, "I would have noticed it during my inspection."

"There are paint chips on the ground," Kate chirped. "I used some packing tape to hold them in place where I found them."

Detective Connolly squatted towards the ground observing the tape Kate laid down. Eyeing the de facto evidence log for a moment, he carefully pulled at an edge stringing the tape and the paint chips adhered to it in the air in front of his eyes as he inspected it, "I may have to introduce you to my forensics team, Ms. Harper. That was good thinking."

Kate gushed, swaying slightly, "I just thought it best to preserve the scene as well as I could. The afternoon breeze might come along and whisk them away."

"Might," Detective Connolly nodded. Glancing up at Nick, he pressed, "You found this?"

"I did," Nick smiled. "I shared it with Kate as soon as I noticed it…given everything that has been going on around here."

Connolly rose from the ground, assessing the handyman, "Thanks for bringing it to everyone's attention. If you don't mind, Ms. Harper and I can take it from here."

Nick was taken slightly aback before nodding, "Sure. I have plenty of work to do. Installing a security system for Kate, I hope to have it online by nightfall."

"Hmm," the detective considered, "I might like to check out this alarm system when you're finished. Being an expert sort of comes with the job."

Nick shot Kate a glance before squaring his eyes on the detective, "Sure. I'd love to get your *professional* take on my work."

Grabbing his tools from the ground, Nick smiled at Kate, "I'll be out back if you need anything. The moment the system arrives, I'll get to work on it."

"Thanks, Nick," Kate smiled.

Detective Connolly watched the exchange, his eyes following Nick until he disappeared around the back of the house. Turning to Kate, he said, "So, I couldn't help but notice that he had all the tools necessary to try and gain access to the house. The small pry bar in his bag would slip right into this gap and with a slight pull, make those gouges in the wood and most certainly chip away the paint."

Kate's mouth hung agape, "You can't think that Nick tried to break into the house. I mean, he's been helping me since the first day I arrived at the beach house."

The detective's head snapped towards Kate, "The same day you saw someone chased on the beach directly behind this house and I had to open a murder investigation?"

"Well, yeah, but…Nick couldn't have been involved in all that," Kate argued.

"Couldn't? Or you hope he wasn't?" Detective Connolly asked. "The difference between a professional detective and an amateur is a professional understands that everyone connected, no matter how indirect and incidental are all very much still suspects."

"I guess that makes me a suspect, too," Kate spat. "All this happened the day I arrived."

The detective smirked, "You tried to break into your own house?"

Kate coughed and looked away, "Still…"

"Look, I'm just saying, your handyman has unprecedented access to your house. Has been swirling around since you arrived and has all the tools to try and gain entry," Detective Connolly stated.

Kate smirked, "I have to think if Nick wanted to get in, he wouldn't have failed."

"Maybe something spooked him and he ran off. Realized he left some evidence that might get found and called your attention to it in order to avoid detection," the detective said.

"Detective Conolly-" Kate started.

"Please, call me Sam," the detective cut her off.

Kate cocked her head slightly, "*Sam*, let's focus on the facts instead of speculation. Isn't that what a professional would do?"

Connolly frowned, "To be clear, I am all about the facts. The fact is, everyone is a suspect until ruled out."

"Let's start with the victim. Who is she? What do you know about her?" Kate asked.

The detective studied the woman for a moment, "How about we go inside and chat? I've seen what I need to here."

Kate frowned, "You don't want any photos? I have some…"

Connolly snapped his head, "Sure, send them to me and I'll pass them on to forensics."

With a nod, the detective suggested Kate lead him inside.

Kate obliged, pushing through the door and heading up the steep steps to the house. Looking over her shoulder, she asked, "Can I get you an iced tea or lemonade?"

"Got any coffee? Still early morning for a detective. Seems my work hours tend later in the evening," Connolly admitted.

"Not hard to make some," Kate admitted, filling the pot with water and sifting some ground into a filter. Spinning, she propped her palms on the counter and faced the detective, "So, you were about to tell me what you know about the victim and the murder that took place not far from my beach house."

Detective Connolly laughed, "Was I? There isn't much I can say about an ongoing investigation."

"I need to know if there is someone tied to the murder that may pose a threat to me. I have had people eyeing me at restaurants, watching my house from the beach, hiding behind bushes and apparently, trying to enter my house while I was asleep," Kate snapped.

Studying Kate, the detective relented, "Okay, I will tell you what I can. The victim was a young woman, a tourist in town with her boyfriend and a couple of their friends. Her name is…was Joann Marrs, or JoJo to her friends. By all accounts, an American sweetheart with her full life ahead of her."

"And her boyfriend?" Kate pushed.

Detective Connolly sighed, "His name is Dane Smithfield…of the *Smithfields*. They are a prominent southern family with their hands in over a billion dollars in business dealings throughout the region."

"Money often breeds motive," Kate shrugged.

"Ms. Marrs didn't have much," Connolly said.

"Seems she might have been about to have a whole lot," Kate surmised.

"The ring?" Connolly asked. "Yeah, it seems Dane was going to propose on their vacation. He's high on the suspect list, but to be truthful, he seems genuinely broken up about her death."

"Even if he had a hand in it, he could still regret it and be pained by it," Kate suggested.

Detective Connolly laughed, "You might make a good detective yet. It's true. In fact, probably more common than not that the murderer had intense feelings for the person who they victimized."

"Any other suspects on your list?" Kate pressed.

The detective looked more reticent to divulge any additional information. Biting his lip for a moment, he said, "We have to look at the friends they were traveling with. John Trigg and Stacy Karp. They are both single, traveling as a group. Initial interviews didn't reveal any tensions or arguments with each other. They were all pretty tight friends."

"Hmm," Kate hummed thoughtfully. "Any chance chummy could have been too chummy?"

Detective Connolly nodded, "Yeah, maybe. I kind of thought the same."

The pair looked at each other for a quiet moment while the discussion baked in their minds.

The detective shook himself, "Look, I have already said a whole lot more than I typically would on an investigation."

"I appreciate it, Detective. I feel a bit under siege here," Kate admitted.

"Maybe you should stay at a hotel until all of this blows over? I could have the department set something up," Connolly suggested.

"No, if I can't feel safe here at the house, I can't in good conscience rent it," Kate said.

The detective looked past Kate's shoulder as Nick walked into the kitchen, a large box cradled in his arms.

"The question I have," Nick asked, "Is why would someone target Kate in the first place? The 911 call could have come from any house along this stretch of beach or from a passerby that isn't even a resident."

"I've asked myself the same question," the detective admitted. "The adage is true, criminals do often return to the scene of the crime. Either out of fear of being caught, wondering what evidence they left in their wake...or witnesses."

"Or?" Nick pressed.

"Some enjoy the process. They like seeing the chaos, the heartbreak, the thrill of the chase as law enforcement closes in," Connolly added.

"Evidence *and* a witness. My face was plastered all over the news when I handed you the ring I found on the beach," Kate snapped.

The detective nodded, "Evidence and a witness."

"You should really stay at a hotel, at least until Detective Connolly and his department close this case," Nick suggested.

"You two reading off the same page…" Kate mused.

The thought made both men sour.

Kate dashed excitedly to the cupboard and pulled out a plastic baggie. Thrusting it towards the detective, she said, "Here."

Connolly frowned as he snatched the baggie. Eying the contents, he scowled, "You kept these?"

"I thought they might be evidence," Kate rocked on her heels, feeling rather proud of herself. "And they are."

"*Maybe*," Detective Connolly cautioned.

"Those the ones I found by the bushes?" Nick asked.

Kate nodded.

"I'll run them through the lab," the detective nodded reluctantly as he slid them into his pocket. Spinning towards Nick, he asked in a pointed tone, "Say, what brand do you smoke, Mason?"

"I don't," Nick snapped.

"Hmm," Connolly considered Nick's response. Turning to Kate, he asked, "Are you sure you won't consider moving out for a bit? I'm confident I'll get this wrapped up soon."

Kate shook her head, a steady hand clapped on Nick's shoulder, "Nick will have the security system up and running. I'll be fine right here. That what's in the box, the security system?"

"This and the other two boxes in the driveway," Nick nodded.

"See," Kate beamed. "I'll be fine."

Connolly studied Kate and Nick for a moment. "Ms. Harper, as I said, you call *anytime*. I'll be here."

Kate offered a polite smile, "I will. Thank you. That gives me great relief."

Connolly looked at Nick for a moment before turning on his heel and walking down the hallway. "Police Academy is looking for new recruits, Ms. Harper. Just saying..."

Nick and Kate watched the detective leave through the front door.

"He is an interesting character," Kate said.

"He's something," Nick chortled. "That's for sure."

Ten

Nick quickly tore open boxes and began distributing the security equipment around the house in the strategic locations he planned on installing them. He was thorough and thoughtful in his work, wanting to ensure Kate was and felt safe in the beach house.

Modern tech made it easy to work fast and cast a wide net in installing a security system, but Nick was concerned about cracks in the secure foundation. The worst thing with security was being lulled into a sense of false impermeability. He wasn't sure how far the snooper would go. If it was indeed the murderer, he might perceive the most viable eye witness as a life-and-death asset worth risking anything to silence.

Nick knew there was no way to defend against the desperate, but he could make it so there was no chance an intruder wouldn't be detected and the cavalry called. He hoped he could take Detective Connolly at his word that he and his officers would be at Kate's call at a moment's notice.

The problem with Nick, was that he didn't like leaving control in others' hands, never mind fate's. His only real control in this situation was to ensure he made the security system as tight and foolproof as he possibly could.

Scouring every nook and corner of the house, Nick ensured that every viable path into the house was covered. If someone tried to make entry, Kate and the police would know about it. Giving his work a meticulous inspection, reviewing his master plan notes to ensure he included everything he had intended, he chewed his lips as his thumbs hung from his belt loops.

With a mighty sigh and the slightest bounce in his step, Nick went to find Kate to walk her through her new security system. Expecting to see her at the kitchen table she used as her de facto office, he frowned as the space was empty.

"I'm in here, Nick!" Kate called.

Following the voice that echoed through the large house, he walked through the kitchen and into an adjacent alcove. What he found there took him aback. Kate had turned the beach house's dining room into a side project. News reports were printed and spread out on the table.

Photos of the found cigarette butts, attempted door entry and even a snapshot of the card handed to her by the phony home association rep were tacked to the wall. A large print of waves lapping on the beach was scribbled on with a dry-erase marker.

Kate hardly noticed Nick standing in the doorway as she focused intently on her notes. Her brow furrowed as she toyed with a marker in one hand, the other pulling on her lip as she studied the board.

Raising an eyebrow, Nick asked, "What's going on in here?"

Kate snapped out of her thoughtful trance and glanced at Nick, "This is me taking control."

"Of…a police investigation?" Nick pressed.

"Of understanding what actually happened the other night, who might be involved, and most certainly who is likely watching me and trying to break into the house," Kate replied.

"I see," Nick responded, his voice declaring how unsure he was of the idea. "What have you come up with so far?"

"Not much, at least not of new information. Having everything all mapped out, *that* I am finding most helpful," Kate said, her eyes once more landing on the makeshift dry-erase board.

Nick's eyes followed Kate's as he stepped forward, "Who are all these names?"

Kate sighed when she identified the first name at the top of the board, "Joann Marrs. She's the young woman who was murdered the other night."

"Poor thing," Nick whispered. "And these?"

"The boyfriend and two friends they were traveling with," Kate replied.

"Lovers' triangle?" Nick suggested.

Kate nodded, "That's what I thought. They denied it when interviewed by Detective Connolly. He hasn't ruled it out as a possibility, though."

"Hmm," Nick scratched his chin, taking in the sparse information Kate had assembled to that point. "Now what?"

"Now I do what anyone trying to get the bottom of it would do, I investigate what I know and use that to expand the story until either the police get to the bottom of it…or I do," Kate said, folding her arms in front of her.

"Sounds like you might be poking the bear and you already know the bear has been sniffing right outside your door. Are you sure that is a good idea? You should leave this to 'ol Detective What's-His-Face," Nick suggested.

Kate looked Nick in the eye, ignoring the fact that Nick knew exactly what the detective's name was, "Didn't you come to show me how you turned this lovely beach house into a veritable fortress?"

Nick chuckled, "Something like that. Come on, I'll show what I've been up to."

Like a parent excited to watch their child open presents on Christmas, Nick led Kate through the house. Stopping in the foyer, just inside the front door, Nick tapped a panel mounted on the wall. A full screen popped up, giving them access to manage the entire system. "Everything you see here and more can be connected on your phone through an app," he explained.

"Along with turning the alarm on and off as well as the standard panic button, you can cycle through the cameras mounted around the house. They all record in real-time and can be pulled off the web whenever you need," Nick swiped the screen from camera to camera. The front door, the driveway, the side yards and the rear beach access were all captured.

"Impressive," Kate approved.

"And, your company can use it too. If a renter locks themselves out, you can unlock the door remotely. If they leave and you want to ensure the house is locked up, you can do that too. I don't have it hooked up, but you have the ability to add lighting controls and even music or television screens with a welcome message for your guests. With the touch of a button, your office can video conference with guests as well," Nick added.

Kate looked stunned, "Wow. That is way more than the audible alarm I expected if a door was opened."

"Well, these things have come a long way," Nick shrugged.

Kate placed her hand on his arm, "Nick, this is amazing. Thank you so much for doing this. It is above and beyond. We'll pay you for more than the standard time."

Nick shook his head, squaring up with Kate, "You guys can pay for the equipment. The time was me wanting to make sure you were safe."

The sentiment shook Kate for a moment. Her lips parted as her mind whirred, trying to make full sense of Nick's words as his eyes were locked on hers. Her autonomic defense response burst out in a retort, "I just hope it doesn't start calling me Dave and locking the doors on me."

Nick cocked his head, frowning at the comment.

Kate wrinkled her nose, almost horrified at her own response, "I mean, you know…like the movie."

She felt even worse when Nick seemed genuinely crestfallen by her glib outburst. Her hands instinctively reached and grabbed him by his arm, "This…this is great. It is way more than what I expected, but in a good way. You are right, I already feel safer with it in place and it will benefit the company once everything blows over and we can open it up to renters."

They were frozen there for a moment, her fingers wrapped around his arm. Despite his modest frame, Kate couldn't help but notice the definition in the surfer's biceps and triceps. The realization didn't encourage her to let go, though embarrassment did. Releasing her grip, her hands splayed out in the air almost apologetically.

Nick's expression fell more into his usual affable state, giving Kate a much-needed sense of relief. "Please, will you show me how all this works?" she looked up into his eyes.

"Of course," Nick nodded. "First, we'll walk through the keypad. Then we can download the app to your phone and finally I'll show you how you or your company can tap into it from any computer anywhere."

"Great," Kate sighed, her shoulders falling from their tense position. "Thank you, Nick."

For the next hour, Nick meticulously walked Kate through the security system and all of its many high-tech tools. When he was done, he leaned against the kitchen counter proudly, "Not bad for a surfer, huh?"

"This is nothing short of amazing," Kate agreed. "You really deserve to be paid for all your time."

Nick looked thoughtful, a grin crossing his lips, "How about we say the labor for the install is worked out in trade?"

Kate frowned, "In trade for what?"

Nick's grin widened. Casting a glance out of the kitchen window, he watched as the offshore breezes had worked up attractive late afternoon waves rolling in, "Go surfing with me."

"I don't know," Kate hesitated, a mild look of fear crossing her face.

"Come on. It will be fun," Nick encouraged. "I'm a great teacher. And besides, you could stand to get your mind off of things for a bit. There is nothing better than the ocean to clear your mind and instill a healthier perspective."

Kate looked out at the water. It both beckoned and frightened her.

"On top of the waves, you and the ocean work together to tame the world. Trust me, there is nothing better," Nick pressed.

"Oh, I can think of a few things better," Kate bit her lip. With a heavy sigh and eyes that declared her reservation, she nodded meekly, "All right, fine. But I warn you, I'll probably spoil your fun by being awful."

Nick bounced excitedly, "Nonsense. Like I said, I'm a pretty good teacher! I'll grab the boards and meet you out back."

"I guess I'll go change for the beach," Kate murmured, sounding like a child sent off to do her chores.

Eleven

Nick stood on the path to the beach, holding up a pair of surfboards on either side of him.

Kate stopped short, her sarong blowing in the breeze. Looking up at Nick, she pursed her lips, "You just happen to carry a spare board?"

Nick shrugged, a grin escaping his lips, "Yeah. You never know…"

Squinting, Kate scrutinized the surfer, "I get the feeling this isn't the first time you've lured an unsuspecting lady out into the surf."

"You're unsuspecting? Not sure I'd use those words to describe you. Dudes have borrowed it before, too," Nick defended. "Surfing is equally fun on your own or with friends. I like to be prepared and share when the mood hits."

Kate rolled her eyes, "Let's get this over with."

Nick leaned a board towards Kate, "You'll have fun. I promise!"

Studying the board with trepidation, Kate grasped the fiberglass in her hands and scooped it up, tucking it under her arm as she had watched surfers do hundreds of times.

"See," Nick grinned. "You're a natural!"

"Tell me that once we're in the water," Kate grumbled.

Leading her out to the beach, Kate felt almost like a traitor taking the worn surfer path that cut through the beach house's yard. The sun leaned westward, beginning to paint streaks of orange against the blue sky.

The breaking surf crashed against the beach and ran up onto the sand with a melodic force. She watched Nick carry his board above his waist as he nearly tossed it forward before diving onto it chest-first.

Kate emulated his technique and glided alongside him just as a wave crashed. Reaching out his hand, Nick grabbed her board and instructed her to duck. As the wave passed by, he centered the nose of Kate's surfboard, allowing the water to crash over her.

"Now, paddle out before the next wave!" Nick said, letting go of her board.

Kate nodded, straining her eyes forward to keep an eye out for oncoming waves and began stroking arm after arm into the water projecting her board forward. Nick, a couple yards ahead of her, called, "Hold the front of your board and duck. Keep your nose down!"

Seeing a wave rolling towards her, she did as she was told, leaning forward so that the nose of the surfboard dipped and allowed the waves to rumble over her, leaving her on track to keep up with Nick and reach the more gentle rolling swells.

"Good, your first duck dive. Nice work!" Nick beamed. "Now, we'll study the sets."

Kate frowned, "Shouldn't we have started on the beach, practicing my launch onto the board?"

"We could have. I find getting into the rhythm of the waves is far more important," Nick said. "When we find one that looks and feels right, we'll start paddling out ahead of the wave. When you feel a bit of lift and the slightest tug, you'll scramble up onto your feet standing sideways. Crouching like you're playing softball or about to catch a medicine ball at the gym and let the ocean flow through you. You'll feel what it wants you to do. Just don't fight it," Nick suggested.

"It's just that easy?" Kate snapped, looking rather uncomfortable as they bobbed along the swells.

"No. It's not easy. But it is a feeling thing. You have good instincts and it seems you tend to listen to them. They will serve you well on the water," Nick said.

"Maybe I should just watch you first," Kate winced.

Nick scanned the horizon. Seeing a handful of surfers set up a Frisbee throw down the beach, he nodded, "Watch them. And then we'll watch the waves. When we're ready, I'll be with you every step of the way."

"Are you sure about this?" Kate scowled.

Nick cast an innocent smile with the slightest sideways bob of his head, "The worst thing that can happen is you fall off your board and swim. Well, the worst thing is you clonk your head on a board, but I won't let that happen."

Kate's eyes told how not reassured she was.

"Watch… that guy right there!" Nick urged, and pointed as a young man spun his head from the open Gulf to face the beach. With smooth, aggressive strokes, he streaked ahead of the wave. As the wave caught up and lifted the board, he hopped to his feet. One arm forward, one back, his knees bent, he allowed the wave to carry him. Once atop the wave, he pressed on his back heel to pivot the board and worked the nose and tail to stay within the maximum power of the wave. Steering toward the wave's natural longitudinal curve, he spun just enough to allow the wave to carry him in that direction. Right before it crashed on shore, he hopped off, spinning both himself and the board to once more face the ocean.

"Well, he made it look easy," Kate scoffed.

Nick paddled back to Kate, bobbing the swells. Seeing an unsure look on her face, he smiled.

"Don't worry about steering with the wave. Just worry about hopping up, finding your balance and letting the wave take you. Right before you feel the wave give out and displace with air, you want to hop off," Nick said.

"Or..." Kate scowled.

"The wave will toss you face-first into the sand," Nick grinned.

Kate did not look humored.

"It will be alright. I'll be with you," Nick assured.

"What are you going to do, yank me off?" Kate scoffed.

"Something like that," Nick nodded.

Kate rolled her eyes.

Looking over his shoulder, Nick instructed, "Let's watch the waves come in."

"That looks like a good one!" Kate exclaimed, pointing at an incoming wave.

"Don't be fooled. See how the next one builds bigger? Sometimes it's the second...or the third wave that you want to ride. Behind that first wave, there is a bit of a trough. Then it climbs and really gets rolling. That is the power we're looking for," Nick said.

Kate's eyes went wide, leaning hard on the board and making a few strokes, "Should we take it?"

"No!" Nick cautioned. "We would be too late and you'll get stuck either idle somewhere between here and the beach or worse, pummeled into the sand in the bottom of the trough."

"That sounds pleasant," Kate cursed, maneuvering her way back to Nick's side. As the set moved on, the Gulf flattened. Kate snapped back, looking perturbed. "We missed it!"

Nick laughed, "Another set will roll in. Keep an eye on your back and be ready."

The slightest ripple in the water began to grow, rising to a decent sized wave.

"Here's one," Nick said. "Be ready. Go when I say go...now!"

The pair paddled ahead of the wave. As it lifted them up, Kate tried to scramble to her feet, hopping on the board as she had watched the other surfer do. When her board failed to move forward, she frowned. Nick planted his heel hard and spun his board out of the wave.

"What happened?" Kate asked, dropping to her knees as her board bobbed in the wake of the set.

"A little too late, that's all," Nick said. "Come on, let's set back up."

Paddling back out to where the waves were just rolling swells and their curls threatened to begin, they again pointed their noses towards the beach and their eyes to the water.

"I kind of like floating out here. It's rather pleasant," Kate said, sitting atop her board.

"There are some days that's all I want to do. It's kind of peaceful. Away from the beach and the roads beyond that and the cities they lead to. I never feel more one with nature than sitting right where we are. Human without all the human strife," Nick admitted.

Kate eyed him, "You are an interesting man, Nick Mason."

"Aw, all of us surfers get a little introspective while we're riding the swells," Nick gushed.

Kate's eyes widened. The largest ripple yet barreled towards them, "How about that one?"

"That's a good one!" Nick agreed to give her board a shove forward before dipping his arms into the water alongside his board.

Keeping an eye on Kate, Nick kept pace while trying to encourage her forward. As the lip of the wave caught up to them, he called, "Now, Kate, now!"

Jumping to his feet, Nick craned his head over his shoulder to monitor Kate. She stood atop her board, her arms instinctively stretching out in the air east and west as her knees wobbled.

"Bend your knees!" Nick encouraged.

Kate lowered, helping her center mass of gravity meld with the board and accept the power of the wave. Flipping his natural foot position so he could face her, Nick reached his hands out and grabbed Kate's as their boards ran alongside the other.

Like a dance, he led her. Her knees dipped as his dipped. Her balance adjusted in unison with his. For a moment, they were one with the ocean. Feeling as though she was on a cushion of air, Kate watched as the golden sand came closer and closer. Nick grasped her hands tighter and gently led her off the board, over his and held her as they slipped into the water just before it hit the slope of the beach and rolled into a froth of breakwater. Face to face, chest to chest, their hands still laced together, they stood, bracing against the churn of the waves.

"That…was…fun!" Kate gasped, her heart pounded against Nick's.

Nick's smile was as pleasant a smile as Kate had ever witnessed, "Welcome to surfing, Kate."

Kate blinked, realizing how close they were to one another. Pulling away, she pointed, "My board!"

Her untethered surfboard headed toward the shore and slowly began making its way in waist high water down the beach. "I'll get it. Paddle mine out past the swells," Nick said.

In a mighty plunge, Nick kicked his way, arms forward to slice through the water to retrieve the errant surfboard. Reaching it, he immediately hopped on board and began paddling out past the breakers before turning north to rejoin Kate waiting for him at the edge of the swells.

Exchanging boards, they straddled them and once again perched above the swells.

"Well?" Nick asked.

"That was wonderful!" Kate exclaimed, exasperated.

"In all your years of beach property management, this is the first time you tried your hand at surfing?" Nick asked.

"Yeah," Kate shrugged. "I enjoy the beach. The environments I get to visit are amazing. I work a lot. Play a little. Sunbathing…sure. Surfing…no."

"Well, you don't know it yet, but I assure you, you are now hooked," Nick said.

"It's fun, but hooked?" Kate questioned.

Nick grinned, "You'll see. The power of the wave under your feet, tugging at you. Working *with* you to embrace its power as it gracefully guides you to shore. Oh yeah, you're hooked."

"It was a lot of fun. Exciting, heart pounding and peaceful all at the same time," Kate said. "The peace only lasted as long you pulling me off and me gasping for breath, but, it was nice."

"Any longer and that peace would have been broken up with a face full of sand," Nick warned.

"You *are* a wonderful teacher," Kate admitted.

"Wanna go again?" Nick asked.

"Oh, yeah!" Kate exclaimed.

"Hooked," Nick proclaimed knowingly.

Kate's second ride was much like her first, with Nick riding his board backward to face Kate in their delicate above-water dance. Again, he used subtle tension on her hands to help her flow, bend her knees and achieve balance atop her board.

After her third ride and time to appreciate the gentle swells, Kate figured she was on her own. Nick rode several lengths to her opposite side and let her tackle the power of the waves on her own.

At first, it looked like Kate was going to tame the set, riding high, and ever so wobbly, she maintained poise. Embracing the feeling of riding the water, she aimed straight for the beach.

So immersed in the experience, the world seemed to slip away. The increasingly pointed words from Nick had a delayed response from her ears to her head. "Bail, bail, bail…"

By the time the instruction resonated, Kate's board dipped. The power of the wave swept by plummeting her face down towards the trough the wave had left behind. With insufficient water to display her gravity-compliant body, she pierced through the froth and hit the sand hard. She picked her head up just as another wave crashed over, sending her spinning and disoriented.

She stumbled as her salt stinging eyes, bell rung brain and wave jostled body fought to regain a semblance of control in the situation. A pair of powerful hands grasped her shoulders and steadied her.

Kate unceremoniously spit a spray of saltwater from her mouth, wiped her eyes. She opened them to see very hesitant Nick Mason studying her for a response. A burst of giggling from Kate gave Nick instant relief.

"*That* was fun. A little rough at the end, but very fun," Kate grinned, her hands resting on the arms that supported her.

Nick instinctively gave her a wet hug as she soaked in the experience, "Welcome to surfing."

Realizing their awkward beachfront embrace, Kate let go and took a step back even as a new set of waves crashed in to sway them. Suddenly aware of the world beyond her and Nick and the waves, Kate spied her board enjoying its own ride in the froth down the expanse of beach.

"It won't go far," Nick said. "If you're going to go on your own, we should probably use the leash, just be aware of the board when you splash down so it doesn't hit you in the head."

Kate nodded and streaked after the board. When she caught up to it and returned to the spot she had left Nick, she grinned, "One more ride?"

Nick laughed, "Let's do it. Let's make it a good one."

Kate followed Nick beyond the surf to the rolling swells. Letting a modest set flow by, they found their ride home. As before, they stroked ahead of the lead wave, hopping up just as it began to lift the board and steadied themselves low, letting the wave carry them toward the beach.

This time, Kate kept a wary eye on the breakwater, sidestepping off her board into the shoulder-high water, her right arm wrapped around her board as she did so. Nick hopped off right beside her, a confirming nod as he steadied himself, "That was perfect!"

Kate smoothed her wet hair out of her eyes, "I can see why you like this so much."

Nick nodded.

"It's thrilling and peaceful and relaxing and exhausting all at the same time," Kate said. "I think…I think I might be done."

Nick smiled, "Fatigue out on the water has a way of sneaking up on you and you don't want that. We can head in."

"You stay, ride a few more. I'm just going to catch my breath on the beach for a minute," Kate said.

Nick stood, unsure.

"Go, I'll be right up there," Kate assured.

With the steadiness in Kate's voice, Nick complied, spinning, he hopped on his board and swam out along the line of the other surfers dotting the section of Sunset Beach.

Kate tucked her board under her arm and hiked through the surf onto the bleached sand. Using the board as her perch, she sat watching the waves, a new appreciation for their power and reasonable acceptance of providing human joy rides.

She watched Nick, his well-sunned body looking even more tan in the ever-increasing amber light of evening. The sun setting behind was an impressive backdrop as the blue-green waters of the Gulf adopted a dark hue in the fading light.

Nick pressed his heel, guiding his surfboard to dance with the wave, maintaining its peak power to extend his ride. Kate was happy enough to stand frozen still atop her board and just let the waves control her path dead straight toward the shore.

Nick looked graceful, as though he were meant to be a part of the ocean's world. Rather than fighting the power of the current he melded with it. Towards the end of the ride, he squatted low, his fingers extending to the edge of the board stretching out every inch of the ride before rolling off in knee deep water, board in hand.

Kate giggled slightly as she found Nick's silhouette, the shape of his board and the edge of the sun squared off by the horizon worthy of a surfer movie poster.

"I'm pretty sure I looked nothing like that when I was out there," Kate called as Nick made his way onto the beach. "Smooth."

Nick chuckled, "You looked way better than I did the first time out there, I promise you."

Kate looked up at him, accepting his hand to pull her up. Launched to her feet, she stood looking into his eyes, "You were right. You are an excellent teacher."

Turning, they began walking towards the beach house. Nick cocked his head toward Kate, "You did fantastic."

"The board would have done just fine by itself, I was just a passenger along for the ride," Kate scoffed.

"Nah, it's like riding a horse. Sure, the horse does most of the work, but it takes a subtle partnership with its rider to get it to go where it needs to," Nick said.

Slamming to a halt, Nick cast a raised brow as Kate looked at him blankly, "You've never ridden a horse, either."

Kate shook her head.

"Guess we're going to have to fix that too one of these days," Nick laughed.

"However I looked out there, one thing is for sure, I am famished," Kate exclaimed.

"It can certainly build an appetite," Nick admitted.

"Dinner…my treat…for your wonderful lesson," Kate suggested.

Nick grinned, "I know a place…"

"Of course, you do," Kate laughed.

Twelve

Salt and sand showered off, Nick picked Kate up from her beach house and followed the coastal frontage road south and hopped the causeway to St. Pete Beach. Stopping at a little bungalow nestled right on top of the beach, Nick scrambled around the hood of his truck to snatch the passenger door before Kate could swing it all the way open.

Despite the somewhat awkward exchange, Kate flashed a smile, "A surfer *and* a gentleman."

Nick shrugged.

"I like it," Kate assured. Her eyes danced along the front of the building covered in beach-toned paint, well-weathered along the sunshine coast.

"It's not about the building," Nick said, walking through the front door and motioning to the waitress for them to be seated outside. The waitress gave Nick a warm smile and grabbed a pair of menus, leading them to a large back patio that spilled onto a cement boardwalk that ran right along the beach.

Locating a table right alongside the sand, the hostess paused.

"This is great, thank you," Nick nodded, pulling out a chair for Kate.

Kate accepted the seat and scanned the open-air restaurant. An acoustic band set up in a corner of the patio crooning songs of beaches, boats and the Florida Keys. The setting and the beach crowd were a keen balance of festive and casual.

"This is a perfect spot to end a day of surfing," Kate said enthusiastically.

"I thought it would be fitting," Nick said, settling in his own chair.

Kate kicked the sand at her toes, "Reminds me of one of my favorite places in Hawaii. It's perched right on the edge of the Pacific with tables and chairs on the sand. I could sit there for hours."

"I've got all night," Nick shrugged.

Kate smiled and turned her gaze to the ocean. Lights flickered along the water and the constant soft rumble let you know it was there. The moon hadn't risen to a point where its reflection would paint the swells.

"Are you two ready to order?" a voice called behind Kate. She was so lost in her environment, she almost jumped.

Glancing at the menus still stacked where the waitress sat them, she admitted, "I haven't even started looking."

"No rush. Something to drink?" the waitress asked.

Nick looked at Kate, who shrugged, "What do surfers drink after a day on the water?"

Nick just laughed.

"How about something tropical?" the waitress asked.

"Why not?" Kate beamed.

Nick held up his fingers, "How about two of whatever you think fits the bill?"

The waitress nodded and spun on her heels to put her order in.

Kate leaned back in her seat, "All the places I have visited over the years. Being at the beach, along the water…it never gets old."

"So easy for people to take for granted what lies before them, but yeah, me either," Nick agreed, also settling back in his seat.

"Thanks again for taking me out on the water. It was against my better judgment, but I really enjoyed it," Kate said. "So, have you always been a Treasure Island surfer slash handyman?"

Nick laughed, "No. I cut my teeth surfing the Outer Banks of North Carolina. Did a stint in the military. Was fortunate enough to be stationed near the beach. Went out a few times with my buddies and fell in love with it."

"Military man. Thank you for your service," Kate crooned. She frowned, "How'd you end up here?"

"When my billet was up, I finished my law degree. Got my first big job in Tampa. Closed a few cases, one really big one and realized I didn't like my job all that much. Moved from the high-rent condos downtown to something I could easily afford on Treasure Island. I can live my life without a ton of outside pressures. Take it a day at a time," Nick shrugged.

"Hmm," Kate crossed her arms and contemplated this new information. "Not so much the vagabond I originally took you for."

"Still a vagabond at heart. Gotta give me that," Nick grinned.

Kate laughed, "I'm fine to live without confining titles."

"But not so much to prejudge a trespassing surfer," Nick pressed.

Scowling, Kate defended, "It *was* the middle of the workday, and you were in the middle of my company's new property."

"It wasn't really the *middle*," Nick winced.

Making room for the waitress to deliver their umbrella-clad beverages, they ordered whatever the special of the day was. The waitress promised that it never disappointed.

Without wasting time on perusing the menu, they were able to continue their parrying inquisition on each other.

"So, how about you? How'd you end up touring beach houses for a living?" Nick asked, taking a sip and approving his drink.

"I was in real estate. Let's just say I needed to make a geographic change and that meant completely rebuilding the book of business I had spent years earning. The rental management company had an opening that took the right kind of person to fill. One that wasn't anchored to one place and could move freely around the country. That really appealed to me," Kate said. "Plus, the properties are all brilliant."

Nick looked over his drink, "Where is…home then?"

"A storage unit in West Palm Beach. According to the IRS, a little postal store right down the road from it," Kate shrugged.

"I see," Nick mused. "It doesn't feel a little weird not to have roots anywhere?"

"Says the vagabond surfer…" Kate teased.

"A vagabond surfer with a title and deed," Nick quipped.

"Touché," Kate laughed. "I'm sure one of these trips, I will find a location that trumps all others and I'll call it home. Until then, an SUV full of bags takes me from beautiful location to beautiful location unless it entails a plane flight. Or a boat trip."

"Boat trip?" Nick wiggled in his seat intrigued.

"Molokai, Catalina, Mackinac…," Kate rattled off.

Nick was impressed, "You have houses in each of those?"

"Been to each one," Kate nodded.

"Hmm. If you ever need a traveling handyman…" Nick joked.

Kate laughed, "I'll be sure to put your resume on top of the stack."

Nick looked hurt by the insinuation.

"We hire local when we can," Kate said, softening the blow.

As their food arrived, they each pulled back from their lean-forward positions. Kate looked over her plate of grilled grouper and fried conch. With a fork in one hand and knife in the other, she looked ready for battle.

Nick chuckled, after bowing his head and saying a soft prayer, which caught the eye of Kate, he popped his head up, "Dig in!"

"Yeah, not going to lie, I'm hungry," Kate said, slicing a piece of the conch.

When their plates emptied and their personal stories took a decidedly surface-level depth, they pushed back, napkins on the table. The moon had taken its place and hung high over the Gulf leaving a silvery streak of water to shimmer toward the shoreline.

"This was lovely, thank you," Kate said.

"No problem," Nick said. "I should probably get you back."

The words caused a definitive change in Kate's demeanor. Nick eyed her closely, "Got your app?"

Kate pulled out her phone and nodded.

"Check it out," Nick said.

Sliding her finger along the screen, the security alarm app was lit with a variety of green icons.

"All looks safe and sound," Kate reported.

"Good," Nick nodded. His confident smile seemed to boost Kate's mood.

Kate's comfort vanished as Nick pulled into the beach house driveway. The beams of his truck's headlights added to the house's own litany of lights chasing away the night. Glancing at the screen on her phone, she climbed out of the truck to find Nick holding the door for her.

"You didn't have to do that…" she feigned.

"Yeah, yeah I did," Nick pressed.

Following her up to her steps, Kate hit the "I'm home" button on the system. The lock whirred as it released the deadbolt from its steel encasement.

Hand on the door, Kate gave it a shove, swinging it open. Turning, she looked at Nick who appeared anxious, standing on the bottom step. "Did you want to come in?" she asked.

"I do, I mean, if you want me to…to check things out," Nick stammered.

Kate looked thoughtful for a moment, studying his response. "No, I do not need you to 'check things out'. I'll be fine. But…"

"Right, okay," Nick nodded and spun on his heels. "I'll see you tomorrow. Remember to lock up!"

Retreating to his truck, Nick seemed to mutter to himself. Kate stood just inside the doorway, watching him. As he gave an awkward wave from the cab of his pickup, she offered a return wave before slowly shutting the door. With a swipe of her phone, the deadbolt slid back into place and the security system settled into "home" mode.

As she stood with her back to the door, Kate heard Nick's pickup start and back out of the driveway, the shine of its headlights retreating from the façade of the house. With a reassuring glance at the security system panel on the wall, she decided it was time that she embraced the feeling of protection that she was grateful for Nick installing. She was no expert, but it seemed as though he was very thorough.

Kate set her bag down on the kitchen table. She eyed the bank of French doors spanning the back wall of the beach house. Recalling the pleasant evening breeze off the Gulf at the restaurant, she would have loved to invite it into the house. Even with the security system in place, she was still too unnerved to open the accessible doors and windows of the lower floors.

Retiring to the third floor for the evening, Kate threw open the patio doors. Stepping out onto the balcony, she leaned against the rail. Watching the waves she had been riding atop hours before that, the moon so kindly highlighted for her, she breathed deep. If not for that poor girl's death and the creepiness that lurked around the dark corners since, this would have been one of her favorite property assignments.

She laughed to herself, begrudgingly admitting the surfer-handyman played a part in that favoritism.

The beach was quiet that evening. Kate shared the ocean with the waves, the breeze and the handful of birds that stretched their daily hunting in the moon's light. The peace and lack of suspicious figures finally settled Kate's mind. Her eyes were no longer filled with cataloging every body that walked by as a potential suspect or threat and instead could become consumed in the crashing waves.

Subconsciously, she began studying the waves for their rideability. From her limited experience, they all looked rideable. Kate looked at them through the lens that Nick had taught her. Watching fresh sets roll in, she noticed how it was often a second or third trailing set that arrived with the most energy and pushed the furthest up the beach, delivering the longest ride.

As much as she spent time on luxurious beaches, she rarely took the time to play in the water and truly enjoy them. The experience helped shape her view of representing the properties. It helped change how she thought about how she spent her time at the beachfront homes she visited.

With a laugh, she shook her head and moved into the bedroom for the night. Content to catch up on work after all the distractions,

Kate froze. In the corner of her eye, her pleasant reflection was broken by a figure in a hooded sweatshirt scuttling along the beach.

Hands shoved in his pockets, and his rapid pivoting of his head was difficult to tell friend from foe, harmless beach stroller versus a nefarious stranger. Kate's eyes followed him intently until the hooded figure slowly made his way down the beach and out of view.

Kate didn't feel frightened. She felt empowered. The house was set so that if the figure reversed course and attempted entry, she would know. She was well on notice, so there was little chance in her waking hours that she would be taken by surprise.

Content in her feeling of security, she returned to her bedroom and hopped onto her bed. Free from the stress and distractions of recent days, she was determined to catch up on her work. Sitting cross-legged, she opened her laptop in front of her. She considered hitting the button to listen to her favorite playlist, instead, she deferred to the music from the sea.

A glance lighting on her phone and the watchful eye of the security system declared the beach house safe, and Kate settled into focusing on her laptop. Experiencing first-hand the visceral experience the location offered heightened her zeal to sink her teeth into her work, as well as the words that tumbled out in her write-up. The beach house was beautiful, the view was stunning *and* it was the perfect place to grab a board and enjoy the waves until the golden sun began to spill from the Gulf's horizon.

Thirteen

Kate woke with a start. Her senses were screaming at her, demanding she open her eyes. Staring at the ceiling, Kate tried to reconcile what was calling for her to be alert.

She heard it again, this time not from a deep sleep state. A metallic scraping sound followed by a click like two pieces of metal coming together. The noises weren't loud, but they were abnormal, enough so that her slumbering mind urged her to investigate.

She realized that was not what woke her.

Kate kicked out from under her covers and slid her legs over the edge of the bed. Remembering her new security system, she snatched her phone from the bed stand and swiped the screen to life. A red symbol flashed, and with it, a chime alerting her that the cameras had detected a presence and had begun recording.

Clicking on the phone, Kate studied the live feed. Not seeing anything, she scrolled through each of the house's cameras. Seeing nothing amiss, her heart finally slowed.

Chewing her lip, Kate opened the saved file. Locating the image, she slid the toggle back to the time stamped on the initial alert. Out from the bushes of the adjacent yard, a shadowy figure appeared. Clearly trying to avoid the glow of the exterior lights that Kate had left on, its movements were careful. The infrared cameras had no trouble fighting through the dark picking up a person, hood pulled over their head, passing by the camera's lens before disappearing along the side of the house.

An alert on Kate's phone told her a second camera had begun recording. Switching to the live feed, she found a hooded figure hovering over the lock on the side door. Her eyes were wide, her heart was throbbing to its peak. She watched as a person inspected the side entrance to the beach house.

Leaping to her feet, Kate ran down the steps, allowing her feet to land heavily, maximizing the noise she made on her way down. Flipping on the lights, she monitored her phone and the security camera feed.

The figure looked startled and spun toward the rear of the house. As the hooded assailant left the frame of the side camera, the feed switched to the rear in time to see whoever was alongside the house dash toward the beach.

Kate studied the video from the phone app before she dared turn the corner, exposing her to the view from the rear of the house. Keeping the kitchen lights dim, she could see out, knowing the bright exterior lights would make it difficult for anyone to see in.

Leaning against the bank of glass French doors, she peered outside. Confident the system worked and it, along with her quick reaction, scared whoever was lurking, Kate clicked out of her app. For a moment, her thumb hovered over her contacts. Scrolling between Detective Connolly and Nick, she mulled sharing the most recent episode with them.

Deciding she had no real reference as to whether the figure was a threat or merely a nighttime beachgoer cutting through the property, she elected to not disturb either one. Instead, she sat at the table and replayed all of the footage from the moment the security system had sprung into action.

As she watched the hooded figure first come into frame, head bowed, the individual fidgeted with their hands as they slunk through the side of the house. They seemed to understand they weren't supposed to be there. Pausing by the side door was suspicious, but they were soon startled by what Kate assumed was her descending the stairs. Moments later, the figure had disappeared.

Kate set the phone down, her fingers tapping lightly on its casing as she considered the evening's event in context with everything else that had occurred since she had been at the beach house.

The late-night encounter didn't make her more afraid. It made her more resolute. She was going to take control of her situation. The security system made her feel more comfortable, not invincible, but just knowing she was more aware of her surroundings made her feel more confident.

Slinking back upstairs, she slipped into bed. Setting her phone on the nightstand, she tilted the screen so that it faced the bed. Resting her head on the pillow, she closed her eyes, one remaining open a slit alert for any more alerts from the security app.

Fourteen

Despite sleeping with an eye open and an ear peeled, Kate woke surprisingly refreshed. The light blanket of security gave her enough peace to allow her mind to finally get some rest.

Waiting for the coffee to brew, she swiped through the late-night alerts. Only twice, after Kate finally fell asleep, did the system capture a visitor. One inquisitive raccoon emerged through the darkness and right at sunrise, an enterprising pelican darted past en route to fish the calm morning waters of the Gulf.

Pouring a cup of coffee, she heard a knock at the door. Glancing at the clock on the kitchen range, she smiled. Nick was right on time. Pouring a second cup, she walked to the door. Hand on the knob, she froze with a chuckle. Punching in her code so that she didn't set her own alarm off, she pulled the door open.

"Good morning!" Nick called, his hands laden with tool bags.

"Good morning," Kate smiled, opening the door all the way for Nick to come in and set his bags down.

"Is that coffee I smell?" Nick craned his neck so that his nose followed the scent down the hallway.

"Already poured you a cup," Kate nodded.

"You are amazing…I mean, for pouring coffee…you…" Nick struggled. Finally, he just dropped his head and breathed, "Thank you."

Kate laughed, "You're welcome."

Leading Nick to the kitchen, she handed him a cup.

He pulled the mug in with both hands appreciatively, "So, how did it work?"

"The security system?" Kate asked instinctively, knowing exactly what Nick meant. "It worked great. Caught a raccoon, a pelican and… someone."

"Someone?" Nick exclaimed, setting his cup down.

Kate looked hesitant to share. "I don't know whether they were just passing through or what," Kate shrugged her shoulders. "I flagged the recording."

"Let me see it," Nick requested, leaning over the counter.

Kate studied Nick for a moment before relenting and swiping her phone open. Setting the screen in front of Nick, she stood back, watching his observation of the evening visitor.

Nick crossed his arms as he watched the recording. Chewing his lip, he seemed to be deeply considering what he had just viewed. Shaking his head, he said, "Without all the prior events, I probably wouldn't think a lot of it. Whoever it was slowed down at the same side door that was tampered with a couple of nights prior. After my tweaks, they'd have to use detonation cord to go through there. It is odd, though."

Kate nodded slowly, trying to interpret his eyes.

"I can't think it is a coincidence. Besides the surfers who know the path to reach the breaks, no one else would think to traipse through that location," Nick said.

"Maybe it is a surfer," Kate suggested.

Nick almost looked stunned at the consideration.

Kate was concerned she offended him in some way.

"I'll have to take a closer look at the photos and try to match them to the surfers I know that run Sunset Beach," Nick replied.

Taken aback at the seriousness that the surfer-handyman took her suggestion, Kate leaned in. "You really think it could be?"

Nick shrugged, "What is it the crime shows say? Everyone is a suspect?"

Kate raised a brow.

"Everyone but the ones installing security systems in the subject homes, clearly," Nick defended.

"You installed it," Kate grinned. "That gives you the perfect way to circumvent it without anyone being the wiser."

Nick frowned.

Kate laughed, "It's okay. You are *really* low on my suspect list."

The words did little to relieve Nick of his feeling of being implicated as someone who would do harm to Kate.

"Are you going to send that to Detective Connolly?" Nick asked.

"He already thinks I'm a crackpot. Should I?" Kate asked.

"It's just so hard to discount anything at this point," Nick shrugged. "Besides, I have a feeling if you call, he'll come running."

Kate shot Nick an inquisitive glance, but understood the meaning behind his words. Reluctantly, she dialed the detective's number. After describing the late-night visit and what was captured on the video, she hung up the phone.

"Well?" Nick asked, a wry smile across his face.

"He's coming right over," Kate admitted.

Chuckling, Nick swirled the remaining coffee in his cup. Noticing Kate's mood becoming decidedly more pensive, he leaned forward, "Are you okay?"

Kate looked at Nick for a moment as though she had to deeply consider the question, "I am. I'm just no longer in the mood to keep jumping at shadows."

"I can understand that," Nick said. "You're in good hands. The police will get to the bottom of it. I mean, Detective Connolly is racing over here as we speak."

"Thanks," Kate rolled her eyes, lifting her own coffee mug to her lips. Looking across the counter, she studied Nick. "I am."

Nick shot her a puzzled look.

"In good hands," Kate said.

For a moment, their eyes connected. A hearty rap at the front door followed by an earnest ring of the doorbell shattered whatever thoughts they were about to share.

"Thank you for the coffee," Nick said, placing his empty mug in the sink. "I should get to work."

Kate nodded, watching Nick grab his bags and saunter off toward the next house project he was set to tackle. Another stab at the doorbell hastened her pace down the hall, "I'm coming...I'm coming!"

Swinging the door open, she found Detective Connolly standing on her front step. Whipping off his sunglasses, he offered a reassuring smile.

"Thanks for coming over," Kate said, holding the door wide for the detective to enter the beach house.

"I owe you an inspection on the surfer's...handiwork," Connolly said, following her to the kitchen.

"Coffee?" Kate offered.

"Sure, that would be great," Detective Connolly set his sunglasses on the kitchen island counter.

Filling a cup, Kate handed it to the detective as he waved off cream and sugar.

"All right, let's see what you've got," Connolly said, wiggling close to Kate as she brought up the video feed on her phone. Clicking on the saved clips, she showed the detective what she had seen the previous evening.

"Hmm," Connolly considered the images of the figure walking through the sideyard. "Well, in a vacuum, not sure I'd think much of it. Given everything else that has gone on, I'd be remiss to discount it."

"That's what Nick said," Kate agreed.

Connolly shot Kate a look, "The surfer...handyman."

Kate nodded.

"Can you email those clips to me? I'd like to have our tech team review them in closer detail," Connolly said. "If you don't mind, I'd like to poke around, just to see what I can see. Maybe check out this security system of yours."

"I don't mind," Kate said. As the sound of a circular saw ran from outside where Nick was prepping some boards, she added, "You boys play nice."

The detective frowned as he snatched his glasses from the counter, "Thank you for the coffee."

"Thank you for taking all of this seriously," Kate said.

Connolly whirled around, halting placing his sunglasses back over his eyes, "I take your safety...er...the safety of all our constituents very seriously."

Kate simply offered a smile in return as the detective awkwardly pivoted and retreated out of the house.

Detective Connolly eyed the camera positions and studied each door and window for the alarm sensors of Kate's beach house. Walking around the front of the house, he entered the side yard where the camera had picked up the late-night visitor.

Following the same path that he had witnessed in the video, he paused where the suspect had paused – right in front of the side entrance to the house. Lifting his sunglasses so that he could inspect the fresh locks that Nick had installed, he didn't see any signs of tampering. Continuing along the path, he eventually found himself on the path that led to the beach.

Spinning, Connolly caught a figure in the corner of his eye. Nick returned to his sawhorses to grab another board.

"Detective," Nick acknowledged.

"Mr. Mason," Connolly nodded. "Nice system you installed for Ms. Harper. I assume you had her reset the passwords?"

Nick laughed at the insinuation, "Yes, I did. She's as secure as a security system can make her."

"Hmm," Connolly nodded. "How about you… You see any signs of disturbances?"

"Nothing new," Nick shook his head. "I am glad you're taking her safety seriously."

The detective frowned, unsure as to the tone and inference from the handyman. He elected to simply nod in response. Scanning the rear of the home, he offered, "Sure is a nice piece of property."

"It is," Nick agreed. "I didn't think much of the surf access and its implication on the homeowner, but seeing what Kate has gone through, I kind of get it."

Connolly eyed the handyman, "Who else uses this path?"

Nick shrugged, "Outside of a few diehard locals, no one. There is a beach access a block or two in each direction."

"Why the sudden traffic, then?" Connolly pondered.

"I think if you were studying the houses from the beach, you might stumble upon it. No reason unless you had some interest in this spot," Nick said.

The information seemed to impact Connolly and how he thought of the recent swath of visitors. "Or it's a surfer."

"I'll line up the images Kate saved with the surfers I know that cut through this area," Nick suggested.

"If anyone matches, you be sure to let me know," Detective Connolly instructed.

"Of course," Nick agreed.

With a final eye cast around the back of the beach house, Connolly nodded to himself, slipping his glasses over his eyes.

Nick grabbed the piece of lumber he needed, watching the detective exit.

Fifteen

Kate grabbed her keys and her list. Pushing through the front door, she bound down the steps toward her car. Nick was rustling through the bed of his truck for a saw blade to make precision cuts on the finish work.

Lifting his head, Nick paused as Kate stood with her driver's side door open. Flashing a smile, he held the blade in the air, "Found it!"

"I'm not sure I'd even know what you had. I'm good with ordering work to be done, I'm not so much the one to know how to do it," Kate confessed.

"I suppose I should be glad for that, otherwise you wouldn't need me around so much," Nick grinned.

"I suppose not," Kate laughed. "I'm heading out to run a few errands. Need anything?"

Nick looked thoughtful for a moment, "If you're heading past a hardware store, we could use some superfine sandpaper. Never seem to have enough of that stuff."

"Alright, I will," Kate nodded. "See you in a bit!"

Turning back to her car, about to slip into the driver's seat, she paused as she spied a vehicle parked across the street from her driveway.

The engine running, she couldn't quite make out the driver through the tint of the windows. She couldn't place why the car looked familiar, but she could see that the driver was focused on her and the beach house.

Walking away from her car, she strode quickly toward the suspect vehicle, her thumb swiping open the camera on her phone. Without breaking stride, Kate made a beeline to the center of the road while she hit the record button.

The car was suddenly put into gear and the engine roared, jutting the nose of the car erratically in Kate's direction as it pulled from the curb. A pair of powerful arms wrapped around Kate, spinning her away from the speeding vehicle.

Kate twisted to ensure her camera lens was focused on the rear of the car as it sprinted down the road.

"Are you all right?" Nick gasped, setting Kate gently down in the safety of her driveway.

Kate's focus was on the now empty road. "Yeah," she nodded. Holding her phone in the air like a trophy, "I'm fine!"

"What were you thinking?" Nick snapped.

"I was just doing a little investigative filming," Kate replied, unmoved by the experience.

"The door camera would have captured the car without your endangering yourself," Nick scolded.

Kate looked defiant, "It wouldn't get the plate. *I* did."

"You could have been killed!" Nick exclaimed.

Kate shook her head, "They weren't trying to hit me. They just pulled out a little wildly."

"Too close for my comfort," Nick pressed.

"Thank you," Kate looked up at Nick. "I appreciate you being worried. I'm fine. But, thank you."

Hands on his hips, Nick looked away in the direction the car had sped away.

"I'll be careful," Kate promised.

"Sending that to Officer Connolly?" Nick asked.

Kate chewed her lip, "Think I should?"

"The idea of coincidence has fled a long time ago," Nick said.

"Yeah, that seems to be the growing sentiment," Kate agreed. Pulling the footage up on her phone, she sent it to the most recent communication with the officer. "Well, I'm safe now. Time to go hunt down some sandpaper."

Nick watched Kate climb into her car and back out of the driveway. When her car disappeared, his eyes swept the street for any other oddities before spinning to return to his work.

Kate completed her errands, but she was distracted the entire time. Her mind was circulating around the events of the afternoon and over the course of the week.

Driving past the Treasure Island Police Station, she realized she hadn't heard from Detective Connolly. With an apologetic wave, she abruptly cut across traffic and pulled into the station parking lot.

Pulling open the doors, she found the small police department buzzing with activity. Amidst the action was Detective Connolly. He was trailed by several people scribbling hasty notes while he marched toward an older man sporting a bushy mustache who waited by a board.

Kate paused, looking past the police department staff. Her eyes were locked on the board. With a sly smile, she noticed it looked a lot like her own. She took in the photos and notes, comparing it to what she had assembled on the dining room wall.

Across the room, the detective stopped his rattling of instructions and held up a finger to the man who was waiting for him. The mustached man bristled at the notion he had to wait.

"Ms. Harper," the detective sighed. "I suppose I owed you a phone call. Things have been…a bit hectic."

Kate's eyes widened, "You have a lead?"

"Worse, I don't, and pressure is mounting from the mayor's office. Which explains my chief's sunny disposition," Conolly lamented.

"I see," Kate nodded solemnly. "What about the plates?"

"We're running it down. They belong to a rental company, so we have a call in to see who rented it. Gives me something to report at least," the detective said. "If you'll excuse me, I really need to get my chief."

"What about the engagement ring? How does that fit into the situation? Why are people snooping around my beach house?" Kate persisted.

Conolly looked perturbed, "I couldn't comment on any of that if I wanted to. Thank you for filling me in on what you find- it is helpful. But from there, you have to let us handle it. I'm sorry, but I *really* have to go."

The detective turned away and walked quickly back toward the mustached man who wore a sour scowl as he watched the interaction.

Kate didn't yield her ground. She watched from her vantage as she studied the board and even took a few steps closer to try and hear what was being reported to the station chief.

As Conolly began his report, the chief cast his head toward Kate.

"She's still standing there, isn't she?" the detective asked.

The chief nodded, causing Detective Conolly to spin on his heel. Seeing Kate standing within earshot, he scowled. She seemed to study a message on her phone. Rolling his eyes, the detective marched over to her.

"Ms. Harper, I get your concerns. I am doing everything I can to keep you safe and to close this case. In the meantime, I need to conduct my investigation," Connolly said. "Again, we can put you up in a hotel until this all gets sorted out or maybe it's time you go home."

Kate winced, "I'm not going home because some deviant is afraid of what I may have seen! For whatever reason, there is heavy activity around me and my beach house, quite possibly by the killer themselves. No, I'm not going anywhere. I can, however, be helpful in this investigation."

The detective cast a wary glance toward his boss before returning his gaze to Kate, "That's not how it works. We can up patrols during the day in addition to the extra watch we have posted at night. Other than that, I have to get back to my investigation. I need you to go somewhere safe and stay away from any aspect of this investigation."

Frustrated with the detective's stance on accepting her help, she turned in a huff. The detective opened his mouth to speak, envisioning the piercing eyes of his chief burrowing into the back of his skull.

"Look!" he called out. Kate spun on her heel, still fuming. "I'll run the plates off of your photo."

"And you'll let me know what you find?" Kate pressed.

Detective Conolly stammered, "If it is in direct relation to the case, I won't be able to do that."

"This person has been outside my house since the…murder!" Kate steamed.

"I understand that. If I find something that suggests there is a danger to you, I will address it. We'll keep you safe," the detective said.

Kate looked at him for a long moment before conceding, "Let me know what you are allowed to, detective."

"I will," Connolly nodded as he watched the woman leave as quickly as she stormed in. Turning to face his boss and the techs, his face flushed. "You can't blame her. By being a witness and finding that ring, she is in a precarious position."

"Being one of the only witnesses and magically finding that piece of evidence, places her on the suspect board," the chief told his detective.

The idea of Kate being a suspect made Detective Conolly cast a glance over his shoulder where she had confronted him. With a knowing nod, the detective returned to the board to fill his boss in on the investigation.

Kate started her car with her eyes locked on the front door of the police station. She had little doubt the detective and the officers of the Treasure Island Police Department were doing all they could, but she felt as though turning a deaf ear to her and her observations were a miss on their part.

"Alright, if you don't want my help, I'll just have to do this on my own!" Kate cursed, slamming her car into gear.

Kate pulled into the beach house driveway. Seeing Nick turn the corner of the house, she waved a variety of sandpaper packs in the air, "One of these should do the trick!"

Nick laughed and nodded, "If I can't make one of those work, I'm not very good at my job."

He paused the moment that both of their hands had grasped the sheets of sandpaper. There was a distinct look in her eyes.

"You alright?" Nick asked.

"I'm good. I realized waiting makes you helpless. I'm not waiting on the bad guys to make their move. I'm not waiting on the police to take care of me. Like it or not, the mystery seems to be surrounding me, so I'm all in," Kate declared.

Nick wasn't sure whether to laugh or be alarmed. Instead, he strode forward, "What can I do to help you?"

Kate grinned, "We're going to catch a killer!"

Sixteen

Kate printed out the photo of the license plate she captured off the car that veered close to hitting her. Adding it to her wall of clues, she stepped back, trying to figure out how it all fit together.

Walking up behind her, Nick observed her studying the board.

Pinching her lip with her fingers, Kate huffed, "I know he won't share with me who that car belongs to."

"The detective?" Nick frowned.

Kate nodded. "He is under a lot of scrutiny and I'm pretty sure I am a suspect anyway."

"You a suspect?" Nick was taken aback. "You're sort of a victim in all of this, by circumstance at least."

"Think about it. I'm the only witness. I found the clearest piece of evidence, that I'm aware of, at least. I'm a stranger from out of town and I am an overall thorn in the department's side, peppering them for information," Kate said.

"If you committed the crime, shouldn't you have left by now?" Nick asked.

"Not necessarily. Some criminals stay close to observe the investigation and see if the authorities are closing in before they decide to flee," Kate shrugged. "Some are sickly fascinated with the aftermath of the crime. They like the attention they stirred up. They get off on the pain they caused."

"I see," Nick wrinkled his nose. Lightening the mood, he joked, "Should I be concerned?"

Instead of reacting negatively to the insinuation, Kate spun, looking Nick in the eye, "I don't know, should you?"

Nick reeled, "Touché. I guess I deserved that one."

Kate's face fell into a pleasant smile.

"You know, I might be able to help," Nick shook his finger as he stepped toward the board. "If Detective Conolly won't share who the owner of the car is, I have a buddy I can call."

"You have a buddy who can run plates?" Kate was doubtful.

Nick smiled, "An old surfer pal of mine. I'll see what I can do."

"Alright. You do that, I am going to see if I can find out more about the group the victim was traveling with," Kate suggested.

"How do you suggest you do that?" Nick asked.

A grin escaped Kate's lips, "I saw a few notes on the police investigation board. It showed where they are staying."

"You're not going alone. What if one of them is the killer and they recognize you?" Nick's concern was evident.

Kate tossed her keys lightly in the air to illustrate she accepted his offer to join her and she was ready, "Let's go."

Kate pulled up to the St. Petersburg Pier. As she got out of the car, she cast a glance toward Nick, "Up for a boat ride?"

"Boat ride? I thought we were staking out the victim's friends," Nick frowned.

"They are staying on a boat moored at the Isla Del Sol Yacht Club," Kate replied.

"I know that marina. Nice place," Nick said. "What are we doing here?"

"I rented a boat. I thought it would be a good vantage to check up on our possible suspects," Kate shrugged. "Worst case, it's a great day for a boat ride."

"You know how to drive a boat?" Nick asked.

Kate twisted her lips, "Not really. I figured it was like driving a car."

Nick laughed, "Driving it isn't so bad. Parking it...that's the real trick."

"Then I'm glad I brought you along," Kate smiled, locking her car and striding to a series of boats moored along the docks.

Locating the slip listed on her rental agreement, she found a young man prepping it. "You Ms. Harper?"

"I am Kate Harper."

"Great, you're all set. She's gassed up, have her back by sunset," the deckhand said.

Nick held out a hand for Kate to grasp as she stepped from the dock and into the boat. With a nod to the deckhand who began untying the mooring lines, Nick started the engine. The inboard motor roared to life, and a gurgle bubbled to the surface as the propeller spun.

"Have fun!" the deckhand called, tossing the lines onto the boat.

Standing with a hand on the throttle and one on the steering wheel, Nick brought the boat out of the slip and guided it through the marina and into Tampa Bay. Skirting the southern edge of the St. Petersburg peninsula, they slipped under the Sunshine Skyway Bridge.

Knifing between Tarpon and Indian Keys, they wrapped around Isla Del Sol.

Cruising past the yacht club, Kate was relieved they weren't out of place with the afternoon boat traffic. Countless boats and jet skis dotted the area in front of the yacht club marina.

Nick stopped their boat in an area of flat water just off the tip of Long Key.

"This is great!" Kate said, pulling a camera out of her bag. Popping off the primary lens, she snapped a long telephoto lens into place.

Swinging it in the marina's direction, Kate slowly swept the camera until a broad smile crossed her lips. "There it is, the *Sunny Dream*," she declared.

"The *Sunny Dream*?" Nick asked.

"That is the name of the boat the victim was staying on with her friends. It looks like her friends are still staying there," Kate said.

"Well, I'm sure the police said they couldn't leave town," Nick suggested.

"They don't appear very mournful over their friend's death," Kate said, pulling away from the camera. "Here, take a look."

Nick settled in next to Kate and peered at the screen. Two young men and a young woman lounged on the bow of the boat, one of the men tossing beers from a cooler to his friends.

"Yeah, they don't look very torn up, do they?" Nick agreed. "Nice boat, though. Even as a rental, that is a pricey place to hole up for a bunch of kids."

Kate nodded, "There's got to be some family money among that group."

"Money can be an excellent motive for murder," Nick said.

"Money, relationships, jealousy…there are a lot of possible ingredients here," Kate mused as she watched the trio on the yacht.

"Jealousy?" Nick craned his neck toward Kate.

Shrugging, she admitted, "Just one theory. Put a bunch of attractive people into a group like that and things happen."

Nick shot Kate a look.

"It happens," Kate snapped. "Not to me. Just saying…"

Nick laughed. Peering at the screen, he asked, "What is it you are hoping to see?"

"Part of it, I already have. I wanted to get an idea of where they were staying and see if that would provide clues to their background. Secondly, I wanted to see how they were acting in the wake of their friend's tragedy," Kate replied.

"Their background is clearly one of wealth, for at least one of them," Nick observed.

"The boyfriend. At least, that is who rented the yacht, according to the board at the police station," Kate answered.

Nick looked at Kate with appreciation, "You got a glimpse of that board."

Kate grinned, "I may have taken a picture of it with my phone."

"Clever woman," Nick smiled. "So, what do you make of their behavior? I mean, it has been a few days and they are remanded to stay local."

"I suppose imbibing their way through pain would not be so unusual. It's just, I can't see the pain part," Kate said, zooming in as tight as she could to the group. The image was close enough they could see the expressions on their faces.

"They don't seem too distraught, do they?" Nick admitted.

"Like you say, it has been a few days and what else are they supposed to do? I mean, we may have just caught them in a sublime moment," Kate questioned her shaky conclusion as to the lack of mourning they observed on the boat.

"Maybe," Nick said, settling back into his seat. The sun, the bobbing of the boat, and the company nearly coaxed him into forgetting they were staking out a possible murder suspect.

"I'm curious if the rest of the friends come from as equally...affluent backgrounds," Kate mused.

Nick rubbed his chin, "You have their names?"

"On my phone," Kate nodded.

"I may know a guy...," Nick pondered out loud.

Kate chuckled at Nick's propensity to have a solution in his network of acquaintances.

Pulling up the photo from the police station again, Kate zoomed in on the suspect photos.

Nick loomed over her shoulder. He sighed when he eyed the photo on top of the board, "She was a pretty girl."

Kate stopped on the photo with a large red circle etched with the word 'victim' next to it.

"Yeah. It's a shame anyone so young should be taken away from the life that awaited them," Kate nodded. Scrolling down the photo, she highlighted the first face on the suspect board and read, "Dane Smithfield, the boyfriend. He must be the blonde guy near the beer chest."

"Might be that he's a few beers in, but he doesn't seem very affected by his girlfriend's death," Nick observed.

"The girl between the two guys, is Stacey Karp," Kate compared the photo with the girl on the yacht. She's an awful pretty girl, isn't she?"

Nick swallowed hard, "On account that this might be a test, I decline to answer. Let's just say, she doesn't break the camera lens."

Kate laughed as she framed the phone photo to compare to the other young male on the boat, "Our other contestant is John Trigg."

"Doesn't seem to quite carry the same swagger as our friend Mr. Smithfield, does he?" Nick noticed.

"No, he doesn't seem to," Kate said as she watched the image on her camera intently.

"Might bear watching," Nick suggested, settling back in his seat.

As the group on the yacht seemed content to lounge in the sun and toss empty beer cans on the deck of the boat, Kate eased back in her seat as well.

Their boat bobbed up and down gently in the swells that spanned from the wakes of passing boats. The Florida Gulf Coast sun beat down on them, but on the water with the light breeze that carried through, it never felt unbearable.

As they rocked back and forth, they were joined by brown pelicans diving for food. The large birds splashed down in almost comically inelegant landings, yet they happily lifted their heads to allow fish to fall into their wide-open gullets. Anhingas, with their long necks, were far more graceful, slicing into the water, gliding nearly as smoothly as the fish they were chasing. Surfacing with their prizes, they craned around in all directions, keeping a wary eye for predators but their next meal as well.

Kate and Nick almost succumbed to purely enjoying the afternoon instead of the reality of sleuthing.

"They're rather cute, aren't they?" Kate called, watching the anhingas bob around.

Nick laughed, "They're one of my favorite birds along the Gulf. Especially when they stretch out their wings to dry out. They remind me of little dragons…if dragons were adorable."

"Adorable?" Kate scoffed. "That's a word I didn't think I'd hear escape your lips."

Nick blushed, "Yeah, wait 'til you get a load of those…"

Pointing to the water just off their boat's stern, Nick directed Kate's attention.

"Dolphins!" she shrieked.

"Pantropical spotted dolphins," Nick added.

"Now *those* are adorable," Kate admired.

Nick smiled in response. Kate scooted closer to him so that she could get a better view. He had to admit, he didn't mind. In fact, he thought he owed the marine mammals a bit of gratitude.

Glancing over his shoulder, his eyes widened and he scrambled toward the bow, which pointed directly at the yacht club marina. "Uh, oh!" he exclaimed. "Our subjects are on the move!"

Kate spun, ramming her eye towards the screen of her camera. Zooming out so she could see the entire boat in the frame of the lens, she realized the suspects were no longer lounging in their chairs. Adjusting the camera, she located them on the side of the boat, descending the gangway. With loose clothing over their swimwear and sandals, they left the boat and walked up the wooden dock.

"You hungry?" Kate asked.

"I could eat," Nick replied. Frowning, he asked, "What do you have in mind?"

"What's close to the yacht club?" Kate asked.

"There is a bar and grill right on the grounds," Nick shrugged.

"Let's go there, now!" Kate said.

Nick started up the boat. Pointing its nose directly at the marina, he swung the boat toward the dock that led to the small island's boardwalk. Cutting the power and spinning the wheel, he slid the boat sideways close to the dock marked for guests of the bar and grill.

"What do I do?" Kate asked, nervously positioning herself to move in any direction she was asked.

"Grab the bowline, that's the rope in front and wrap it around one of the cleats on the dock," Nick said. Pulling the key from the ignition, he stuffed it in his pocket and launched himself off the rear of the boat, scooping the stern line in his hand as he did so. Glancing at Kate wrapping the rope in the front of the boat to the dock, he pulled the boat tight to the rubber bumpers and tied his line tight to the dock.

Joining Kate, he smiled, "Nice job." Taking her rope in his hand, he unwound it a few feet and tied the boat to the dock in a neat cleat hitch.

With a hand towards the shore, he gallantly led Kate up the ramp to the boardwalk.

"Why thank you, captain," Kate quipped.

"Milady," Nick said, offering his arm out for her.

Hesitating for a moment, Kate slipped her arm into his, "Lead the way, good sir."

Nick smiled, pulling Kate ever so closer to him as they ascended the ramp to the boardwalk. Like leading his dance partner, he swayed her toward the bar and grill.

Standing in front of the hostess stand, Kate stood on her tiptoes, scanning the restaurant. "How about that little table in the corner there?" she asked.

Given there were tables overlooking the water, the hostess was confused with their selection but shrugged. Grabbing a pair of menus, she escorted her guests to the table in the corner of the restaurant closest to the restrooms. Setting the menus down, she had the slightest roll of her eyes, "Here you go, your waitress will be right over."

"Thank you. Been in the sun all day, a few moments in the shade is kind of nice," Kate shrugged.

The hostess offered a thin-lipped acknowledgment and walked away.

Nick followed Kate's eyes. Their table had an ideal vantage to position their view of the three suspects from the yacht.

"I see," Nick nodded. With a slight frown, he asked, "How'd you know they would be here?"

"They didn't bother to clean up after being in the sun. They barely tossed coverings over their bathing suits. The flip-flops and sandals wouldn't be comfortable for too much of a walk. No one bothered to lock up the yacht when they left," Kate explained.

Nick looked shocked, "You got all that through the lens of your camera?"

"Yeah," Kate shrugged. "Didn't you?"

"Yeah, of course," Nick choked.

Sitting back in their seats, they looked around the bar and grill that catered to the boaters and golfers that visited the yacht and country club. Kate leaned her phone against the laminated flip drink menu, facing it toward the suspects from the yacht and hit the record button.

"I suppose that means I should watch what I say…" Nick quipped.

Kate laughed, "I can edit it."

Nick looked shrewd, "Wouldn't it need to be raw footage for evidence?"

"Fine, I guess you're just going to have to behave," Kate winked.

A waitress walked over to take their orders. Kate shifted the phone so it wasn't obvious she was recording the other table.

"Are you sure you wouldn't like a table closer to the water?" the waitress asked.

Kate feigned sun-weary, "Out on the boat all day. It's good to catch a little break."

"Ah," the waitress nodded absently.

As she left, Kate made sure the phone and its camera lens were once more targeting the friends of the murder victim. She looked morose, "Life just…goes on, huh?"

Nick's gaze followed hers. "I suppose it does. I'm not sure it would be so easy for me. Losing someone I cared about, I mean."

"Yeah, I get it. Is the next generation so desensitized to death?" Kate gasped.

"I don't know about that. Maybe they are just coping the only way they know how," Nick shrugged.

"By having cocktails on the water?" Kate wasn't so sure.

"Remember, they *are* remanded here. Maybe there is just so much sulking in a yacht stateroom you can do," Nick suggested.

"Maybe," Kate said, her eyes not hiding the fact that she was intently watching the table across the restaurant.

"I mean, they did order a cocktail in her honor," Nick said, motioning toward the umbrellaed beverage that sat in front of the empty chair at the table. Cocking his head, he watched as the trio grasped each other's hands and bowed their heads, "Are they praying?"

Kate leaned forward, gazing at the group, "It kind of looks like it."

"I guess they aren't completely remiss of their friend's absence," Nick observed.

"No, I guess they're not," Kate breathed.

As the group of young adults settled back into their chairs, they instantly returned to their revelry, raising their cocktails in the air. The man Kate identified from the police station photos as the victim's boyfriend tossed his beverage down his throat and slammed his empty glass on the table. Craning his neck, he looked for the waitress to return to add to his order.

Finding the waitress not readily available, the boyfriend reached across the table for the cocktail perched in front of the empty seat. The move drew immediate ire from the man sitting beside him, which caused the woman at the table to whip her head at the interaction.

Despite the friend's fervent plea, the boyfriend laughed, carrying his voice audibly across the room, "It's a gracious gesture, but come on, she's not *actually* going to drink it."

Pulling his arm away from his friend, glass in hand, the boyfriend plucked the umbrella out of the drink and tossed it irreverently on to the table. Tilting the glass up to his lips, he took a big drink.

His friend fumed with narrow eyes as he glared at him. The lone female at the table seemed more interested in the friend's reaction than the unsympathetic notion of the boyfriend.

As the boyfriend finished his girlfriend's commemorative drink and before he added the empty glass next to his own, he raised it in the air, "Fine. To JoJo!"

The friend half-heartedly raised his glass, the displeasure clear in the expression he wore on his face.

"Come on, Johnny," the boyfriend bellowed as he landed a jab to his friend's arm. "She would want us to celebrate her life."

The friend shook his head, "Life just goes on?"

"No. I want to know what lowlife killed her. I want to tear him apart. Until then, I'm going to soak up the Florida sun that Jo loved so much," the boyfriend said.

"I just want to go home. Get out of this place. It makes me sad," the woman said.

The friend's head swiveled.

Tilting her half-drunk glass toward him, she said, "Just like you, Johnny. I'm drinkin' away the pain."

Pouring the liquid down her throat, she slammed her glass down. Johnny followed suit with him as their friend held his arm high in the air to flag down the waitress.

Kate did her best to shrink into the shadows as she watched, open-mouthed at the exchange. Looking at Nick, who was hiding behind his drink, her eyes were wide.

"There are some interesting dynamics in that group," Kate observed.

Removed from gawking at the table of supposed mourners, Nick set his glass down and turned his attention to Kate.

"Some tension among the friends," Nick agreed.

"Did you see that interaction between Johnny, the friend near the aisle and Dane, the victim's boyfriend?" Kate asked.

Nick nodded, "And how the woman reacted?"

"Stacy," Kate replied.

"Right, Stacy. There is more going on amongst those friends than is on the surface," Nick said.

"Dane Smithfield seems like a callous jerk. He is high on my list of suspects right now," Kate said. "Crime of passion, the would-be engagement ring and he seems the least broken up over all of them."

"If you asked me who just lost their girlfriend by watching them, I'd have said it was Johnny," Nick added.

"How does Stacy fit into their web?" Kate asked.

"And who among them is harassing you and your beach house?" Nick glowered.

"If it is any one of them," Kate cautioned.

"If not them, then who?" Nick reasoned.

Kate wrapped her fingers delicately around the step of her glass and leaned in, "One way or another, we are going to find out."

Seventeen

Kate Harper closed the front door of her beach house. Her palm lingered on the oak frame as she watched Nick head down the steps to his truck. Turning the deadbolt, she paused by the alarm panel and ensured it was set for the evening.

With a renewed sense of security, she retreated into the beach house. The moon played along the waves offering a soft shimmer with each incoming set. The froth of the water pushing up the sand seemed brilliant white in the moon's gleam in contrast to the dark blue night sky.

Grabbing her laptop from the counter, she draped her fingers around a bottle of wine and the stem of a glass. Making her way up the steps, she made a cozy nest for herself in the plush master bed. Confident in the rest of the house being secure, Kate flung open the French doors leading to the upper balcony. With a smile, she allowed the Gulf's rhythmic symphony to be her background music while she settled in front of her computer.

Pouring a glass of wine, she let out a deep sigh. It was the most comfortable she had been since the first night on Treasure Island in the house, before the tragedy unfolded outside her beach house. Putting the glass to her lips, she took a sip before turning her attention to the screen on her laptop.

A wave of contentment washed over her. Just to be relaxed in her own space. Her mind and senses were not hijacked by fear. The simple task of focusing on her work felt good. Kate was at peace. The soft roll of the Gulf waves was music filling the room. The moment was inspirational, leading Kate to her best marketing prose on the beach house since she had arrived.

Lost blissfully in her work, the night melted by. By the time Kate had reached the bottom of her wineglass, she had well surpassed her expectations for check marks on her still lengthy to-do list.

Bobbing her head back and forth, she contemplated another glass and an hour of work or shutting it all down and diving into bed for a solid night of sleep that her body yearned for. Sliding out of bed, she was pulled to the master bedroom veranda. The moon playing on the slow roll of the waves was too much to resist. Walking to the rail, she breathed deep, the hint of sea air a fine pot pourri.

Staring at the beach and wide-open Gulf was both invigorating as well as soothing, only compounding the dilemma of more work or sleep. Kate's decision was made for her.

The sound of glass shattering on the main floor tightened every nerve in Kate's body. Her heart beat so hard in her chest that it hurt. Whipping her head around, she fought for direction- what she should do. Back-pedaling, Kate instinctively pushed against the rail of the veranda before leaping into the master bedroom and slamming the French doors shut.

A cacophony of fresh sounds filled her ears. Her eyes were drawn to her phone which was lit up. Slowly, her mind took over the chaos of initial fear. The sounds were an uneven chorus of phone chimes and security system alarms ringing.

Snatching her phone, she swiped on the security icon that overtook her screen. Hands trembling, Kate keyed on the video feed. The system automatically flowed to the camera whose sensors were tripped. A figure, clad from head to toe in black, including a Balaklava covering their face stared at the broken glass for a moment, their scowling eyes nearly staring directly at the infrared camera lens of the security system.

Despite the alarm's piercing call erupting into the night, the figure froze for just a moment before leaping through the window. The deviant ignored the alarm, bent on their desperate task of silencing Kate.

Kate's heart seized, clutching her chest with her palms. She knew the murderer of the young woman was most likely in her house and making their way to her room.

Her fingers dancing along her phone's keypad, Kate's dialing for help was interrupted by an alarm company operating calling through the speaker.

"This is First Security. We have a glass breakage alarm at your location, is everything all right?" a woman's voice nearly sang through the phone.

"No!" Kate's voice trembled even worse than her shaking hands. "Someone is in my house!"

"Someone is in your house?" the operator repeated.

"Yes!" Kate gasped.

"Try and find a safe place. The police are on their way," the operator said. "I'll stay with you on the phone until they arrive."

"Please!" Kate said, tears streaking down her face.

A window on her phone popped up as the cameras picked up a second figure jumping through the shattered window. Kate could hear thundering footsteps on the main floor followed by a shout. More footfalls were heard ascending the stairs towards the floor the master bedroom and Kate's veranda were on.

Suddenly, a loud crash on the floor below was followed by more shouting. The camera once again popped up with the figure in black leaping through the window, launching themselves over the deck rail and disappearing out of frame.

"Ma'am, are you okay? The police are one minute out, help is almost there," the operator called into the phone.

"I…I don't know. There is someone else," Kate stammered.

"Someone else, ma'am?"

"Kate!" Nick's voice bellowed throughout the house.

"Nick?" Kate called. "I'm upstairs!"

The bedroom door flew open. Kate could see Nick streaking toward the French doors of the veranda.

Flinging the glass doors open, Kate greeted Nick rushing to her. Wrapping her in a secure embrace, Nick asked, "Are you okay?"

Kate swiped at the tears on her cheek and nodded, choking out a hoarse reply. Leaning into Nick's chest, her heart still pounding.

"Ma'am, the police are at your door. Can you make it to them?" the operator's voice barely audible from the phone in Kate's hand.

Realizing she didn't know the answer, Kate looked up at Nick. Offering a nod, Nick escorted Kate from the veranda and into the house. "Yes, I can go meet them," Kate said into the phone. "Thank you."

Peeling away from Nick's comforting arms, Kate cleared her throat and did her best to reset herself. "The police are here," she announced.

Nodding, Nick led Kate down the steps, scanning the lower floor as they made their way to the door. Kate fumbled with the deadbolt before swinging it open. Several police officers were huddled on her front steps, parting as Detective Connolly marched through.

"Ms. Harper, is everything alright?" Connolly asked, surprised to see Nick at Kate's side.

"Someone smashed a window and came into the house," Kate replied, her voice still shaky.

The detective glanced at Nick.

"I have it on the security system video," Kate said.

"Speaking of, would you mind turning the alarm off?" Connolly asked.

Kate nodded, pausing as her brain fought to recall the numbers under stress. Finally punching in the code, the system reset.

After giving orders to the officers to maintain a perimeter, the detective turned to Kate, "Walk me through what you know."

"I was on the veranda, upstairs. I heard a crash. The alarm went off and my phone started beeping. I saw on the screen a person in a mask crawling through the window. I heard their footsteps down below. Then I saw another person, Nick on the camera. There was a commotion and the person in black jumped back through the window and over the railing," Kate said.

"Nick. Rather fortuitous you were…so close by," Connolly gave Nick a discerning look.

Nick seemed unsure of what to say before straightening and admitting, "I was concerned, especially after that lurker last night. I sort of parked down the street in my truck."

Both Kate and Detective Connolly craned their necks at the handyman.

"I saw the police cruiser wasn't assigned to watch the house…so I did," Nick confessed.

The detective frowned, "What lurker?"

Kate sighed, "The security cameras picked up someone going through the alley last night. It didn't seem like a big enough deal to alert you."

"It could be something, it could be nothing. The signs are starting up add up. Someone is very concerned about what you know or don't know," Connolly said. "I'll make a statement to the press stating the witness information was not useful to the investigation, see if that doesn't cool things off for a bit."

"And you," the detective swung his gaze toward Nick. "I'm not one to look good fortune in the eye, but I'm not one to believe in good fortune, either. You lurking around can cause trouble, too. For you and for Ms. Harper.

Nick shuttered a look to brush off the criticism.

Connolly stared at Nick for a long moment. "So, you parked outside Ms. Harper's home and then what?"

"I could just hear the alarm through my open window. It took me a second to realize what it was. I ran toward the house, checking the front and side doors first. Going up the steps of the back deck, I found the window broken. I peered through and saw a shadow heading up the stairs. I jumped through and chased after them," Nick declared.

Continuing, he added, "I lunged at the steps and was able to catch their foot. They fell, but before I was able to tackle them, they kicked me in the face. I was knocked back just enough that they were able to brush by and run back toward the window. I considered giving chase, but I wanted to make sure that Kate was okay."

"I see. This shadowy figure kicked you in the face and hopped up and ran right by you," the detective questioned, noting a red mark near Nick's temple.

"Yeah, when I lunged to trip them, I was extended landing hard on the stairs. I was not in a great position. They were quick to take advantage," Nick said, looking a bit dejected.

"What can you tell me about this person? Were they big, small, heavy?" Connolly pressed.

"I couldn't really tell," Nick thought hard about the brief encounter. "Wiry, I'd say. I should have been able to handle them better."

Connolly nodded subconsciously, "Well, you aren't a trained officer. I wouldn't take your loss too hard."

"Loss?" Kate scoffed. "He chased away what was very possibly the murderer. Clearly not swayed by the house alarm."

"I gotta say, aside from handyman Nick stalking you, the suspect ignoring the alarm is…unsettling," the detective mused.

"What does that mean?" Nick asked, ignoring the disparaging comment toward him.

"It means Ms. Harper is in real danger," Connolly answered, his voice direct.

Kate felt her body tighten at the response.

Connolly brightened, "You say the security system had the suspect and Mr. Mason on camera? Do you have the recording?"

Kate nodded. Finding the saved clips in the security app, she handed the phone to the detective.

Connolly watched as the figure appeared, smashed the window as quickly as they appeared, and paused only for a moment as the security alarm sounded. Hitting the next clip, he saw Nick arrive on the scene, shine his phone's light through into the house and launch himself out of the frame and into the beach house. The last clip showed the first figure leap back through the window, catching a piece of glass that hung from the top of the frame as they jumped through.

"If you don't mind, send those to me and I'll have our digital forensics team see what they can scour from those clips," Connolly said. "I'd like to see the footage from last night, too."

Kate nodded.

"Mr. Mason, if you don't mind, I'd like to have my forensics team have a clean space. You are free to leave," Connolly said.

"I'd like to stay and see what I can do to repair that window, if it's okay with Kate," Nick replied.

"I'd like that. To tell the truth, I'm not too fond of being on my own right now," Kate said.

"I'll have patrols on the beach and a cruiser permanently parked out front. My team will dust for prints or anything else. It looked like the suspect was wearing gloves in the video, I'm not sure if anything will turn up," Connolly said.

"Thank you for coming, Detective," Kate said.

Connolly eyed Kate carefully and shot a wary glance at Nick, "Be careful, Ms. Harper."

The detective spun as his team had already studied the window and collected any fragments that climbing through might have been left behind.

When the police finally left, Nick and Kate looked at each other.

"This is getting dangerous," Nick stated, his voice serious.

"Thank you for being here," Kate said.

"Sometimes intuition pays off," Nick shrugged. "You have to listen to the nagging voices in the back of your head."

Kate nodded, her shoulders slumping. Looking out the windows, the indigo of the late-night was relinquishing to a deep blue.

"Well, we're up. Sunrise is in a couple of hours. I guess I'll put on a pot of coffee," Kate said. Placing her hand on Nick's forearm, she looked up at him, "Thank you, again."

Nick nodded. As Kate pulled away and started filling the filter with grounds, he set to work on the window. Grabbing his shop vacuum from the truck, he began cleaning up the shards littering the bamboo floor. On one knee, he carefully maneuvered the hose to ensure no bits had found their way into the crevice along the floor. Suddenly, he stopped. Snapping off the vacuum, he pulled out his phone, shining it in the crease of the baseboards.

Pulling out his utility knife, he carefully scooted a piece of glass free from under the molding. A speck of red had caught his eye. Nick grinned, with any luck, the shard had the DNA of Kate's would-be assailant.

"Coffee is ready," Kate called, carrying two mugs across the room.

Slipping the shard into a little baggy that once held screws, Nick shoved it in his pocket.

"Sit with me on the deck? Not quite sunset looking west over the Gulf, but the colors are still beautiful," Kate said. Her voice dripped with exhaustion, but calm.

Nick hesitated for a moment, not knowing where strangers might lurk, but decided that was the only time the culprit would get the best of him. With a nod, he held the door for Kate to walk through.

Settling in chairs overlooking the beach, Kate scooted her chair next to Nick's. Cradling her mug between her hands, she leaned over so that her head was resting against Nick's shoulders.

In peaceful silence, they watched the pinks and oranges of daybreak spill across the Gulf. The wisp of white atop the waves glistened as they picked up fragments of the sky's colors.

Eighteen

Nick ordered a new window, covering the open space with a sheet of plexiglass buried in the bed of his truck. Turning to report to Kate, he was surprised to not see her at the kitchen island.

Following the light sound of shuffling paper, Nick found himself in the dining room. Kate held a fistful of papers in one hand; the other was held so that her thumbnail could subconsciously play on her lip while she studied the details of the crime wall she had created.

"Getting anywhere?" Nick asked.

Kate spun, deep in thought, she jumped slightly at Nick's voice. Dropping her hands to her side, she shook her head admitting, "No. Not really. All signs point to the boyfriend. But he is not the man at the bar or sitting outside my house."

"Are you sure? They were fleeting glances," Nick asked.

Kate tapped on the picture of the victim's boyfriend, "Dane Smithfield was not the one staring at me from the bar. He wasn't the one in an economy rental car parked outside my house."

Nick studied the photo, "No, I guess he wasn't. It wasn't his friend John Triggs either."

"Then who is watching me? Who broke into the beach house?" Kate frowned, her eyes covering the photos and clippings pinned to her wall.

"I don't know," Nick admitted. "I need to pick up the replacement window. How about you ride with me? We'll stop at the police station. See if they came up with anything. I can give them the shard of glass that I found."

Kate looked at Nick, "Yeah. It beats staring at the same photos hoping for some mystical answer to jump out at me."

Nick offered a warm smile, "No mystical answers, but maybe some good, honest investigating."

Breaking into a wide grin, an injection of energy uplifting her, Kate replied, "Let's go!"

Detective Connolly wheeled around the corner of the busy police station. Coming to an abrupt halt at seeing Kate and Nick at the front desk, he cocked his head disapprovingly. Seeing Kate's weary eyes meet his, the detective's demeanor softened. All that the woman had been through, she earned the right to some civility.

Striding toward the lobby, Connolly addressed the front desk clerk, "It's alright, Clarice. They're here to see me."

The clerk turned to find the detective welcoming the pair to come with him.

Connolly shot a brief wary look toward Nick but relented. "We can talk in the conference room. Would you like some coffee? Pretty sure we hold the distinction for worst in the city."

"Well, since you sold it so well, I'm fine. Thank you," Nick chimed.

Kate merely shook her head.

Detective Connolly led them to a windowless room and closed the door behind them. With a gesture of his hand, he suggested they take a seat.

"What brings you here? My forensics team hasn't completed their analysis, though I expect it soon," Connolly asked.

"Well, that's part of our visit. Your team missed something. Not entirely their fault, I had to dig it out with a knife," Nick said, fishing the small fragment of blood-stained glass from his pocket.

Connolly reached out and accepted the small, sealed baggie. Holding it up to the light, he inspected it. Seeing the infinitesimal speck of blood on the glass, he nodded his approval. Relenting, he affirmed, "Good job. I'll have the lab run it. If the owner is in the system, we'll be able to identify them."

Kate leaned forward, looking directly into the detective's eyes, "I need answers."

"We don't have answers," Connolly shrugged. "Not yet."

"Tell me what you know," Kate pressed.

The detective leaned back in his seat, putting the tips of his fingers together in front of him as he contemplated the request.

"I'll start," Kate snapped impatiently. "Two people raced by on the beach a few nights ago. One dropped a ring. One died. You have three visitors from out of town that came as a foursome. Joann Marrs is dead. Her boyfriend, Dane Smithfield, and his two friends John Trigg and Stacey Karp are staying on a yacht in Isla Del Sol. Someone, *not* one of the three remaining friends from out of town has been casing out my beach house. Someone or multiple people are surveilling my house. Several attempts have been made to gain entry. Last night, despite the security alarm, one got as far as my stairwell. If Nick hadn't, right or wrong, been keeping an eye on the house, who knows if we'd be having this conversation?"

Connolly nodded slowly at the animated summation.

"Alright. I can't share every detail of the investigation. What I can tell you is we were able to track down the license plate. According to the rental company, the car was recently rented by Frank Driscoll. It turns out, he is a private investigator from Charleston," Connolly shared.

"That's where the Smithfields are from!" Kate's eyes widened. Turning into a scowl, she asked, "What does the private investigator, this…Frank Driscoll, want with me?"

Connolly straightened, "We intend to find out. We've been trying to bring him in for questioning, but he's been evasive. He has swapped out the rental car and we don't know where to find him."

"Couldn't you track him through his credit cards?" Nick spat.

The detective had to fight to not roll his eyes, "Of course. If he used a standard bank card. He hasn't used any credit or debit cards attached to his name. He did have to show his driver's license at the car rental counter, but he used a credit gift card. You can buy those with cash at any grocery or convenience store."

Kate's shoulders slumped, dejected.

"We'll find him. We've reached out to his office, but it appears he's a one man show," Connolly said. Turning on the conference room monitor, he put in his passcode and opened a file. "Here is his picture."

Kate nearly jumped out of her seat, "That's him. He's the guy from the restaurant."

"And outside of your house," Nick added.

"Our primary suspect is Dane Smithfield. This entire case stinks like a crime of passion. We are working through channels to bring him in, but the Smithfield legal team has been…challenging to work with," Connolly admitted.

Nick looked thoughtful, "You suppose they hired the P.I. to try and sweep up evidence ahead of the official investigation?"

"Maybe," Connolly nodded. "I've thought the same. We won't know until we can bring him in."

Kate looked disappointed at the results levied by the police department.

"It's a process. We're getting there. I just wish you weren't caught in the crossfire," Connolly tried to console her.

"What about the two friends? Smithfield might be lawyered up, but does that apply to the other two?" Nick asked.

"The Smithfield team put a blanket around the whole crew. They have a story to tell. The District Attorney's Office is working to get us a warrant to bring them in," Connolly said.

"Even if they do, the lawyers will have them clamped down," Nick frowned.

"Then maybe someone in a non-official capacity needs to chat with them," Kate perked up.

Connolly wasted no time shaking his head, "I know what you're thinking. Don't. You have had enough danger swirling around you and it could interfere with our investigation."

Kate nodded, but the wry smile on her face told the detective she had no intention of adhering to his directive.

"As soon as we have anything, we'll let you know," Connolly assured. Turning to Nick, he said, "Thank you for finding the glass fragment. Let me get this to the lab right away."

The group stood up from their chairs and Detective Connolly held the conference door open for them. Stepping slightly in front of Kate, he looked directly at her, "I mean it. Stay away from anyone and anything to do with this case. I would still encourage you to move out until all of this blows over."

"Thank you for your concern, Detective," Kate offered a half smile and followed Nick out of the conference room and out of the police station.

Barely in the parking lot, Nick glanced at Kate and let out an enormous sigh, "We're going to the marina, aren't we?"

Kate's lips broke into a wide grin, "Yes, we are. I could use some lunch, couldn't you?"

Pulling into the parking lot of the posh yacht club, Nick wished they had swapped his truck out for Kate's luxury SUV. The work truck with surfboards strapped to the bedrails was an obvious anomaly against the expensive cars filling the other spaces.

Even their attire was out of place for the clientele. Kate paused outside the truck's mirror. Tussling her hair and undoing a button on her blouse was a start. Untucking her shirt, she tied the bottom ends to overhang her waist. Glancing at Nick, with his perma-surfer appearance, he just needed to lose his work belt.

"How do we play this?" Nick asked.

Kate's response shocked the handyman as she pressed tight against him, an arm around his back and a hand on his chest. With a giggle to finish the part, she flashed a wicked grin, "Lovers tend to get a pass on out-of-place attire."

"I see," Nick swallowed hard. "We're lovers, huh?"

"For the day," Kate winked.

A willing participant, Nick slung his arm around Kate and drew her closer as they slipped into the grand yacht club's main foyer. Acting oblivious to anyone around them other than themselves, they made their way toward the main restaurant. Pausing as if to study the menu, they surveyed the seated tables. Not seeing Smithfield and his friends, they excused themselves from the hostess and meandered out of the restaurant.

"It is possible they aren't leaving the yacht," Nick warned.

"No," Kate shook her head. "Dane doesn't seem the type to stay penned in. They might be sequestered to the grounds, but they won't stay on the boat the whole time."

Making their way to the more casual restaurant overlooking the marina, they paused as familiar voices declared they had hit pay dirt.

Dane Smithfield, John Trigg and Stacey Karp were at a table by the boardwalk rail.

Barely noticing the hostess as the pair appeared entranced by their own company, Nick and Kate waved toward an adjacent table before returning their gaze to each other.

"Uhm, you'll have to give us a moment to finish putting that table together," the hostess said.

Pretending not to hear, the couple sauntered over to their requested table. Only having one seat in its place, Nick swung to the nearest table. "Is anyone else coming? Do you mind if we take this chair?"

The pair at the table looked up at the newcomer. "Have at it," Dane Smithfield waved him off.

Nick grunted a thank you and wrapped his hands around the top of the chair. Pausing, he eyed a bottle on the table, "Diplomatico Ambassador?"

"Yeah," Dane nodded. "You know your rum."

"Aged in ex-bourbon casks before being finished in Pedro Ximenez sherry casks. Good stuff," Nick said and proceeded to pull the chair away.

"I'll have the waitress grab another couple of glasses," Dane offered. "This bottle's about empty, though."

"Next one is on me," Nick grinned.

Dane shrugged, "Pull up a chair. We aren't going anywhere."

Nick left the chair he was pulling and instead swung the lone chair from their intended table. Holding it for Kate, he helped her slide into place beside him.

Stacey Karp froze for a second. Bobbing her finger up and down, she studied Kate, "I recognize you…"

Kate shrugged, "I get that. I'm in real estate."

"No, that's not it. You're the one from the news. You found the ring!" Stacey exclaimed.

Both Dane and John Trigg cocked their heads, examining Kate.

"Yeah, that is you," Dane finally said. "I guess I should thank you. That ring belongs to my family. If I lost it, my father would kill me. How it got there…is a mystery."

Kate and Nick were cataloging every eye movement, every wince, every sign that might suggest the group at the table was taken aback by their presence.

Dane just shook his head, "It's just a shame JoJo will never get to wear it."

The waitress excused herself and dropped off two highball glasses on the table.

Dane picked up the bottle and poured a few drams of rum in each before topping off the glasses already in front of the trio. Lifting his glass in the air, he said, "To JoJo!"

Kate shot Nick a quick glance before joining her glass over the table, "To JoJo. I'm sorry for your loss."

Dane turned his glass up, sliding the entire contents down his throat. Flipping the rum bottle up, he only managed a modest dribble. Nick raised a finger toward the waitress and pointed at the bottle requesting she bring another to the table.

"So, how did you happen to come by the ring? Seems like an impossible bit of luck," Dane said, licking remnants of rum from his glass.

"I like walking on the beach at night. I literally stepped on it. I thought it was a shell or a piece of glass. It is an impressive piece of jewelry. It shone like a beacon in the moonlight when I looked down," Kate shrugged.

"Do you live right there? Where you found the ring?" John Trigg asked.

Kate and Nick struggled to not react with visual cues to the question. Instead, Kate shrugged, "Down the way a bit. I love how everything is within walking distance on Treasure Island."

"Hmm, yeah. Do you walk there every night?" John asked.

Kate studied the young man, her eyes calculating the intent of the questions. "No. Whenever the mood strikes. You know how that is," she played off the inquiry.

Stacey's eyes widened, "You might have seen JoJo and maybe even her attacker that night!"

"Stacey! Let's respect Jo's memory and quit peppering this woman with questions," Dane snapped and shot an equally disapproving look toward John. "I'm sorry. We haven't even introduced ourselves. I'm Dane. These are my friends John and Stacey."

"I'm Kate, this is…my boyfriend Nick," Kate replied. She could feel Nick's arm tense as she wrapped her fingers around his biceps.

"Nice to meet you," Dane said. Glancing up at the waitress carrying a replacement bottle.

Nick quickly accepted it, thanking the server. Popping the top off, he wasted no time filling Dane's glass. John and Stacey weren't so quick to empty theirs.

Glancing around, Kate eyed a stoic man wearing a suit at the bar. He seemed to pay their table a fair amount of attention as he sipped what appeared to be a glass of iced tea. Giving Nick a soft kick, she panned her head around the room urging his eyes to follow hers, "I like this place."

"Yeah, it's all right. Since…Jo's death, we just haven't felt much like going anywhere else. Except for maybe home, but that's not in the cards right now," Dane admitted.

"You're staying here at the resort?" Nick asked.

Using his glass, Dane pointed to their yacht at the end of the pier, "Home sweet home is over there. You like boats? You should join us sometime."

Nick smiled cordially, "Maybe we will."

Seeing John and Stacey's glass slowly empty, Nick was quick to refill them. He didn't miss the man in the suit at the end of the bar bristling as he did so.

"What brings you guys here?" Stacey asked.

"Any town with beaches and ideally a little surf, I like to check out," Nick said.

John frowned, "Surfing? Aren't you on the wrong coast?"

Nick laughed, "A bit, yes. There are a few spots that are fun to surf when the weather is right. Do you surf?"

"A little. Dane's the group's resident athlete. If it requires strength, speed or body control, he's the reigning hero," John quipped.

"I'll take you guys out sometime. I'll show you the best spots," Nick offered.

John shot Dane a glance before responding, "Maybe."

Dane set his glass down and stretched, "Well, if ya'll will excuse me, I've got to shed the first few glasses of rum."

As Dane left the table, John seemed to relax a bit.

"Yeah, I enjoy surfing. I'm not real good at it, though," John admitted.

"I could teach you a few tricks," Nick said.

"He's an excellent teacher. He taught me and I'm terrible at things like that," Kate chirped. "Do you surf, Stacey?"

"I like to play in the swells, but I'm more the beachcomber type. Like you, it sounds," Stacey said. Her eyes said there was more in her statement than what appeared on the surface.

"It's terrible what happened to your friend," Kate said, her voice soothing. "What was she like?"

John twitched in his seat as he let Stacey respond.

"JoJo was a sweetheart. I was a little surprised when she started dating Dane, to be honest. He is charming and comes with a lifetime supply of money, but JoJo was deeper than that. Dane's great; I just didn't see JoJo with him," Stacey said.

"Yeah, she was special. Dane was lucky," John replied, his voice a bit mopey. "I was surprised to learn he was going to pop the question."

"Oh?" Kate pressed.

John wrinkled his nose, "He's my best friend and all, but he is still in the sowing oats phase of his life."

Glancing at Stacey, who looked uncomfortable at the conversation, John suddenly straightened up as Dane returned to the table.

"What happened to the table? You all seem uptight. Do we need to move to shots?" Dane asked as he slid back into his seat.

"Just reflecting on Jo," Stacey said softly.

"Well, knowing her as well as anyone, I can tell you she wouldn't want us sulking. You two want to join us on the boat for a bit? Maybe a little poker with some…entertaining wagers?" Dane suggested.

Suddenly, Dane's phone buzzed before Kate or Nick could answer. Glancing at the screen, he grimaced. "Maybe another time. We should get going. Thanks for the drink. I like your eye for quality, Nick," Dane announced. "You know where to find us."

Dane, Stacey and John rose from their seats.

"Take the bottle. Maybe we'll join you to finish it off sometime," Nick offered.

Dane scoffed as he accepted the bottle of rum, "Yeah. Thanks, though don't expect this bottle to still be full."

As the trio left, Nick waved the waitress for the tab.

Still admiring the lounge, Kate watched as the man in the suit stayed for just a moment to observe them before tossing a handful of bills on the bar and slipping out after Joann Marrs' friends.

"Did you see that?" Kate asked in a hoarse whisper.

"The uptight man at the end of the bar watching us?" Nick asked.

"He also pulled out his phone just before Dane received a text," Kate added.

Nick brightened, "Legal firm babysitter!"

"That's what I'm thinking," Kate agreed.

"They are on a short leash," Nick mused. Thanking the waitress, he reached for the bill.

"Oh, no. This is mine," Kate snatched it away. "My investigation, my bill."

Nick frowned, "You know, I'm not a *poor* surfer."

Kate paused her scribbling on the receipt and looked at Nick, her lips pursed, "That's not what I meant, but I'm the one embroiled in all this. You shouldn't be paying for the cost of chasing the evidence down."

Placing his hand on her forearm, Nick gazed at Kate, "That's what boyfriends do."

Pulling her arm away, Kate smacked Nick on the shoulder with a laugh, "Stop!"

With a slight shrug, Nick just grinned.

"I guess this part of the investigation is over," Kate conceded.

"I think we got a few nuggets. We just need to keep digging," Nick said.

"Yeah, if babysitters don't spoil all the fun," Kate said, her voice sour.

Nineteen

Back in Nick's truck, he turned to Kate, his expression dead serious, "Does this mean we're broken up?"

Kate rolled her eyes and laughed, "Just drive."

"You know, we never did get lunch," Nick observed as he started his truck. "I know a place…"

Kate smiled, "Of course you do. Let's go."

Nick put the truck in gear.

"Nice move with the chair and then the rum," Kate said. "If I had known how expensive it was, I may have let you pay the bill. Yeesh!"

Laughing, Nick replied, "Yeah, it's not cheap."

"It was good, though. Would've kept the bottle for as much as I paid for it," Kate scoffed.

"You pulled the bill out from under me. It was a choice," Nick shrugged as he pulled out onto the road leading back toward Treasure Island.

Kate stared out the window as the road turned from beach to causeway. Her mind was rapidly analyzing and tabulating each comment, each twitch of an eye or shift in posture the Joann Marrs' friends exhibited at the table in the yacht club restaurant.

Pulling into a parking lot along the Blind Pass Causeway, Nick killed the ignition.

The truck coming to a stop snapped Kate to attention. "You good?" Nick asked.

"Yeah," Kate nodded. "I just want to make sure I capture all of it."

Nick cocked his head questioningly.

"There was so much said and not said at that table. Joann Marrs' friends have a lot of stories to tell," Kate said.

"Well, I understand a good meal is excellent for talking through things and preserving memories," Nick offered.

"I'd be lying to say I wasn't starving," Kate agreed.

Still deep in thought, Kate stepped out past the bed of the truck. Nick's arm flashed out against her chest as a car rushed through the parking lot.

Sheepishly looking up at Nick, Kate flushed, "Thanks."

"Let's get some food into you," Nick said. Given her state, he escorted her with a palm softly planted on her back. Kate didn't seem to mind.

Finding their way to the upstairs balcony overlooking the causeway, they found their seats. Nick paused to slide Kate's chair under her as she settled to the table.

Kate shook herself to focus on the moment. Looking at Nick, she asked, "What's good here?"

"Well, they have some of the best beers from Maine to Florida. Food-wise, their burgers are great, but I'm a big fan of their grouper sandwich," Nick suggested.

"I'll go with that," Kate said, tossing the menu in front of her. "Order me whatever beer you think pairs with that."

Nick laughed, "How about we get a flight? Then you can pick your favorite."

"Sounds good," Kate replied. Her voice was a bit distant as she watched a boat slip under the causeway.

Nick surveyed Kate for a moment and elected to let her have her moment to come to terms with everything her mind had digested. He knew the situation couldn't be easy for her.

As the waitress stopped by, he didn't disturb Kate and put their orders in.

It wasn't until the waitress returned with glasses of water and their home-brewed flights of beer that Kate was present at the table. Grasping her water, she took a big pull from her straw and turned her gaze to Nick.

"Sorry," she winced. "Guess my mind is on overdrive."

"That's okay. When my mind is overwhelmed, I like to write things down. I brought a notepad from the truck. Where do we start?" Nick asked.

Kate smiled, "You really are...resourceful. I like that."

Nick chuckled his response.

"Before we dive into murder suspects, where do I start with all this?" Kate asked, eyeing the assortment of tiny beer glasses placed in front of her.

"Move left to right. Mild flavor to more robust, though I would say the middle one is quite good with the Grouper," Nick suggested.

"I see," Kate said, moving the middle glass out of the tray it came in to save it for their meal. "In terms of our visit with Joann's friends…it was way more interesting than I would have expected. They didn't seem very taken aback to see me. Never mind inviting me to the table with you."

"That was interesting. I was purposely looking for a defensive response or anything to suggest they were nervous to have us in their space," Nick said.

"They really didn't. Their questions, especially John and Stacey's, were a little pointed," Kate responded.

"They were," Nick nodded. "John was twitchy. Very reserved, almost sullen until Dane left for the restroom and then asserted himself a bit."

Kate considered their experience, "He definitely appears to live in Dane's shadow."

"Did you see how he responded each time Joann's name was mentioned?" Nick asked.

"It looked like he was going to come out of his skin," Kate agreed.

"Guilt?" Nick pressed.

Kate shook her head, "John was in love with Joann. His visceral response to his best friend proposing to Joann was unexpected. He did not like those two together."

"When he talked about Dane still sowing his oats, John shot Stacey a rather pointed look," Nick added.

Nodding, Kate declared, "Stacey and Dane were more than just friends."

"Quite the triangle," Nick said, tasting one of the samplers.

"Square until one corner was removed from the equation," Kate corrected, her eyes narrowing.

"Any one of them could have a reason to lose it and kill Joann," Nick surmised.

Kate's gaze was again lost on the causeway, "They could."

"Dane threw me," Nick announced. "Despite his gregarious party attitude, he seemed genuinely choked up when mentioning Joann."

"Wouldn't you gasp a bit when you talked about someone you killed?" Kate snapped.

Nick coughed a relenting laugh, "I suppose so. They all remain on the suspect list. You think Dane was really surprised the ring was found on the beach?"

"Maybe," Kate shrugged. "He certainly seemed genuine in his response, but he seems rather clever."

"It was John who was peppering you with questions about you finding it," Nick offered.

"Yeah, that struck me," Kate admitted.

"I'm not sure that narrows the field," Nick said.

Kate looked distant, "It qualifies the field. They are all suspects. I came into it with Dane as the runaway winner, but now, I think anyone of them could have been the killer."

"Could any of them have broken into the beach house?" Nick asked.

"Maybe. If not, any of them could have paid someone to, especially Dane," Kate replied.

Nick nodded thoughtfully. Pursing his lips, he frowned, "So, are we any further than we were?"

Kate looked resolute, "We know there are tensions among the victim's friends. We know that they are being carefully watched. I couldn't imagine Dane Smithfield taking orders from anyone, never mind from a phone text. Whoever the man in the suit was, had Dane on a tight leash."

"And Dane conceded to follow," Nick said.

"He did," Kate said. "I can't see too many people tugging a leash like that with a wild child like Dane."

"Someone who controls his bank account," Nick snapped his fingers.

"Mommy or Daddy...or whoever administers his trust," Kate nodded.

As their meals were placed in front of them, Kate hadn't realized how hungry she had become. "This is really good," she told Nick. "I may have to have you write our visitor's guide."

Nick's face dropped into a look of mock horror, "Oh, no. We should have all of our excursions under a strict non-disclosure agreement. You can't let out the secrets of the locals' favorite spots. They'd be overrun by tourists and I'll have to move again."

Kate looked over her plate of fish, "Well, we can't have that now, can we? How about let just a few of my closest renter friends know?"

With a shrug, Nick conceded, "All right. But if your company begins buying up more beach homes, we're going to have to renegotiate."

"As long as you pick the local eatery for our negotiation meeting, I'm in," Kate grinned.

"You're just trying to scoop another local hangout," Nick teased.

Kate wrinkled her nose, "You've got a good eye for locations. Magnificent views, relaxing, yummy food... can't blame a girl for trying!"

Her phone buzzing on the table almost made her jump, "It's Detective Connolly!"

Holding the phone to her ear, she answered.

"Ms. Harper, this is Detective Connolly. I wanted to give you a call as our lab has sent me their results."

"Thank you for calling, Detective," Kate replied.

"First, results of the blood on the glass fragment. Unfortunately, whoever's DNA it belongs to isn't in our system, but as we get warrants for serious suspects, we should be able to change that and identify a match," Connolly shared.

"I see," Kate said into the phone.

"The cigarette butts are interesting. Again, there are no owners of DNA in our system, but, we did find those butts belonged to different individuals," the detective reported.

"What does that mean?"

"It means you have more than one person interested in you and what you may have seen at that beach house," Connolly said.

The thought gave Kate a shudder.

"Unfortunately, that's all we have so far. We are processing the warrants but the legal blocks have been frustrating," the detective said. "We have patrols out for that private investigator as well. We'll have answers soon."

"Thank you for calling, Detective," Kate hung up the phone. Her eyes peered across the table at an impatient Nick.

"Well…" Nick pressed.

Kate summarized her call with Detective Connolly had shared with her. "He also said the cigarette butts belonged to more than one person."

Nick's face fell, "There has been more than one person lurking in the shadows outside your beach house."

"And one made their way inside," Kate reminded him.

"Kate, this is serious," Nick looked concerned.

"Yeah and they still haven't been able to locate that private investigator," Kate said.

"His DNA might be on one of those cigarette butts," Nick added. "And might possibly be on the glass shard."

"There's only one way to know," Kate said.

"Wait for the police to bring him in," Nick nodded absently.

Kate shook her head, a devious look on her face as she leaned across the table, "No. *We* are going to find him."

Nick looked incredulous, "Kate, haven't we done enough sleuthing for the day?"

"It's time we moved this investigation along. I want to know what that P.I. knows," Kate said, a sparkle in her eye. "I have a plan."

Twenty

Nick spent much of the drive back to Kate's beach house trying to convince her not to go through with her plan. His pleas were met with deaf ears.

"Honestly, I feel better being proactive than sitting in my house waiting for the next thing to happen," Kate said. As they pulled down her street, they scoured the area, especially as they closed in on her house.

A car parked well into the shadows, caught their eye as they drove by. "Recognize that one?" Nick asked.

"No," Kate said. "It does have a view of the beach house."

"I couldn't tell if anyone was inside or not," Nick said.

"Me either. I guess maybe we'll find out," Kate suggested.

Nick put his truck in park. Turning to face Kate, he started to speak, but she cut him off.

With a firm smile, Kate said, "We're doing this. You know the plan."

Nick sighed. Watching Kate walk up to her door, she gave a little wave as she punched in her code and disappeared into the house.

Backing up, Nick sped away, taking a hard look at the suspect vehicle, unable to learn any more than when they drove in. Pulling out of the neighborhood, Nick looped around the block and aligned himself far from Kate's beach house, but with a view of the entire length of road. Hesitating, he shut off the ignition and settled back into his seat.

Kate closed the door behind her. Snapping on lights throughout the house, she ensured her silhouette was prominently displayed in the windows as she passed. Holding her phone to her ear, she wanted anyone watching to think she was on an animated call.

Rummaging through her office supplies, she found what she was looking for. Glancing around, she snatched the first thing within reach and stuffed it in the legal-sized manila envelope.

Retracing her steps, Kate moved quickly through the house, switching off lights in her wake. Pausing to set the alarm system, she stepped out onto the porch. Under the amber lights, she spun with her package held out in front of her.

Gliding down the steps, she unlocked her SUV, the perimeter lights flashing in the night. Starting the SUV, Kate backed out of the drive and drove casually down her street. Her eyes couldn't help but to gravitate to her rearview mirror. Pausing at the stop sign near the end of the street. Lingering a few moments longer than she felt she should, she reluctantly pulled onto the major thoroughfare.

Disheartened that she didn't see headlights blazing behind her, Kate hoped that she hadn't dragged Nick into a hapless goose chase.

Nick watched the street intently for any movement, in a vehicle or on foot. No shadows produced themselves, no glowing embers from a lit cigarette, and no slight shake of a car suspension to indicate someone was shifting in their seat.

He didn't have long to wait as Kate stepped out of her beach house. Whirling on her porch steps, a package in her hand was clearly seen in the house lights. Seconds later, Kate was in her car and pulling out of her driveway.

No brake lights flashed as an ignition was pushed. No figure slipped out from behind a tree. No car pulled out after Kate.

Hitting the call button, Nick was about to let Kate know the plan had failed. Suddenly, from the corner of Kate's house, a shadow darted across the street. A car was brought to life, spinning sand in its wake as the rear tires were urged forward with a hearty stab at the accelerator.

For half the block, the vehicle's lights remained off before blazing to life. Taking a hasty right turn in the direction Kate had, the vehicle disappeared from Nick's view.

Punching the button for his own ignition, Nick launched to chase the chaser.

Accelerating hard, he sped to the stop sign. With no oncoming traffic, he barely paused before turning on to Gulf Boulevard. Locking Kate's pursuer's taillight style in his eyes, Nick was hyper-focused to keep the car in his sights without following too close.

Driving the length of Treasure Island, Kate wondered if any of the scant headlights behind her might belong to the private investigator. All she could do was complete her plan and see if anyone took the bait.

Swinging into an offshoot just before John's Pass, she drove past the shops and restaurants to a narrow, fenced section of a boat dealer. The flickering light at the chain and padlocked gate gave the area a surreal feeling. Even though it was her plan, her heart pounded in her chest.

Slipping out of her SUV, packet in hand, she spun to face a pair of headlights entering the same narrow lane. Assuming it was just Nick's truck, she quickly realized the lights belonged to a much smaller car than a pickup truck. Her pulse quickened and her chest tightened.

The driver of the car paused a few car lengths behind Kate as if contemplating what their next step should be. Suddenly, another pair of lights sped toward them. The driver of the car slammed their vehicle in reverse and accelerated backward.

The approaching truck was too quick, cutting off the smaller car's escape. Nick edged just so his bumper was barely clear of Kate's pursuer. Whoever followed her was boxed in.

Nick hopped out of his truck as the driver ahead of him opened their driver's door and attempted to slip passed him. A quick thrust with Nick's palm to the man's chest pinned him to the tall chain-link fence that penned his car in.

Jostling him toward the front of the car, its headlights still burning, Nick studied the man as Kate approached.

"Frank Driscoll," Kate exclaimed, as the man's features were clear in the glow of the headlights.

Holding his hands out, he glared at Nick, who held the private investigator's shirt in his clenched fists. "All right, all right. You got me. You can let go," the investigator said.

Nick hesitated for just a moment before releasing his grip.

Driscoll smoothed out his shirt where Nick had grabbed him, relaxing his posture to indicate he was defeated. As Nick glanced toward Kate, Driscoll darted away, leaping as high as he could up on the chain-link fence.

"Really?" Nick cursed, racing after the man. With his own lunge, he grasped Driscoll's pant leg just as the investigator lurched toward the top of the fence.

Ripping him back to the ground, Nick maintained a firm grip on the man's shirt.

Kate walked calmly up to Driscoll, "Are you done? You aren't going anywhere, obviously."

Driscoll dropped his head, "Sure. Yeah. I'm done. I assume meathead here is going to keep a hold of me now, anyway."

Nick grunted, closing his fist tightly around the fabric he had a hold of.

Kate stood directly in front of the private investigator. Staring him in the eyes, her brows creased in suppressed anger, she repeated, "Frank Driscoll."

The detective slumped even further, "Yes. I am Frank Driscoll."

"The police are looking for you," Kate informed.

"I'm sure they are," Driscoll scowled.

"Too bad for you, so were we," Kate sneered. "Why have you been watching me?"

"Watching you? Why would I do that?" Driscoll shrugged.

Nick slammed Driscoll against the chain-link fence, "Did you break into her house?"

Driscoll's eyes widened with Nick's sudden physicality, "Break in…no. Nasty stuff. I was about to call 911 when I saw the hero here launch into action. If I was, say, to break in, I'd pick the lock and circumvent the security system. I *am* a professional."

"I'll ask again before my friend here gets too angry. Why have you been watching me?" Kate growled.

"Look. I was hired to monitor you. See if I could find out what you know about what happened down the beach. Some people think you might be…a danger if certain people were taken to court," Driscoll said.

"Who hired you? Do you know who killed that girl on the beach?" Kate snarled.

Driscoll waved his hands in front of him, "No, I don't know nothin' about what happened or who did what. My job was simple. Tail you and find out what *you* know."

"And?" Kate asked.

"As far as I can tell, you don't know nothin'. That's been my report. Still, my job was to make sure of that," the private investigator said.

"You didn't break into my house?" Kate demanded.

Driscoll looked her straight in the eye, "I did not."

Kate stepped back, trying to determine her next question, when a series of blue lights and stressed engines came roaring toward them. She glanced at Nick, who shrugged, "This was your plan. As soon as I had him cornered, I called it in."

Nodding, Kate relented to greet the officers. As had become customary, Detective Connolly strode through the uniformed officers.

Looking more cross than usual, Connolly scowled, "What is going on here?"

"We, uh, did what you have been trying to do. We got Frank Driscoll," Kate replied.

Connolly stopped directly in front of Kate. Silently, he looked her up and down as if trying to ascertain what made this woman tick. Realizing he wasn't going to get anywhere with that enigma, he swung his attention toward Nick and Driscoll, "Let him go, Mr. Mason."

Nick promptly released the private investigator.

"Frank Driscoll, you are wanted for questioning regarding the murder of Joann Marrs. We can do this here or at the station. What'll it be?" Connolly asked.

Driscoll shrugged, "I have nothing to hide. You driving, or am I?"

"I think we'll drive. We'll make sure your rental car is taken care of," Connolly said.

"Can I sit up front?" Driscoll asked, a hop in his step.

Connolly rolled his eyes, "I think you'll be more comfortable in the back."

An officer began escorting the private investigator to a patrol car.

"Hey, I gotta ask, what was in the envelope?" Driscoll asked as he was led past Kate.

A wide grin crossed Kate's lips. With a shrug, she replied, "My stapler."

Driscoll's head dropped, dejected. Lifting up, an appreciative smile spread across his face, "Nice work, kid."

As the procession of officers cajoled Driscoll toward their patrol cars to escort the P.I. back to the station, Connolly spun to address Kate and Nick. The police detective was clearly fuming.

"Did you ever once think that whoever was following wasn't the private investigator but the killer themselves? Or maybe that Driscoll might be the murderer?" Connolly's words rang through the alley, dripping in anger.

Kate's heart sank at the proposition she might have lured the murderer to the enclosed alley. The notion had never crossed her mind.

As the detective's attention turned to Nick, the handyman huffed, "I don't disagree with you, detective. I tried to talk her out of it. She was doing it with or without me. Would you have preferred I let her go on her own?"

Connolly studied Nick's eyes for several moments before turning in disgust, "I suppose you're right. Reining Ms. Harper in seems like an insurmountable task."

"So, you'll just make us part of the team?" Kate brightened.

The detective scowled, "*That* is not what I said.

"Can we come to the station and see what Driscoll has to say?" Kate countered eagerly.

Connolly hesitated. "You can listen in from the observation room. I don't want a peep out of you."

Kate moved her fingers across her lips to insinuate they were zipped.

With a roll of his eyes, Connolly sighed, "I'll see you at the station."

Twenty One

Detective Connolly escorted Kate and Nick into the observation room. A small alcove with four steel chairs and a modicum of computers, cameras and sound equipment in an otherwise sparse room.

"Not a word from you two," the detective was clearly still not happy with their most recent exploits. Eyeing the equipment in front of them that allowed other detectives and police resources to interact with interrogations, Connolly said, "If in the course of the questioning you feel like you have something to add...don't."

Turning on his heel, the detective exited the room.

Kate and Nick looked at each other and then through the one-way glass at a sparse room save for a table and chairs that were bolted to the floor along with a sundry of recording equipment. Frank Driscoll was already in the room, tapping impatiently on the table.

Kate framed her finger in front of her face as she studied the private investigator.

"What are you doing?" Nick asked, his face screwed into a confused look.

"I'm trying to picture him in a ski mask," Kate said.

"Hmm," Nick frowned, cocking his head slightly to the side as he examined the man in the interrogation room. "Is it helping?"

"Not really," Kate admitted, dropping her hands to her sides.

Connolly burst into the interrogation room, a single coffee cup in hand. Freezing on Driscoll, he feigned, "I'm sorry, I should have brought one for you. Next time."

Setting the cup down, the detective slipped into a seat directly across from Driscoll. Leaning back as though he was thoroughly comfortable in the metal chair, Connolly played with the cup on the table in front of him.

With a sigh, he began the interrogation, "Why don't we start with the easy stuff? Who hired you to spy on Ms. Harper?"

Driscoll's demeanor was unmoved save a slight smirk that quivered in the corner of his lip. Shaking his head, he replied, "I can't answer that. Client privileges and all."

"Client privileges that could well land you in jail," Connolly said.

"For what?" Driscoll frowned.

"Murder. Breaking and entering. Stalking. Interfering with an ongoing police investigation..." Connolly countered.

"If you had me on any of that stuff, you'd have arrested me, not politely stuffed me in the back of a patrol car without reading my rights, dragging me here for a friendly discussion," Driscoll sneered.

"I can charge you for the interfering with a police investigation and stalking right now, if you like," Connolly said.

The P.I. waved his hands in front of him, "Come on. I was just doing my job. I'm a licensed investigator."

"You're licensed in Florida?" Connolly asked.

"It's in process," Driscoll snapped.

Connolly sighed, "Most of that stuff I could hardly care about. What I do care about is a young woman found dead near one of my beaches and someone threatening Ms. Harper!"

Driscoll laughed, "Yeah, it seems like you gotta soft spot for *that* one, huh, Detective?"

Squirming in his chair, Connolly turned back toward the investigator, "Did you break into Ms. Harper's home?"

"Where is that?" Driscoll shrugged.

Connolly reached into a folder and tossed Kate's photo of the rental car license plate.

"That supposed to mean something to me?" Driscoll scoffed.

"That is the license plate of a car that you rented. You were clever to use credit gift cards, but you still have to provide your license. Not too hard to track," Connolly said.

"So what?" Driscoll shrugged. "I was in the neighborhood. Sunset Beach is a nice place."

"Did I say this was taken at Sunset Beach?" Driscoll asked.

The private investigator's head dropped with his mistake.

"You know what?" Connolly started. "I'm done with this. I have a dead girl and a woman in danger. I don't have time for this nonsense. I'll just arrest you for whatever charges I can pin on you. Wait here. I'll get the papers started."

The detective was at the door when Driscoll called out, "Detective, wait. I'll tell you what I can."

Connolly paused with his hand on the doorknob. Slowly turning on his heel, he faced the P.I.

"I can't tell you hired me, but yes, I was hired to watch Harper and see what she knew about the murder of that girl," Driscoll said.

"That girl- was Joann Marrs. She had her life ahead of her and you're playing games," Connolly snapped.

"No games. I was hired the day after the, uh, the day you found Joann. A lot of money for an expedited trip. That's why my license extension is still pending. Yes, I cased Harper's beach house. Followed her and that handyman around town. Followed her to this police station a couple of times," Driscoll admitted.

"Did you enter Ms. Harper's home?" Conolly asked pointedly.

"No," Driscoll shook his head. "I never did. I looked inside once or twice, might have tried a door handle to see if it was unlocked, but I never went in."

Connolly scrutinized the private investigator's face, "You never tried to gain entry- like maybe through the downstairs door?"

Driscoll maintained innocent, "I didn't. You gotta believe me. I ain't guilty of anything but doing my job and yes, that means staying away from you and this police station if I can help it."

The police detective tapped against the folder, "You mind committing to a DNA test?"

Driscoll was taken aback. His eyes squinted, "Why do I get the feeling I should have an attorney for this?"

"That's your choice. You say you're innocent..." Connolly pressed.

"I am innocent, but I also know enough to make sure legal boxes are checked," Driscoll said.

Connolly rose from his seat, "Suit yourself. We have enough to hold you for forty-eight hours. Should be enough time for you to get an attorney...or will Mr. Smithfield be supplying you one. I think there are several in town."

Driscoll soured, "I'll get my own."

"Make yourself comfortable," Connolly said, readying to leave the room.

"I'll...I'll take that coffee..." Driscoll called.

"Humph," Connolly grunted, leaving the room.

In moments, the police detective burst into the observation room.

Kate stood grinning, "Well?"

Connolly scowled, "Well, what?"

"Did we do good? Helping you bring him in?" Kate asked.

"No. You didn't do good. You put yourself in potential danger. Surfer boy there laying hands on him can complicate legal matters...no, definitely not good," Connolly scolded.

"We found him for you," Nick offered.

"Yes, you should have called me. Called 911. Taken a photo from a window within the safety of the beach house. You should not have played cat and mouse with him, especially while there is a killer out there," Connolly snapped.

"To be fair, that is what Nick said to do," Kate conceded.

"Well, occasionally, I agree with Mason," Connolly admitted.

"What happens now?" Nick asked.

Connolly sighed, "Now the legal fun begins. We'll put out warrants based on Driscoll casting plenty of suspicion on himself to get his DNA samples. Hopefully, we get to do the same with the victim's friends sooner than later."

"Can you find out who hired him?" Kate asked.

"We can try. He doesn't have any legal responsibility to tell us. We can search his financials, phone calls, things like that. Speaking of which, I need to make sure all of his electronic devices are part of the warrant. I'm sure you don't need pictures of you on some creep's phone or laptop," Connolly said.

"I would prefer not," Kate admitted.

"Go home," Connolly told Kate. "If Driscoll doesn't happen to be the killer, the next person snooping around your beach house might be. Unless it's handyman here creeping in the shadows."

Nick scowled.

"Look, no more heroics on your part. This is dangerous stuff. As we close in, things tend to get more dangerous as people get desperate. I'm not joking. You need to be careful," Connolly warned. Turning to Nick, the detective asked, "You want to be responsible for Ms. Harper getting hurt…or worse?"

"I don't," Nick shook his head softly.

"Then help her make good decisions. She seems to struggle with herself," Connolly said.

Without another word, the detective spun and left Nick and Kate standing in front of the open observation room door.

Kate cast a glance at the disgruntled private detective in the interrogation room.

With a deep breath, she admitted, "I don't believe he's the killer. He was sent here to somehow protect the killer."

"Maybe. How far would that protection go?" Nick asked. "Taking you out if you knew too much?"

Kate looked Nick in the eyes, a slight tremble coursing through her spine.

"Let's not find out," Kate suggested.

Nick laughed, "Somehow, I think you are going to keep sticking your finger into that flame."

Kate bobbed her head in a slight shrug.

Stopping outside of their vehicles, Kate surprised Nick as she laid her hand on his arm as he was about to open the door of his truck.

Nick shot Kate a quizzical look.

"Connolly is about to cut Driscoll loose. He doesn't have enough to hold him on after questioning," Kate said.

Frowning, Nick asked, "Isn't he still a suspect?"

"He is," Kate nodded. "Based on the formal interview, Detective Connolly will have to present as much as he can to a district attorney and a judge to get anything more."

"So…what are we doing waiting here?" Nick asked.

Kate answered by pulling the door open and leaping out of the truck.

Nick looked across the parking lot to see the private investigator exiting the police station looking quite flustered. "Thanks for including me in the plan," Nick muttered, jumping out after Kate.

"Frank Driscoll!" Kate called, making a beeline for the P.I.

Driscoll hesitated before slowing to allow Kate to walk up to him. His face morphed from alarmed to nervous to a forced smile. "Ms. Harper, can I help you?"

"Probably," Kate said, her voice dripping with confidence. "You are a private investigator from Charleston. No coincidence, who showed up at my home right after…right after a young woman from Charleston was slain on the beach? The police brought you in as a suspect. I don't think you did it."

"You don't?" Driscoll seemed surprised by the statement. Laughing uncomfortably, he glanced at Nick, who stood by Kate's shoulder and said, "I hope you share that with the detective in there."

Kate looked directly at the private investigator, "I think that you are here on behalf of the murderer or at least the murderer's family. You know more than you are letting on."

Driscoll shrugged, "This is a sensitive situation. I don't want *anyone* getting hurt."

"Anyone *else*, you mean?" Nick snapped.

"Right," Driscoll's head bobbed. "Ms. Harper is right, though. I didn't kill that young woman. I arrived in town the day after her life was taken."

Nick crossed his arms. The posture made his forearms look immense across his chest. "Then what are you doing at Kate's house? If you care so much about no one else getting hurt, why didn't you intercede when her house was broken into? She was in real danger!"

Driscoll shook his head, "I didn't know what was going on at first. And then I saw you show up. I decided to monitor the situation. I was going to call 911 and see if you had the incident in hand. I…I'm sorry. I should have been more reactive."

Both Kate and Nick studied the detective for several long moments.

The investigator stumbled over his words and shrugged, "I'm sorry. Your house getting broken into…that's too much. This has gotten out of hand."

"Then tell us what you know!" Kate demanded, her eyes cross.

Driscoll thought about the request as he eyed Kate and Nick. Finally, he nodded, "All right. I will tell you what I can. I *was* hired by someone in Charleston. Like I told the police, that is privileged information. I don't know who killed that young woman. If I did, I wouldn't protect them. As I said before, I was hired to watch you, Ms. Harper. To see what you knew. To see if you had information on the case."

"Why spy on *me*?" Kate asked.

"Initially, I was sent to Treasure Island to observe the case. After that news clip with you handing the detective evidence reportedly related to the case, my objective changed," Driscoll shared.

"To spy on me," Kate scowled.

Driscoll shrugged, "It's part of my job."

"Why does Kate have your employer so concerned?" Nick asked.

"I don't think they know themselves. They want to know what she saw on the beach that night and how exactly she came upon the ring," Driscoll admitted. "That's all I know. My job is to investigate, but that does not include unlawful searches or breaking and entering."

Suddenly, the front door to the police station flung open. An irate Detective Connolly strode down the steps. "Ms. Harper! What are you doing here and why are you speaking with my suspect?"

Kate flashed Connolly a weak smile, "We just ran into him on our way out."

The detective addressed all three standing in the police station parking lot, "If any of you are not completely forthcoming or if any of you interfere with this investigation, I will have you arrested. Go home or the next time we speak, I'll be putting cuffs on your wrists!"

Driscoll was more than happy to have the conversation end and to slink off into the night. Immediately, he turned on his heels toward the police impound, where his car was parked.

Connolly stopped him, "Mr. Driscoll, before you go, I need your phone."

Pulling a piece of paper out of his jacket pocket, the detective handed Driscoll a summons.

"A warrant to search my phone," the private investigator read. With a sigh, he fished his cell phone out of his pocket. Sliding it into a plastic bag the police detective held in front of him, Driscoll conceded.

Kate looked hopefully at Connolly.

Connolly's stern look reinforced he was in no mood for her impending inquisitive request. Snapping with his finger, and waving it in the air, he said, "No. Go home. All of you!"

Mouth open to rebut, Kate thought the better of it and simply nodded. With a hand on Nick's arm, she pivoted to return to the pickup truck.

"I mean it, Mr. Mason. If Ms. Harper can't keep out of trouble, I am counting on you to nudge her in the right direction," Connolly called.

Nick looked perplexed, "I'll do what I can, detective."

Connolly stood on the police station steps to observe both groups retreat to their respective vehicles and do as he had requested. Only when the taillights of Nick's truck and Kate's SUV disappeared out of the parking lot and down the road, did the detective return inside the station with his new potential evidence in hand.

Twenty Two

Kate looked out a window on the front of the beach house. Peeking through the curtain, she could see that Detective Connolly had stuck to his word and posted a patrol car across the street.

Hurrying to get herself together for the day, Kate bounded down the steps in time to greet Nick before he could even rap his knuckles against the door. Surprised, Nick took a slight step backward.

"You're ready to set off early this morning," Nick said.

Kate looked at Nick, "I want to get to the station and see what they were able to pull off that P.I.'s phone."

Nick looked displeased, grumbling, "Isn't it time we let the police handle it?"

Kate scowled, "They weren't handling finding Driscoll until we wrapped him up and delivered him with a bow."

"Come on, they have rules to follow and procedures. They are doing what they can," Nick said.

"I know. We are just helping them along a bit," Kate smiled.

"Fine," Nick's head bobbed.

"I'll drive. We'll even pick up coffee along the way," Kate offered, locking the door behind her.

Reluctantly, Nick followed her to the SUV and climbed in.

Carrying a tray full of coffees into the police station, their presence was instantly met with the ire of the police chief. His mustache bristled above his lip as he eyed the pair. "Ms. Harper and Mr. Mason. I'm sure my detective was clear in that you were not to interfere in the investigation," Chief Reynolds said.

"Yes, Chief Reynolds. He was very clear. I am only coming down as a witness. I am sure Detective Connolly will want me to be able to identify anyone captured on the images from Frank Driscoll's phone," Kate said.

"Hmph," the police chief grunted from behind, arms folded across his chest. Eyeing the trays of coffees Kate and Nick were holding, he said, "Tantamount to bribing police officials. Especially since you two are still on the suspect list."

Kate's mouth was agape at the notion of remaining a suspect. Her face softened as the chief grabbed a cup from her tray anyway.

Pausing after turning away, Chief Reynolds said, "I'll let the detective know you are here. Stay put."

"Yes, sir," Kate beamed, looking as innocent as she could.

The moment the police chief's head was turned, Kate's eyes were busy exploring the station for any nuggets related to the case that she could find. Purposely walking forward to offer a coffee to an officer typing away at their desk, Kate leaned so that she could see into the front conference room lined with glass walls. A whiteboard was littered with scribbles, a long list of suspects with very few lined out, Kate assumed those were people with verified alibis. She did notice that she and Nick were not among those.

The names with asterisks were ones that caught her attention. Dane Smithfield was at the top of the list. Frank Driscoll and a name she didn't recognize were listed directly below Smithfield's.

"Ms. Harper, what a surprise. And I see you brought your sidekick with you," Detective Connolly called from across the station.

Kate quickly averted her eyes, but the police detective was sharp. With a snap of his fingers, an officer compiling files in the conference room rotated the board so that no information was visible.

Thrusting her tray of coffees toward the detective, Kate smiled, "I thought you might want me to review the images from Driscoll's phone. I could be helpful in recognizing what was captured."

"I don't recall calling and asking that you come in for that exercise," Connolly scowled.

"I like to be proactive," Kate chimed in, her voice exuberant.

"That you do," Connolly sighed. "Fine. You might as well come and check out what we have so far. You too, Mason. Your lurking might pay off yet."

Nick rolled his eyes at the detective's condescension but followed Kate just the same.

"You can leave the trays of coffees on that table," Connolly nodded toward a counter that separated the two glass conference rooms.

Leading the pair to the windowless conference room as he had previously, he turned on the monitor and projected the files they had pulled from the private investigator. The initial photos made Kate's stomach hurt. Images of her getting out of her SUV and walking up the steps to the beach house. Oblivious to the fact that someone was watching her. Photographing her.

The detective flashed through a series of innocuous shots of Kate and Nick. Pulling his finger off the button, he paused on an image of someone sneaking across the side of the beach house driveway.

Zooming in, Connolly asked, "Whoever this is stuck close to the shadows and had their back to Driscoll most of the time. This side view is one of the few that captured a portion of the person's face. Recognize this person at all?"

Kate leaned forward. Nick squinted, his eyes fighting through the haziness of the photo. Both shook their heads.

"What do you think, Nick? About the size of who broke into Kate's house?" the detective asked.

Nick studied the image and nodded, "Yeah, roughly. Sure, it could be."

Reviewing additional images, mostly of shadowy figures, none were more conclusive than the first.

"Well, that wasn't terribly helpful," Nick sighed.

Connolly looked serious, "What it does show is that someone other than Frank Driscoll was sneaking around the beach house. Well, Driscoll and you, Nick. The figure in the images Driscoll captured is shorter than you."

"That is a lot of interest in my beach house," Kate muttered.

"It is," Connolly looked directly at Kate. "You need to take your safety seriously."

Kate nodded absently, her mind was elsewhere, "What else did Driscoll's phone tell you? Did it give you an idea about who hired him?"

The police detective looked hesitant to answer. Shaking his head slowly, he replied, "No. Texts and phone calls went to a burner phone purchased and dumped in Charleston."

"Well, we know someone in Smithfield's hometown hired him," Nick offered.

"Can you track the burner phone and determine when it was purchased?" Kate asked.

Connolly's face fell into an almost impressed expression. "We could and we did. It was purchased at a convenience store the morning after Joann Marrs was murdered," the detective replied.

"So, someone other than the murderer purchased it," Kate's eyes brightened.

"They did," Connolly admitted.

"That should mean the murderer is connected to someone from Charleston," Nick suggested.

"Not necessarily. Driscoll could have been hired out of concern for the remaining friends. He could have been hired to recover something lost during the murder. He could have been hired to ensure Smithfield and his friends weren't implicated," Connolly countered.

"Hmm," Nick frowned, taking in the broad swath of possibilities.

"Let's be honest. Driscoll was hired by someone connected to Smithfields, be it one of them or even Joann Marrs' family," Kate said. "But as Detective Connolly illustrates, Driscoll could have been hired for any number of reasons. Someone might have even thought I was the killer."

Connolly smiled, "Welcome to my life. Answers aren't just sitting there most of the time. Even when they are, they can be twisted in countless ways. For me to get a conviction, never mind warrants, I need that evidence to be clear."

The detective's phone rang. Glancing at it, he picked it up and placed it to his ear, "Connolly. I see. The marina. That is interesting. I'm on my way. Have the officers hold him. I'll be there in ten."

Hanging up the phone, Connolly looked at Kate and Nick as he stood, "I need to go. How about I walk you out."

The detective walked briskly through the police station. With scarcely a second glance, he slid his sunglasses over his eyes and made a beeline for his unmarked police car.

Kate shot Nick a look. Nick's head slumped.

With a grin, Kate exclaimed, "You know what marina he is heading to?"

"He almost seemed okay with us reviewing Driscoll's information. Are you sure you want to whack the hornet's nest with a baseball bat?" Nick asked.

The unwavering smile on Kate's face told Nick everything he needed to know.

Pulling into the parking lot of the yacht club, the same marina where Smithfield's yacht was moored. Positioning the nose of her SUV so that she and Nick could spy on the action without being intrusive, they watched as the relatively raucous scene was unfolding.

Several police officers struggled to detain a wiry man. Kate took in the man's appearance, who was starkly out of place for the elegant yacht club. The snarl on the man's face and constant wriggling against the firm grip of the officers shared his state of mind.

Detective Connolly had parked in front of the lobby, where much of the commotion was taking place. Without hesitation, he strode up to an officer who was standing with the yacht club's security and who Kate assumed to be a manager based on the man's crisp suit.

For several minutes, Nick and Kate watched from the confines of her SUV. In a huff, Kate opened the driver's side door.

"Where are you going?" Nick hissed.

"I can't hear what's going on. I want to know who that man is and why he is so important that Detective Connolly raced right over here," Kate replied. "Stay here."

Stooping so that she was below the top of the cars in the parking lot, Kate snaked her way closer to the action. Pressing against a large luxury SUV parked close to the lobby entrance, she kneeled as far forward as she dared and craned her ears to take in what was being said.

Most conversations were veiled by the man in custody's constant griping and arguing with the police officers that held him. Detective Connolly, clearly tired of the man's demeanor, ordered the officers to stow the suspect in the back of a patrol car.

Kate leaned in even further as she tried to listen to the conversation the Treasure Island detective was having with the hotel staff and officers who arrived on the scene.

"He was caught trying to board the *Sunny Dream*," an officer shared.

"It isn't the first time we've seen him sneaking onto the property," the hotel security shared.

Detective Connolly pulled at his bottom lip as he took in the information, "When did he start showing up?"

The man in the sharp suit shrugged, "Around the time the *Sunny Dream* pulled in, give or take a day."

"Has he been seen interacting with any of the passengers or anyone else at the marina?" Connolly asked.

"No, not that we can say," the man in the suit said.

"We can pull up security footage and scan through the times we noticed Huck on the property," one of the security guards offered.

"Have those files sent in a link to the precinct. Put my name in the header," Connolly said, handing the guard a card.

The security guard nodded, slipping the card into his jacket pocket.

"You called him 'Huck'. You've seen him around before?" Connolly asked.

The hotel security guard answered, "The first time we caught him, he played it casual. Even volunteered his driver's license. Said he was here to work on a boat."

"What boat?" Connolly asked.

"The *Sunny Dream*," the guard replied. "We checked with the captain and he denied any work was scheduled. We figured it was a scam. By the time we returned to Huck, he was gone."

"He hadn't targeted any other boats?" Connolly asked.

"No," the guards shook their heads.

Connolly considered the situation, "I'd like to speak to the harbor master. And send me those security videos starting with the day the *Sunny Dream* arrived."

Turning to the police officers, Connolly said, "Take Huck to the precinct. Throw him in interrogation. I'll be there soon enough."

The officers nodded and didn't hesitate to remove the unruly man from the yacht club premises. Kate slowly rose above the beltline of the SUV so that she could peer through the vehicle's tinted windows. Her heart sank as a voice called out to her.

"You might as well come, too, Ms. Harper. At least that way I can keep an eye on you," Detective Connolly barked.

Reluctantly, Kate rose to her full height. Offering a sheepish grin, she greeted Connolly, "Hi there, Detective."

Even through his dark sunglasses, Kate could tell the police detective's eyes were piercing her with disdain.

The man in the distinguished suit asked, "You know this woman, Detective?"

"She has a sideline attachment to a case I am working on and an insatiable curiosity," Connolly said as they followed the man into the yacht club. "Mind if we poke our heads into your security office before we visit the harbor master?"

"Of course," the man in the suit shrugged.

Pushing their way into the security suite, one of the guards that had been in front of the prestigious club looked up, surprised to see the entourage, "I'm compiling the footage now. It will take a bit."

Connolly nodded, "I was hoping you could do me a favor. Ms. Harper here needs a place out of the heat until I conclude my visit."

"I see," the guard said, clearly not fully understanding the request.

"If she could sit in here under your watch, that would be fantastic. I will collect her on my way out," Connolly pressed.

"Yes, absolutely," the guard nodded.

"If she claims she has to use the restroom or anything else until I collect her, ignore her. If that doesn't work, put her in cuffs," the police detective ordered.

"Hopefully, it won't come to that," the guard smiled.

"Don't be so sure," Connolly snapped, tilting his sunglasses so that Kate could see the ire in his eyes. Turning to the man in the suit, he nudged, "The harbor master?"

"Right this way," the man in the suit agreed.

The detective ensured the door closed behind them as they left.

Kate slumped in her seat, dismayed that Connolly had somehow spied her behind that SUV. Retracing their steps, her mind followed the path from the SUV that concealed her to where the detective was standing. As she joined him and they made their way to the lobby, an image she hadn't internalized made her head droop. When the man in the suit swung the door open for them to enter the lobby, the front row of cars was visible in the door's reflection.

Connolly noticed her as someone came through the doors. Despite all the elements capturing the detective's attention at that time, he still had the wherewithal to spot her hiding behind the SUV. With a grunt, she had to hand it to the detective.

Her attention swung to the bank of monitors capturing nearly every square foot of public space around the yacht club grounds. She could follow the suited man and Connolly as they made their way toward the marina. Moving from one screen and camera angle to the next, she watched them.

On a trailing screen, something caught her attention. Shadowing the detective, a familiar figure splashed across the screen. Nick Mason slunk carefully behind Connolly. Using hallways and corridors for concealment, he tailed the detective and the man in the suit through the hotel.

Stepping out onto the back of the property, there were fewer options for hiding places. Seeing a man set his fishing gear down as he entered the yacht club restaurant, Kate watched as Nick donned the man's hat and grabbed his pole as he made his way toward the marina docks.

As the security cameras surveilled Detective Connolly and the man in the suit paused at the harbormaster's office, Nick passed through the frame only to duck behind the marina office.

"Well played, Nick," Kate whispered to herself.

"What?" the security guard asked, looking up from the files he was linking for the police as instructed.

"Nothing. Just a nice setup you have here," Kate admired the security office.

The guard's eyes bounced around the office. "Yeah, we have a lot of important clients. We want to maintain their safety and security. They shouldn't have to worry about a thing when they are here."

"They are likely thrilled to have you take such good care of them," Kate said, her eyes glancing at the screens that captured the detective and Nick occasionally appearing from his concealment.

The guard followed Kate's eyes instinctively to the bank of cameras. Nick bobbed in and out of frame suspiciously outside of the harbormaster's office. Kate lurched forward and grasped a joystick mounted to the security panel. "What does this do?"

The guard spun to wrap his hand around Kate's grasp, "That allows us to pan certain cameras. It would be best if you didn't touch things in here."

"Right, sorry," Kate nodded, backpedaling into her seat. A glance at the screen told her the distraction worked as Nick was no longer in frame and at risk of being seen by the guard. "I'm sorry. I'll let you focus on your work."

The guard nodded and turned his attention from Kate and the screens to the files he was transferring for Detective Connolly.

Kate settled back in her seat, a knowing smile creasing her lips.

After a stern lecture from Detective Connolly, who was eager to return to the police station and question the man detained by club security, Kate was freed to return to her vehicle. A rather smug Nick Mason was already seated inside, waiting patiently in the passenger seat.

"How was your visit with the detective and security?" Nick asked with a grin spread across his face.

"Probably not as fruitful as your stealth mission to the harbor master's office. Were you able to catch anything?" Kate asked.

Nick nodded, "They had to talk fairly loud over an air conditioner unit that's probably on its last leg. They mentioned a man, a Dan Huck. I guess he is a notorious hothead in this area. Known for trying to make a quick buck without actually having to work for it. The harbor master said he had been seen a few times at the marina. As far as he could recall, Huck only started coming around after the *Sunny Dream* steamed in."

"That's what I picked up from security," Kate said.

"I guess Huck has tried to sneak aboard via a skiff from the water, too," Nick added.

Kate was thoughtful as she draped her hands on the steering wheel, "So we have a name, but other than eyeing the fanciest boat in the marina, how does this 'Huck' fit into the murder investigation?"

"And if he targets fancy boats, why is this the first time the yacht club has had a run-in with him? Seems like he would have shown up before," Kate pondered.

"Maybe he had," Nick shrugged. "Maybe the lavishness of the *Sunny Dream* was too much to pass up and Huck got careless chasing his silver tuna."

"Maybe," Kate repeated. Her mind was absently trying to connect the dots. "I don't suppose we'd get anywhere at the station."

"Oh, I have no doubt," Nick nodded. "Locked up in a cell is where we'd get. I think we've pressed our luck as much as we can with this one."

"Then I think we need to dig up something else that grants us access," Kate declared.

Nick frowned.

"Every time I have been able to turn something over to the police, Connolly has begrudgingly let me in on some insight," Kate said.

Nick's frown only deepened, "How are we supposed to 'dig up something' useful?"

Kate sighed as she started her SUV and admitted, "I don't know. We'll have to figure that out."

"While you unearth some monumental evidence that will enamor the detective so much that he gives you keys to the investigation, I have a window to fix," Nick said.

Kate nodded, still deep in thought. Nick wondered if she had even heard him.

Twenty Three

Kate leaned up against the wall of the dining room. Staring at the wall that she had turned into her crime diorama, she groaned. Two names were circled with large question marks scrawled next to them.

"Window's fixed!" Nick said with a triumphant grin as he walked into the room. Pausing, he tilted his head and asked, "What's wrong?"

Scowling, Kate tossed her pen on the table, "I can't get information on Dan Huck, or this mystery man, Vincent Aguilar."

Nick frowned, "Who is that?"

"I don't know," Kate shrugged. "It was a name on the whiteboard in the police station."

"You don't want to just ask Detective Connolly nicely?" Nick teased.

Kate shot him a look that summed up her response succinctly, "I don't think that is going to fly. I searched online. I didn't find out anything new on Huck. Only what was reported in newspapers. As for Vincent Aguilar, there are one hundred and eighty-three matches in the greater Tampa area alone. Thirty-five of them with arrest records."

Nick looked thoughtful, "I might know a guy."

Kate looked curious and then rolled her eyes, "Of course you do. I should have known."

"Yeah, a guy from my unit. He owes me a favor or two," Nick shared.

"He works at the Treasure Island Police?" Kate asked, raising an eyebrow.

"Better," Nick grinned. "He's with the CIA."

Kate just shook her head and chuckled, "It's worth a shot."

"Let's just hope it's worth burning up one of those favors," Nick said.

"It will be better than waiting for my Freedom of Information Act request to be processed," Kate added.

"In the middle of a police investigation?" Nick scoffed. "Yeah, that will get misplaced real quick."

Kate changed her tone, "I did find out one interesting thing."

Nick cocked his head, "What's that?"

"There is a candlelight vigil scheduled for Joann Marrs tomorrow night," Kate said.

"And I suppose you want to go," Nick looked displeased with the idea.

"I do," Kate said.

"What could possibly go wrong…" Nick breathed. "Let me see if I can get my buddy on the phone."

Nick paced through the beach house as he dialed his friend. Mindlessly peering out of the windows at the front of the house, he saw an old man pause outside of Kate's house as he rested on his cane.

When he closed his call, he called Kate to the front room.

"Can your friend help?" Kate asked.

"He's going to look into it," Nick said. Peeking out the window, he wrinkled his face and asked, "Do you see anything strange about that old man?"

Kate followed Nick's gaze, both stayed within the frame of the window to avoid being obvious that they were spying on the man. Kate squinted, "The one stooped over on his cane?"

"Yeah," Nick said. His voice sounded more resolute.

"Wait, is that…?" Kate cursed and made a beeline for the door.

Nick pulled out his phone and snapped a quick picture of the man who began moving briskly away from the beach house as Kate flung the front door open.

In nearly a single leap, Kate descended the steps. Nick raced to keep pace with her. By the time they reached the sidewalk, the old man was ambling quickly toward a nearby car.

"Frank Driscoll!" Kate snapped.

The old man ignored Kate and continued to shuffle off.

Catching up to him, Kate slapped her hand on the man's shoulder. "Frank, you can give it up."

"Eh?" the old man rasped. He paused to look at Kate through thick glasses shrouded by bushy eyebrows. His arched back looked genuinely painful in his stooped position.

Rolling her eyes that the private investigator was intent on continuing with the charade, Kate kicked the cane away from the man, much to Nick's horror. He was sure they were correct, but if by some shred they were wrong, Kate's brash move would have been a horrible mistake.

"Do we need to detain you again for Detective Connolly and his officers?" Kate demanded at the man who had fortunately not crashed to the ground without his cane.

Slowly, a reluctant Frank Driscoll rose to his full, un-stooped height. With a gasp, he admitted, "I'm almost glad you caught me. That was getting painful. I was worried I might be stuck that way."

"What are you doing here?" Kate asked. Her face twisted as though she had just bitten into a lemon, "And why are you dressed in that pathetic disguise?"

"Pathetic?" Driscoll was offended. "I thought it was quite good."

"We could tell it was you from the house," Nick chipped in. "Mostly."

"Look, I still have a job to do. My...employer is expecting reports with photos to back them. You don't have to call Connolly. I'll leave," Driscoll promised.

Kate squared up with the private investigator, a shrewd look across her face. "I tell you what, I have a deal for you. If you provide us with information, we won't call Connolly."

Driscoll eyed Kate carefully, "What do you want to know?"

"I don't suppose you'll tell us who hired you..." Kate asked.

Shaking his head, Driscoll said, "I'd lose credibility with my clientele. I'd rather Connolly lock me up for obstruction."

Nick scoffed, "I'm pretty sure posting your ridiculous costume would tank your credibility on its own."

Driscoll rolled his eyes and shifted uncomfortably.

"What do you know about Vincent Aguilar and how is he connected to the case?" Kate asked.

Driscoll's eyes widened under his taped-on bushy eyebrows, "You know about Vinny Aguilar."

"Not enough," Kate snapped.

The private investigator smiled, "If I tell you about Vinny Aguilar, I was never here...deal?"

Kate looked at Nick and back at Driscoll, "Deal."

"Alright then," Driscoll began. "The night before...the...uh..."

"Before Joann Marrs was needlessly murdered," Nick snapped, helping the private detective find his words.

"Yes, Joann. Dane Smithfield loves to take risks. He heard of a street race that uses a stretch of the Gulf to Bay Parkway. Reports are he made a spectacle, calling out the leader of the illegal race and wagered pink slips in an all-or-nothing race," Driscoll shared.

"Let me guess, the leader of the street races is Vinny Aguilar," Kate said.

"He is. He's a bit more than that. He is suspected of being a notorious drug dealer, owning much of south Tampa as his territory. No one has been able to pin it on him, though," Driscoll said. Looking up at Kate and Nick who were enthralled by his story, he continued in dramatic fashion, "Vinny accepted. Lined up his best car. Smithfield pulled up in his stock-looking luxury sedan. Apparently, it was anything but stock. The moment the race began, it was like Smithfield hit a switch. It lurched forward, let out a helluva racket and streaked down the raceway."

"Beating Vinny Aguilar," Nick nodded.

"Worse, *showing up* Vinny Aguilar in front of all the racers. Never mind taking his best car in the process, fooling a shark like Vinny himself... The people watching the race thought Vinny was going to kill Smithfield right there. Fortunately, with a hundred witnesses or so there, Vinny's people held him back. Smithfield was laughing the whole time. He tossed his buddy John Trigg his keys and climbed into Vinny's car himself, with Joann Marrs in the passenger seat. He sped away with a triumphant arm reaching out of the driver's side window," Driscoll said.

Kate and Nick took in the story.

"I can see why Vincent Aguilar was asterisked on the board at the police station," Kate said.

Driscoll nodded, "Smithfield seems to leave a wake of angry people behind him."

"You think Joann just got caught in the crosshairs?" Nick asked.

The private investigator looked as serious as he could underneath the ridiculous disguise, "It is a strong possibility."

"You don't happen to have a picture of Vinny Aguilar, do you?" Kate asked. "Or a middle name, at least?"

Driscoll laughed, "You tried looking him up. Might as well be named John Smith. I'll dig up a photo and get it to you."

Kate and Nick looked dubious.

"I promise," Driscoll pleaded. "My job might make me seem nefarious, but I am a man of my word."

"Can we have your word you will stop surveilling Kate?" Nick pressed.

"I'm afraid not, but at least I am being honest," Driscoll admitted.

Nick huffed at the response.

"You're going to have to work a little harder on your concealment," Kate chided.

Driscoll nodded, "Seems like it. If you don't mind, I'd rather like to get out of this stuff. It's not the most humidity and heat friendly disguise."

"You can go," Kate said.

Driscoll picked his cane up from the sidewalk and hurried down the street.

Kate and Nick watched him disappear down the street.

"Strange man," Nick sighed.

"He did get us valuable information on our mystery man," Kate countered.

"There is no shortage of people that Dane Smithfield has made angry," Nick said.

"The question is, why is Joann Marrs dead instead of him?" Kate asked.

Nick's phone buzzed as they walked back into the house, "Well, that was quick."

Kate looked up from her expanded wall of suspects in the dining room turned crime lab, "Information from your friend?"

Nodding, Nick worked through the process of opening a secure file.

"Dan Huck. Resident of Pinellas Park across the causeway. Ah, his rap sheet," Nick held his phone out and waved it. "I see why he is high on the suspect list. Huck is not a nice guy. Larceny, larceny, breaking and entering…sound familiar?"

Kate looked on with keen interest.

Nick continued scrolling through his phone, "Weapons charges, more larceny…ooh, assault. It looks like it was a case tied to a B&E."

Kate looked horrified, "During a breaking and entering, he assaulted someone?"

"This is just his record. The story isn't in this file," Nick shrugged.

Kate looked off at a blank spot on the wall as she contemplated the news about Dan Huck. The thought of a man like that inside her beach house gave her a shudder.

"We need to find that story," Kate said.

Nick nodded solemnly. He had a good idea what unpleasant thoughts were running through Kate's head. "We'll get to the bottom of this," he promised.

"I know," Kate said softly. Her arms wrapped tightly against her chest.

Nick set his phone down on the table. Wishing he knew how to soothe Kate's frazzled nerves.

"Anything on Aguilar?" Kate asked, her voice almost choking.

"No," Nick shook his head. "My friend reiterated that unless there was a warrant filed with this case, there is no way for him to know which Vincent Aguilar was mixed up with Smithfield."

Kate cracked an awkward smile, "We could always enter a street race."

Nick laughed, "In my work truck or your SUV?"

"It would be quite the spectacle," Kate admitted. "Hopefully, Driscoll will keep his word and at least get me a photo of Aguilar."

"I hate the idea that some of these people could be in the same room with us and we might never know," Nick said, instantly regretting his choice of words.

Kate's shudder returned.

"Let's...let's take a break from all this. Let all this new information sink in," Nick suggested.

"What do you have in mind? I am afraid if I tried surfing right now, I'd drown," Kate said meekly.

"I know a place," Nick grinned.

"Of course you do," Kate laughed. "Sure, I could use some time to reset."

"Perfect. Wear sandals..."

Kate shot Nick a curious look but he was already off to prepare for their excursion.

Twenty Four

Kate's trepidation with Nick's mysterious respite quickly subsided when they left the busy parking lot of Fort DeSoto Park and meandered to a remarkably serene piece of beach.

A light breeze rolled in off the Gulf, making the afternoon pleasant despite the Florida sun baking the stretch of white sand they strolled along. Kate's hair played lightly in the air as she followed Nick.

Despite the excited grin on the surfer's face, he was silent as he urged Kate along. Finding a series of modest dunes, Nick slowed his pace as he walked gingerly along, eyes peeled in the valleys of each dune.

Suddenly, he crouched, pulling Kate down with him. In almost a whisper, he pointed, "There. That's what I wanted you to see."

Covered in sand, just at the edge of a ridge of sand, a turtle gazed lazily up at them.

Kate's eyes widened.

"She's a loggerhead sea turtle. Sitting on her clutch," Nick breathed.

Kate squeezed his arm, finding herself whispering, "She's beautiful."

"She is," Nick nodded. "We have a little over a hundred of them between Clearwater and St. Pete Beach. When the babies hatch, you can watch them make their way into the water for the first time. It's amazing, especially at night with the moon lighting their path."

"I bet," Kate admired the dutiful mother monitoring her clutch. "I'd add it to the rental book, but somehow, I think I'd just as soon let the turtles have their space."

Nick smiled, "They deserve it."

Squatting a safe distance away, they watched the turtle dust herself with sand as she settled in for an afternoon nap.

"Thank you," Kate sighed. "This is just what I needed."

"A far cry from nefarious criminals," Nick said.

"Quite the opposite of all that," Kate admitted. Looking out at the Gulf, her mind reeled. She was torn between soaking up the peace and serenity of nature and returning with energy renewed to complete the investigation.

"Time to go?" Nick asked, eyeing the change in expression on Kate's face.

Nodding, she said, "This was great."

Reluctantly, Nick rose from his squat to begin making their way back to the main trail leading to the parking lot. "What's next?"

Kate frowned, the gears in her mind spinning back to speed, "We have a lot of suspects. None higher than Dane Smithfield."

"That Vinny Aguilar is way up there for me," Nick interjected.

"And Dan Huck. He is vying for Detective Connolly's top spot," Kate said.

Nick shot Kate a glance, "Not yours?"

"He is a great patsy. His outbursts and violent rhetoric make him the perfect suspect. Something there just doesn't add up for me though…" Kate considered.

"Too easy for you?" Nick pressed.

Nodding, Kate affirmed, "Yes. Way too easy."

"What about the private investigator?" Nick asked.

"Frank Driscoll is, I think, who he seems to be. An annoying man hired to do a job. A bit of a parasite, perhaps, but not a killer. At least not Joan Marrs'," Kate said.

"And then you have the other two friends," Nick said.

"There is more than meets the eye, for sure. I can't quite put my finger on that," Kate said, her serious expression suddenly lifting as she nudged Nick. "And then there is us. We're suspects too!"

"I don't much like being a murder suspect," Nick admitted. Opening the passenger door of his truck, he let Kate in. Circling the hood, he climbed into the driver's seat. Kate eyed him with a suspicious, scrutinizing look. Rolling his eyes as he started the truck, he laughed, "Stop it!"

Kate giggled as she leaned her arm against the open window of the pickup. The trip to prep the beach house was not as she planned, but there were parts of it, she had to admit, she rather liked.

It didn't take long for Kate to find herself once more in front of her suspect board. She was convinced there was something she was missing. The ping of her cell phone shook her out of her gaze.

A glance at the screen displayed a now familiar name- Frank Driscoll. A simple attachment was all that the message contained. Pulling open the image, she sent it to the printer. In moments, the machine came to life, spitting out a piece of paper.

Snatching it, Kate studied the photo as she held it up to the wall. Absently reaching for a thumbtack, she placed Vincent "Vinny" Aguilar's picture right next to Dane Smithfield and Dan Huck.

Carrying a load of lumber through the house, Nick paused and leaned into the dining room, "Who's that?"

Kate looked at Nick, stepped back and looked at the photo she had just placed, "Meet Vincent Aguilar."

"Ah," Nick said, setting the boards down. Walking into the room to get a closer look, he added, "So, Driscoll came through."

"I guess he did," Kate nodded.

"This is the street racer and local crime lord," Nick eyed the photo.

"Alleged," Kate scowled mockingly.

"Right," Nick grinned. "Alleged local crime lord. He looks the part. He look familiar to you at all?"

Kate shook her head, "No. I don't know that I have ever seen him. You?"

"No. It seems like he fits the profile of a killer more than Dan Huck," Nick mused. "Though I'm not sure I'd put it past, either."

"Anyone can be a killer when circumstances present," Kate said, stepping back to take in the entire wall of images and clippings.

Nick cocked his head at Kate, a brow raised, "You could be a killer? You think I could?"

Shrugging, Kate said, "Killer, yes. Cold-blooded murderer, no. To save someone else's life or in defense..."

"Well, sure," Nick frowned. "Those are special circumstances. Not petty theft."

"Or misplaced passion, as the case might be," Kate added. "I think most sane people have buffers and filters."

"Some don't," Nick said.

"Some don't," Kate affirmed.

Nick crossed his arms, eyeing the wall, "I can't convince myself definitively among the top three. Dane Smithfield, Dan Huck and Vincent Aguilar could all have had opportunity and motive."

Kate scrunched her face, "Aguilar had motive to go after Smithfield, but his girlfriend?"

"Caught in the crosshairs? Convenient revenge?" Nick suggested.

"That ring. It would be more than enough to pay for a new race car or at least the start of one," Kate added.

"Attractive mark for a guy like Huck, too," Nick suggested.

"According to Smithfield and his friends, he hadn't proposed yet. How did the ring end up on the beach?" Kate asked.

Nick considered the situation, "Maybe Smithfield was carrying it and it got swiped. Maybe Joann found it or maybe it was stolen from the boat?"

"If it was stolen from the boat, why would the thief be hanging out at the beach?" Kate asked.

"Maybe Joann witnessed the theft," Nick offered.

"And didn't tell anyone?" Kate was dubious.

"It is a mystery," Nick said, rubbing his chin.

A loud knock at the door broke their concentration. Sharing quick glances, they made their way to the foyer. Peeking at the security panel screen, they saw Detective Connolly pacing impatiently in front of the door.

"Detective Connolly," Kate called as she swung the door open. "News to share?"

The detective nodded, "Mind if I come in?"

Kate ushered Connolly into the beach house. The detective gave a weak nod to Nick.

"The District Attorney is confident we have our man. We are charging Dan Huck with the murder of Joann Marrs," Connolly said.

"I see. Are *you* confident you have your man?" Kate asked.

"The evidence adds up. We have motive, opportunity, means… a long history of criminal activity, including physical violence," Connolly shared. "I thought you should know. The Chief is pulling the nighttime detail from your beach house."

"What if you're wrong? Shouldn't you maintain the patrol a little while longer?" Nick asked.

"That would illustrate we didn't think we had the right guy. That is not good for our case against Huck," the detective said.

Nick scowled, "There's a lot riding on that hunch."

"It's not a hunch, Mason. It is evidence. That is how *real* detectives handle things," Connolly snapped.

Nick bristled.

Kate stepped in before the conversation escalated, "Detective Connolly, since your investigation is almost over, do you mind showing us what else you found on Driscoll's phone?"

"I can't provide that information, Ms. Harper," Connolly started.

"The private investigator was hired by someone and he was stalking me, taking pictures of me. I have no doubt that those photos have been shared. I'd like to know where," Kate fumed.

Connolly's face twisted as he considered Kate's position. Slowly he nodded, "Truth is, we didn't get much. Most of the calls were to the Charleston area. A majority of them to a burner phone, the rest to a law firm in Charleston."

"The one retained by the Smithfield family," Nick pressed.

The detective nodded.

"Since you are confident in your case and feel assured I am now safe in my beach house, is there anything else you can share that would increase *my* confidence in my safety?" Kate asked.

Connolly studied Kate for several long moments. "We are as sure as we can be. I will keep a personal eye out for anything we may have missed. You have my card. Call me anytime. *Anytime*, Ms. Harper."

Kate stared blankly at the detective.

"I'll, uh, I'll show myself out," Connolly nodded awkwardly and shuffled out of the room and out of the beach house.

Nick just looked at Kate, trying to decipher what she was thinking. He didn't have to wonder for long.

"I think I am only more confident that Huck isn't the guy. He's a *bad* guy, to be sure. Just not *the* guy. He didn't murder Joann Marrs," Kate stated. "I think Detective Connolly feels the same way."

"Every time he used the word 'confident', it was a collective we, the D.A. or the chief of police," Nick nodded.

"Exactly," Kate said.

"Where does that leave us?" Nick asked.

"Still on the case," Kate declared defiantly.

Twenty Four

Kate was already in front of her laptop when the light rap on her door echoed down the hall of the beach house. Setting her work aside, she turned off the security alarm and swung the door open to see Nick smiling on her front step.

"Good morning," Kate sang.

"Good morning, Kate," Nick echoed. "You seem in good spirits."

"I am!" Kate beamed. "No one set off alarms or smashed windows. I was able to concentrate on my work this morning, which I admit has been in a bit of neglect chasing murderers and all."

Nick followed Kate into the kitchen. "The focus on work is refreshing. I should be able to finish the last of the decking today. That means I'll need to access the master bedroom deck," Nick said.

Pouring a cup of coffee for Nick, Kate suggested, "What do you say we enjoy coffee out back before we get too busy?"

Raising his mug in the air, Nick nodded, "Sounds good to me."

A second to the brilliant sunsets that slipped into the Gulf, calm mornings with the sun not yet directing its full attention on the beachside of the house delighted Kate. Slipping into a chair, she curled her legs under her and cupped her mug as she enjoyed the morning.

"Man, it is nice out here," Nick breathed.

"It's great," Kate admitted. "I may be a little jealous of the renters who will get to come and enjoy this house."

"The term million-dollar view isn't an accident," Nick scoffed.

Kate savored the coastal breeze, "It is so much more than that. The peace and serenity. The dolphins and the birds. Watching couples and families and children leaving whatever cares they had at home. Aside from stealing moments like this myself on amazing properties, knowing that these homes give people a much-needed escape and a place to reconnect and recharge is very rewarding."

"I'm not sure I ever looked at property management like that," Nick said, his voice thoughtful. "I think people who live near beaches imagine these properties as almost stolen bits of paradise hoarded by those with a lot of money."

Kate laughed, "I suppose that is partly true. Even in my company, there are bean counters and aggressive buyers. My boss puts a lot of thought and love into her properties. She wants each rental to be an experience. Give those who can't afford to purchase this kind of lifestyle a taste of living on the water, listening to waves crash outside your open bedroom window. It is magical."

"Wow, you made property management almost poetic," Nick said, leaning back in his chair.

"Yeah, don't take my experience to be gospel across the industry," Kate warned over her coffee cup.

Nick took a sip and stared out at the water, "I suppose that is true of anything. Good and bad in all things."

"Yeah. Who would have thought something so terrible could have happened right out there past my windows," Kate said, the beach quiet and peaceful.

Not wanting the conversation to rehash the horrific events of the previous week, Nick just offered a slight nod, directing his gaze at a trio of sandpipers dancing along the water's edge.

Kate broke the mood herself, "Windows...I still can't believe someone broke into the house. So desperate to ignore the alarm..."

Nick pivoted to Kate, unsure if he should take the bait.

"Smithfield...Huck...Aguilar...someone Aguilar hired?" Kate pondered.

With a sigh, Nick shrugged, "John Trigg, Stacey Karp or Frank Driscoll?"

Kate nodded, "I guess no one has been officially ruled out."

"Including us," Nick laughed.

"Including us!" Kate smiled.

Nick's face fell as he squinted, "Seeing the cast of characters, who knocked on your door posing as the neighborhood watch?"

Kate's expression mirrored his, "You know, I'm not sure. He wore a hat and glasses. His frame could have been any one of them."

"One of Frank Driscoll's amazing disguises," Nick said.

Nodding toward the beach, Kate grunted, "Speaking of which…"

Nick swung his attention out to the beach. A man in Bermuda shorts, athletic socks and a broad sun hat took an inordinately long time to locate the prize left by the small dog he was walking. Though shielded by a dark pair of sunglasses, the man spent as much time staring at the pair on the deck enjoying their coffee as he did being a good steward in cleaning up his dog's mess.

Kate stared directly at the man as he abruptly averted his gaze. "Frank! Cute dog!"

The man seemed stunned, looking up and down the beach. One hand holding a leash, the other a weighted baggie the man seemed to not know what to do.

"Seriously, Frank, why don't you just come up? I'll pour you a cup of coffee," Kate called.

Shoulders slumping, the man urged his dog to head up the beach toward the stairs leading to Kate's beach house.

With a wide grin, Kate chastised, "You really need to work on your disguises."

"Humph," Driscoll grunted. Holding the bag out awkwardly to the side, he scanned the area, unsure of what to do with it.

"There's a trash can on the side of the house. I know you know your way," Kate snapped.

With a nod, Driscoll began walking in that direction.

"I'll hold the dog for you," Nick offered, holding his hand out. "What's its name?"

"That is Gladys," the private investigator declared. "I offered to walk her for a little old woman staying in the hotel room next to me."

Nick bent over to pet the dog while Driscoll disposed of the baggie and Kate appeared with a third cup of coffee and a bowl of water for Gladys.

Driscoll thanked Kate for the coffee and slumped against the deck rail, sheepishly drooping his head.

Looking up from Gladys, Nick asked, "With Huck in custody, I am surprised you aren't headed back to Charleston."

The private investigator lifted his head, his eyes squinting as he discerned what to say. "There are a number of remaining threads that…my client wants to ensure don't blow back on them or their associates," Driscoll finally drawled.

"Remaining threads? Like what?" Kate leaned forward.

Driscoll studied Kate before he spoke, "Vincent Aguilar remains a concern. With tonight's vigil planned, my client thought it best that I stay local to…keep an eye on things."

"I see," Kate nodded. "Is there a concern regarding the vigil?"

"As in a bonified threat? No. I don't think so. Just a potential cast of unsavory players," Driscoll said.

"What do you think? Do the police have the right guy?" Nick asked.

Driscoll looked serious as he replied, "They have a viable suspect, to be sure. The right guy… I don't know."

"You think Aguilar?" Kate pressed.

"Or Smithfield or one of his friends?" Nick added.

Driscoll nodded absently, "Could be."

Kate cocked her head, "Do you *know* who the murderer is?"

"I do not," Driscoll shook his head adamantly. "I presume my suspicion board looks a lot like Detective Connolly's."

"I see," Kate said.

Driscoll stood up abruptly, "Thank you for the coffee. I should be getting Gladys back."

The fluffy dog panted happily at Nick's feet. Grasping the leash from Nick, Driscoll excused himself and coaxed Gladys down the steps and back out onto the beach.

Kate and Nick watched the man saunter down the beach in his Hawaiian shirt, oversized hat and cliché beach ensemble.

"He is an odd man," Nick observed.

"Not unlikeable in his own way. But he is odd," Kate admitted.

"Well, I suppose it is time to get some work done around here," Nick stood.

Kate looked up at the sun rays that had just begun clearing the roof of the beach house. "I feel guilty. I should have allowed you to work while it was cool out."

"That's okay. I enjoyed the company. Oddities and all," Nick smiled.

Kate smiled back, gathering up the coffee cups so that Nick's hands were free to gather his tools. Casting a glance over her shoulder at where the private detective had disappeared, she shook her head.

Twenty Five

Nick swiped at his forehead with the back of his wrist as he placed another board in tight to a spacer. The Florida sun was making its presence well known as it beat down directly on the back of Kate's beach house. The coastal breeze might have been helpful if it too wasn't approaching ninety degrees itself.

He didn't complain as Kate kept him freshly stocked with lemonade and water as he worked. Nick certainly couldn't complain about the view. Framed with palm trees, the blue-green waters of the Gulf were brilliant against nearly pure white sand. As offices went, this one was pretty spectacular.

Fastening the board down with screws, he paused to appreciate the view before retrieving the next piece of the deck puzzle. Perched on the third-story deck, the vista was expansive. Sunbathers, beachcombers, swimmers and paddleboards dotted the scene. The location of the beach house was nearly ideal. There was enough activity nearby to feel you were in good company, but scant enough that you never felt crowded.

Turning to grab a board, something made Nick pause. Scanning the beach, his eyes locked on what stood out to him. A man in a fishing cap sat on a cooler, sipping a bottle of water. A rod shoved into the sand by its handle stood behind the man's shoulder. As the man saw Nick pause in his work, the fisherman slowly spun, his feet dancing along the sand until he faced the water.

Rolling his eyes, Nick cursed, "All right, Driscoll. Enough is enough!"

Flinging the veranda doors open, Nick stomped through the house, making a beeline for the main patio and the walkway to the beach.

Kate looked up from her work, seeing that Nick was on a mission, "What's up?"

"Driscoll just doesn't quit!" Nick growled as he marched out of the house.

Kate got up and followed him out onto the deck. Leaning up against the rail, she surveyed the beach. Seeing a man in a fishing cap quickly amble away, a cooler tucked under one arm like a football and a rod dangling in the other, he had disappeared by the time Nick reached the beach.

Scanning both directions from where he had seen Driscoll, Nick gave a kick to the sand, fuming. With nothing else to do but return to the beach house, Nick saw Kate watching him and his mini-tantrum.

"Enough is enough. We've tolerated Driscoll, even been *nice* to him. I'm going to put an end to this. Frankly, it's gotten a bit creepy!" Nick snapped, pulling out his phone.

Kate continued to watch Nick, occasionally casting a glance toward the beach.

"Detective Connolly, please," Nick bellowed into his cell phone.

After a few minutes of waiting, Nick spoke hastily, "Detective Connolly, Nick Mason. Listen, I've been working at Kate Harper's place and for the third time in two days, I've caught the private investigator Frank Driscoll spying on her."

"When? The last time was a few minutes ago. What? I…
I see. No, I couldn't be sure. I am sure someone was watching
the house. When I caught them, they scattered, I thought for
sure it was Driscoll again. Yes, the other two times, I am
positive. Okay, okay. Thank you," Nick called into the phone.
"Oh, detective, if you have Huck in custody, why is there still so
much attention on Kate? Yeah, I don't know either. I will.
Thank you."

Nick hung up the phone, looking more perturbed and
confused than before he made the call.

Looking up, he flashed a sheepish glance at Kate.

"What's going on?" Kate asked, her voice curious but
gentle, given Nick's agitated state.

Nick looked at Kate, "I thought for sure that was
Driscoll sitting on the beach in a fisherman's get-up."

"And it wasn't?" Kate asked, a little surprised.

"Not according to Detective Connolly. He said Driscoll
was sitting right in front of him. Connolly had some photos
from Driscoll's phone that he wanted to access in order to
corroborate the package for the district attorney," Nick said.

Kate cocked her head, she suggested, "Maybe it was just
a fisherman on the beach."

Nick considered the thought. Finally, he shook his head,
"No. Something was off. First, what fisherman sits with his *back*
to the beach? No, they are always dreaming and plotting about
the catch they are going to pull from the water. If he was a
fisherman, his timing was a bit off. There's not much to catch
this time of day right off the beach. And then, there was his
gear. His pole was so shiny, the reflection caught my eye. The
cooler was brand new. There was no other gear. No ties, no
lures, no tackle box."

Kate chewed her lip, "When he left the beach, he did seem in quite the hurry and he didn't carry the cooler by the handles, he picked it up and tucked it under his arm."

"If it was full…drinks, bait, whatever… he wouldn't carry it that way," Nick said.

"It's probably just a tourist," Kate shrugged.

Nick shook his head, chewing on his lip as he looked out toward the beach, "No. I'm over coincidences."

They both moved toward the house to get back to their respective tasks. Nick held the door, eyeing Kate, concern dripping from his look.

"What?!" Kate scrunched her face.

"I'm…I'm just worried about you, that's all," Nick gasped. "If Connolly is wrong, there is still a murderer out there. And there seems to be no shortage of people concerned about this beach house and what you know."

"I'm a big girl. I can take care of myself. Especially with that state-of-the-art security system you installed," Kate argued.

"I have no doubt that you can take care of yourself," Nick agreed. Pressing, he added, "Under *normal* circumstances. We all have challenges that are bigger than ourselves. There is no shame in that."

Kate tried to brush Nick off.

"If Driscoll is still poking around and other people have an eye on this house, then that suggests that not everyone thinks this case is closed. Or worse, the real *murderer* knows it isn't but wants to keep it closed," Nick countered.

"Fine," Kate relented. "I'll be careful. What else can I do?"

"Go away. Go home. Anywhere until all of this blows over," Nick pleaded.

Kate laughed, "I can't do that. I'm sorry."

Nick crossed his arms trying to think of what to say. He wasn't happy when Kate shifted gears back to the case.

"If Driscoll was hired by the Smithfields, then they most likely still have something to hide," Kate snapped her fingers.

With a sigh, Nick realized the amount of breath he had just wasted trying to convince Kate to stay as far away from the case as she could.

"It's a P.R. play," Nick shrugged. "For families like that, they have an image to uphold. Whether anyone had anything to do with Joann Marrs' death or not, paints a black mark across the entire family."

"Maybe. Or Dane Smithfield really is the murderer, after all? He makes the most sense. He had from day one," Kate said. She sounded irritated with herself for being led astray in the investigation. "Maybe that's what Driscoll is actually here for- to paint the evidence every color but Dane Smithfield."

"I thought of that," Nick admitted. "On the surface, Smithfield is the logical suspect. Dating Joann. About to propose. Was supposed to be in possession of the ring..."

"So many reasons that scenario could get out of hand and emotional. Lead to a chase down the beach and..." Kate gasped, imagining the scene she had witnessed all over again, only carrying it to the unseen conclusion.

Kate's face fell. Instinctively, she wandered into the dining room where her wall of clippings and images surrounding the case were pinned into the sheetrock. "This is the thing I have never been able to wrap my head around. If the murderer already had the ring, why chase after the victim?"

"They weren't after the ring," Nick shrugged. "They were specifically after the victim. But if the victim already had the ring..."

"Then a whole host of suspects rises to the surface," Kate finished.

"But according to the reports. Smithfield hadn't proposed to Joann Marrs yet," Nick looked confused.

Kate frowned, "Maybe he did. Maybe he stole a moment with Joann and proposed."

"Then the whole trough of suspects once again becomes viable," Nick nodded.

"Then why, especially with counsel, would Dane Smithfield not have shared that? It takes so much pressure off of his case," Kate said.

Nick shrugged, "Because either he didn't. Or he did, but it turned out not the way he pictured it and things got out of hand. Whether it would help his case or not, his instinct would be to clam up about the entire experience."

"Which leads us exactly nowhere," Kate concluded. Brushing her hair off of her forehead, she was exasperated.

"Nothing to do but let Detective Connolly and the police sort all this out," Nick said.

"Or..." a wicked grin splashed across Kate's face. "We attend tonight's vigil and take a whack at sorting this out with most of the players present in one place!"

Nick's eyes rolled in the back of his head.

"The vigil is planned for Joann at the site of...well, where she died. The family and friends have been sequestered by the police while they were sorting things out. I think I should go and pay my respects," Kate announced.

Nick looked horrified, "I'm not so sure that is a great idea. There is a strong chance the murderer will be there. *Whoever* has been stalking you will be there."

"I know," Kate grinned. "It will be a great opportunity to listen and observe. Ask questions and see how people respond."

"That's...no. Kate, you can't be serious," Nick protested.

"I'll be fine," Kate insisted. Her eyes perked up, "Unless... you want to go with me?"

Nick scowled, "I don't *want* to go, but I don't really want to read about you in the news, either."

"It's a date!" Kate beamed and then her face fell. "Well, not a date..."

"It's sort of a date and I will be going under protest," Nick said, his voice firm.

Kate shot him a sideways grin.

Twenty Six

Nick stood in front of the door as it was flung open by a frazzled Kate Harper. Putting earrings on while she slipped into high heel shoes, she paused as she took in the full sight of the man on her front porch. "Wow, you clean up nice!" she exclaimed.

Straightening his shirt cuffs protruding from his suit sleeves, Nick grinned, "As do you, though I don't think your ability to arrive at elegance was ever in question. I'm just a ragged handyman-surfer."

Setting the security system, Kate swung the door behind her. Giving Nick a final once-over, she let out a mischievous smirk, "You'll do."

Eyeing a bouquet of flowers cradled in his arms, Kate raised a brow.

"For Joann," Nick said, his voice cracking slightly.

"At least one of us was thinking ahead," Kate kicked herself for not coming up with something for the vigil.

"You've had a lot on your mind," Nick offered.

Holding his arm out for her to hook hers into his, Nick led her down the steps. Dangling her keys, Kate declared, "I'll drive."

Nick eyed the work truck with surfboards lashed to the roof and Kate's gleaming SUV, "Probably the right choice tonight."

Sliding behind the wheel, Kate watched Nick climb in next to her. "This should be interesting," Kate said, as she started her car.

"Around you, it always is," Nick sighed.

Accepting the statement with a slight shrug, Kate eyed her rearview mirror and backed out of her driveway.

Kate was surprised at the presence at the vigil site. "I guess we should have just walked from my house," Kate said as she stretched in her seat, searching for a parking spot.

"Head across Gulf Boulevard. Most people won't cross the road," Nick suggested.

Nodding, Kate pulled into a beach shop parking lot. The shop had closed down for the day and a handful of vigil attendees had adopted the same idea.

Nick hopped out of the SUV the moment it stopped rolling. Hurrying to Kate's side of the vehicle, he pulled the door open.

"Wow, how chivalrous? That suit of yours is getting to your head," Kate teased.

"Oh, come on now. Surfer shorts or a suit, I'm still a gentleman," Nick protested.

Kate wrinkled her nose and eyed the open button on his shirt, "That you are. No tie though, huh?"

"After leaving the suit and tie world, I promised myself weddings and funerals only," Nick quipped. Thinking about the event they were walking toward, he dipped his head, "Oh, gosh!"

Kate slipped her arm into his, "I know what you meant."

With a nod, Nick straightened, and they followed a small contingent of attendees as they waited for the crossing signal to make their way across Gulf Boulevard and towards the beach access where Joann Marrs was found.

A large police presence was nearly matched with news crews maneuvering to capture the scene. Kate watched the rapidly growing crowd force the police to expand their barricaded area dedicated to the service. The amoebic throng was clearly filled with curious onlookers who were seeing the vigil as an event, the site of a well-publicized murder, as much as they were paying respects to Joann Marrs.

Several well-dressed men and women Kate figured to be in their early sixties stood at the roughly configured entrance to the service site. While they offered nods and flat smiles, their scowls and eyes welled with tears couldn't mask their pain, and at times, disdain for the attendees.

"Families?" Nick whispered in Kate's ear.

Nodding, she replied, "That's my guess."

Behind the older group at the front of the service space, the faces of Dane Smithfield, John Trigg and Stacey Karp peered at the unending flow of people streaming into the site. Their curious looks were quickly washed with frustration. The vigil, while eagerly declared by the news channels, was supposed to have been about the families and friends closest to Joann.

Seeing Kate and Nick, Joann's friends' faces softened slightly. Kate made a quick beeline for the group, their eyes lighting on the bouquet of flowers clutched in Nick's hands.

"Again, we are so sorry for your loss," Kate said to the group.

"Thank you," Dane replied. His voice struck Kate as the words were the most genuine she had heard tumble out of his mouth in any of their interactions. The cockiness was almost entirely replaced with a sunken introspection.

"This is…quite the turnout," Kate said, her eyes panning the packed vigil site.

"A bunch of people attending a news report like a ride at Disneyland," Stacey snapped.

John Trigg shook his head, his eyes a mix of watery flames belying his anger, "None of them even knew Joann, never mind cared about her. They shouldn't be here. Frankly, neither should you."

Kate breathed in, her kind eyes directly focused on Trigg, "I understand your feeling. I wanted to pay my respects. While I didn't know her personally, I feel a connection somehow."

"You're fine to be here," Dane snapped. "It is almost as much a show for the families that came down as for anyone else."

John and Stacey swung their heads toward Dane.

Dane shrugged, "Look at them. Greeting people as they come in, smiling while occasionally giving sad eyes to the cameras. I mean, Mrs. Marrs' tears are real, but come on."

"Your parents weren't close with Joann?" Kate asked.

"They're barely close with me," Dane shot back. "They could care less about Joann other than her family's status in the Charleston area."

Kate frowned, "Does the Marrs family walk in the same circle as your family?"

Dane laughed, "Not at all. Her mom is a schoolteacher, her dad is a sales rep for a lumber company. They do okay, but they aren't exactly members of the country club."

"How'd you guys meet?" Nick asked.

"I liked to mix it up and visit some of the local hangouts outside of the gated communities. Honestly, usually to get in trouble. I met Joann one of those nights and decided she was more interesting than trouble," Dane said, his voice cracking as he spoke.

Nick smiled, "You can meet special people just about anywhere, even just passing by on a beach access trail."

"Or trespassing…" Kate teased Nick. Turning back to Joann's friends, she said, "You all seem close. That's nice."

"We were," John spat.

"We *are*," Stacey said.

"Right," John's head sagged.

Kate studied him as he averted eye contact. He was sad and angry.

"Well, thank you for coming. You can place the flowers by the fence line," Dane said.

"Come on, let's get some space," Stacey tugged at Dane's arm. She shot a glance at John.

"I think I need a few minutes to myself," John muttered.

Stacey offered a nod and pulled Dane toward the beach access nearby.

Kate and Nick watched the group of friends dodge the onlookers, some taking selfies at the site. John Trigg's fist tightened as he pushed past a group of college-aged kids trying to squeeze into a photo.

"Hey!" a girl with a camera exclaimed.

A boy close to her tapped John Trigg on the shoulder. The young mourner spun around and without warning, swung a haymaker into the boy's face. Police stepped in almost immediately and suggested the group taking the photo leave as they stepped between them and John Trigg. Trigg surveyed the situation for a moment and shrugged, continuing on his way.

As the group dispersed, Kate led Nick to the spot designated for Joann's vigil. Flowers, teddy bears and lit candles filled the area. Nick placed the bouquet he carried down. Kate wandered to the rail that overlooked the beach and the wooden walkway that led to it. At the edge of the sand, she watched Dane Smithfield and Stacey Karp huddle shoulder to shoulder, looking out at the Gulf. Swaying back and forth, the glow of cigarettes visible as they shuffled.

"They both smoke," Kate said.

Nick's eyes followed hers, "So, they do."

"One of the people snooping around the beach house smoked," Kate said, as she watched the pair share a moment out on the beach. With a sigh, she looked at Nick, "I'm not sure who is taking all of this harder, Dane or John."

"It looks like Dane is in good company," Nick said.

"John Trigg definitely had a thing for Joann," Kate said.

Leaning against the rail with his back to the beach so that he could monitor what ears might be close and could take in the crowd, Nick mused, "So, either John or Dane could have acted in a moment of passion."

"As could Stacey," Kate added.

"Mix in Dan Huck, Vinnie Aguilar, shifty detective Frank Driscoll and you got a heckuva party," Nick said.

"No one is legitimately off of Detective Connolly's list," Kate nodded.

"Speaking of Connolly..." Nick nodded toward the Treasure Island Police Detective making his way through the crowd, looking as disgusted as most of the Joanna Marrs' family and friends at the curiosity seekers.

Seeing Kate and Nick didn't seem to improve his mood. Making a direct line towards them, he strode with purpose. Crossing his arms, he cursed, "You too?"

"I've got more affinity with Joann Marrs than most of these people," Kate defended.

Scanning the crowd, Connolly shook his head, "This is ridiculous."

"With the newshounds relishing every moment of this case in their broadcasts, are you really surprised?" Nick asked.

"No. No, I guess I'm not," the police detective admitted. "The families arrived in town. The station has been a zoo."

"I imagine," Kate said.

"At least we have Dan Huck," Connolly said.

Kate looked at the detective, "And everyone is satisfied with that?"

"Makes sense," Connolly shrugged.

"A little too much sense," Kate said.

Connolly raised an eyebrow as he looked at Kate, "You have seen too many mystery shows. In the real world, the facts typically tell the real story, just as they seem."

"Does Dan Huck smoke?" Kate blurted.

"What?" Connolly frowned.

"Does he smoke? Whoever was sneaking around my house smoked," Kate said. Her gaze drifted to Dane Smithfield and Stacey Karp on the beach.

Connolly rolled his eyes, "I see where you are going. Those butts could have been left by a passerby. You know, riff-raff who use your property to access the beach."

Nick scowled at Connolly's shot.

"The butts weren't found where people walk through," Kate said.

"It just doesn't prove anything," the detective said. Looking around at the vigil, he said, "Look, I've got to pay my respect to the family. Show that I was here as directed by my chief and make sure this circus doesn't get out of hand."

"Good luck with that," Nick said.

Connolly looked at Nick slowly before shuffling off.

"Look, they're coming back up," Kate said. She nodded toward the walkway to the beach where Dane Smithfield was escorted by Stacey Karp.

"Yeah, I suppose the vigil is about to begin," Nick said as the audience gathered around the site where Joann Marrs had breathed her last breath.

"Come on. I want to get some samples!" Kate said in a hoarse whisper.

"Samples?" Nick frowned as he was tugged by Kate moving towards the beach walkway.

As most eyes were on the area that was amassed with flowers, notes and other gifts commemorating Joann Marrs, Kate searched the beach with the light from her cell phone. Pulling a sandwich bag from her pocket, she scooped up a pair of cigarette butts.

"You keep sandwich bags in your pocket?" Nick scoffed.

"I do after all this stuff," Kate grinned.

Shaking his head, Nick was once more yanked along. Skirting the crowd that had closed in on the vigil site, a pastor was sharing words on behalf of the family to kick off the main part of the vigil.

Kate took the opportunity to circle the audience. John Trigg remained on his own, distanced from the crowd. He looked more miserable than ever. Dane Smithfield stood near his family with Stacey Karp directly at his side. Joann Marrs' family stood on the opposite side of the vigil from the Smithfields. Several men in suits that were familiar were dotted throughout the periphery of the crowd.

"The Smithfields brought their legal team?" Kate hissed.

Nick spied the men that Kate had identified, "I guess. They are scattered like Secret Service."

"Oh, my…" Kate froze, making Nick collide with her. Looking straight ahead, she saw a group clad in jackets over tank tops. The man in the center eyed the proceedings with a look more like he had business to conduct than to pay respects to Joann Marrs. "That's Vincent Aguilar!"

Nick studied the group, "They look friendly."

"Why aren't the cops paying more attention?" Kate whispered.

"They have their man," Nick said.

"I'm going to talk to Detective Connolly," Kate snapped, storming off to find the police detective.

"I'm sure he is going to love that," Nick muttered, setting off after her.

Twenty Seven

The police detective hovered at the edge of the crowd. He was acutely studying the crowd, to Kate's opinion, like someone waiting for a shoe to drop.

"Ms. Harper," Connolly acknowledged, taking his eyes off the crowd and applying them to her. Largely ignoring Kate's shadow in the form of Nick, he said, "So far, everything seems in order."

"Maybe. Did you see Vincent Aguilar is here?" Kate spat.

"I saw. I have officers monitoring him and his crew," Connolly acknowledged.

Kate didn't look pleased with the response, "What is he *doing* here?"

"Exercising his rights as a citizen," Connolly shrugged. "Look, it is probably disrespectful for him to be here. I doubt it is in reverence to the passing of Ms. Marrs. But, he isn't a suspect anymore. There isn't anything I can do. If he, or anyone associated with him acts out of line, we'll handle it. Beside the Smithfields gave the mayor an earful and the mayor gave Chief Reynolds who..."

"Gave you an earful," Kate finished.

"Exactly. We aren't in Charleston but the giant legal team still has sway, regardless of where they hail from," Connolly said. Turning his attention to them, he squinted, "Why are *you* two here? Sick curiosity like the rest of these rubber necks?"

Kate sighed and looked Connolly directly in the eyes, "I feel somewhat responsible for Joann Marrs' death and someone or some people who are here have been terrifying me at my house! *That* is why I am here. The case may be closed for you and the department, but for me, something is still fishy around here and it isn't coming from the Gulf."

"Kate… Ms. Harper, let us do the police work," Connolly said, his voice stern.

Kate started to walk away in a huff.

"Oh," Kate spun. Jamming her hand into her pocket, she produced the baggy of cigarette butts. "I got these off the beach. They belong to Dane Smithfield and Stacey Karp."

Reluctantly accepting the package, the detective glanced around before shoving the bag into his own pocket, "I'll…I'll have the lab run these just to be safe. Now, stay out of trouble, if you will. Not being woken up for a late-night emergency call at your beach house has been…refreshing."

Nick led Kate away with a soft hand on her shoulder. To his dismay, her path took them straight toward Vincent Aguilar. Standing in front of the alleged drug runner and street racer, she stood watching the vigil with Aguilar at her back.

Constant chatter behind her while the pastor and members of the victim's family spoke, caused Kate to spin abruptly. Looking directly up into the purported gangster's eyes, she spat, "Do you guys mind? This is a vigil for a girl who lost her life!"

Nick swallowed hard as he reluctantly joined her side as Vincent and his crew stood tall in front of the fiery woman.

"That's why we're here, paying our respects," Aguilar snarled.

"Part of paying respects is *being* respectful!" Kate shot back.

Nick winced.

Aguilar squared up in front of Kate, his crew closing in behind him. Studying her, his head bobbing from side to side as he considered how to address the woman. Finally, he grinned, "All right. You know what? You're right. We should be more respectful. In fact, that's what brings us here. A little chat about respect with the boyfriend up there. You understand."

Unflinching, Kate looked directly into Aguilar's eyes. Squinting slightly, she replied, "Your business is your business. I just want to celebrate Joann's life in peace."

"You got it, princess," Aguilar conceded. With his grin growing wider, he added, "I like your spunk. If you like fast rides, you should look me up. I think you might like it."

Kate looked Aguilar up and down, "Yeah, you seem like you'd be a quick one."

Without waiting for a reply, she spun as Aguilar's crew gasped at her parry.

Spinning on his heel, Nick was happy to move away from the reputed gangster. "Did you have to antagonize him?"

"I wanted to see how he'd respond, if he recognized me," Kate shrugged.

"I don't think he did," Nick replied.

"I don't think he did either," Kate admitted. "But then again, a guy like Aguilar isn't the type to do his own dirty work."

Making their way once more within the mix of the crowd, many who came out of pure curiosity and little connection with Joann Marrs, had left. The push to wriggle within the thick of the vigil was easier.

They saw Stephen Marrs, Joann Marrs' father address the crowd, his wife gripping his hand tightly as he spoke. "My daughter…Joann was an amazing soul. She lived life through kindness. Whether in her words or action, she wanted the best for everyone. She saw the best in everyone, whether anyone else saw it or not," Marrs said, his eyes briefly lighting on Dane Smithfield.

"Her loss is a tragedy. Not just to this family, but to the world," Stephen Marrs wiped tears from his eyes. His lips trembled as he oscillated from sad to angry, "How such a dark, *pathetic* person could rob Joann of life? Her untouched dreams, all the souls she has yet to touch, we will never know the enormity of the good, the positive impact that she would have brought to this earth that so desperately needs it. She was an angel, here, she *is* an angel in heaven."

Marrs took a moment to scan the crowd, "If you came here to genuinely pay respects, offer a gasp of earthly love to Joann…thank you. Our whole family thanks you."

Stephen Marrs squeezed his wife tightly as her emotions boiled over, breaking down in his arms for what Kate was sure was the millionth time in the past week.

Dane Smithfield's father nudged his son to scoot into Marrs' place. Dane shuffled unsurely to address the crowd. "I…" Dane cleared his throat. "I don't really have words to share. There are none that make sense right now. Joann was a gift. She put up with so much of my nonsense when she didn't have to. When she shouldn't have. She was just so full of love and I feel like… like my heart has been ripped out. For those that know me, you know emotion is not part of the Smithfield way, but… damn it!"

Dropping his chin to his chest, Dane quickly moved out of the limelight, seeking a shadowy spot where he could sob in private. Stacey Karp touched his shoulder as he brushed by.

Taking that as her cue, Joann's best friend wandered to the center of the space. She was patient as she panned the crowd. Her expression was serious but somehow more stoic than the others that shared their thoughts.

"Where do I begin? Joann was my best friend. Some would argue that we didn't have a lot in common, but as others have said, she looked beyond boundaries and barriers. I'm not even sure I wanted to like her when I met her in school. She didn't give me much of a choice. From helping me with my homework, to celebrating when I made cheer and being a kind shoulder when I had boy problems which seemed to be all the time," Stacey took a breath and re-scanned the audience.

"Jo Jo was sweet, funny and kind. I'm with Dane. We might drive to school in BMWs but I have no idea what that girl saw in *us*. A stuck-up, unruly, self-absorbed crew that lost our anchor. As challenging as I'm sure we are to our parents, I can only imagine where we'd be without her. Unfortunately, we are going to find out as we are cast out, adrift with the tragic loss of Jo Jo," Stacey clamped her lips tight as her eyes quivered, a tear fighting its way through her otherwise numb visage.

Stacey looked at John Trigg, who trembled slightly as he took a step forward. Like so many others, his face was awash in sadness, pain and anger. It appeared as though he wanted to speak, but instead whirled around and stormed off in the opposite direction.

The pastor took over, suggesting the crowd take a moment before inviting others to speak.

Kate couldn't help but scan the crowd. In one corner, John Trigg paced at the edge of the vigil space. Stacey Karp leaned against the railing and lit a cigarette as she stared out at the Gulf. Dane had disappeared onto the solitude of the beach after speaking.

Her eyes working overtime, she nudged Nick, "Where'd Aguilar go?"

Nick shrugged, "After Dane spoke, he kind of nodded for his crew to disband."

Kate frowned, "Did they all go together?"

"Not really. They sort of separated and made their way away from Aguilar. A few moments later, he left himself," Nick said.

"Toward the parking lot?" Kate asked.

"No," Nick shook his head. "Now that you mention it, he went down the other walkway to the beach."

"Dane is on the beach!" Kate exclaimed.

Twenty Eight

Darting through the periphery of the crowd, Kate made her way to the beach access that Dane Smithfield had used. It didn't take her long to scan the beach and find him along with three other silhouettes.

Nick, on Kate's heels, whispered, "That's Aguilar!"

The four figures were having a spirited discussion, though Kate and Nick couldn't quite make out what was being said. Walking out onto the sand, they closed in on the group of men.

"You want it? Here!" Dane Smithfield dug something out of his pocket.

Smithfield dangled a set of keys in the air, glistening in the moonlight. Aguilar took a step forward. Before he could close in and grasp the keys, Dane reeled back and sent the keys sailing in the air, landing beyond the breakers in a satisfying splash.

Aguilar was enraged, "You little punk! You'll regret that. Damned rich, spoiled brat!"

"It's all right. I've got plenty of regrets," Dane sneered.

The gang leader lunged forward, delivering a fist to Dane's gut. The other two men held Smithfield up by grabbing either side of him.

Vincent Aguilar drew back for another unencumbered swing, "I thought you would have learned by now what happens when someone crosses me. You lose things… that are important to you."

"Hey!" Nick shouted, taking rapid steps toward the skirmish.

Kate followed close behind, her cellphone camera recording the incident.

Aguilar looked at Nick and then at Kate. A broad grin swept across the reputed gangster's face as he released his fist and dropped his arm to his side. "We were just sharing our condolences. Seemed like Dane here was real upset. You know, like doubled over in pain kind of upset," Aguilar said.

"Yeah, I see that," Nick glowered.

"No, really. Weren't we, Dane?" Aguilar pressed.

As Aguilar's men let go of Dane, he held his arms up and shook his head at Kate and Nick, "No, it's all right. I probably deserved that and much worse."

Aguilar squared up as he considered how to complete his mission with Dane. He glanced out at the water where the keys to what was presumably the car that Dane won in the illegal street race were settling into the sand under the breakers.

"The car is parked in the marina lot. I'm sure you have another set of keys. Just take it," Dane spat heaving air back into his lungs. Digging into his pocket, he pulled out a valet slip, "Here, this will get you in and out. You shouldn't have any trouble."

Frowning, Aguilar asked, "And how is this supposed to square us up? You still made me look like a chump in front of the race crowd."

"Yeah, well, they can take that at face value," Dane laughed.

Aguilar and his men closed in again, only to be separated by Nick. Nick's effort was enough to give the men a moment's pause before they continued to try and get at Dane.

"Look, tell them you beat the keys out of me. Tell them we raced again and this time… I didn't cheat. Here, take the keys to my car.

That should do it," Dane said, tossing another set of keys at Aguilar's chest.

Glancing at the set of keys in his hand, Aguilar grinned, "Yeah. That should do it."

With a nod, his men stood down. Aguilar walked up to Dane with Nick at the ready to separate them once more. "Kid, I better never see your face around again. Otherwise, a few sore ribs would be the least of your concern. Thanks for the ride, though."

Spinning in the sand, Aguilar walked away, his men in tow.

Dane stooped over, still feeling the effects of Aguilar's punch. Looking up at Nick and Kate, he said, "Thanks, I think."

"Vincent Aguilar is no one to mess with," Kate scowled.

"I know," Dane grinned. "That's what made it so fun. Figured I'd have a chance to be floating in a canal somewhere after showing him up at the race."

"Why antagonize him by throwing the keys in the water?" Nick asked.

Dane shrugged, "I figured he should work for what he wanted. Besides… after everything, I kinda feel like I deserve to get beat up a bit."

"Why would you say that?" Kate was barely able to conceal suspicion in her voice.

"I never treated Jo Jo right. Hell, I don't treat anyone right. Aguilar is right. I'm just a spoiled rich kid. I didn't deserve Jo and she definitely didn't deserve what happened. It just isn't right," Smithfield's voice trailed off. Looking up, he said, "I should probably get back up there. Besides, I'm gonna need a ride."

Walking away from Kate and Nick, the pair stood absorbing everything that happened.

"Oh, thanks again for stepping in," Dane said over his shoulder before ascending the walkway leading back toward the vigil.

Kate and Nick looked at each other.

"Well, you had good instincts," Nick said.

"I hate to think what might have happened if we didn't show up when we did," Kate breathed.

"It would be pretty gutsy to do much more than rough the kid up with all the cops up there," Nick said.

"Maybe. A gangster with a bruised ego, who knows?" Kate shrugged.

"True," Nick said. Moving toward the boardwalk away from the beach, he gently placed a hand on Kate's back. She moved into the gesture instead of away.

The moment was abruptly shattered by Detective Connolly's voice ringing down from the top of the walkway, "Everything okay down there? Dane Smithfield looked a little rough."

"He had a little chat with Vincent Aguilar. A chat with their fists until we showed up," Nick said.

Instinctively, Connolly looked over his shoulder at the sizeable crowd and large police presence within reach of the beach. Meeting Kate and Nick midway along the walkway, he pressed, "Why don't you two tell me what happened?"

"Kate noticed Aguilar and his guys disappeared not long after Dane finished speaking. She thought there might be trouble and there was," Nick said.

"I even got part of it on video," Kate grinned, waving her cell phone.

Connolly grabbed the phone as Kate hit play on the recording.

"Aguilar was pressing Dane for making amends to cheating him out of the car he lost. Smithfield responded by tossing a set of keys in the Gulf," Nick narrated as the police detective watched Kate's brief clip.

"That's a good way to get yourself roughed up... or worse," Connolly grunted. "Got a give it to that kid. He's got stones. Not the brightest maybe, but he's got some guts."

"Aguilar said something about taking things away from Dane that were 'important to him'. Dane seemed to reel from that comment and then he handed Aguilar the keys to his own car. Along with the claim ticket to get Aguilar's ride out of the marina parking lot. Aguilar decided that was sufficient to square things up between the two of them and garner his respect back amongst the racing community," Kate added.

"I see," Connolly considered. "I guess it's a good thing that you two came along when you did."

The detective paused and gave a scrutinizing look at Nick, "Just stepping in on a guy like Vincent Aguilar is enough to get on his nasty list."

Nick shrugged, "While I don't seek them out like Dane Smithfield, I can handle guys like Aguilar."

The bold statement gave the detective pause.

Shaking himself out of his thoughts, he said, "The formal part of the vigil seems to be finishing up. We should probably get up there. I still need to speak with the families as per the chief."

Connolly stormed up the walkway.

Kate and Nick shared glances and shrugged, following the detective. A disgruntled Connolly looked over his shoulder telling them that tailing him was not exactly what he meant.

As they re-entered the vigil area, the formal speeches had concluded. A mass of reporters swarmed around them, initially focused on Detective Connolly and peppering him with questions regarding Dan Huck and if the case was officially closed. They questioned why such a large police presence was at the vigil and if that meant the potential for more violence was a concern for residents and tourists on Treasure Island.

Connolly assured them that they had their man and no, the department was not concerned with crime on Treasure Island. The resort area was a perfect haven for families.

With a half-hearted smile, he walked on, ignoring additional questions.

As the cameras panned towards the police detective's exit, the reporters spied Kate. With eyes widened, they hastened the cameramen to turn to Kate.

Microphones were thrust in Kate's face and pens were whipped out to record her responses. "Kate Harper, you were there the night of Joann Marrs' murder. You were seen providing what many think to be key evidence to the Treasure Island Police. Can you comment on what you provided them?"

Kate winced at the lights cast on her, "No, those questions need to be addressed to the Treasure Island police."

"What exactly did you witness on that horrific night?" a reporter asked.

"Did you see it from your beach house or were you on the beach at the time?" another spat.

"I… I'm sorry. I really can't comment on any of that. You really need to consult with the police. This is their case in an ongoing investigation," Kate said. Trying to move along in the direction Connolly escaped, she was walled in by reporters.

"Ongoing… so, does that mean the police are not confident in the arrest of Dan Huck, as reported?" a reporter pressed.

Kate frowned, "I didn't say that…"

"You didn't say that, but what do you think as one of the only eyewitnesses to the event that evening?" the reporter spat.

Nick stepped up, his arm wrapped around Kate's shoulders, "Ms. Harper is not able to field questions at this time. I suggest you reach out to the Treasure Island Police P.R. department for answers to your questions. Now, if you'll excuse us, this evening is about honoring Joann Marrs."

"Are you Ms. Harper's attorney?"

"What is your name?"

"Who is that man?"

A rattle of questions was tossed out as Nick shouldered his and Kate's way through the gauntlet of reporters.

Kate followed Nick's lead as he grasped her hand and pulled her away from the fracas. Pulling away from the media crews, they caught up with Detective Connolly. He was paused just outside the circle of the families.

Whatever Joann Marrs' mother had bottled up was violently uncorked, a deluge of anger spilling over Dane's parents, "You can save your fake tears and heartfelt speeches; I know you never liked Joann!"

"Gina," Dane's mother tried to calm the broken-hearted mother down. "We adored Joann. She was the one person who seemed to remotely keep Dane on a healthy path."

"Look where that got my daughter!" Gina Marrs said. She spun toward Dane's father with a finger pointed at his unwaveringly even expression. "You, I can't tell you how many times Joann came home crying after visiting your house. You never minded sharing your contempt for Dane dating someone whose family was not part of Charleston's royalty."

Beau Smithfield looked calm in the face of the outburst, "Mrs. Marrs, I respected your daughter's kindness and appreciated the positive direction she nudged Dane in. I will be forever grateful for all that she had done for him. Rehashing their relationship is not what tonight is for."

Stephen Marrs held his wife back from furthering the altercation, "They're right. This isn't the time for this."

Joann's father's eyes couldn't hide his own anger at the Smithfields.

"If you'll excuse us, this has been an emotional evening. I think we will head back to the hotel. Let us know if you'd like a car sent to bring you back," Beau Smithfield smiled, his hand in the small of his wife's back nudging her away from Joann's parents and the cameras that had swung to capture the outburst.

One young man hung back for a moment. Leaning into the Marrs', he said in a soft, pleasant voice, "Mr. and Mrs. Marrs, I am genuinely sorry for your loss."

With a respectful nod, he sauntered off after the Smithfields.

Mrs. Marrs wiped the tears from her cheeks, "At least *some* of the Smithfield family has decency."

Looking up, she realized she had attracted an audience. Detective Connolly strode forward, "Mrs. Marrs, Mr. Marrs… the Treasure Island Police Department wanted to share our deepest sympathies. We are so sorry for your loss."

Mrs. Marrs looked up at the detective. Tears continued to well up in her eyes. Stephen Marrs extended his hand, "Thank you, Detective. As you can see, this is all still pretty raw for us."

"As would be imagined. I don't believe anyone can appreciate what you are going through right now," Connolly said.

"At least you caught the guy, right? A thief," Joann's father shook his head. "Such a tragedy over something as unnecessary as a robbery. Still, we are grateful for your service in catching Joann's…"

Stephen Marrs' voice trailed off as he cast his own hurt glance away.

"I wish I wasn't needed and such cases didn't exist," Connolly said. With a warning glance to Kate and Nick, he added, "We'll leave you to your evening. Please, let me know if there is anything the station can do for you."

Taking the detective's lead, Kate and Nick spun to dutifully follow. Mrs. Marrs' voice froze them in place.

"You were the one who found the ring on the beach. You saw... what happened?" Mrs. Marrs asked.

Kate hesitated, sharing a glance with Connolly. Turning to face the grieving mother, Kate admitted, "I did find the ring. I wasn't sure at the time what the significance of it might be, so I brought it to Detective Connolly. I saw something on the beach that night, but no, I didn't see what happened. I couldn't even be sure it was your daughter that I saw."

"I see," Mrs. Marrs said thoughtfully. Her eyebrows twitched, "You should have done something!"

Detective Connolly stepped in front of Kate, "She did. She did exactly what she should have done. She did *all* she could have done. She had the instinct to sense that something was off and she immediately reported it. We sent a patrolman to the scene right away. By then, it was too late. I'm sorry."

The answer didn't seem to allay Gina Marrs. Her husband nodded a thank you and an apologetic look toward Kate, "I think we have reached the end of our very fragile rope tonight. We should call it a night as well."

Carting his wife away from the crowd, Stephen Marrs steered her on a path leading them out of the vigil.

Kate, Nick and Detective Connolly looked at one another, no one knowing quite what to say.

"You two certainly know how to stir up trouble," Connolly cursed.

"Don't look at me," Nick shrugged, a sideways smile on his face. "I just follow it."

"Hey!" Kate scowled. "We likely saved Dane Smithfield from a beating tonight."

"I feel bad for the Marrs family. Their reactions are certainly understandable," Nick said.

Connolly studied the pair, "Okay. Show's over. Go home. Please. I'm not even sure why you let her attend."

Nick looked at the detective, "*Let* her attend. She was going to come anyway."

The detective nodded slowly, "Yeah, you're probably right about that. Good *night*, you two."

Nick looked at Kate, "Well, should we go?"

Kate's gaze was paused at a figure standing in the shadows. Beyond the small palmettos used for cover, she spied what the figure was doing. The Smithfield family stood by a pair of limousines parked by the curb.

Beau Smithfield stood in front of Dane, his cool demeanor amid the vigil escaped him as he was visibly angry with his son, "No. You and your friends are no longer on the yacht. We'll send a driver to collect your things. You'll spend the rest of your police-remanded sequester at the Don Cesar with us."

"We're good on the yacht, thanks," Dane Smithfield quipped.

The elder Smithfield leaned in, his eyes menacing, "You think it's a request? You and your riffraff have caused enough problems for this family, don't you think?"

"Why do you suddenly care what I do now?" Dane asked.

Beau Smithfield, who had turned toward his awaiting vehicle, spun and lunged within inches of his son's face, "Because an entire police force, a slew of news reporters and heartbroken family lie in your wake! If this isn't a wake-up call, I don't know what is!"

"Dad…" Dane started as his father pivoted for the car, intent on leaving.

As he reached the limousine, Beau placed a hand on the car and turned to his son, "I'll see you at the hotel."

Absent of a parting glance, he slipped inside. The driver closed the door and whisked Beau Smithfield, his wife and younger son away from the curb.

Dane stared at the disappearing taillights, turning to see his friends watching the scene, their mouths agape, he shrugged meekly, "I guess the afterparty is at the Don Cesar."

Without another word, he walked to the second limousine. Several paces back, his friends followed. In moments, the car was off in the same direction as the first limo.

The man quietly observing the scene from the small palm turned to find that he wasn't the only one watching the Smithfield family drama.

Kate cocked her head as she studied the man. Suddenly, her eyes went wide.

Nick followed her gaze, trying to see what she was seeing. Noting that she clearly recognized the man, he looked closer. The reporter wore a hat and glasses. Clad in a tweed sports jacket with a press badge dangling from his neck, a recorder and pad of paper constantly at the ready. He looked as frenzied as any of the others trying to capture the details of the event and score interviews with whoever would stop and talk. Thinking he had a scoop on the Smithfields, a smile parted his beard.

"Frank Driscoll!" Kate hissed as she strode toward the reporter.

Nick did a double take, frowning, "Driscoll?"

The reporter nodded sheepishly as he waved the pair over.

"Frank," Kate smiled. "Nice job. If I hadn't caught you spying on the Smithfields, I never would have known it was you."

The private investigator beamed at the praise, "You both walked past me half a dozen times tonight. For once, I didn't have to coerce details from people. I introduce myself as a reporter and they just spill. With the exception of the Smithfields, of course."

"They seemed pretty worked up as they were leaving," Nick observed.

Driscoll nodded, "Seems like Beau Smithfield is finally laying down the law. Probably a decade too late."

"Tough life, ripped from your yacht in the marina to one of the most iconic hotels in St. Pete Beach," Nick said.

"The Don Cesar…" Kate chewed her lip.

"The large, gleaming pink building at the entrance to Passe Grille, the southern edge of St. Pete Beach," Nick said.

Kate's eyes widened, "That place is gorgeous!"

"We should go sometime," Nick suggested.

"We *should*," Kate gleamed.

"Oh, no. I know that look. Kate…" Nick started.

Driscoll put his hands up, "You two are on your own. That is a crowd I probably should not be caught spying on."

Kate twisted her face, "Spying on *me* is okay, though…"

"I tell you what, the next time I spy on you, I'll give you a call ahead. I feel like I owe you that much," Driscoll smirked. "Be careful out there. The police *may* have their killer, but there are still some unsavory types connected with this case."

The private investigator sauntered away, melting into the remaining fragments of the reporter pool.

"Well, this was quite a night," Nick breathed.

Kate looked up at him and grinned, "The night is not over yet."

Twenty Nine

Pulling up to the Don Cesar was like stepping back in time, driving up to a Mediterranean castle. The grand, ornate building flanked by the aquamarine waters of the Gulf of Mexico stood both iconic and stunningly beautiful.

Instantly met by a valet, Kate relinquished her keys and followed Nick into the lobby of the hotel.

"Welcome to the Pink Palace," Nick said as he nodded to a doorman.

Once inside, they were met with a long hallway that ran the length of the hotel. Skirted by registrar and concierge stands, the marble corridor led Kate and Nick nearly immediately to the prize they sought. Just outside of the lobby bar, in a small alcove fashioned with a sofa and a pair of wingback armchairs, Beau Smithfield stood with his arms crossed in front of his son Dane.

Kate tapped Nick on the arm and pulled him between a plant and the wall that formed the shell of the semi-private alcove.

"Enough, Dane! It is time you began to grow up," Beau raged at his son.

"You're so worried about family image. Have you once asked how I am doing during all this?" Dane spat back.

"How you're doing? We'll have time for feelings later. After we shore up our legal affairs and make sure your stupidity doesn't bring the entire family down with you!" Beau fumed.

"Legal... Joann is dead, Dad. I was going to propose to her on this trip," Dane said.

"Yeah, thanks for letting us know about that. I'm glad you can set up this elaborate trip on my dime and not even tell me about it," Beau said.

"I would hope you'd be happy for me," Dane pressed.

"Are *you*? Are *you* happy now? Who knows what unsavory characters you let into that girl's life," Beau snapped.

Dane groaned and paced around the sitting room, "Figured you'd have me pegged as the bad guy in all this."

"Fortunately, the police have a bad guy in custody that they've fingered for the girl's death," Beau said.

"Yeah," Dane sighed. "Fortunately."

"You know, Dane. This is the last time I'm cleaning up one of your messes," Beau said.

"One of my messes? The girl I was going to marry is dead, Dad. Do you care even the slightest about that?" Dane asked.

"I care. I do. But I have the burden of caring about the rest of the family. All that I have given to you and you just take and take and take. Without asking, whether it is yours or not, you just take," Beau lamented.

"What is that supposed to mean? You want to know about..." Dane started before a calm voice interceded.

"Excuse me, Dad...Dane. Mom wants us to join her at the Society Table. Some sort of family meeting. She isn't in a mood to take 'no' for an answer, if you know what I mean," the voice said.

"Fine. We were about done here. After *you*, Dane," Beau growled with his hand out for Dane to go in front of him.

"I'll be right behind you," the voice said.

Kate and Nick spun around the plant as they were about to be discovered. They nodded in deference and made their way down the hallway. The pair had clearly heard part of the argument, but it wasn't clear how much.

Dane led his father out of the alcove and through the hotel to where his mother was waiting for him. Geoffrey Smithfield, who had summoned the pair, slipped out the door leading to the balcony overlooking the pool and the beach. Lighting a cigarette, he breathed it in and exhaled.

Kate and Nick pushed out of the doors as though they were headed for a stroll down the beach.

Geoffrey looked up for the rail, his cheeks flushed. Squinting, he said, "Hey, I saw you two at the vigil. Sorry for my family. They can be kind of intense. Never short of theatrics, even if they mean well."

"It is a challenging time," Kate acknowledged.

Turning his back to the rail so that he could address the pair directly, Geoffrey nodded.

Nick asked, "Did you know Joann well?"

"No, not really. My brother and I...and his friends... we run in different circles. Still, it's a shame. She seemed like a nice girl. She might have been good for my brother," Geoffrey admitted.

Nick smiled, "Yeah, sometimes a good woman in your corner makes all the difference."

Kate shot Nick a quick glance.

"Did you know your brother was going to propose?" Kate asked.

"I found out about it when everyone else did. When that poor girl was… was killed. I was hoping they would have stayed together. If you can't tell, Dane is kind of an untamed horse. Joann made him almost… tolerable. We're all sad about her passing," Geoffrey admitted.

"Your parents didn't know?" Nick asked.

"The less they knew about Dane and his exploits the happier they were. I'm not sure they would have been thrilled with the engagement, even if some of us were happy about it," Geoffrey said. Tamping out the cigarette, he exhaled a funnel of smoke, "Look, I better get back to my family. One black sheep is enough, I think."

The Smithfield boy moved quickly past them and into the building.

Kate and Nick took a moment to lean over the rail and watch the movement of the Gulf against the hotel lights and the moon hung high in the night sky.

"Why do I keep thinking the further we get into this mystery, the more complicated it all gets?" Kate asked.

"Even with Dan Huck in custody, there doesn't seem to be an end to clandestine side conversations, threats on beaches and family feuds," Nick nodded. "What do we do?"

"We follow the leads until we are satisfied," Kate said. "For now, how about you buy a girl a drink? It's been a long day."

Gently grasping her hand, Nick led her back into the Don Cesar. Making their way through the hotel, they found themselves in a charming beach bar. Snaking through the guests, Kate followed Nick onto a deck that overlooked the sand dunes. Finding a cozy spot opposite a gas firepit with colorful flames furthering the inviting aesthetic, Nick pulled out a chair for Kate.

A friendly waitress took their order and shuffled off.

Kate gazed around the beachfront bar, enjoying the evening sea breeze as her body sunk into the cushions, "This is fabulous. Thank you."

"This old place is always reinventing itself. I like this spot. It is so relaxing, yet full of energy at the same time," Nick nodded.

"Come here much?" Kate raised a brow.

"No," Nick laughed. "Mostly pass by it on the beach side. I knew a guy that was working on a movie being filmed here. I got invited to the crew party."

Kate smiled, "Of course you did."

Their drinks arrived and they thanked the server.

Taking a sip, Kate melted even further into the comfortable sofa, "This was an interesting, long night."

"They always seem to be with you," Nick teased.

"Lately," Kate had to admit. "I mean, it's not every day you get to stop a gangster from roughing up a socialite's kid."

Nick laughed, "I would hope not."

"I just keep thinking about what Aguilar said to Dane Smithfield. He warned, 'I thought you would have learned what happens when you cross me. You lose things important to you.' I can tell you the first thing that ran through my head when he said that," Kate said.

"Yeah, it was pretty ominous. Guess if Dane was afraid for his life, not a big stretch to give a car to save yourself," Nick said. "Especially when Dad bought the car. But do you really think Aguilar murdered Joann Marrs?"

Kate looked over her tropical beverage, "He's certainly right at the top of my list, assuming Dan Huck wasn't the actual killer."

"Maybe he was," Nick shrugged. "He could have been hired by someone like Aguilar. Use a fall guy not attached to you and your gang. Not a bad way to send a message to Dane and keep yourself clean."

"But why go after Joann at all? Besides, remember what Aguilar said? He didn't even know Joann was Dane's girlfriend. He thought Stacey was," Kate questioned.

Nick scoffed, "Not the first time we heard that."

"And what about Dane's father- Beau Smithfield? When he was getting into it with Dane, he said, 'It's your fault.' What was his fault? Does he blame Dane for Joann's death?" Kate pressed.

"Directly or indirectly… maybe," Nick said. "What else did he say to Dane? 'We've given you everything and yet you take and you take, even what's not yours?' What did he take?"

Kate's eyes widened, "The ring! Dane took the ring without asking for it!"

"A multimillion-dollar ring, essentially stolen. Could be worth killing for," Nick said.

"Several million reasons," Kate agreed.

Nick chewed his lip thoughtfully as he sat up excitedly in his seat, "Did you get a load of John Trigg's demeanor at the vigil? He didn't seem to be in the same state as Dane or Stacey. Didn't even seem like they were part of the same circle."

Kate nodded, "He's kind of been that way the entire time we've been keeping an eye on that group. He seems more emotionally disturbed by the whole thing than either of his two friends."

"Remorseful killer?" Nick cocked his head.

"Maybe. It's run through my mind," Kate said. "The entire group is a bit off. Stacey and Dane Smithfield had something going on behind the scenes. I think they had an affair, maybe right up to the time Dane was set to propose to Joann. I mean, even Vincent Aguilar saw that."

"Who is John Trigg broken-hearted over, Joann or Stacey?" Nick frowned.

"Joann Marrs. I'd bet the beach house on it," Kate said.

Nick swirled his drink, "Think he and Joann…"

"No," Kate answered quickly. "It has the hallmark of an unrequited, even unvoiced affection."

"So, what about Dan Huck? Did the police get the wrong guy?" Nick asked.

"Maybe. Maybe they got the guy that pulled the trigger but not the person who hired him to," Kate shrugged. "Or they hired him to perform the robbery and things went awry."

"Wouldn't he instantly rat out the person behind the check? He might go down, but not alone for the ride?" Nick asked.

"Perhaps. Unless Huck is frightened of that person or that person has leverage on him," Kate said.

Nick looked thoughtful, "Aguilar and Beau Smithfield could fit both of those bills. So many unanswered questions."

"Yeah," Kate nodded. Her mind drifted briefly before turning to Nick. Placing her hand on his arm, she shot a sheepish look at Nick, "I'm sorry. We are in this fantastic place- a coastal breeze, firelight, delightful drinks- and I have us talking whodunit clues."

"It's all right. You get a lot of flak for finding trouble, but the truth is, I think trouble finds you. Lately, at least," Nick said.

"Still, I think we deserve a moment," Kate said, as the waitress brought another pair of drinks.

Handing Kate hers and picking his up, Nick smiled at Kate, "To a few moments of respite amidst a world of chaos."

"I'll drink to that," Kate smiled, raising her glass to Nick's. "Thanks for rescuing the damsel in distress on her balcony. You never would have thought it would have embroiled you in a murder investigation."

"I never would have thought it would have introduced me to someone that would make me *want* to get embroiled," Nick said.

"Oh, you *want* to be involved," Kate grinned.

"With you, not the investigation, necessarily… I mean…," Nick stuttered, his cheeks glowing slightly red.

Kate leaned in closer to Nick, his eyes dancing in the flicker of the firepit flames, and whispered, "I've enjoyed getting to know you, too."

Reciprocating, Nick moved closer to Kate.

Kate smiled, taking a deep breath as their lips hovered dangerously close. His hand cupped her head gently as they drew in. She willingly followed the flow of his hands until their beverage-tinged breath mingled.

Frozen in place, Kate closed her eyes as her phone rang horrifyingly loud. Biting her lip, Kate pulled away, grappling for her phone to not allow it to disturb the other guests of the beach bar.

Frowning, she announced, "It's Driscoll."

"Hello," Kate called into the phone. "I see. At the beach house. Yes, Nick is with me. Okay. We'll be there."

Turning to Nick, she said, "Frank Driscoll has information. He wants to share it in person."

"Now?" Nick scowled.

Kate shrugged, "He's on his way now."

Nick set his drink down, "Well, let's go."

Frank Driscoll's car was parked on the street across from Kate's beach house when she wheeled into the driveway.

"He was eager," Kate said, as she slid out of her SUV.

Nick walked to the edge of the driveway to peer into the windows of the private investigator's rental. Not seeing him on the front porch, Nick suggested, "Must be out back."

Kate waited for Nick to meet her at the corner of the beach house before proceeding down the side walkway toward the beachfront back patio. The Gulf breeze blew softly through the corridor, reminding them what a pleasant evening it was. Kate's hand dropped to her side, brushing against Nick's.

Suddenly, Nick slammed to a halt. His arm cast out across Kate's chest like a parent protecting their child in the front seat of a car.

"Stay here," he said, his voice even.

At that moment, Kate saw what made Nick stop. A pair of legs protruded through the shadows on the backside of the beach house.

Hand clasped to her mouth, she ignored Nick's command and jogged to his side.

Squatting down, Nick studied the body of Frank Driscoll. With fingers to the private detective's carotid artery, Nick sighed. Looking up at Kate, he shook his head, "Driscoll's dead."

Thirty

Dialing 911, Kate walked away from the body of Frank Driscoll. Her voice trembled as she reported the finding to the police.

Nick scanned the house and the nearby access to the beach to ensure whoever struck the private detective wasn't still there. Wanting to stay close to Kate, he kept a constant eye and ear out for danger.

"It couldn't have happened more than a few minutes ago," Nick said.

"You're sure... he's dead?" Kate trembled.

"Yeah," Nick offered a solemn nod. "He's gone."

Kate clicked on her phone and turned on the app for her security system. Flipping through the camera notices, she found three within the time frame since Frank Driscoll called her. Nick leaned in as she reviewed the clips.

The first image showed Frank Driscoll arriving and waiting in the driveway by the front of the house. Something appeared to get his attention on the side of the house and right of the frame. The next clip followed the private investigator along the side of the house. He appeared to move with caution as he walked between the beach house and tropical bushes that separated the house from the neighboring property.

Kate gasped as she clicked on the next clip. A figure, clad in black with a hoodie covering the head and face, lunged out of the bushes, hitting Driscoll on the head with a heavy board. Barely in frame, Driscoll was bludgeoned several more times as he lay on the ground.

"That's terrible!" Kate turned away from the screen and gasped.

"Let's wait out front for the police," Nick suggested, leading Kate toward the front of the house.

Flashing blue lights were already streaking through the night, she felt a sense of relief as several patrol cars stopped in front of Kate's house. The officers wasted no time in corralling Kate and Nick away from the scene while several cased the property and began securing the scene.

"Did anyone access the house?" an officer asked as she began taking a statement.

"No, I don't think so. Not according to the security system," Kate replied.

"Okay, we might send a team through to be sure, if that's okay,' the officer said.

Kate looked at the chaos and tragedy once again at her doorstep, this time literally. She glanced at Nick, "Detective Connolly is *not* going to like this."

"I don't like this, Ms. Harper!" a voice bellowed from a set of additional police cars that arrived on the scene. "Not one bit!"

"Detective Connolly," Kate greeted the police officer.

Connolly gave both Kate and Nick a disapproving look, "One of you mind telling me what is going on here?"

"Frank Driscoll gave me a call. It couldn't have been more than thirty minutes ago. He had something he wanted to share with me. It sounded like a break in the case," Kate said. "I agreed to meet him here. Nick and I left the Don Cesar and came right here…"

Connolly did a double take, "What? You were at the Don Cesar? Where the Smithfields are staying? Of course, you were!"

"I know. What a coincidence, right?" Kate said sheepishly.

The detective's mood was not improved by Kate's nonchalance.

"Driscoll's car was here when we pulled up. When he wasn't standing in front waiting for us, we circled around back and… and we found him. Laying near the back corner of the house. He was dead by the time we got here," Nick said.

The police detective tried to collect himself with Kate and Nick, yet again embroiled in the case. Finally, he spoke, "Do you have any idea what he wanted to share with you?"

Kate shook her head, "I have no idea. He seemed urgent."

"You two stay here with Officer Jenkins," Connolly ordered. The detective made a beeline for the side of the house where the patrol officers were securing the site.

Kate's eyes widened, "I have video!"

Starting after the detective, Officer Jenkins attempted to stop her, but Kate was on the detective's heels. Giving in, she was allowed to escort Nick in their wake.

Connolly heard Kate call out and was prepared for her presence, "Just… don't touch anything!"

The detective walked over to the body. After a brief inspection and scan of the area, he began giving orders for a wider berth of quarantine for the crime scene. Walking back toward Kate, he grumbled, "All right, let me see what you have."

Looking over Kate's shoulder, Connolly studied the video clips from her security system.

Scowling, he said, "Driscoll called you when?"

Kate scrolled through her phone, "9:47."

"And your video was time-stamped at 9:59. When did you get here?" Connolly asked.

"We paid the tab and drove right over. Must have been five...seven minutes after ten," Nick suggested.

Connolly digested the information that had been supplied to him. "You didn't hear or see anything?"

Kate and Nick shot each other glances and shook their heads, "No. Nothing."

The detective scratched his chin thoughtfully, "Whoever it was must have known Driscoll was coming here to meet you."

"It seemed like in the video, something- or someone-drew Driscoll's attention over," Nick said.

"A great place for an ambush," Connolly agreed. "You have no idea what he wanted to share with you?"

Kate shook her head slowly, "No. He seemed pretty worked up about it, though."

"It must have been something he discovered this evening. We had just spoken to him at the vigil," Nick pointed out.

"I saw him posing as a reporter. Almost slipped by me," Connolly said.

Hands on his hips, the detective assessed the situation, "Did you see anything on or around Driscoll? His phone?"

"No," Nick shook his head. "Checked for a pulse and left to call 911."

"We'll check it out. In the meantime, why don't you two go inside? My officers have given the beach house an all-clear. I am going to post a patrolman with you. It is going to be a long night out here," Connolly said.

Kate nodded, "I'll put some tea on. And some coffee for the officers."

"I'm sure they'd like that. Just for once, you two stay out of the way," Connolly said, his voice stern.

Kate led Nick and the assigned officer inside the beach house. Making a beeline for the kitchen, she began making beverages. The busy tasks made her feel better, a glimpse of normalcy amidst the tragic chaos of the evening.

When Kate offered to take the drinks outside to share with the forensics team and officers on duty securing the scene, the officer ordered to watch Kate and Nick remanded her to stay in the house. Pondering for just a moment, Kate set up a coffee stand inside the foyer so that officers could pop in as their shifts allowed.

The officer thanked Kate and found a seat in the corner of the room, where she had a view of the kitchen and the main hallways.

Kate leaned across the kitchen counter pulling closer to Nick, cupping her mug of tea. "I keep thinking of poor Driscoll. He was an odd man, to be sure. But, he was kind of growing on me," Kate sighed.

"Yeah, he was quirky, but I was beginning to get the sense that he meant well," Nick agreed.

"Why did he have to go around the side of the house?" Kate groaned.

Nick shot her a scowl, "Sounds like something you would have done."

Kate flashed a weak smile, "Yeah, I suppose I would have."

"The bigger question is, how could anyone have known he was going to be here?" Nick asked. "Unless they were here for you and he happened to stumble onto them."

"I don't know. The exact moment Driscoll has a break in the case... I think the killer figured out that they had tipped their hand somehow at the vigil and Driscoll was on to them," Kate said.

"And the killer followed him here?" Nick asked.

A chill shuddered down Kate's spine, "It almost seemed like they were here waiting for him."

"Hard to say. Maybe Connolly can piece it all together," Nick shrugged.

Kate looked distant in thought, "Someone at the vigil…"

"All the players were there, except for Dan Huck," Nick said.

"Dan Huck… kind of puts a hole in Connolly's case," Kate said. "Even if Huck was the one who killed Joann Marrs, he certainly wasn't the one who took out poor ol' Frank."

"Every time we look for answers, we get more questions," Nick bemoaned. "Either way, there is a murderer loose on Treasure Island."

Thirty One

Kate Harper was refreshing the pot of coffee she put out for the crime scene investigators as Detective Connolly pushed through the door. He paused as Kate tidied up the side table she used as a service station. Connolly chewed on his lip as he considered whether to be amused and appreciative of her hospitality or frustrated with her continued meddling in the murder case that had become increasingly dangerous.

When Kate was done straightening the table, the detective followed her into the kitchen. Both Nick and Kate stared at him with demanding eyes.

With a sigh, Connolly slumped his shoulders and breathed, "All right. I'll tell you what I can. I have some questions for you both."

Nick leaned against the counter across from the detective as Kate stood next to him.

"Driscoll was hit repeatedly from behind with a blunt object. The forensics team is working to get a better identification of what the murder weapon might have been," the detective reported.

Nick frowned, "Is that consistent with how Joann Marrs was killed?"

Connolly paused, studying both Nick and Kate before answering, "Yes. Yes, it was."

"Does that mean it was the same person?" Kate's eyes widened.

The detective shook his head, "Not necessarily. The crime scene unit will put together some metrics on size, height and force relative to the victims. The reality is, it may help rule out suspects, but not necessarily identify them."

"Did you find the weapon?" Nick asked.

"No," Connolly once more shook his head. "Aside from Frank Driscoll's body, there was little at the scene. Even impressions that might have been left on the ground when the attacker moved in from the bushes were swept. No footprints, no pieces of fabric snagged on the foliage."

Kate tugged at her lip, "Did you find anything on Frank?"

The detective sighed, "Nothing. No notes, no photographs. His cell phone and his wallet were both missing as well."

"So, we have another dead body, but no clues," Nick sighed.

"The question is, what did Driscoll want to share with Kate tonight? Did he give you any indication of what it might be?" Connolly asked.

"No. Like I said, he was pretty excited. He wanted to meet right away," Kate replied.

Connolly scowled, "Why go to you and not to the police?"

"I'm not sure," Kate shrugged. "Something connected to me and who has been lurking around the beach house? Feeling bad about spying on me, his guilt driving him to clue me in? I don't know."

"Maybe he wanted to confide in someone who didn't believe the case was closed with Huck locked up. He might have wanted to flesh out his thoughts before going to the police," Nick suggested.

"Maybe. Whatever his reason, he chose wrong. He could have put you in danger," the police detective looked at Kate. Swinging his gaze to include Nick, he added, "Both of you."

"I wish there was something else I could do to help you. I feel so bad about Frank," Kate said.

"You can help by staying out of danger, so I can concentrate on actual police work. Unfortunately, Frank Driscoll is an example of what can happen when untrained people stick their noses into police work. I wish it hadn't come to that," Connolly stated. "I'm going to send a unit to Driscoll's hotel. Hopefully, I'll find something out there. His rental is loaded on a flatbed. Forensics will sort through it at the police impound."

Kate looked at the detective through weary eyes, "I'm sorry someone else got hurt."

Connolly looked directly at Kate, "I strongly encourage you to reconsider checking into a hotel and staying somewhere else."

The detective's eyes flashed on Nick for support.

"He's right," Nick said as he stood up from his position, leaning on the counter. "I think we'd all sleep better knowing you were somewhere safe."

"I have the alarm that you installed. I can't imagine whoever killed Frank is still lurking around," Kate snapped.

"Just the same, I'll have a patrolman parked outside," Connolly stated. Taking a step to leave, the police detective paused and turned to Kate, "If you leave the house before daylight, I'll have my officer arrest you."

Kate's eyes narrowed at being put on house arrest.

Turning his attention to Nick, Connolly grumbled, "You go home."

Nick looked at Kate who nodded that she'd be okay.

Reluctantly following the detective through the house, Nick stopped at the front door. Looking at Kate, he said softly, "You be careful."

Kate nodded. With both men on her front porch, she closed the heavy front door and clicked the deadbolt into place. Tapping at the screen of the security system, she placed the alarm on nighttime stay-at-home mode.

Hearing the system arm, Nick left his perch by the front door and walked down the steps toward his truck.

Kate leaned against the window in the front of the beach house. Peering out into the night, she watched the taillights of Nick's truck disappear down the street. The police forensics team seemed to be wrapping up, delivering equipment and what little evidence they could find into the back of a van.

She watched as an ambulance parked alongside the driveway. An EMS crew rolled a gurney toward the side of the house. A few moments later, the gurney was rolled back and lifted gently into the back of the ambulance. Detective Connolly followed it out, climbing into his unmarked police car. Pausing to look glance at the house, he conferred with a patrolman. With a nod, he pulled away, following the ambulance to where Kate assumed would be the morgue where an autopsy would take place.

Seeing the shape of Frank Driscoll's body carried unceremoniously out on a gurney made Kate's stomach hurt. She considered that Connolly was right. This was no case for non-police officers. Even Frank Driscoll, a salty private investigator met his end at the hand of whoever was lurking around Treasure Island. An amateur like herself had no business sticking her nose into a murder case.

She watched as a patrol car pulled directly into her driveway.

Pulling herself away from the window, she grabbed the tray of coffee service she had put out for the crime scene team. Placing the tray on the kitchen counter, she considered cleaning up. Only then did she realize how exhausted she was. The already long day turned impossibly long as the police were outside of the beach house until the first fragments of dawn began to break somewhere on the Atlantic side of the Florida peninsula.

Following her body's lead, Kate left the dishes for the next day. Trudging up the steps, she made her way to the master bedroom. With an instinctive glance toward the bathroom, she eschewed her routine. She licked her unbrushed teeth and imagined the shower water cascading over her tired body.

Nothing daunted her from her goal. Led like she was being pulled by a rope, she spun and collapsed backward into her bed. Ignoring her impulse to shed her clothes and crawl under the covers, she just lay there. Watching the ceiling fan spin, she drifted into an odd, pre-sleep daze.

Each rotation of the ceiling fan blades flashed in the soft light that filtered into the room. Like a filmstrip, the flashes brought images into Kate's head- the silhouettes on the beach preceding Joann Marrs' death, holding the diamond ring up shining in the moonlight, the flashing lights of the police cars at the crime scene, all the faces that attended the vigil—each of them a possible suspect and finally, Frank Driscoll.

From his goofy disguises to his proud grin when he finally found one that worked, Kate thought of the man that had called to meet her. She grimaced as she thought of Driscoll lying on the ground outside of the beach house. Minutes prior, she was on the phone with him. The fragility of life had never felt so real.

As she slipped in and out of sleep, the same thought tugged at her, trying to keep her from yielding to the oppressive need to shut her eyes. What did Frank Driscoll want to share with her?

Thirty Two

Kate woke with the sun shining directly into the beach house's master bedroom. With a groan, she pried her eyes open. Staring out the window at the Gulf, she took a moment to admire the gorgeous view while coming to terms with the fact that the sun tilted to that side of the house meant that she had slept through half the day.

Slapping at the bed, she found her cell phone slipped under her pillow. A glance at the phone that she had neglected to plug into the charger confirmed that it was, in fact just past noon. Several missed texts and calls encouraged her to sit up and note who was so intent on reaching her. Alternating pings from Nick and Detective Connolly littered her messages and call list.

Reading through the messages, she found Nick's in particular became more insistent.

Dialing Nick first, Kate yawned, "Hi. I'm sorry I missed your calls."

"Are you okay?" Nick asked.

"Yeah. Clearly tired. Everything okay with you?" Kate asked.

"I'm fine. I had stopped by but you didn't answer the door and the patrolman Connolly had stationed out front shooed me away after a few tries," Nick said. "I was worried."

"Sorry, I just slept like a rock," Kate admitted.

"You probably needed it. I'm sorry to disturb you," Nick said.

Kate pulled her head away as she received another ping from Detective Connolly, "It's okay. I need to get up. Detective Connolly keeps asking me to get with forensics to pull data from my security system."

"Want me to come with you?" Nick asked.

"No. I'll wash up and head down there. I'm hoping he has some news that can return all of us to peaceful nights and proper sleep," Kate said.

"All right. I have some more supplies to shop for to finish your projects. Let me know if you need anything," Nick said.

"I will. Thank you, Nick," Kate hung up the phone.

Texting Detective Connolly, she let him know she'd be at the station within the hour.

With a stretch, Kate lifted herself off the bed. Shedding her slept-in clothes, she squirted a dab of paste on her toothbrush and stepped into the shower. The steady flow of hot water felt good as it soaked her tired muscles. Her clean teeth may have trumped the power of the shower as she regretted the decision to avoid the ritual the evening prior.

Balancing her toothbrush on the edge of the shower stall, she pushed against the tile wall, angling her spine to receive the luxurious deluge of hot water as she stretched.

For a precious few moments, the gravity of the previous evening and the sight of Frank Driscoll's lifeless body escaped her. She turned the water off and the water fall slowed to a few scattered drops splashing at the bottom of the shower.

With a deep breath, Kate grabbed at her towel. With renewed vigor, she was ready to go find some answers from Detective Connolly.

Greeted immediately by the front desk officer, Kate was whisked through the halls to the forensic tech's office. Ignoring her requests to see Detective Connolly and her craning neck scanning the station, the clerk made a beeline, closing the door behind her as she was delivered to forensics.

"Ms. Harper, thank you for coming in. Detective Connolly said to expect you," the tech said. Wheeling his chair in close to his computer terminal, he rubbed his hands, "All right, let's see what you've got."

Kate provided the tech with the login for her security system so that they could navigate to the video clip library. Locating the folder for the previous evening, the tech began the process of copying the clips captured during the time surrounding Frank Driscoll's death.

Spinning away from the images that she didn't care to watch again, she choked, "Can…do you mind if I step out for a glass of water?"

The tech looked up from his work, "Sure, this will take a few moments and we'll want to reset your password."

Kate nodded as she reached for the handle and swung the door open. Stepping out of the dark forensics' tech room, she watched as a series of policemen with Detective Connolly in the lead jostled a snarling man into the station.

"I wasn't doin' nothin', you got nothing on me!" the man snapped at anyone who would listen.

Connolly grinned, his voice even, "You were caught rummaging through the victim's hotel room conveniently right after he was murdered."

"I had nothin' to do with that. Me and…uh…Driscoll…we're friends," the man spat.

"Yeah, so good friends that you had to think hard on what your pal's name was," Connolly said as he marched the man in the direction of the interrogation room.

"I get confused," the man said.

"You take orders from Vinnie Aguilar. It just took you a second to remember the name of the guy you were sent to kill. What were you looking for in Driscoll's hotel room? Your boss worried the P.I. might have had something incriminating?" Connolly pressed.

"Nah, it wasn't like that. I had nothin' to do with that. I ain't the killer type," the man pleaded.

Connolly glanced over his shoulder to see Kate taking in the scene. Returning his gaze toward the man he had just taken into custody, he said, "We'll get to all that in a moment. Sit tight."

"Where am I gonna go? I'm handcuffed to the table!" the man yelled as Connolly slammed the door shut.

Without a wasted movement, the detective strode across the police station and stood in front of Kate, "Shows over, Ms. Harper."

Kate stretched to look over Connolly's shoulder at the interrogation room, "That one of Vincent Aguilar's men? I recognize him from the vigil."

"He was rifling through Driscoll's motel room when my patrolmen got there. They held him until I could get to the scene myself," Connolly admitted.

"Did you find anything? What was he looking for?" Kate asked.

Connolly sighed, his hands dropping to his hips, "Kate, go home. I thought after what happened to Driscoll, you would have learned to back off."

Kate pulled out her phone with the flurry of texts the police detective sent for her to come in to provide forensics with the security footage from the beach house, "I came because you were clearly adamant that I came in."

"Right," Connolly dropped his head, his cheeks flushing. "Fine. Did you give forensics what they needed?"

"He's finishing up right now," Kate nodded.

"Great. Once you're done, *please* go home," Connolly pressed.

Kate smiled, "Of course."

Spinning on his heels, the detective began heading for the interrogation room. Feeling her eyes on him, he called, "*Goodbye*, Kate!"

Kate felt awkward lingering in the hall after being dismissed by the detective. She wanted to learn what Aguilar's man had to stay.

With a grin, she called out, waving a finger at the detective, "Oh my gosh! In all the chaos of last night, I never was able to share with you what Nick and I overheard while we were at the Don Cesar."

Connolly froze. He stared at the interrogation room door for a moment before sighing and turning to face Kate. In exasperation, he intoned, "That's right. When you and Mason were stalking the Smithfields. In direct disobedience of my order to stand down."

Kate wrinkled her nose and corrected, "I like to think of it more like we were having cocktails conveniently close to where the Smithfields were."

The detective paused, leaning toward the interrogation room. Finally, he slumped, "Fine. Carlos isn't going anywhere. Let's talk in my office."

With an outstretched hand, he beckoned Kate to march in front of him.

When Connolly and Kate were in his office, the detective closed the door and offered her a seat across from his. Settling into his desk chair, he impatiently folded his hands together and asked, "So, what did you and the surfer 'overhear' last night?"

Kate leaned forward excitedly, "Well, first, we heard Beau Smithfield arguing with his son. It didn't sound as though he was aware of Dane's ill-fated proposal to Joann Marrs. He was very unhappy about the money Dane was spending and he said something about his son taking things that weren't his."

"I'm sure ringing up untold dollars on platinum cards and losing not one but two cars probably didn't sit well with Mr. Smithfield. I can't imagine any father being thrilled about that," Connolly shrugged.

"Still, something with that family is just… off," Kate said.

"That is hardly usable evidence in any way," Connolly blew her off.

Kate squinted, "The brother, Geoffrey, I think, he seemed to think his brother was in pretty hot water with Beau."

"I'm sure he is. How is that relevant to how Joann Marrs was killed? It sounds like, other than being surprised, the family liked Joann as an influence on Dane," Connolly said.

Kate shifted gears, taking the detective by surprise, "Where does Aguilar's man and what happened last night fit in with your case on Dan Huck?"

Connolly bristled, "The D.A. wants me to consider releasing Huck. Just because… well, last night, doesn't mean Huck *wasn't* Marrs' killer."

"If he was who murdered Joann Marrs, what would be *so* important to track Driscoll down and… and…" Kate stammered.

"I don't know," Connolly shook his head. "Could be anything."

Kate looked thoughtful, "Unless you got the wrong guy and *the* guy was trying to keep Driscoll from getting the truth out there."

"*Or,*" Connolly countered. "I have Joann Marrs' murderer in custody. In the process of investigating Marrs' murder, Driscoll tripped across something else, some other information that someone didn't want out."

"Someone like Aguilar," Kate snapped her fingers. "That would explain his man snooping around his motel room. Did you find Driscoll's phone or wallet on Aguilar's man?"

"No," Connolly admitted.

"If it wasn't on Driscoll, then it would make sense that Aguilar would want the motel room searched. If nothing was on him, then maybe the evidence is still out there!" Kate exclaimed.

"Perhaps," Connolly replied, tight-lipped. "I see Driscoll's murder and the murder of Joann Marrs as two separate investigations."

"That would be an incredible coincidence for their deaths to not be intrinsically connected in some way," Kate said.

"Dane Smithfield seems to be a negative energy field that tends to pull these cases together in the form of a coincidence. It wouldn't be the first time that someone was found to be a magnet for trouble," Connolly said.

"I thought *I* was the magnet for trouble," Kate teased.

Connolly scowled and grumbled, "I still have a jail cell with your name on it."

"I wonder if Aguilar got Dane's cars…" Kate wondered as her eyes drifted to the ceiling.

"What?" Connolly snapped.

"I wonder if Aguilar was able to pick up Dane's cars after the vigil," Kate said.

Connolly shrugged, "I'll look into it. You think that has some bearing on all this?"

"I don't know," Kate squinted. "He was pretty worked up. I think the only reason Dane walked away was because we showed up. Getting the car back, including Dane's, would be the minimum a guy like Aguilar would need to save face in his community."

"You're a criminal profiler, now?" Connolly scoffed. "I'll look into it. But, I'm serious Kate. You *need* to stay out of this. I don't want to find your body added to the investigation. This has been a tragic enough of a week."

Kate looked at the detective and nodded, "It has."

Looking dubious, Connolly looked across his desk, "You're done playing investigator?"

"Absolutely," Kate smiled. "I trust you have the case well in hand."

The detective continued studying Kate as if trying to judge her sincerity. "I have a suspect to interrogate," he said, rising from his chair. Walking across the room, he opened the door for her.

Kate walked through, "Thank you for your time, Detective."

Connolly nodded. Standing outside of his office, he watched Kate cross back to the interrogation room. Nodding toward an officer, he said, "Officer Janus, make sure Ms. Harper exits the station the moment she is done with forensics."

The officer looked up from her desk, "Understood, sir."

Satisfied the officer would escort Kate out of the station, the detective made his way back to the interrogation room. Flinging the door open, he grinned at Aguilar's man, "I'm sorry to keep you waiting."

Thirty Three

Kate was distracted the entire drive back to the beach house. Her mind whirred as she tried to piece together the facts of the case. There were so many strands that just failed to connect.

She knew she was supposed to stand down, in fact, after Driscoll, she *wanted* to. Climbing out of her SUV, she walked to her front door, absently greeting the policeman sitting on the hood of his patrol car, maintaining watch over the beach house.

She thought of Aguilar's man at the station. It was difficult to disagree with Detective Connolly, the man being at Driscoll's motel room shortly after his death was damning evidence on its own merit. Even if the man, Carlos, did kill Driscoll, did he also kill Joann Marrs? Why? Even then, he would be the triggerman, but the order would have come from Vincent Aguilar. Mumbling to herself, she thought of a question she wished she had tossed out to Connolly, "Was bludgeoning victims Aguilar's gang's modus operandi?"

Kate stood in front of her crime wall, tugging her lip as she studied the links of Aguilar to Joan Marrs. The line ran directly through Dane Smithfield. Given Driscoll's role in Treasure Island to sort out Joann's death and keep the Smithfields out of as much trouble as possible, it was plausible that the private investigator had evidence tying Aguilar to Joann's death.

"Am I, uh, interrupting?" a voice called softly from the hallway.

Kate turned to find Nick standing just outside of the dining room turned crime lab.

Smiling, she laughed, "No. I was just trying to connect the dots."

"Kate, as annoying as Detective Connolly can be, he is right. Let him and his officers get to the truth. They are trained and carry guns," Nick pleaded.

Nodding absently, Kate said, "Yeah. I know. It's just... something's bugging me."

"Well, one thing is for sure, you're going to need a bigger wall," Nick quipped.

"I know, right?" Kate grinned. "But really, the pool of suspects isn't actually growing. Their true motives and opportunities to potentially commit the crimes are getting deeper."

"Maybe that's how investigations go, peeling away the layers. You might have your suspect, but then you have to gather all the facts to get them convicted," Nick suggested.

"Yeah, the layers are slowly coming into focus," Kate agreed.

"You feel like you're closing in?" Nick asked.

"Maybe," Kate shrugged. "Not all the strings want to connect. If Driscoll had something on Aguilar, that is clear motive. But Joann Marrs... that is asking for trouble and misplaced revenge at that for Aguilar."

"I don't know," Nick defended the theory. "For Aguilar, murdering a high-profile person like Dane Smithfield might seem too risky, but attacking his non-social status girlfriend... might not seem as dangerous. Plant a stooge like Huck or better yet, hire him to do it and bam! Aguilar has his revenge that cuts his opponent Dane Smithfield deeply and he gets to maintain arm's length distance from the capital crime."

Kate nodded, "That would make sense. But why go after Dane again on the beach? And why send a guy to Driscoll's motel room?"

Nick laughed, "That's an easy one. Aguilar is a bad guy and a snoop like Driscoll, God rest his soul, could easily trip across something Aguilar would not want out in the open. Maybe even his ties to Huck."

"Like a money trail," Kate suggested.

"Sure. That would be as much a smoking gun as anything," Nick shrugged.

Kate looked thoughtfully at the wall.

"But you're going to leave all that to the police, right?" Nick asked. "Kate?"

Kate pulled her attention away from the wall and looked at Nick. With a grimace, she admitted, "Detective Connolly said he would arrest me… and you, if we ignore his stand-down orders again."

"Great," Nick sighed. "I wear a size large prison jumper because you don't seem to be standing down and I am pretty sure Connolly will be ready with his cuffs."

"You don't *have* to follow me," Kate offered a sultry grin.

Nick shook his head and smiled. His expression veiled the depth of his concern. With reservation in his voice, he asked, "So, what do we do?"

Kate stepped back from her wall of evidence to take a broader look at the variables lined out in front of her.

"I'd like to pick things up from the vigil. It wasn't long after that when I got the call from Driscoll," Kate said.

"All right," Nick said. Stepping next to her, he focused on what he recalled from the vigil attendees. "Starting with Joann's friends, you have Dane, the flamboyant boyfriend who always seems to find himself in trouble. He was allegedly set to propose to Joann on this trip, yet he's getting into trouble. Doing the kinds of things that would not sit well with Joann."

"Maybe he was testing the boundaries of their relationship before he proposed," Kate suggested.

"When he spoke, he had a sense of sincerity in his words," Nick observed.

"He is impetuous. No one said he was dumb. An impassioned speech is just what he needed to throw people off his trail," Kate said.

"Vincent Aguilar certainly wasn't buying it or at least didn't care," Nick added.

Kate's eyes bounced from Dane's photo to Aguilar's, "I'd go with the latter."

"His family doesn't seem happy with him or with the concept of him marrying Joann," Nick said.

Kate nodded, "Again, maybe not a surprise given Dane and his exploits. Then again, it was said that Joann gave them hope that she could make him a better man."

"Who's next?" Nick asked, studying the wall with no shortage of options.

"Stacey Karp. She is *way* more chummy with Dane than a friend, never mind a friend mourning her best friend, should be," Kate said.

Nick agreed, "There was definitely something going on there. But the one that really struck me was John Trigg. He is dripping with anger toward his friend Dane. He glared at him the entire vigil, at least when he wasn't obviously overcome by the loss of Joann."

"He had a thing for Joann. I can see it in his eyes," Kate said, her voice firm.

"You can see when someone likes someone from their eyes?" Nick asked.

Kate shrugged, "Yeah. Can't you?"

Nick shifted uncomfortably and his eyes darting to the evidence wall. "I don't know. But I do know that John Trigg seems to be the most visibly upset over the loss of Joann Marrs."

"Upset enough that Joann Marrs marrying Dane Smithfield might have set him off in a moment of passion?" Kate rubbed her chin.

"He seems ready to snap... or snap again, if that is the case," Nick agreed.

Kate sighed heavily, "And then there is Aguilar. It was a bit brazen for him and his crew to be at the vigil. Even more so to attack Dane on the beach, just steps from the site."

"And then his man showing up at Driscoll's motel," Nick added.

"Driscoll...," Kate's head dropped. "What did he want to share with me?"

"Whatever it was, it must have been important enough to kill for," Nick said.

Kate looked thoughtful and shook her head, "I can't see how it is anything but something tied to the murder of Joann Marrs."

"Like a payoff to Huck," Nick suggested.

"Huck was the perfect patsy in all this, until Driscoll was killed, at least," Kate said.

"Not the sharpest tool in the shed. No fear. A thief with a long rap sheet...," Nick shrugged.

Kate's eyes narrowed, "No one would know a local thug like..."

"Another local thug!" Nick broke in.

Staring at the board, Kate looked despondent. Nick recognized the look, her wheels were churning on overdrive, "Kate?"

A plan of action coming into focus, Kate turned toward Nick, a grin washing over her face, "How do you feel about cars?"

"Cars?" Nick shrugged. "I drive a work truck with surf racks on it."

"We are going to a street race!" Kate exclaimed.

Nick's face fell, "Oh, no. No, we're not, Kate."

"Just to watch, unless you want to mix it up a bit," Kate gave a mischievous smile.

"I think that falls in the Detective Connolly toss us in the paddy wagon category of things we can do," Nick groaned.

"We need to know what Aguilar was so worried about that he sent one of his thugs to ransack Driscoll's hotel," Kate said.

"And, don't forget, most likely killed Driscoll. Outside of your beach house just minutes before you and I arrived, I might add!" Nick argued.

"Of all the people on that wall, Vincent Aguilar is the most likely to have been either directly or indirectly involved in murder. He clearly has a penchant for violence. He is just smart enough to not get caught, or at least avoids evidence trails. It seemed like his business with Dane might not have quite been over *and* he insinuated that he might have had something to do with Joann's death. He took *something* of importance away from Dane. What would have been more important than Joann?" Kate reasoned.

"Great. Share all of that with Connolly. Let him do his job," Nick defended.

Kate shook her head, "Aguilar has a way of keeping the police at bay. Someone, or some*ones* who can fly under the radar might have a better chance. That is what is needed to take a guy like Aguilar down. Or at least to uncover the evidence."

Nick bit his lip. He regretted the words as soon as they spilled out, "That is probably exactly what Frank Driscoll thought."

Kate looked at Nick. Her eyes trembled as she considered they might be following in Driscoll's footsteps.

Thirty Four

"I can't believe we actually found it," Kate whispered as she followed Nick through the construction site in downtown Tampa.

"Well, I knew a guy," Nick shrugged. "Truth is, there are several spots notorious for street racing. The police have a difficult time knowing which spot at which time and day to patrol."

"And of course, you knew a guy," Kate laughed.

Nick nodded as they paused at the tear in the fence line meant to keep trespassers out of the work site. Kate peered into a section of the expansive construction project where, nearly hidden from anyone passing by, there was a rowdy collection of hot rods, LED-trimmed modified cars and a genuine sports car or two.

Amidst the vehicles, a party atmosphere was assembled, lit by headlights with plumes of colorful smoke streaming into the air. Vincent Aguilar and his gang were the centers of attention. He was sitting on the hood of a late model European car more likely to be seen driving along Sunset Park than at an illegal car rally.

Aguilar seemed to be enjoying showing off his new vehicles along with the return of the one that he lost in the race with Dane Smithfield. While Kate and Nick couldn't quite hear from the spot in the shadows, they could tell Aguilar was regaling the crowd with how he dealt with the rich, snot-nosed cheater.

Inching closer, Kate and Nick moved from shadow to shadow until they were within earshot of the crowd. A pair near the edge of the gathering whispered to each other in between puffs of smoke, "Vinnie talks a good game, rumor is, the rich kid just handed the keys over. Signed another check from daddy and just walked on."

"Nah, I heard some chick caught Vinnie and a few of pals about to work the kid over and dusted him off like they were old buddies," the other said.

"He shoulda buried that kid, showing him up like that."

"Nah, only a rematch with a 'dub' for Vinnie and then a public beating would square things with a guy like him."

"I heard he took out that chick on the beach."

"The dude's girlfriend? Brutal. No wonder he just handed over his keys."

The hair on the back of Kate's neck raised as the conversation reached its crescendo. Glancing around, she pulled out her cell phone to take photos of Aguilar and the cars.

Aguilar stood up on the hood of the expensive car he relegated from Smithfield. With arms spread wide, the gang leader hopped to the ground as a pair of scantily clad young women filled in on either side of him.

"All right! Let's get this show literally on the road!" Aguilar called out to a chorus of cheers.

Edging around the pair that had been whispering, Kate lined up her shot. Hitting the button on her phone, she began capturing the scene.

"Uhm, Kate…," Nick started, gently tugging on her arm. "Your flash is on, Kate!"

Aguilar's head snapped in Kate's direction. Fighting through the dark, his eyes narrowed. Raising a menacing finger, he growled, "That's the chick from the beach! Get her!"

Nick was already yanking Kate through the maze of construction zone equipment and half-built structures. They could hear a scramble of footfalls behind them. Further in the distance, engines roared to life, followed by the squeal of tires. Never slowing, Kate and Nick spun sideways to knife through the narrow opening in the fence line.

Leaping over a pile of gravel, using their heels on the downhill slope to slow their descent, they raced for Kate's SUV. Never happier for the proximity of auto-unlock, Kate never had to break stride until she was sliding behind the wheel.

Just as she closed her door and Nick hammered his hand on the lock button, a mass of angry fists began pounding on the SUV's windows. Mashing the start button and slamming the car into gear simultaneously, Kate drilled her foot to the floor of the powerful SUV sending a spray of gravel in the air until the tires found pavement and bit down hard.

The relief of getting away from the angry mob was brief, as a series of headlights appeared in the SUV's mirrors. Nick eyed the reflection outside his window, recognizing some of the LED lighting from the racers, he called, "We have company, Kate!"

"I see them," Kate said, her calm voice belying her heart pounding in her chest.

Squeezing tighter on the steering wheel as her palms were slick with terror-induced perspiration. Turning the wheel hard, she avoided the brakes, pushing the SUV to its limits to drive away from the dark and quiet area of South Tampa renovation for busier main streets.

The racer's cars were considerably more adept at negotiating the tight corners and narrow streets, closing quickly on her tail. One car's headlights shone brightly through her side mirror as it attempted a pass. Spying another intersection, Kate turned the wheel hard right, just as the vehicle sped alongside. Too fast to make the turn, the vehicle slammed on the brakes and spun the car in reverse.

More cars appeared in Kate's rearview. A hot rod with a massive blower rising up from the hood sped through a gap as the pursuers parted allowing it through.

"That's Aguilar's car," Nick said, looking over his shoulder. "I don't think he's happy."

"Good," Kate said. Hitting the call button on her steering wheel she commanded the car to dial Detective Connolly.

"Ms. Harper, I...," the detective began.

"Yeah, I don't have time for that," Kate cut Connolly off. "I have Vincent Aguilar and about a half dozen very angry street racers on my tail."

"You what? Where are you?" Connolly asked.

"I'm about to take a hard turn onto the Gandy Causeway," Kate exclaimed.

"I have Hillsborough Deputies en route, I'm on my way. Stay safe!" Connolly hung up the phone.

As Kate's tires hit the on-ramp for the causeway, her right foot pressed hard on the accelerator. The force pinned Nick against his door as he reached up to cling onto the overhead handle.

While Kate's luxury SUV was powerful, the cars bred for street racing weren't at all struggling to keep up. With her hazards flashing, she tried to make the chase as safe as possible for innocent travelers along their route. Aguilar and the trailing vehicles had no sense of consciousness weaving in and out of traffic, menacing Kate to pull over.

Streaking along the narrow roadway flanked by water on either side was exhilarating. As Kate witnessed several near misses with other commuters, she realized how foolish and dangerous it was as well.

Leveling her foot off the pedal, she realized Aguilar's crew would give her no choice but to keep up the pace. Slamming into her rear quarter panel, the SUV's warning lights and automatic systems fought to keep the vehicle in a safe line.

"They are trying to pit maneuver you," Nick said.

"What?" Kate exclaimed, her eyes wide as they digested the highway in front of her.

"If they hit you hard enough on the rear of the SUV, it will put you into a spin," Nick replied.

Kate chewed her lip, "That's not good."

As a car to her left dove its nose into her lane, she quickly pushed her SUV to the right, avoiding a firm hit. A car from her right attacked, Kate again adjusting to absorb the impact without spinning out.

Blue and red flashing lights gleamed in the night sky as they passed the last turn-off on the causeway until it emptied on the other side of the bay. As Kate closed in on the end of the long stretch of road connecting Tampa to Clearwater-St. Pete, she saw a row of flashing lights waiting for her.

With one final press of the accelerator, Kate created distance between her and her pursuers before slamming on the brakes and sliding to a stop in front of the roadblock formed by police cruisers.

Two patrol cars quickly separated her vehicle from Aguilar and his gang who had begun braking and searching for a way off the causeway. Police cars from the Tampa Bay side closed in around them, shutting off their escape route.

A man walked up to Kate's driver's side window and rapped on the door. The policeman wore an expression of anger mixed with relief.

Kate glanced at Nick and gulped. Turning her head to the window, she hit the button to roll it down and smiled, "Detective. You made good time."

"I have lights, training and the authority to move fast when lives are at stake," Detective Connolly said.

With a slow nod, Kate looked contrite.

"Out. Both of you," Connolly demanded.

Kate and Nick slowly opened their doors and slid out of the SUV.

Connolly paced back and forth in front of the pair as he seethed, "I'd ask 'what were you thinking?' but I'm getting a bit tired of the lack of answers that come from that question. How did you happen to have Aguilar and his men chasing you this evening?"

"We, uh, well, I- Nick was only here for support- went to watch Aguilar at one of his street races," Kate said, her head bowed as though she were a child being scolded by her parent.

Connolly shook his head violently as his eyes blinked, trying to comprehend the words that Kate expressed, "You what? You have got to be kidding me. You know what? We're done here. We have the entire causeway blocked. You've put lives in danger... Oh, we're done."

Kate exchanged a quick look at Nick before they realized what Connolly meant. With a quick order, two officers escorted Kate and Nick to the rear of a patrol car and stuffed them in the back as another officer moved Kate's SUV to the side of the road as a tow truck made its way up to the roadblock.

Nick fidgeted in the plastic seat of the patrol car, staring at the metal cage separating the front and rear of the vehicle.

"I am so sorry," Kate breathed. "This is all my fault."

Nick remained transfixed on the steel grating in front of him.

With a slight nod of understanding, Kate gazed out her window. A procession of vehicles from the Hillsborough County Sheriff's Department and Tampa police rolled through the disbanding roadblock. In the rear of one vehicle, the piercing eyes of Vincent Aguilar stared at Kate Harper as it passed.

Thirty Five

Kate had dozed off, her head in her arms that were crossed in front of her as they lay on the interrogation room table. She didn't know how long she had drifted to sleep or how long she had been in the holding room of the Treasure Island Police Station.

The door flung open, revealing a still very cross Detective Connolly. He stood in the doorway looking at Kate who raised her head off the table and blinked her eyes awake to study the police detective.

"What do you say I lock you and your friend away until all of this is cleared up," Connolly said, kicking the door shut with his heel. Setting two coffee cups down on the interrogation room table, he sat on the edge while he peered over Kate.

"Thank you," Kate said, her voice crackling.

With folded arms, Connolly drew a deep breath before speaking, "I get it. You witnessed the precursor to a murder that you wonder if you could have done something to prevent it. The fact is, you couldn't. You called the police and we investigated. Sadly for Ms. Marrs, we were too late. Then you were threatened. Many... *most* people would pack up and leave at that point. Not you. You're strong. You're bright. Not too bright, clearly..."

Connolly took a sip of coffee, "It's one thing to put your own life at risk. That's your choice. What about the families on that freeway this evening? Where was their choice in your sleuthing expedition?"

"I'm sorry. I'm sorry for all of that," Kate said.

"Sorry wouldn't take back someone getting hurt or worse on that freeway," Connolly snapped.

Kate nodded, "I know. You're right. I didn't think snapping a few pictures and listening in on Aguilar at the race would lead to a full-on car chase. He recognized me and Nick and I feared for our lives."

"Nick," Connolly growled. "I would expect *him* to be smarter than all this."

"He argued against going. I told him I was going to go anyway. I guilted him into joining me," Kate said.

"Well, he's an adult. He should override those feelings of guilt and do the right thing," Connolly said.

Kate sighed, "I think he did what he felt he had to."

"Well, those fluttering eyes of yours are going to cost you. Both of you," Connolly said. The detective's shoulders slumped and his entire demeanor changed. "I would just as soon charge you both with obstruction of justice and reckless endangerment. Unfortunately, the District Attorney is so excited to finally have irrefutable evidence on Aguilar in catching him chasing you red-handed, he wants to drop all charges against you and Mason."

Kate's eyes lit, "That's great news!"

Connolly rolled his eyes.

"Did you get Aguilar to talk? Did he admit to killing Joann Marrs? What about Driscoll?" Kate asked excitedly.

The detective frowned, "You just never stop, do you?"

Kate looked expectantly.

Connolly looked up at the ceiling before letting out a deep sigh, "He won't talk. We're waiting for his lawyer to show up."

"I can get him to talk," Kate blurted.

"What? You... no way," Connolly shook his head.

"He's more likely to talk to me than you or any other person in law enforcement. If nothing else, he's angry enough at me, he might let something slip out before he can filter what he says," Kate offered.

Connolly stared directly at Kate, refusing to flinch. Finally, he chewed his lip, glanced at the door and conceded, "All right. We can give it a try."

Kate bounced in her seat as a broad grin crossed her face.

"No, see that. Don't do that. It's like me condoning what you've done. The department is just using you to get to Aguilar," Connolly said.

"I'm ready to do my civic duty," Kate sat erect in her chair.

"I'm going to regret this," Connolly sighed. "Come on. Before his attorney shows up."

Vincent Aguilar looked up from the table he was shackled to. His face morphed from surprise to a twitch of anger to a sardonic smile.

"And they say my street racers, excuse me, *alleged* street racers are dangerous," Aguilar said.

"How often are they running for their lives?" Kate snapped back.

Aguilar snarled, enjoying the exchange, "More often than you might think."

"So tough until someone gets the better of you. Dane Smithfield beat the unbeatable. How did that happen?" Kate asked.

Aguilar bristled, "That little brat cheated. He had some high-tech boosters attached to electric motors on the wheels. No way I could match that instant torque. I almost caught him in the end, but it was too late."

"But you couldn't prove it at the time, so all people saw was you getting beat. And you losing your prize car in the process," Kate pressed.

Aguilar scowled, "Not one of my better nights."

"Of course, it couldn't stop there, right?" Kate asked.

"You mean the little fracas on the beach," Aguilar said. "He had that coming and more."

"What would you have done if Nick and I hadn't shown up?" Kate asked.

Aguilar smiled, "That Smithfield kid and I would have had a much more in-depth conversation, but it seemed to turn out all right. I walked away with not one, but two cars and got my baby back. It's all good."

Knowing Connolly was watching from behind the one-way glass, she texted the photos she had taken at the street race to show that Aguilar was in-fact in possession of the two cars that Smithfield gave him.

"That night, you said something about Dane Smithfield should have learned his lesson about people who cross you losing things that were close to them. Did you mean things like Dane's girlfriend Joann Marrs?" Kate pressed.

Aguilar screwed his face, "You mean the girl the vigil was for? No. I didn't even know that was Smithfield's girl. I thought he was with the other one. She was draped all over him the night of the street race. She was the one cheering and prodding him along. The other chick didn't seem real interested. In him or the race."

Kate looked surprised, "So, what did you do? No way a powerful guy like you could leave it there. Let a punk like Dane get over on you."

"No, I sent some guys to steal my car back. When they couldn't find it, they took his. I didn't realize he had two. Probably made a fat insurance claim and didn't think twice about it," Aguilar boasted.

Kate could feel Connolly looking at her through the glass.

"At the race tonight," Kate continued. "There was talk that you hadn't done enough."

"Yeah, that's probably true. Sometimes rumors take care of that nasty business for me. If people thought I had a hand in that broad's death, so be it. Did me a favor," Aguilar shrugged. "In this case, people just wouldn't let it go. That Smithfield kid was seen around town, lounging on his daddy's yacht. Bragging about taking my car from me. It wasn't a good look."

"Well, surely, you couldn't let *that* go," Kate scoffed.

Aguilar's face fell, "That's why I sent my guy. See if that Driscoll guy had any of Smithfield's secrets. I could use it as…leverage."

"You mean *blackmail*," Kate's brows flattened.

"Tomato, tom*ah*to," Aguilar grinned.

Connolly, clearly not amused, stepped into the room.

Aguilar looked up, realized the entire exchange was in full view of the police detective and straightened in his seat. Turning his attention to Connolly, who closed the door behind him, the gang leader announced, "Look, I didn't know Driscoll had just gotten whacked. If I had, I never would have sent my guy. I mean, look where it got me?"

"Pretty convenient," the detective said.

"It's bad luck, I'd call it. If I was going to send a guy, hypothetically, it would have been to take out that snotty brat Smithfield. Not that little weasel Driscoll. That guy was harmless. I definitely wouldn't have had anyone connected to me snoop around the first place the cops would go after a murder. I have my faults but bein' dumb ain't one of them," Aguilar defended.

A rap at the door caught the room's attention. All eyes watched a squirrelly man in a suit step in and set a briefcase down on the table. He looked at Connolly and rasped, "Surely, Detective, you know that anything you asked my client after he called me is inadmissible."

Connolly smiled with a brief glance toward Kate, "*I* didn't ask him anything."

Excusing themselves while Aguilar and his counselor debriefed, Connolly reunited Kate with Nick, who was left waiting for her in a chair outside of the detective's office.

Kate beamed at the detective as she bounced excitedly on her heels, "Well, that was exciting!"

Nick frowned at Kate.

Detective Connolly did not share Kate's exuberance. His scowl declared how very angry he still was with her, "We picked up some good nuggets with you in there, I'll admit."

"Nuggets? I had him admitting to an entire rap sheet full of offenses," Kate argued.

"You did all right. I'll have that noted in your file with the district attorney," Connolly said.

"I have a file?" Kate gasped.

Connolly grinned, "You do now."

Nick looked confused by the conversation, "*You* interrogated Aguilar?"

"I had a friendly conversation with Aguilar," Kate beamed.

"He probably wants to kill us," Nick winced.

Kate pondered the statement, "Probably still does."

Detective Connolly took the moment to express his ire, "I would have thought that a dead body outside of your beach house would have been enough to discourage you from sticking your nose into police business. But no, you go and antagonize a notorious gang leader. What is wrong with you Kate? If you won't save yourself, I will. I'm putting you in police custody. I've already cleared it with Chief Reynolds."

"You can't do this," Kate argued.

"Oh, I can. And I did. By the way, you did this to *yourself*, Kate." Connolly said. Turning to Nick, he snapped, "Nick, go home. You give Kate a false sense of security and don't seem capable of injecting the slightest bit of common sense into her decision-making."

Nick sighed, looking between Kate and the detective. With an inability to argue, he accepted the word.

"An officer will take you to your beach house to collect what you need, and no, leave all that stuff on that wall of yours. You don't need that. You will then be taken to an undisclosed location until all this is over. Bye Kate. Bye Nick," Connolly shooed them out of his office with his hands.

Waving to a uniformed patrolman, he called, "Officer Travis, she's all yours."

Without another word, Detective Connolly disappeared towards the interrogation room where Vincent Aguilar was meeting with his attorney.

Officer Travis held his arm out, suggesting that Kate and Nick make their way out of the police station. They conceded. When they reached the parking lot, the officer instructed them to wait while he pulled his cruiser up to take them to Kate's beach house where Nick could retrieve his truck and Kate could collect her things before she moved to the police safe house.

"Are you okay?" Nick asked as the officer walked away.

Kate nodded, "I'm okay. I'm tired. I'm grateful no one was hurt during the chase."

"Did you uncover anything?" Nick asked in a low tone as the officer disappeared around the corner.

"Aguilar is every bit the thug everyone thinks he is. But I don't think he killed Joann Marrs," Kate admitted.

Nick cocked his head, "Then who did?"

"I don't know. According to Aguilar, he had no idea Joann Marrs and Dane Smithfield were a couple. He thought Dane was with Stacey Karp," Kate said.

"Anyone at the vigil might have assumed the same," Nick shrugged.

"The point is," Kate continued. "If Aguilar was to exact revenge, it wouldn't have been directed at Joann Marrs."

"What if she was just in the way? The wrong place at the wrong time?" Nick suggested.

Kate looked thoughtful as her head bobbed, "True. I still don't get the impression Aguilar was motivated to kill *anybody* over being shown up by Dane Smithfield. He would have preferred a more public display of power. Dane showing up with a black eye, a broken arm *and* losing his cars. Ideally, a rematch where Aguilar had the opportunity to prove Dane was cheating and *then* rough him up- that was Aguilar's plan. Murder didn't seem to be on the table."

"One of his goons went too far," Nick shrugged.

"Maybe," Kate conceded.

Officer Travis pulled up. Climbing out of his police Interceptor, he said, "I'm sorry, one of you will need to ride in the back."

Kate looked at Nick and said, "We'll both ride in back."

Agreeing, Nick opened the door and allowed Kate in. Climbing after her as she scooted across the bucketed seats, he said, "Let's have this be the last time we ride in the back of one of these."

Kate shrugged, an apologetic grin creasing her lips, "I can't promise that…"

Thirty Six

Officer Travis pulled alongside Nick's truck parked in Kate's beach house driveway. Putting the police cruiser in park, he climbed out and reminded the pair of Detective Connolly's instructions.

"Mr. Mason, you need to go home. Ms. Harper, you need to remain in my sight the whole time," the officer said, his voice almost apologetic.

Kate smiled and nodded, "I understand, Officer Travis. Is it okay that I walk Nick to his truck and tell him goodbye?"

The officer bobbled his head and rolled his shoulders in indifference.

Kate looped around the cruiser and followed Nick to the driver's door of his pickup truck. Placing her hands on his chest, she glanced at Officer Travis before looking up at Nick, "I am *so* sorry. For everything."

Nick looked down at Kate, almost begrudgingly wrapping his arms around her, "Kate, I just want you to be safe. From the moment I met you, your foot poking through those rotted boards, that is all that I've wanted."

Closing her eyes, Kate digested Nick's words. With a sigh, her chest heaved against his. "I know," she whispered.

"So, be safe," Nick whispered back.

Kate lifted on her heels, her lips close enough to Nick's to feel the heat of his breath.

Nick moved closer, to the point where their lips nearly touched. Tilting his head ever so slightly, he kissed Kate on her cheek. "Take care of yourself, Kate."

With an appreciative nod to Officer Travis, Nick released his arms from Kate and climbed unceremoniously into his truck. Hitting the 'start' button, he concentrated more than he needed to in order to back out of Kate's driveway and accelerated down the street and out of view.

Kate's eyes followed Nick's truck until he vanished from her sight. Even then, she allowed her focus to linger on his departure longer than she should have. With a heaving breath, she spun on her heel and forced a smile at Officer Travis.

"Thank you for waiting," Kate said.

"Of course, ma'am," the officer bowed his head.

Kate marched up the steps to her front door. Inserting her key and hitting the disarm button on her cell phone app, she opened the front door. Officer Travis held out his hand to suggest that she should go in and he would follow.

Walking through the house with speed, she called over her shoulder, "I'll only be a moment."

Officer Travis shook his head, "Detective Connolly was explicit. You were to remain in my sight at all times."

"All times?" Kate spun and frowned as she took a step up the stairs.

The young officer's face reddened, "Well, not *all* the time, ma'am."

Kate smiled and continued her ascent up the steps. She whirled around the room, shoving her toiletries and clothes in their respective bags. Intentionally laden, she waddled to the doorway, barely squeezing through with luggage pressing against either side of the doorway.

Looking beleaguered, she shot a sheepish look at Officer Travis, "You wouldn't help me, by any chance, would you?"

Officer Travis shrugged, "Of course, I'd be happy to help."

As the officer reached out to grab one of Kate's bags, she allowed the lot of them to slip off her arms and fall to the floor. "Great!" she smiled, stepping over the luggage.

Gliding down the steps, Kate left the young officer in the third-floor hallway, collecting a random assortment of baggage. Streaking through the house, Kate slid into the dining room. Phone in hand, she took meticulous photos of her "crime wall" and evidence she had strewn on the table. Scooping up what was handy, she raced to the kitchen as Officer Travis struggled down the steps.

Shoving her loot into her workbag, Kate spun as Officer Travis ambled into the kitchen. Bags strewn over each shoulder and more gripped in each hand, he looked expectantly at the woman he was tasked with securing.

"I'm almost done," Kate sang, sliding her laptop into the bag she had crammed with photos and documents she had printed in reference to the case.

Zipping the overstuffed bag close, she smiled, "Ready!"

Travis nodded as he turned and began his burdened trek toward the door and his patrol car.

"Will there be food?" Kate asked, scooping up her travel printer as she hurried down the hallway after the officer. "If not, my friend showed me this delightful bistro along the causeway... my treat!"

After helping Kate carry her things into the hotel room, Officer Travis informed her, "I'll be right outside in the hall."

"Great. I feel much safer... and constrained," Kate said.

The officer merely offered a slight nod and closed the door behind him.

Pulling open her laptop and setting up her printer, she began recreating as much of her suspect tree as she could. Following the conversation with Aguilar, as much as the detective warned her to take the gang leader's discourse with a grain of salt, she found sincerity in what was said in the interrogation room.

Aguilar killing Joann Marrs didn't make a lot of sense, though anyone caught in the act of another crime could resort to murder. She couldn't rule the gangster out. Nor could she completely ignore the trail to Driscoll. One of Aguilar's men at the private detective's hotel room so soon after his death was difficult to overlook.

Kate thought of Aguilar's response, if he had known Driscoll had been killed, he wouldn't have sent his man to search the motel. Connolly had countered with the fact that Aguilar might have hoped for a longer lead time from the body discovery to the police showing up at the motel. The police detective also warned Kate that men like Aguilar will often send others to do their dirty work and are therefore likely to take greater risks.

Kate tapped at the photo of Aguilar sitting on the hood of Dane Smithfield's car. For a gangster that was so difficult for the police to make a case on, it all seemed a little too sloppy to Kate.

Sorting through the photos, she began fanning out pictures of Joann Marrs' friends. Their individual emotions and actions at the vigil just didn't make sense to her. She thought of Driscoll and what evidence he had wanted to share with her. It was the trio in the photos in front of her that the private investigator had spent the most time with. He had noted the same thing that Kate had.

Sliding the photo of John Trigg from the pile, she studied it. Joann Marrs' friend and best friend to Dane Smithfield was so full of anger and remorse. There was something gnawing at the young man. Kate wondered if that something was guilt.

Kate looked at the pool of suspects on the hotel coffee table. No matter what direction the case took, it always came back to these three.

Chewing her lip, Kate considered what to do. "I wish Nick was here," the words tumbled out of her mouth in a way that caught her by surprise. She felt safer with Nick by her side. She felt better.

Picking up her phone, she dialed Nick's number.

"Hello?" Nick said.

"You're still picking up my calls. That's a good sign," Kate smiled.

"No one said spending time with you would be dull. Or safe. Or legal," Nick said. "Speaking of which, I just picked up a to-go order at Caddy's for dinner. Guess who came in as I was leaving?"

Kate frowned and then shrugged to herself, "I don't know. Connolly?"

"Good guess, but no. Joann Marrs' friends. Followed by an entourage of legal team babysitters," Nick said.

"Hmm. I'm surprised Beau let them out at all, supervision or otherwise," Kate said.

"They seem like the type that largely do as they please anyway," Nick said.

Kate laughed, "Sneaking away from Dad."

"Likely," Nick agreed. "Look, with the crime scene and all and without you here, I haven't been able to get much done at the house. I'm sorry."

"These are unusual circumstances. I can buy a little more time with the management company. Besides, I'm pretty sure me dragging you along clandestine adventures has taken a toll on the schedule too," Kate said.

"I will say, knowing you are locked up under police supervision, I might get a good night's sleep for the first time since I met you," Nick teased.

Kate pouted, "Well, I'm glad *something* good is coming from my house arrest."

"You're just itching to do some sleuthing, aren't you?" Nick asked.

"What?" Kate scoffed. "Nonsense. I'm catching up on my favorite mystery series on the romance channel."

"Ha, I bet you are," Nick laughed. "Well, I should let you go. Get this meal in me before it gets cold. See you tomorrow?"

"If Detective Connolly allows me," Kate said.

"All right. Goodnight, Kate."

"Goodnight, Nick," Kate ended the call, looking at the photos of Joann Marrs' friends on her coffee table thoughtfully.

Mumbling to herself, she said "Man, I'd love to see what those three are up to."

With a burst of inspiration, she scanned the hotel amenities. Finding what she was looking for, she dialed the concierge. "Yes, is the spa still open? Just the sauna. There is a lady's and a gentleman's. Thank you, that sounds perfect."

With a grin, Kate dashed to the bathroom, grabbed the plush hotel bathrobe off its hook and pulled it over her clothes. Stuffing her shoes into the robe's pockets, she hoisted up her pants to ride high on her knees, above the bottom of the robe. Sliding into a pair of slippers that matched the robe, she shuffled toward the exit.

Grabbing the hotel key, she flung open the door and started down the hallway, marching directly past Officer Travis. The patrolman was on his feet in an instant.

"Uhm, ma'am. Ms. Harper, you can't go anywhere," the officer stammered, catching up to her.

Kate smiled at the young man, "I'm just going to the hotel sauna. You want to join me?"

Officer Travis' eyes widened, "What? No. No, ma'am."

"It's okay. You can sit right outside until I'm done," Kate said and spun on her heels, continuing her defiant march to the elevators.

"I, I guess that would be okay," Officer Travis scratched his head.

As they entered the elevator and it made its slow descent, Kate smiled at the policeman, "Do you sauna? It's quite relaxing."

"No. I like the hot tub at my apartment's pool," Officer Travis said.

"That's nice," Kate said. "Ooh, here we are."

In a flash, Kate was out of the elevator and down the hall. Officer Travis jogged after her to keep up. When they arrived at the spa, Kate nodded her head toward the lady's entrance, "I'm going to be right inside."

Adjusting her robe as though she were preparing to loosen it, the officer instinctively averted his eyes.

"See you in a bit," Kate sang as she disappeared into the spa.

"How long are you going to be?" Officer Travis called. "Ms. Harper?"

Kate didn't respond as she knifed through the doors.

With a shrug, the officer found a chair and sat right outside the entrance of the lady's spa entrance.

Inside the bowels of the women's locker room, Kate let the robe fall to the floor and kicked off her slippers. Pulling her pant legs down, she slipped on her shoes and hurried to the hallway that intersected the woman's spa with the restrooms for the outdoor pool.

Walking briskly past the families enjoying an evening swim, Kate smiled and gave a half wave. Marching directly to the gate to the outdoor sitting area, Kate slipped through. Circling the side of the hotel, she found the car she had hired and jumped into the backseat.

"Caddy's on Treasure Island, please," Kate said, as she settled into her seat.

Thirty Seven

Kate thanked the driver and took in the beachfront restaurant. Open air with seating under the cabana or directly on the sandy beach, Cabbie's was as close to dining on the beach as you could get. Popular with locals and tourists, the atmosphere with the tropical music playing was like a vacation in itself.

Finding a spot in a corner that suffered from poor lighting, Kate looked at the hostess, who nodded a welcome. Sliding in, a quick scan quickly found the trio of men sticking out of place in their business suits. None of them looked happy with their assignments, especially as the Florida evening had yet to yield the heat and humidity of the day.

Following their glowering eyes, Kate found Dane Smithfield, Stacey Karp and John Trigg. As usual, Dane Smithfield's presence was front and center of the trio. Finishing a beer, he quickly replaced it with a fresh one from the ice bucket in the middle of the table.

Kate wasn't surprised to see Stacey Karp sitting closer to Dane than seating would suggest she should be. John Trigg looked even more distant, a continued progression from the first time that Kate had seen the group of Joann Marrs' friends.

From her vantage, Kate couldn't hear their conversation, but watching their body language told the story quite well. Stacey was using Joann's absence to move in closer to Dane Smithfield. Both appealing to his emotions about losing his would-be fiancé while also preying on his character that fed on adoration and attention.

John Trigg only seemed more tired of his friend's antics. The disgruntled looks that he cast when others weren't looking had spread to Stacey. Eschewing the table's bucket of beer for what looked like two fingers of whiskey, John Trigg drained the fluid. Slamming his glass down, he reached for a second that was placed in front of him.

When the conversation at the table turned to him, he forced a smile before returning to his unhappy stare when Dane and Stacey's attention wasn't on him.

Kate ordered food and a drink. Less hungry than wanting to look as if she was there for a meal like anyone else. Picking at her plate, she realized that John Trigg had slipped away from the table. An eye toward the restrooms suggested he had gone elsewhere.

Kate glanced at the trio of chaperones, who seemed more interested in their plates of coconut shrimp and fish tacos than where Trigg had gone.

Curious, Kate slipped out of her seat. Taking advantage of the open-air restaurant, Kate was able to make a wide circle around the building and the beachfront that it spilled out onto. Her eyes panned the scene while she tried to remain obscure. Finding a spot in the shadows, she scanned for a sign of John Trigg.

From an alley the staff used to accept deliveries to the restaurant, a shadow caught Kate's eye. Her brain struggled to accept what her eyes were telling her. A chill raced down her spine as she realized the shadow was striding directly at her, wielding an object high over their head.

Kate dodged just as the object swept by her, grazing her shoulder. In a panic, Kate started to run. Instinct drove her toward the relative safety of a crowded restaurant, but the shadow raced to cut her off, another wicked swing of the weapon aimed right at her.

Spinning, Kate raced away from the attacker. The straightest path was the beach itself. Running as fast as she could, tears streaming from her eyes and flying in her wake. She couldn't think about anything other than desperate flight.

Kate wanted to scream. Her mouth moved but no words came out other than a gravelly gasp. She wanted to turn and face her attacker but the first two swipes of the instrument they wielded screamed at her that that would be a tragic mistake. She wanted to pull out her phone, but she knew that action could slow her down enough that her pursuer would catch her and strike her down.

As it was, she could hear the footfalls closing in. Over her own labored breathing, she could hear the assailant's breath. Angry, wheezing, intent on closing the distance. It was only then that Kate realized she was passing her own beach house. The chill already shocking her spine intensified. She was on the same path that Joann Marrs was on, moments before meeting her death. Moments before being struck from behind with a weapon much like the one that had already narrowly missed her own skull on two occasions.

Her brain screamed at her not to take the same path Joann had that fateful night. Kate scanned the horizon, the beach only became darker and more desolate the further she went. Streaking for the beach access was her only chance.

As the footfalls were a mere stride apart from hers, Kate knew she had no chance. Suddenly, she dropped to her knees. The momentum of her pursuer carried them past. By the time they could correct and ready a swing of their weapon, Kate reached down, grabbing a fistful of sand, Kate threw it in her attacker's eyes just as they readied a strike.

Their action paused as the pursuer rubbed at their eyes, giving Kate just the opportunity to pounce back to her feet. Sprinting past, she made her way to the beach access and the dim light of the parking lot.

The pursuer, back on the chase, tried to make up ground. Slamming on the brakes, they quickly retreated as Kate reached a parked patrol car. Panting, she pointed at the beach just as her attacker disappeared into the shadows.

Connolly's appearance at the scene put everyone on edge, none more so than Kate. She could hardly lock eyes with the Treasure Island police detective as he slid out of his vehicle and scanned the beach access parking lot. The expression on his face was one of the grimmest looks Kate had ever seen.

After making a few commands to the police officers, Detective Connolly stared directly at Kate as he made a deliberate walk across the pavement. Standing in front of her, the detective moved his mouth in the manner one would when they were fishing out the remnant of a meal. In Connolly's case, it was to control his emotions and center his thoughts in a professional manner, irrespective of the rage that welled up inside.

"Ms. Harper," Connolly moved his eyes to the beach access as he struggled to maintain his composure as he spoke in front of Kate. "I am not sure how or why you are standing here instead of in the safety of your hotel with my patrolman outside your door."

Kate and Detective Connolly turned their heads toward the parking lot entrance as a police cruiser screeched to a halt with a perspiring Officer Travis leaping out. Head swiveling across the beach access parking lot, he spied the detective and Kate. Seeing the icy stare in his superior's eyes, the patrolman dipped his head and made a contrite path across the pavement to his boss and the woman he was supposed to be protecting.

"Detective. Ms. Harper," Travis acknowledged as he joined the pair.

"I'll be with you in a moment, Officer Travis. How about you man the beach access steps? Think you can handle that?" Detective Connolly snapped.

"Yes, sir!" the officer nodded to his boss, he shot Kate an incensed glare as he walked off to fulfill his orders.

"Yeah," Kate swished her toe across the pavement, "It's really not Officer Travis' fault."

Connolly's head snapped up, "You're here. Not at the hotel. Securing you was his only task. I'd say he holds plenty of blame."

"I'm sorry, Detective," Kate said.

"How many times have you told me that in the…what? Little over a week that I've known you?" Connolly shot.

Kate nodded, "That's fair."

"Let's dispense with your misguided defiance for just a moment and focus on the matter at hand," Detective Connolly said. "What exactly happened out here tonight?"

Kate took a big breath and shared, "As I was reviewing in my head the conversation with Aguilar and thinking about the other suspects, I realized that despite criminals like Dan Huck and Vincent Aguilar stealing the highlight reels, details in the case always swung back to Dane Smithfield and the rest of Joann Marrs' friends."

Connolly frowned, "How did the conversation with Aguilar bring you to Joann Marrs' friends?"

"Frank Driscoll," Kate replied. "Whatever he caught or figured out, came at or immediately after the vigil. He wasn't involved in the Aguilar incident. His focus was on Dane Smithfield and his friends."

"So, how does that get you defying my orders, giving my patrolman the slip and ending up being chased by a potential murderer on the beach? At the very same location Joann Marrs was slain, by the way," Detective Connolly's brows narrowed, displaying how cross he was at the situation.

"It kind of happened by accident…," Kate winced.

"By accident?" Connolly snapped.

Kate bobbed her head, "Nick happened to be picking up a to-go order from Caddy's. He, in conversation, shared that Dane and his friends, along with a trio of chaperones, had just arrived."

"At Caddy's," Connolly repeated. "And you decided it made all the sense in the world to slip your protective detail and come stick your nose, once more, into a police investigation?"

"Yes," Kate dropped her head.

The detective took a step away and let out a heavy exhale as he stared out at the Gulf that had turned inky black as night had taken hold.

Spinning back to Kate, he asked, "So, how did you end up being chased down the beach?"

"I noticed that John Trigg had slipped away from his friends. He seemed off at the vigil. He was even more off this evening," Kate said.

"Off?" Connolly pressed.

"He was a very prickly third wheel. Dane Smithfield was Dane Smithfield. Stacey Karp looked ready to pounce in her departed friend's absence. John Trigg seemed incensed with the whole ordeal. When he disappeared from the table, I got curious. I went to find him," Kate said.

"Did you? Did you find where John Trigg went?" Connolly asked.

"I don't know," Kate shook her head. "I was looking around the restaurant when someone sprang from the shadows. They swung... what looked like a two-by-four at me. And I ran."

The detective studied Kate for a moment. "You didn't recognize who attacked you?"

"No," Kate admitted. "It happened so fast and there wasn't good lighting in that spot. And then I ran. I just ran."

Looking away, Kate's eyes fell on the ocean. Her body trembled as she recalled the chase. "They were so close. Getting closer. When I realized I was repeating Joann Marrs' path, I almost lost it. I realized that I wouldn't make it to help. I fell to the ground. I scooped up a handful of sand and when whoever was chasing me closed in to strike, I flung the sand and ran. Thank God you had an officer there."

"Or you'd be right where Joann Marrs was!" Connolly snapped, immediately regretting his words.

Kate wrapped her arms around herself and nodded as tears welled in her eyes and whispered, "Yeah."

Detective Connolly relaxed his demeanor, his voice was soft, "I'm glad you're okay."

"I'm sorry," Kate whispered. Wiping her tears away, she scowled, "I'm sorry I didn't face my pursuer down and identify them. I should have fought back!"

Connolly cocked his head and held his arms out for Kate to reluctantly move within the grasp of his hands around her elbows, "If you had, you would have met Joann's fate. But you didn't. You're smart. You're resourceful. Maybe a bit too much…"

Kate laughed as she sniffed.

Connolly stepped back. Licking his lips as he thought, he announced suddenly, "I'd like you to join me at the station. My officers are bringing Dane Smithfield, Stacey Karp and John Trigg in for questioning."

"With their team of lawyers," Kate rolled her eyes.

"Exactly," Connolly nodded.

Thirty Eight

Detective Connolly escorted Kate into the Treasure Island police station. Sitting her down in a chair alongside an officer's desk, he said, "Stay here."

Spinning, he marched off to the interrogation rooms where Dane Smithfield, Stacey Karp and John Trigg were being distributed.

Kate bobbed her head absently as she surveyed the police station. She could only imagine what the conversation about her had been, especially given her latest escapade.

Seeing a forlorn Officer Travis walk into the station receiving catcalls and eyes from the other officers, the young patrolman's head only drooped further.

Squeezing her eyes tight, Kate took in a deep breath and rose from her seat. Making a beeline for Officer Travis' desk, she stood quietly in front of him until he lifted his head and acknowledged her.

"Officer Travis, I am so sorry. I didn't mean to cause you trouble by sneaking away," Kate said, her voice soft.

The young officer looked up, rubbing his face, "That's just it, Ms. Harper. The decisions you make and the actions you take... have consequences. Those consequences don't always affect you but anyone who might be standing in their way."

"You're right," Kate's head dropped. "If there is anything that I might do... speak to Detective Connolly or Chief Reynolds..."

"Oh, no. You have done quite enough, thank you," Officer Travis said. He cast a look that Kate had become familiar with seeing. The conversation was over. It was time for her to shuffle off.

With a nod, Kate turned and walked away from the young patrolman. Promptly plopping down in her assigned seat until Detective Connolly popped out from the row of interrogation rooms. With a quick beckon of his fingers, he requested she join him.

"Look," Connolly said, looking over Kate's shoulders as a team of attorneys filtered into the station. "Their focus is on Dane. Not much we can do about that. But we can take a whack at Karp and Trigg in the meantime."

"You want me to join you?" Kate asked, surprised at the request.

"They might tell you things they won't tell me," the detective admitted.

"I'll give it a shot," Kate agreed.

Without another word, Connolly turned and led Kate into a closed interrogation room. A tipsy Stacey Karp leaned back in her chair, a wide grin crossing her lips, "It's about time good cop arrived. 'Cause that guy is, *definitely* bad cop!"

Kate walked in and sat across from Stacey. Connolly sat on the far edge of the table.

Stacey's eyes grew, "Hey, I know you. You're the girl from the marina. And the vigil. You were at JoJo's vigil!"

Offering a nod and a friendly smile, Kate said, her voice soft, "That's right."

"What... what are you doing here?" Stacey winced.

"Ms. Harper was attacked in a manner similar to your friend Joann," Detective Connolly answered.

Stacey cocked her head, "You don't look dead. Oh, my God! Are you a ghost in like one of those detective shows... coming back to help solve the case?"

Kate looked confused and shook her head, "No. I got away."

"Oh," Stacey nodded. "*That* makes sense."

Connolly swallowed hard in frustration. Stacey's inebriated state made for a challenging interrogation. Moving the conversation along, he pressed, "The waitress serving you confirmed that you and Dane were never away from the table for more than a few minutes. Neither of you could have been involved in the attack on Ms. Harper. The question is, where did your buddy John Trigg go and when did he get back?"

Stacey looked at the detective and then at Kate, "Johnny's been real stressed lately. He sort of does that. Gets up and 'takes a break' as he calls it. I don't know. I think he was pining for JoJo. Dane thinks so too."

"You think John had feelings for Joann?" Kate asked.

"Well, yeah!" Stacey smiled. "Everyone could see that. In fact, he was going to ask Joann out. Dane had never paid her a second glance. When Johnny introduced everyone to her, it was game on. Dane doesn't like to lose those sorts of games."

Kate cocked her head, "How did *you* feel about that?"

Stacey paused for a moment to think about her response, "I was okay with it. I mean, Dane had a lot of oats to sow, right? I didn't want to be an oat, if you know what I mean."

"You wanted more," Connolly spat out the obvious, to the chagrin of both Stacey and Kate.

"Did you know Dane was going to propose?" Kate asked.

Despondence washed over Stacey Karp for a moment as she reflected, "Yeah. Dane told me. He seemed kind of... unsure about it, you know? I think I was kind of hoping the trip down here, getting away from home and letting out his wild side would fix that once and for all."

Kate and Detective Connolly shot quick glances at one another.

"What do you mean?" Kate pressed softly.

Stacey looked up at Kate, "JoJo was a sweetheart. Real sweet. She didn't like Dane's bad habits- at all. I think she wanted him to change and to a degree, he did when she was around. What I had hoped, was happening. Dane's impulsive risk taking and partying was taking its toll, until JoJo... until JoJo was killed."

"Could either of your friends have had anything to do with Joann's death?" Kate asked.

Stacey screwed her face, initially disturbed by the question. Frowning, she looked up, "A few weeks ago, I would have said no way. But now... I don't know."

"Assuming you had nothing to do with Joann's death, could Dane or John have murdered Joann Marrs?" Connolly asked, leaning into the table.

Trembling with her words, she coughed, "Dane... no. As much as it killed me, he loved JoJo. I get it. But John. I don't know. He's been so angry."

Stacey suddenly plunged her head down on the table.

Kate looked at Connolly who shrugged.

Moving around the table, the detective checked on Stacey Karp. Looking up at Kate, he said, "She's out."

"They were hitting it pretty hard when I was at the restaurant," Kate said.

"She certainly was not the one chasing you down the beach. From the waitress' statement, neither was Dane," Connolly said as he straightened up from checking on Stacey.

"That leaves John Trigg," Kate finished.

Connolly nodded. Escorting Kate to the door, he called for an officer to bring a paramedic in to check on Stacey. Moving across the hall, he opened the door to another interrogation room. A red-eyed John Trigg looked up from burying his head on the table. Unlacing his fingers from the back of his head, he sat up in his seat.

"You," Trigg's eyes narrowed.

Connolly and Kate reacted to the unwelcome tone dripping in John Trigg's voice.

"You seem upset to see Ms. Harper here," Detective Connolly acknowledged.

"Yeah," Trigg nodded. "She keeps showing up. Like some fan girl over JoJo's death. What's she doing here?"

"She was attacked tonight. On the same beach Joann was," Connolly declared.

Trigg looked at both Kate and the detective, his demeanor unchanged, "She's clearly okay. Did you finally catch the guy?"

Connolly looked at Trigg for a long minute, "Where were you when you left the table at the restaurant tonight?"

Trigg's eyes widened, "I see where this is going. Who told you I left the table? Dane? Stacey? What, they think I had something to do with it?"

"Just answer the question," Connolly pressed.

"I went for a smoke," Trigg shrugged his shoulders.

"By yourself? Did anyone else see you?" the detective asked.

Trigg flung his arms wide, "I don't know. I wasn't exactly looking for company! I just wanted to smoke in peace."

"You're frustrated with how easily Dane and Stacey are moving on, aren't you?" Kate blurted.

"We lost... someone special," John Trigg said.

"She was special, wasn't she? So sweet. So kind," Kate nodded. "How did you feel about Dane proposing to Joann?"

Trigg's head snapped up, "I was hoping she'd say 'no.'"

"And if she didn't?" Kate pressed.

Trigg's eyes squinted and trembled.

Looking away, his voice fell flat, "I'm pretty sure one of Smithfield's attorneys is supposed to be coming in here. I'm done."

"John, we can help you...," Detective Connolly started, wanting the conversation to continue without legal intervention.

"If you can't bring Jo back, then you can't really help me," Trigg snarled, once more burying his head on the table.

Connolly looked at Kate and nodded his head toward the door.

Stepping outside, just in time to see one of the fleet of Smithfield attorneys make their way to the interrogation room. "Both Mr. Trigg and Ms. Karp will be represented by us moving forward. They will be answering no questions without one of us present."

"Yeah," Connolly sighed. "I know the drill."

Kate stood by, watching the interaction.

When the attorney disappeared into Triggs' room, the detective gently pulled on Kate's arm, "Come on. Let's sort this out in my office."

With a nod, Kate allowed Connolly to lead her to his office and shut the door. Hands on his hips, the detective paced around the office. "I think we have narrowed in our suspect," Connolly said.

"Did you see his eyes?" Kate asked.

Connolly nodded, "They were pretty red. Like maybe he had to dig sand out of them."

"He doesn't seem like the type," Kate said.

"They often don't until they snap. He had motive. He had opportunity. No one can corroborate his whereabouts," Connolly added.

Kate frowned, "What about the night of Joann's murder?"

"They were allegedly all passed out on the yacht," Connolly said.

"Then how did Joann get across the island and end up on the beach that night?" Kate asked.

"Only two people know for sure. When we arrived to question them, they were all right where they said they were and looking every bit like the aftermath of a wild night," Connolly said.

"Even John Trigg?" Kate asked.

"They had to go below deck and wake him up. Karp and Smithfield were passed out on the top deck in lounge chairs," the detective replied.

Kate pondered the scenario, "Any one of them could have been salient enough to go to Treasure Island with Joann and get back before the others woke up the next morning."

Connolly looked at Kate, "Maybe a love-struck John Trigg, fueled with some liquid courage, decided to confess his feelings for Joann. Or at the very least, tried to dissuade her from marrying Smithfield."

"Maybe he didn't like the answer she gave him," Kate said, her voice trailing off as she imagined the scene. The scene that very well may have taken her life as well.

Thirty Nine

Nick was waiting for Kate as her new police escort drove her to the beach house. With a sheepish smile, Kate offered the handyman a cheery good morning.

Detective Connolly climbed out of the driver's seat and walked to the end of the driveway to confer with a patrolman who parked alongside the curb.

"What happened to Officer Travis?" Nick asked, noting a new officer was tasked with keeping watch on the impulsive woman.

Kate screwed her face, "Yeah, we aren't talking about that."

As Kate opened the beach house and disarmed the security system, Nick pressed, "Kate… what did you do?"

Pausing mid-span in the doorway, Kate looked up at Nick. Frowning as if to determine if she really wanted to volunteer her adventure from the previous evening. "I kind of snuck out of the hotel to spy on Dane Smithfield and his friends. Someone attacked me and chased me down the beach," Kate admitted.

"Someone attacked you!" Nick exclaimed, his expression a mix of concern and displeasure.

"Yeah," Kate's head bobbed. "Eerily down the same path that Joann Marrs did before she, well, you know."

Nick looked away, a hand on his forehead, "Because I told you they were at Caddy's…"

Kate nodded.

"Who attacked you?" Nick asked, his eyes fluttering into a heated glare.

"I don't know. I was pretty sure it was John Trigg," Kate said. Wandering toward the dining room, she set her bag down on the table.

"The boy wound so tight he looks like he could snap at any moment," Nick shook his head. Glancing out toward the driveway where Detective Connolly was speaking with the uniformed officer, he added, "I can understand why Connolly is now your personal escort. Surprised he didn't just toss you in jail."

"He thought about it," Kate said.

"I know I have played along, but Kate, it's time to listen to the detective. You need to back off. Let the police do their job," Nick said, his eyes searing into Kate's.

"I know. I know. I keep telling myself that, too. But then I have an idea and…," Kate started.

"And you rush off instead of sharing it with the police, like you should," Nick scolded.

Kate winced, "I don't want to send them on a goose chase."

"So, instead, you put yourself in danger, which ends up risking your life as well as the lives of others around you," Nick pressed.

"We're so close! I was able to talk with both Stacey and John at the police station…," Kate began.

Nick did a double take, "Detective Connolly let you speak to them after getting attacked by John Trigg?"

"He thought they might tell me things they wouldn't tell him. With the Smithfield super-attorneys outside the door, he didn't have a lot of time before they would be off limits," Kate shrugged.

"Here I thought the detective was annoying but sensible," Nick scoffed.

Kate scowled, "Don't you want to hear what I learned?"

"No, Kate. I want you to start being safe. Truth is, I like you. But I can't encourage you to put yourself in danger like this anymore," Nick said.

Kate, softened by Nick's words, seemed like she might drop the conversation when she suddenly perked up, "We were right, by the way."

"About what?"

"John Trigg was in love with Joann Marrs. Stacey wants Dane to herself," Kate said.

"And you were alone on the beach with either one of two people who are decidedly emotionally unstable, each with clear motive for murder and forced to kill again in the aftermath," Nick said, folding his arms in front of his chest.

Kate's face fell, "That's not how I was going to frame it, but yes."

Nick nodded silently. His expression declared his dissatisfaction with the conversation.

"You know," Kate slithered forward, placing her hands on Nick's forearms. "I wouldn't have to be alone if you were with me."

Nick looked into Kate's eyes, his heart lurching a few beats faster. For a moment, he seemed to consider the suggestion.

"Come on. We had so much fun together. And we were pretty good sleuths, too," Kate beamed.

Nick shook his head and dropped his arms, causing hers to fall to her sides.

"It was fun, Kate. But it's gone too far. You need to listen to the detective. Let me know when this is all over and I'll finish the work on the house," Nick brushed by, causing a stack of papers to fly into the air.

"Nick...Nick, I'm sorry," Kate called. Bending over to pick up the papers, her hand lighted on an article she had printed out on the Smithfields. The photo imbedded in the article gave her pause. Looking up, she watched as Nick slipped through the front door, letting it slam in his wake.

With a sigh, she stared down the hall. Shaking her head, she picked up the clipping. Torn between her thoughts on the case and chasing after Nick, the debate was settled when Detective Connolly appeared in the doorway.

A wry grin was painted on the detective's face, "Everything all right?"

Kate flitted her hand toward the door, "Nick is not... very happy with me."

"I can see that. He mumbled, 'she's all yours' when he stormed past me. Whatever that means," Connolly shared.

"I told him about last night," Kate said, wiping her hair off her forehead.

Connolly chuckled, "I understand why he's upset."

Kate shrugged.

"At least I finally have an ally in the keep Kate Harper safe battle," Connolly said.

"You've always had an ally in that one. I'm clearly not a compliant subject," Kate smiled meekly.

"No, no, you are not," Connolly agreed. Squinted, he nodded at her hand, "What's that?"

Kate looked at the Smithfield article, "Oh, this. It fell on the floor. But it got me thinking... is there any chance you'd take me by Driscoll's motel or at least peek at the evidence?"

"Now, why would I do that? That all sounds very much like you still being involved in the case," Connolly scowled.

"Yes, but under your direct supervision," Kate said. "And, Driscoll had discovered something that he clearly thought would resonate with me."

"Something that the murderer killed him to retrieve," Connolly reminded.

Kate nodded, "True, but there might be something that I see. I mean, I know I'm not a trained detective, but maybe that would be the value. Looking at the evidence through a new lens. It worked for interrogation room discussions."

The detective considered the proposition. Finally, he relented, "If I'm going to be stuck babysitting, I might as well be working on the case at the same time."

"Exactly!" Kate bounced.

Conolly shook his head, "You're kind of a pain."

Kate just smiled as she made her way to the door.

Forty

Detective Connolly opened the conference room door and begrudgingly let Kate in. Kate took a moment to gaze around the room. It had blossomed since the last time Kate saw it.

"Just don't... touch anything," Connolly demanded. "All of the physical evidence we picked up from Driscoll's motel and rental car is right here."

Kate circled the table. A pair of banker boxes held several baggies full of items. Most appeared benign.

Looking up at the detective, she cast an expectant glance, "Please?"

Connolly let out a sigh and nodded reluctantly, "Fine."

Kate eagerly dove into the contents of the first box. Pulling a stack of photos out first, she shuffled quickly through them. Photos of Vincent Aguilar at the vigil with closeups of his counterparts that were there with him lay on top. Driscoll followed the action of Dane Smithfield walking towards the beach being quickly trailed by one of Aguilar's men. A parting shot showed Aguilar and the rest of his crew descending the beach walkway on the opposite side of the lot.

Photos of Dan Huck lurking around the marina had notes of dates and times that preceded the thug's arrest by the police.

Connolly's phone buzzed in his pocket. Pulling it out, he glanced at the screen and then up at Kate, "You good on your own for a minute? I need to take this call."

Kate laughed softly, "Yes. I'll be right here with these two boxes. I promise."

"Jail cell. With your name on it…," the detective warned as he left the conference room.

Kate watched Connolly leave before digging in for the next handful of photos. This set gave her pause. Sifting through them, she saw herself and Nick sitting on her back porch watching the sun set. There was even a photo of the two of them straddling surfboards atop the swells. She sighed, "If you weren't gone, we'd have words over this, Mr. Driscoll."

In a way, she was glad the private investigator caught the moments. The photos brought a smile to Kate's lips despite the awkwardness of her time being recorded from the shadows.

Slipping the photos beneath the others, she continued pilfering the box. Shots of Dane Smithfield and his crew soaking in the sun on his father's yacht a mere day after his fiancé's death. Stacey Karp and John Trigg appeared like perfectly willing participants.

From the visit she made with Nick to the marina, she knew that John Trigg was not happy about the nonchalance of his friend's attitude following the loss of Joann, but he was decidedly more tolerant. That tolerance faded as the investigation into her death wore on. At first, Kate thought it was because Trigg had doubts as to his friend's innocence. Now Kate was more convinced it was the heavy burden of guilt pressing on him with each passing day.

More shots of the vigil lined the bottom of the first evidence box. Shots of Kate and Nick and of Dane's and Stacey's words of memorial and the families. The Smithfield family dutifully receiving the guests was quickly followed by Joann Marrs' mother's outburst. Something about that photo tugged at her, but she couldn't quite figure it out. Looking closer, she saw John Trigg in the background, a half-smile on his face as the Smithfields were verbally assaulted by Joann's family.

Setting the photo aside, Kate began rummaging through the second box. Pulling out the evidence baggies one at a time, she inspected the items before cataloging them in her mind.

The door opened and Connolly stepped back in, "Finding anything?"

Kate looked up, "I'm not sure. This photo of Joann Marrs' mother tearing into the Smithfields… You see who is in the background looking like he's enjoying it?"

Connolly picked up the photo and studied it, "John Trigg."

The detective shuffled through the photos. Finding a set showing the Smithfields and their friends climbing into their limousines, Driscoll's camera focus trailed Dane in favor of another subject. "Driscoll was all over John Trigg."

"That was not long before he called me to meet him," Kate said.

"And was killed," Connolly reminded.

Kate clapped the sides of the second evidence box, "He has evidence on John Trigg. I'm sure of it."

Retrieving a pack of digital media drives, she held them up, a question in her eyes.

"Backup drives. You link them to your phone if you want a local copy of something. We use them in the field to catalog evidence. We typically have a cloud-based backup," the detective shared.

Kate noted one was missing, "Did you happen to find the other one?"

Connolly shook his head, "No. We searched his hotel room, his car and his clothes carefully. I'm afraid that may have been what got him killed."

"Oh," Kate nodded, crestfallen. Her eyes brightened, "Did he have a cloud backup like you have? Maybe…"

"He did, but it wasn't automatic. There was nothing in his cloud storage that struck out to us. Whatever he had was probably on his phone and on that backup drive," Connolly said.

"And the murderer has both," Kate added.

The detective nodded, "Probably."

"What's this?" Kate produced a sticky note with '310 G's' scribbled on it.

"Street value of the ring. Over three hundred thousand reasons to commit murder," Connolly said.

Kate frowned, "I thought the ring was worth over a million?"

"Sure," Connolly laughed. "If you bought it legally. Most likely, the diamonds would have to be separated and sold on their own. Still worth a good haul, but not the full value of the ring."

With a disappointed frown, Kate continued her search. Pulling out a baggy full of receipts, she held them up, for the detective to see.

Connolly shrugged, "Random cash receipts from a convenience store."

Kate studied them closer, "Cigarettes, water, sunglasses…nothing special."

"All cash. I figured they were Driscoll's for tax write-off or reimbursement," Connolly nodded.

At the end of the evidence box, Kate played with the receipts thoughtfully.

"What?" Connolly asked.

"Did you check at the convenience store… to see if they recognized any of the suspects?" Kate asked.

"I showed the clerk photos of Dan Huck and Vinnie Aguilar, our lead suspects at the time, but they didn't register. It was a leap any ways as they most likely belonged to Driscoll," Connolly said.

Kate pulled out her phone and scrolled through her map. Squinting, she said, "There are at least two convenient stores closer to his motel."

"Yeah, but this one was closer to your beach house," Connolly reasoned.

Kate nodded. Her face screwed into a question, "You never showed them pictures of Dane, John and Stacey?"

Connolly chewed his lip. With a shrug, he said, "Let's check it out. If someone at the convenience store can point to Trigg, we'll have him in the locale the night of Joann's murder. We'd have clear opportunity."

Snatching the baggie of receipts from the smug Kate Harper, Detective Connolly headed for the door, "Let's go!"

Connolly parked his unmarked police cruiser in front of the convenience store. Wading between flip-flop and suntan lotion-adorned shoppers, many with fists full of beer cases, they entered the small beach shop.

The clerk behind the counter waved as he looked up from counting change for a customer, "Be with you in a minute, Detective!"

Kate and Detective Connolly filtered in, waiting behind the small line of patrons waiting to check out their snacks, beverages and suntan lotion. Kate watched as the detective instinctively cased the convenience store, eyeing cameras, entrances, exits and the shoppers themselves.

When they approached the clerk, he smiled, "Did you catch the guy? Been watchin' on the news. Was hoping I could be helpful."

"Sometimes ruling suspects out is as helpful as ruling them in," Connolly informed the clerk. "I have a few more photos for you to review. Have you seen any of these people in the store over the past week, most likely in the evening hours?"

"Well, I'm here most nights. My weekends are typically midweek," the clerk said as he reached for the phone.

Connolly pulled it back, "I'll scroll through it. You just let me know if any of these people are familiar."

The detective took his time with photos of all three of Joann Marrs' friends. The clerk leaned in. Scrunching his face, he considered each photo, even as they included the same person before them. Finally, he shook his head, "Nope. If they ever came in, it wasn't while I was here. Like I said, evening and night shift hours, I'd have seen them."

"What about those cameras?" Connolly waved his phone at the security cameras in each corner of the store.

"Yeah, about them," the clerk leaned over the counter to get close to Connolly and Kate. In a whisper, he shared, "Between you and me, they ain't worked in at least two years. The owner was supposed to move to one of those fancy wireless models where your stuff is in the sky. But nope. They are there for show."

"I see. Well, thank you for your help in any case," Connolly said.

"You bet! Glad to help anytime. This your rookie detective you got following you around?" the clerk pointed at Kate.

"Yeah," Connolly nodded as a line began to form behind them. "Something like that."

"Good luck, Detective!" the clerk called as he started swiping items across the counter to ring up for the next customer.

"Well, that was a bust," Kate said, as they walked out of the store.

"It doesn't mean much. Just not a confirmed sighting of John Trigg... or Smithfield or Karp, that's all. They could have been here. They might not have. Could just have been Driscoll after all, which is still my theory," the detective said as he opened the door to his police cruiser.

Kate was nearly pouting in the passenger seat, "Investigating is a tedious process."

"You're telling me. It's best served by the professionals," Connolly said, shooting Kate a look across the cab of the cruiser.

Forty One

Detective Connolly checked a message that pinged on his phone as he drove away from the convenience store. Glancing over toward Kate, he said, "Looks like we need to make a quick stop."

"I'm a captive audience," Kate sang as she held her hands out.

Connolly gave an absent nod as he turned the unmarked police car south on Gulf Boulevard.

Watching the hotels, shops and restaurants flow by outside her window, Kate enjoyed the moment to appreciate the coastal community. Her wild, at times terrifying, visit aside, Treasure Island and the surrounding St. Pete Beach stretches along the shoreline were amazing places to visit.

From the passenger seat, Kate had the luxury of watching families walking hand-in-hand as they marched in flip-flops and bathing suits for a day at the beach or a retreat to a hotel pool. One thing was consistent amongst the families, they all wore bold smiles with worries of whatever work, school or life stressors completely melted away in the golden Florida sun.

Her gazing was cut short as Detective Connolly wheeled the cruiser into the parking lot of the Don Cesar Hotel. Kate's eyes brightened at the chance to see the case progress while in tow.

Connolly put the car into park and looked over at Kate, "You are my shadow. You stand behind me. You don't say a word. You don't ask questions. Don't even smile."

Kate gave the detective a blank stare.

"Alternatively, I can place you in you cuffs and lock you in the back seat," the detective warned.

"My lips are sealed, and I'll do my best to only give stern, stoic detective faces," Kate promised.

Connolly shook his head and grumbled, "I don't know why I do this to myself."

Kate got out of the car. Glancing over at Detective Connolly, she did her best to match his scowl.

Rolling his eyes, Connolly led her inside the hotel. The doorman was prompt as ever, swinging the doors open as the pair passed through the pink arches of the entrance. With a nod of gratitude, the detective ripped off his sunglasses and focused his eyes on the interior of the grand hotel.

"Detective Connolly," a sharp-dressed man strode forward and received the Treasure Island policeman. Kate recognized the man as one of Smithfield's attorneys. Holding his hand out for the detective to follow, he invited, "Right this way."

Connolly followed the man into a conference room. The detective shot Kate a quick glance and motioned for a set of chairs opposite the conference room door. "Don't move from that spot."

Kate offered the detective a tight-lipped shrug as she followed his instructions and plopped down into what she found to be remarkably comfortable chairs. Hands cupping the ends of the armrests, Kate gave a smile as the door closed, separating her from the wary detective.

Settling into the chair of the posh hotel, Kate tapped her fingers as she watched the guests enjoying their holidays. Some shuffled off like those Kate watched on the drive in, intent on the expansive white sand beach or a pool. Others were sleuthing through the hotel in search of a mimosa or tropical concoction.

One guest who was slithering through the crowd wore a demeanor that stood out from the others who were enjoying their day caught Kate's attention. With a glance toward the closed conference room door, her tapping fingers increased their tempo against the arm of the chair. Cocking her head, she slowly rose from the chair. Giving a final look at the conference room, she walked swiftly down the hall where the individual that caught her eye had disappeared.

Turning the corner, she was just able to see the person step out onto the hotel patio. Hurrying after, she reached the exterior door. Swinging her head to the left and then the right, she squinted to relocate her target.

The expanse of the patio that stretched toward the pool and the beach was clear. The steps down to the lawn were the only direction the person could have gone. In a rush, Kate swooped down the steps and turned along a path flanked by well-manicured bushes and tropical plants.

Rounding the corner, she found she had closed the distance. "John! John Trigg!" she called out.

The young man froze. Pivoting on his heel, he saw Kate, pursuing him.

"I just want to talk with you," Kate said, taking a few steps forward.

Trigg's eyes drew wide in alarm. As Kate closed in, he lurched, brushing past her, knocking her to the ground. In a rush, he was gone, back up the steps they had just descended.

Shaking off the surprise, Kate sprung to her feet. Dusting herself off, she was more determined than ever. Sprinting, she launched herself up the steps and scanned the massive patio. It didn't take her long to find the person she was looking for. Leaning against the rail, staring out at the Gulf was John Trigg.

Striding steadfastly forward, Kate made her way to the rail. Standing a few lengths from John Trigg, she realized the boy's face was buried in his hands.

"John…," Kate called out softly.

Trigg lifted his head. His red eyes were glaring at Kate in anger. He appeared visibly unsure of how to respond. Suddenly, he spat, "Why don't you just leave me alone!"

Kate took a step back.

"I'm sorry," Trigg said.

Kate looked unsure, trying to calculate what he was apologizing for, attacking her on the beach or lashing out.

"I'm sorry I knocked you down," John Trigg clarified. "I wish this trip never happened."

Suddenly, his angry eyes were flushed with tears as he doubled over, facing the Gulf. "I… I loved her so much. Why did this have to happen?"

Kate took a careful step forward.

"You cared for her. For Joann," Kate reasoned.

John shot Kate a shocked look, "I *loved* her!"

Kate watched him for a few moments. She began to see something in him, in his reactions. "You didn't kill her."

Trigg's eyes flashed wide, "I would never hurt JoJo. Ever."

Nodding, Kate soothed, "I can see that."

"I don't… I wish I knew," Trigg balled his hands into fists.

"You don't?" Kate asked.

Trigg shook his head, "No."

"John, could it have been Dane?" Kate asked.

Trigg looked at her for a moment before he answered, "Dane could be a bit of a jerk. JoJo deserved better. But he did love her in his own way. For better or worse, he knew she loved him. Taking that ring could have gotten him black-balled by the family. He chose her over everything being a Smithfield afforded him, which, as you have seen, is quite a lot."

Kate looked at Trigg with a calculated, cautious look, "What about Stacey?"

John Trigg's face twisted and he shook his head, "Stacey is… She has her issues. She always thought she should have been with Dane. But, I can't imagine her killing Jo. They were like sisters. Fought like sisters sometimes, as much as JoJo fought with anybody, at least. But they loved each other like sisters, too."

Kate nodded. She mulled the fact that they were right the entire time. Dan Huck was who killed Joann. Aguilar went after Driscoll for reasons separate from the case.

Trigg frowned at Kate, "The police have the guy. Why are you asking these questions?"

Kate considered her response and decided to weigh the young man's response, "Someone attacked me the other night. In very much the same manner that Joann was attacked. Something doesn't add up."

"I'm sorry that happened to you. It wasn't me," John Trigg reported, his voice calm.

Kate watched his eyes. She was no police profiler, but he seemed sincere.

"Thank you for taking the time to talk to me. Again, I'm very sorry for your loss," Kate said.

Trigg offered her a kind nod before returning his gaze to the Gulf as he leaned over the rail.

Kate spun to head back toward the hotel. A man in sunglasses, his forearms crossed tight across his chest, staring at her.

With a quick smile and wave of her fingers, Kate walked across the terrace toward an unhappy Detective Connolly.

"I just got out of a meeting with some of the country's fiercest attorneys on how we are not to question any of the Smithfields or their friends without their presence," Connolly said, whipping off his sunglasses so that Kate could see the ire in his eyes. "And here I find you speaking with one of those friends instead of sitting in the chair that I asked you to remain in."

"I had to pee and we just ran into each other?" Kate shrugged meekly.

"Let's get out of here before we are both sitting across the aisle from them in court," Connolly said, directing Kate toward the exit.

"On the plus side, I don't think John Trigg murdered Joann Marrs," Kate said softly as they walked along the perimeter of the hotel.

"You found evidence of this? In the ten minutes I was in the meeting with the attorneys?" Connolly pressed.

"He seemed sincere. I don't think he did it. He doesn't see either Dane or Stacey doing it either, but the jury is still out on them," Kate said.

The detective paused to look directly at Kate, "That's the thing, Kate. You aren't a jury. Your *feelings* on the case don't really matter."

"Aw, come on, Detective," Kate said. "You have to admit, I have been helpful at times on this case."

"At times. This, steps away from the Smithfield's attorneys sharing some heartfelt message from a desperate suspect isn't one of those times," Conolly said, returning his gait to the parking lot.

Kate mulled her conversation with John Trigg in silence. She was so sure John had attacked her on the beach. His deep pain and anger could easily be masking a murderer's guilt, yet somehow, she found the conversation convincing. Looking at Detective Connolly, she reasoned he was right. She had no expertise in deciphering truth from lies in someone who was a suspect in a murder case.

Sighing as she climbed into the angry detective's car, she was more confused than ever. All of the suspects were still in play. They all had reasons to indicate that they weren't the killer. Yet, they all had motives for murder as well.

Forty Two

Detective Connolly pulled his car into Kate's driveway. "I have to run papers back to the station. I'll be back in half an hour. I mean it, Kate. If you leave this property, I will arrest you. I mean it this time," the detective warned.

Kate nodded, her mind clearly elsewhere.

"Kate…!" Connolly snapped.

Shaking her head, Kate said, "Yes. Property… arrest… for real this time."

"Yeah," the detective sighed. "Go inside. Work on the house. Pour a glass of wine and enjoy the view, like normal people."

"Okay," Kate assured. "I won't go anywhere."

"Thank you," Connolly said, shifting the car into gear and pulling away from the curb.

Wandering into the beach house, Kate's mind was still working overtime.

John Trigg's defense of himself and of his friends seemed in earnest. Dane risking his status in the family by bringing the heirloom wedding ring to Florida was a different spin on his act. It was one more out of love and hope than defiance.

The thought struck Kate as she laid her purse on the kitchen counter. If Dane ran the possibility of getting kicked out of the family for taking the ring, who would have been so riled up to take action?

Wandering into the dining room, Kate gazed at the wall of photos and notes. Studying a picture of the Smithfield family, Beau, the patriarch, standing tall in the very front of the photo. The rest of the Smithfield family filled in around Beau, Dane looking aloof and disinterested.

Suddenly, her eyes widened. Muttering to herself, she asked, "I wonder if Frank Driscoll figured something out about the family or perhaps Beau himself, the night of the vigil. What did you find, Frank? What did you want to show me?"

Kate thought of Driscoll's items Detective Connolly allowed her to sort through. The missing data drive. That could be the key. Kate wondered if he had it on him the night she was supposed to meet him. If he did, she assumed it was in the hands of the killer.

She thought of the sticky note and recreated it, posting it to her evidence wall. *310 G's.* The ring would have fetched a hefty payday, but it was lost only to fall into her possession on the beach and ultimately given to the police as evidence.

Looking at the note, she crumpled it up. It wasn't as she remembered it. Rewriting it more carefully, her heart skipped a beat. She had a new theory.

Dialing Detective Connolly, she got his voicemail. Pondering what to say, she decided it wasn't worth leaving a message on a hunch. Looking at her phone, she considered calling Nick. Looking at his contact page, her thumb hovered over the call button.

Shaking her head, she decided on a long shot, scouring her beach house. Starting with the driveway, she studied the beach house from Frank Driscoll's perspective the evening he was killed. Starting toward the front porch, she paused at the first step. Pivoting, she walked around the edge of the house.

Studying the walkway along the side of the house, she tried to imagine the limitations of the security cameras at night. With deep trepidation, Kate made her way to the spot where she and Nick had found Driscoll's body.

Wincing, she turned away from the awful memory before dutifully returning her gaze to the spot. The shell border used along the house still had deep depressions from when the private investigator had fallen and grasped at his last moments of life.

Kate shook her head at the senselessness of the act and similarly the murder of Joann Marrs. One of the impressions in the shells caught her eye. Near what would have been Driscoll's furthest outstretched hand as he suffered the bludgeoning, deep in the shadows of the corner of the beach house, a mound of shells looked ever so unnaturally bunched. Kneeling down, Kate carefully sifted through the top layers of the shells with her finger until she hit something different. Pausing to take a photo of the spot before she disturbed the scene any further, she dusted away the shells until she revealed a small piece of plastic.

Pinching the plastic in her fingers, she pulled it out of the shell border. Holding it in front of her eyes, she gently shook it, "Driscoll's data drive."

A crunch of shells behind her sent a chill down her spine. Without turning, she drew a deep breath as her mind fought fight-or-flight instincts.

"I have been looking for that," a voice said from behind her, protruding from the bushes on the edge of the beach house property.

"I really need to have those bushes cut down," Kate gasped. Turning her head, she looked up at a palm thrust toward her, beckoning her to hand the data drive over. In Geoffrey Smithfield's other hand was a section of two-by-four.

Gripping the drive, Kate slowly spun on her heel to face her assailant. "It was all about family honor and who deserved a prized family heirloom," Kate said.

"Just give me the drive-," Geoffrey scowled.

"No matter what you did, how you performed, how perfect you were, Dane always found a way to steal the moment. Or, in the unfortunate case of Joann Marrs, steal a prized family ring," Kate continued.

"You really, *really* need to learn to mind your business," Geoffrey menaced by tapping the piece of lumber against his palm as he eyed Kate.

"You were a star baseball player, too. You were the athlete, the academic, the country club choir boy and even followed in your father's footsteps for the family business. You were going to get what you deserved, of course, except for what Dane *took* from you," Kate pressed.

"I get enough of that in the press. I don't need it from you. Now hand me what that sleazy investigator hid from me," Geoffrey took a step forward, wielding the board high in the air.

"This? This is just the tip of the iceberg. Even without it, I have evidence you were in town, the day *before* Joann Marrs was murdered," Kate stated.

"Enough!" Smithfield growled, lunging forward, the two-by-four arching through the air, narrowly missing Kate's head as she rolled backward and onto her feet.

Scrambling, Kate raced away from Geoffrey as a second swing grazed her shoulder.

Sprinting after her, Geoffrey growled, "I'll just take it from your dead body!"

Kate could feel Smithfield on her heels. She could see the shadow of the two-by-four splashed against the wall of the beach house as the murderer closed in. Dashing alongside the wooden walkway that led to the beach, Kate rushed for the dunes.

Glancing over her shoulder, she saw Geoffrey closing in for another strike. Turning to focus on her only hope to get away, she collided with a body that wrapped its arms around her.

Strong hands held her tight and spun her out of the way of a strike from Smithfield. Instead, the board was caught by a powerful fist. Releasing Kate, Nick Mason squared up to Geoffrey Smithfield as they struggled to control the makeshift weapon.

With two hands grasping the piece of lumber, Smithfield celebrated with a grin as he leveraged the weapon away. His grin slipped away as Nick thrust a leg out, kicking Smithfield in the gut and sending him reeling backward.

Planting his feet, Geoffrey readied for another attack. Nick stood with a hand thrust out toward Kate, keeping her away from the fight. His other hand was poised to block the next swing from the attacker's board.

Shifting his hands to hold the timber like a baseball bat, Smithfield moved in, undaunted. With a mighty swoosh, the board arched in the air. Nick dodged the first blow only to be struck with a thrust of the two-by-four in the ribs. Taking a step back while nudging Kate further toward the dunes, Nick suddenly dove forward, driving his shoulder into Geoffrey's midsection, knocking both men to the ground.

The two-by-four fell to the sand while the two men grappled. Smithfield kicked and punched in a frenzy wriggling away from Nick as both men returned to their feet. Taking a wild swing, Smithfield missed. Countering, Nick hit Geoffrey Smithfield square in the jaw, sending him sprawling back to the ground.

To Nick's chagrin, Smithfield fell within easy reach of the improvised weapon. With a wicked smirk, Smithfield stood, two by four, once more in hand, ready to levy another strike.

"Enough!" a voice shouted. "Uhm, Geoffrey Smithfield, you're under arrest?"

"For the murders of Joann Marrs and Frank Driscoll," Kate added, striding forward.

Smithfield spun with his hands in the air. Seeing a police pistol aimed directly at him, he dropped the board.

"On your knees, Smithfield!" Detective Connolly ordered. Walking forward, he kicked the board out of Geoffrey Smithfield's reach and placed cuffs around the young man's wrists.

With a glance at Nick and Kate, he asked, "You two all right?"

Kate and Nick nodded.

Standing Smithfield up, Connolly gave him a slight shove toward a pair of policemen. "Take him to the car. I need to piece all of this together," the detective commanded.

Facing the pair turned spectator, Connolly asked, "Anyone want to clue me in on what is going on around here?"

Forty Three

With Geoffrey Smithfield safely in custody, Detective Connolly paced, arms folded, in front of Kate and Nick. "I saw that you called. When you didn't leave a message, I figured that could only mean you would be up to something," the police detective said.

Kate wrinkled her nose and smiled, "I didn't leave the property…"

The detective didn't appear to be in the mood for Kate's attempt at humor. Looking at Nick, he asked, "How did you happen to be here, Mason?"

"I was heading to go surfing when I got a call from Kate. At first, I thought she had pocket-dialed me, but then I heard Smithfield threatening her in the background. I rushed over in time to find Kate being chased by Geoffrey Smithfield with a two-by-four in hand," Nick explained.

Turning back to Kate, Connolly said, "I was gone for less than forty minutes…"

"Something that John Trigg said got me thinking. Who valued that ring more than a thief?" Kate asked.

"I don't know, three hundred thousand dollars sounds like a lot of value to me," Connolly shrugged.

Kate grinned, snapping her fingers at the detective, "310 G's wasn't three hundred and ten thousand dollars. The apostrophe was an errant mark. I realized that when I recreated the sticky note. It was 3-10 G.S. March tenth, Geoffrey Smithfield."

"Geoffrey Smithfield was in town the day before Joann Marrs was murdered!" Connolly understood what Kate was suggesting and why it might be damning enough for Geoffrey Smithfield to prevent that from getting out.

"While everyone thought he was in Charleston until the family came down for the vigil," Nick added as he listened to Kate's logic.

Kate handed Driscoll's data drive to the police detective, "I think you will find evidence of that on this drive. It was buried in the shells that border the house. I had just found it when Geoffrey Smithfield crept up behind me. I took a picture of it for your evidence, I can send it to you. That is how I was able to dial Nick. I already had the phone out."

"I'm glad you did," Nick said.

"I'm glad you came," Kate laughed.

"You're sure about all of this?" Connolly asked.

"I wasn't a hundred percent until Geoffrey attacked me. He kind of confirmed my suspicions for me. That's why I didn't leave a message for you. I didn't want you to think it was another goose chase," Kate said. "There's more. I think there is, anyway. If you check the dates on the receipts you found Driscoll was holding on to, I think you'll find the dates align to March tenth as well."

"I never showed the convenience store clerks *Geoffrey* Smithfield's picture," Detective Connolly admitted. He looked thoughtfully in the direction his officers took Geoffrey Smithfield, "He traveled with cash, showed back up in Charleston in time to receive the horrible news with his family and traveled back down here when they arrived for the vigil. Clever."

"Not clever enough to get past Kate," Nick grinned.

"Or Frank Driscoll," Kate said, a twinge of sadness in her voice.

Connolly held up the device that Kate retrieved, "So, what is on this exactly?"

"Honestly, I have no idea," Kate shrugged, a wry smile seeping through her lips. "I can't wait to find out when you open it up back at the station."

Connolly's head drooped at the prospect of Kate's continued presence on the case.

"You have to record my official statement anyway," Kate pressed.

"You'll need mine, too," Nick nodded, stepping closer to Kate.

Shaking his head, the police detective breathed, "Fine. With any luck, I'll be done with you very soon. *Both* of you."

With a glance toward Nick, Connolly asked, "Can you drive her to the station?"

Nick nodded.

"Don't open that without me!" Kate sang. Her request wasn't met with a response as the detective walked away.

Nick turned his attention to Kate, "I don't want to imagine what would have happened if I didn't make it here in time."

Kate squared up to him, stretching up so that their eyes were locked, "You don't have to. You *did* make it here in time."

Nick placed his hands gently on Kate's arms. Taking a step back, he inspected her, "Are you sure you're okay?"

"You caught more the brunt of Geoffrey's fury than I did," Kate said. "Are *you* okay?"

Pulling her close, Nick sighed, "I am, now."

The police station was already buzzing with heightened activity when Kate and Nick arrived. Detective Connolly met them in the lobby and ushered them towards his office, "We don't have a lot of time before the legal team and media circuses show up."

Slipping into his office and closing the door, Connolly confirmed, "I already sent an officer to the convenience store with Geoffrey's picture. The clerk identified him and remembered Smithfield being there. He remembered because he had to break a hundred-dollar bill. They usually don't do that unless it is a large purchase. The clerk said Smithfield grabbed a few more items and said to keep the change."

Kate looked expectantly at Connolly. The detective continued, "That was March 10th. The clerk was able to pull receipts for one-hundred-dollar bills, and that was the last one they had taken in."

Slipping the data drive into his computer, Connolly opened up the files on the data drive. Scanning, he pulled up images that were stored in a folder. "Private flight ledgers from a flight chartered March 10th from Charleston to St. Pete-Clearwater. The only passenger, Geoffrey Smithfield," the detective read.

Clapping her hands, Kate squealed, "We got him!"

The detective bobbed his head, "We have enough to hold him. Outside of attacking you, we don't have enough evidence to convict him of Joann Marrs' or Frank Driscoll's murders. We can prove he was in the area, so we have opportunity. He has a clear motive. He used a similar weapon against you as was used on Joann Marrs and Frank Driscoll."

"The weapon!" Nick pointed at the police detective. "When I was fighting with Smithfield, I noticed imperfections in the wood where he had been gripping it."

"Let's take a look," Connolly shrugged. Leading them to the conference room where evidence was being cataloged, he found the two-by-four retrieved at Kate's beach house that afternoon. Holding the wood up to the light, he saw several little divots in the wood, just as Nick had mentioned.

"Geoffrey Smithfield wears a big class ring…," Kate mused.

"It's pretty soft wood. That could do it, especially the way he was gripping it," Nick said.

"We never found the weapon at the other scenes, including your beach house," Connolly said.

Nick's eyes went wide as he smacked his forehead, "You didn't find the weapon that killed Driscoll because Smithfield dumped it with the scrap wood in my pickup truck."

Connolly became uncharacteristically animated at the prospect, "Are you sure?"

"No, but if he doubled back around the bushes after Kate and I arrived, he would have walked right past as he fled the scene," Nick said.

"Let's go take a look," the detective said.

Marching out to the parking lot, they watched as a procession of limousines arrived. Several men and women in luxurious suits climbed out. Pausing as they eyed the detective climbing into the back of a pickup, they shook their heads and proceeded inside the police station.

Connolly quickly pulled out his phone, his thumb hammering on his text keys before resuming the search. Focusing on boards that were a reasonable length to wield as a weapon, they inspected each end of the boards on all four sides.

"I got it!" Kate squealed as she held the board on a line in front of her eyes. "Just like the one in the evidence room."

Connolly and Nick leaned in, both nodding as they saw the markings that Kate had identified.

"Uh, Detective…" Nick pointed at a single piece of hair wedged into a splinter on the opposite end of the board as the markings.

Connolly grinned, "I'll bet dollars to donuts that belonged to Frank Driscoll."

The detective looked at Kate and Nick, "We got him."

Forty Four

Kate and Nick stood glued to the one-way mirror.

Detective Connolly entered the room and sat across from Geoffrey Smithfield. Flanked by a pair of lawyers, the troubled young man looked less like a vicious killer and more like a child who disappointed their parents. His eyes cast down at the table where his hands were cuffed. He scarcely looked up when the police detective addressed him.

"Geoffrey, you're aware of the charges filed against you. The murder of Joann Marrs. The murder of Frank Driscoll. Two counts of attempted murder against Kate Harper. The full list of additional crimes associated with the primary charges fills up those folders in front of your attorneys," Connolly laid out the groundwork for their deposition. "Anything you want to say before we begin?"

Both attorneys shook their heads as they glanced at Geoffrey, who waved them off.

"I'm sorry," Smithfield choked, his eyes never leaving the grain of the wood on the table he had locked onto.

"We advise you to remain silent, Geoffrey. You don't need to say *anything*," one of the attorneys snapped.

Lifting his head, Geoffrey said clearly as he looked at Detective Connolly through twitching, watery eyes, "It's my fault. I did all of it. It wasn't supposed to happen this way. None of it."

Both attorneys slumped in their chairs. One flung her hands in the air as she realized there was no reeling Geoffrey back in.

"I noticed Dane was acting strangely before their Florida trip-well, stranger than usual," Geoffrey said, his voice soft and clear. "I followed him to Dad's office. I watched him get into the safe, but I didn't see what he took. I figured cash, credit cards, whatever he needed to fund his 'Dane Gone Wild' trip with his friends."

Glancing at his irate attorneys, Geoffrey returned his emotional gaze to the detective, "When he left, I went back and checked myself. It took me a bit to figure out what was missing. I realized it was Grandma's ring. It was a huge symbol for our family. She was beloved and had a way of keeping everyone else straight."

"Clearly, when she passed, the family lost a bit of that moral compass. I was furious. Of all the things Dane had done, this was over the top. At first, I figured he was going to sell it. I found a few crumpled notes in his wastebasket. He was compiling his thoughts on proposing to Joann. He was going to use Grandma's ring... It was going to be *my* ring to give when I got married," Geoffrey continued.

With an arm flung across their client's chest like a parent who slammed on the brakes, the female attorney pressed, "*Mr. Smithfield*, I strongly recommend we confer prior to saying anything else in regard to this case!"

Geoffrey's head turned slowly to look at his attorney. Offering only a brief, blank stare, he returned his attention to Detective Connolly, "I truly didn't know what I was going to do. I was mad. I just wanted that ring back. I didn't want to get Dad involved. Who knows how that would have played out? So, I chartered a flight, paid with cash. I planned on having it out with Dane. But, it's Dane… On the flight, I figured out a new plan, a better plan. It should have all worked out," Geoffrey said.

Eyeing a water glass on the table, he asked, "May I?"

Connolly nodded. Reaching across the table, he slipped his key into Smithfield's cuffs and freed his wrists.

"Thank you," Geoffrey drained the glass quickly.

"Mr. Smithfield… Geoffrey, please stop… talking," the lawyers pleaded.

Setting the glass down, Geoffrey cleared his throat and continued, "Joann was a sweet girl. She was good for Dane. If he grew up at all, she might have been *great* for him. Never meeting parents' standards, but good for Dane. I knew she wouldn't want to accept a ring that was stolen. Instead of going after Dane, I reached out to Joann. I told her about the ring and she agreed to meet me. She slipped out when the evening's partying died down and met me on the beach, away from Dane and the rest of his friends. She was supposed to give me the ring."

The male attorney slapped his hands down on the table, "Detective, our client is clearly distraught and is in no mind to be making a statement right now. I demand time to consult with Mr. Smithfield before we continue!"

"If that is what Mr. Smithfield wishes. How about it, Geoffrey? What happened after you arranged to meet with Joann Marrs?" Connolly pressed.

Swallowing hard, Geoffrey said, "She met me, just as we planned. She opened the box to show me and… it was beautiful-dazzling in the moonlight. She closed her eyes and then pulled her hand back. I didn't understand at first. She said it could be life-changing for Dane to get married. She was worried that breaking his trust might set him off on a downward spiral."

"I got angry," Geoffrey shrugged. "I told her to give it to me. She backed off. I must have scared her because she took off running. I took off after her. Catching up to her at the beach access, I reached out for her. She tripped. Hitting her head on the corner of a steel dumpster, she started bleeding. So much blood, but she was still alive. I reached for my phone to call for help. As I stared at the screen, I saw the photo of my parents... That's my background. It wasn't going to go over well. I panicked. I just wanted her to be quiet. To stay quiet. I hit her."

Geoffrey dropped his head into his hands as he began to sob. "I found a piece of wood and I just kept hitting her until she lie still. I stopped. She was dead. I started to discard the piece of wood, but I realized I shouldn't. I searched for the ring. By the time I realized it was gone, the headlights of a car came into view and I ran. Tossing the wood into a discard pile over a construction fence, I ran."

Smithfield looked up at the detective. "I looked for the ring. I thought maybe that lady at the beach house had it. Then I realized she may have seen me and Joann. I had to go home and act like everything was normal, so I hired Dan Huck to case the beach house and look for the ring. When I learned it was turned in to the police as evidence, I sent Dan to rob the yacht. I knew that fool would leave a trail," Smithfield shook his head.

"It all would have worked if it wasn't for the P.I. and that nosy woman," Geoffrey Smithfield said.

Detective Connolly looked intently at Geoffrey as the attorneys pouted, their backs pressed back into their seats, "To be clear, you just confessed to murder and conspiracy for multiple other crimes."

"Yeah," Geoffrey nodded. "All because my brother couldn't help but to take things that weren't his. Things that he didn't deserve. I did everything right and yet somehow, he just got to keep taking."

"You did everything right until the night on the beach," Connolly corrected.

"Yes, until then," Smithfield said softly as he dropped his head.

Forty Five

"So, it's all over," Kate breathed as Detective Connolly stood on her front porch to deliver the news the district attorney had accepted Geoffrey Smithfield's confession.

"It's all over," the detective nodded.

Kate scrunched her nose, "So tragic. Seemed like he might have been a nice kid."

"Wound a little tight," Nick added.

Connolly agreed, "Followed huge family expectations while his brother enjoyed life with none. Dane walking away with their grandmother's ring was the last straw for Geoffrey."

"A ring that Geoffrey assumed would be *his* wife's one day since he was the dutiful 'good' kid," Nick said.

"For Geoffrey, it was like a crown. One that he thought he had earned," the detective nodded.

"What happens now?" Kate asked.

"We'll proceed to put the evidence, witness statements and the case together as if he hadn't confessed. I think a psych eval is in the cards for Geoffrey. He'll likely spend the rest of his life locked up in a secure mental health institution or a prison," Connolly said. He looked at Kate and at her beach house, a site that had been beleaguered with trouble over the unfolding of the case. "You get to finish putting this place together without fear of shadows lurking outside your window."

"That'll be a nice relief," Kate smiled. "I'm grateful for both of you through all of this. Keeping me safe."

"Despite everything you did to get into trouble," Connolly frowned. "Sometimes, when you see that string hanging off your sweater, you really shouldn't pull it. If Nick hadn't been there…"

"And you, Detective," Nick added.

"I know," Kate nodded, her smile meek. "We were a pretty good team, the three of us…"

"Oh, there's no team," Connolly snapped, quickly dismissing the notion.

Nick shrugged, "She's got a point."

Connolly scowled, "I'll take that as my cue to leave."

"Thank you for everything, Detective Connolly," Kate said.

Taking a long look at Kate and then casting a quick glance toward Nick, the detective said, "Stay out of trouble, Ms. Harper. Both of you."

Pivoting, Connolly made his way to his police car and drove off without a second glance.

Kate looked at Nick, "It feels like a weight has been lifted off this place."

"It feels light. Welcoming," Nick nodded.

"Like a good beach house should," Kate smiled.

Kate leaned over the rail of the main deck of the beach house. The sun was angled against the Gulf, sinking slowly toward the water's surface.

Nick walked out of the house and joined Kate. In one hand, he held a bottle of champagne, in his other, a pair of wine flutes gently chimed together as he walked. A broad smile took over his face, "Congratulations. Your beach house is ready to go."

Kate leaned against the rail and accepted a glass from Nick, "It is stunning. I couldn't have done it without you."

"You might still be stuck with your toe in one of the old boards over there," Nick grinned as he pointed to where the rotted board had been.

"That's a little mean," Kate forced a wounded expression. "True, but mean."

Nick poured sparkling wine into each of the glasses. He studied Kate for a moment before moving his eyes over the beach house and its tropical vista, "To… beauty on the Gulf."

Kate's eyes squinted slightly as she sensed a double meaning in his words, "To amazing adventures at sunset!"

They spun to enjoy their toasts while watching the sun hit the water. With each bit of movement, the colors of the sky danced in new hues of pink, red and purple.

"It really is beautiful here," Kate sighed behind her wine glass.

"It really is," Nick's gaze shifted from the sunset to Kate.

For several long moments, they bathed in the splendor of the evening sky in silence. The surf played like a soft love song in the background, its melodic beat serenading them.

Turning to face Nick, Kate said, her breath soft and wine-tinged, "You know, I have another house on a beach that needs a little work."